BLOOD AND ASHES

Books in the
Reclaimed Legacy Chronicles by
Morgan Emerson Fox

Otherkin's Hunger
Bound by Shadows
Blood and Ashes

BLOOD AND ASHES

Book 3 of the
Reclaimed Legacy Chronicles

Morgan Emerson Fox

Blood and Ashes - Book 3 of the Reclaimed Legacy Chronicles

ISBN-13: 978-1-965280-07-2

Raindrop Books LLC
8401 Maryland Drive, STE S
Richmond, VA 23294

This book is dedicated to the ones we've lost to the inexorable march of time and age, whose memories linger. To the families we were born into and the ones we choose, bound not by blood but by the depths of hearts and the strength of spirit. Here's to the friends who stand by us, embrace our quirks, champion our dreams, and hold us close in times of need.

To our beta readers, editor, and every hand and voice that has touched this manuscript, your insights and dedication have made this story far greater than it could have been without you.

This work is a tribute to tolerance, acceptance, and the beauty of being true to who you are and can become. In a world riddled with division and hatred, this narrative stands as a beacon of hope, urging us to look beyond our differences and find unity in our shared humanity.

We hope you find the same joy, escape, and reflection in these words that we found in writing them. Reject division, embrace love, and always seek the light, even in the darkest times.

DISCLAIMER

This novel is a work of fiction. Names, characters, places, and incidents are either products of the author's imagination or are used fictitiously. Any resemblance to actual persons, living or dead, businesses, companies, events, or locales is entirely coincidental. While the author has utilized real places as settings in this novel, it is important to note that any events occurring in these settings are purely the result of the author's creativity. The representation of these places does not reflect their actual historical or current states, and any similarity to real events that have occurred in these places is coincidental or has been loosely inspired by historical events for narrative purposes.

Historical figures and events may be referenced or depicted within the narrative; however, their portrayal is not intended to be historically accurate. These representations are fictionalized and adapted for entertainment, contributing to the novel's thematic and narrative fabric. The interactions, behaviors, and outcomes involving these historical figures and events are purely speculative and should not be considered factual accounts.

The characters within this novel are entirely fictional creations. They are not modeled after any real individuals, and any parallels to real persons, whether living or deceased, are purely coincidental. The stories and actions of these characters are intended solely for the reader's entertainment. The author neither endorses nor condones the behaviors, decisions, or actions of the characters portrayed in this narrative.

The purpose of incorporating fictionalized historical elements and settings is to enrich the novel's world-building and thematic depth. It is not the author's intention to offer commentary on actual history or suggest alternative interpretations of real events. This narrative is crafted for the enjoyment of its audience, inviting them into a vividly imagined world where history, reality, and fantasy intertwine.

Otherkin.[1] /ˈəT͟Hərˌkin/

n., sing. or pl. A person who holds the belief that they are not entirely (or not at all) human. Usually a spiritual belief pertaining to one's soul and the reincarnation thereof, but may also be a belief that one's genetics are descended from, for example, the Irish fae. The word Otherkin was coined to describe people who felt a connection to mythological humanoids such as elves and faeries, but has expanded in recent years to include dragons, gryphons/griffins and other supposedly mythical beasts as well as animals, angelic/ demonic beings (angelkin/demonkin) and in some cases extraterrestrials.

adj. Of or relating to Otherkin.

[1] Spiritedust. (2004, May 15). Otherkin. Urban Dictionary. https://www.urbandictionary.com/define.php?term=otherkin

Prolog

GRANDMASTER EAMON Vale's thoughts were focused on Helena. The blood oath binding her to Eamon required both allegiance and subservience. She had once been his most trusted enforcer, but her recent failures posed a dilemma. Her punishment had been severe, exceeding his initial plans. She had endured what would have broken most humans, which raised the question—had it?

Eamon zealously championed eliminating all supernatural competition, a cause that masked his true nature. His leadership of an order committed to eradicating the supernatural was the ultimate deception. This masquerade allowed him to remove threats without consequence while maintaining an unassailable position of power. In his view, humans could never truly pose a danger; supernatural entities, those possessing powers that could rival those of his kind, needed to be eliminated. Without the oath, Helena might represent such a threat.

Eamon had not confronted her about his suspicions, as confirmation would require her death. He preferred to control her and use her as a tool, so instead, he opted for subtlety. He needed to uncover the extent of her abilities so that he could harness whatever power she concealed.

In the shadows of Paldiski, Estonia, hidden by remnants of the Cold War, Eamon found strength in the depths of the Vault. This concealed bastion, a relic shrouded beneath the ruins of a Soviet nuclear training center, served as his sanctuary and the nerve center for the Sodality of the Thorns. Eamon's appearance belied the millennia of his existence. His late-forties visage, with meticulously styled salt-and-pepper hair and gray eyes, masked a being far removed from humanity.

As he sat in his study, Eamon contemplated his next move. The Vault mirrored his existence with its history and secrets—a web of lies, power, and survival. Helena was one piece in a larger puzzle, a variable in the equation of control he had been solving for much of his existence on this plane. Her potential, both as a threat and an asset, required careful consideration.

With a sigh that seemed to draw the shadows closer around him, Eamon decided Helena would be given another task to prove her loyalty. Failure would not be tolerated, and success would not guarantee her continued existence. Only those who could survive the labyrinth of Eamon's machinations would be spared in this game of power and dominance. Even then, they were subject to the whims of a being who only craved total domination.

As he rose from his seat, his form blending with the darkness that was his constant companion, he prepared to set the wheels of fate in motion once more.

Eamon considered others within his top echelon. Among them, Igor Krakarov, known to the Sodality as 'Eagle,' represented a knight poised for advancement. Eamon had observed Eagle's ascent in the SVR with keen interest, recognizing a blend of loyalty and ruthless efficiency that mirrored his own. Eagle could be a viable replacement for Helena if she needed to be eliminated.

He had other assets around the globe, but few were aware of the Sodality's existence. His controllers typically managed most of those contacts through cutouts. His influence extended to the highest levels of all major world powers, but Eagle was one of the few pieces in a position of direct power. Soon, there would be others, but for now, Eamon concentrated on eliminating the rising threat.

Eagle's recruitment of Nomad and other similarly trained operatives had cemented his value to the Sodality. Eagle was also bound by a blood oath, and his allegiance to Eamon was beyond question, making him an ideal counterbalance to Helena's wavering fidelity.

He had trusted those mystical oaths, but now paused to question them. Richard's bindings had held even as his memories were altered, something Eamon believed possible only with magic. Nomad, tied only by conditioning and ideology, had disappeared and betrayed his controller. These observations alone were not proof of mystical influence, but they strongly suggested it.

The time had come to address Helena's future with the Sodality. Summoning her to his study, Eamon prepared for the conversation with the precision of a grandmaster positioning his queen—one he did not wish to sacrifice without sufficient gain.

Helena entered, her posture rigid and wary, uncertainty and defiance competing beneath her exterior. It had been over a month since her ordeal at his hands, and her wounds had healed—at least on the surface. Her long black hair flowed behind her as she walked to stand before him. She was indeed quite beautiful, and her ability to withstand tortures that could drive a mortal insane had provided a pleasurable interlude from ennui. She appeared to take pleasure from his cruel attentions and, in that, had become a temptation—one more reason to be wary of her.

"Helena," Eamon began, "your recent...endeavors have left much to be desired."

Helena stiffened. "I have served the Sodality to the best of my abilities. My loyalty should not be in question."

Eamon circled her slowly, a predator assessing his prey. "Loyalty, Helena, is a spectrum. And your recent actions have cast a shadow upon yours. Your best has not been enough—success or failure matters. However, I am inclined to offer you one final opportunity."

"What would this 'opportunity' entail?"

"You are to locate Lucian Miller and his allies. Discover their capabilities. And, more importantly"—he leaned closer, his voice dropping to a whisper—"uncover their weaknesses."

"And if I succeed?"

"Then your standing in the Sodality will be restored," Eamon replied. "Fail, and, well, I trust you understand the consequences."

The air was thick with the unspoken threat, the veiled promise of retribution beneath his words. Helena nodded. As she turned to leave, Eamon called out, "Helena, it would be wise to consider your moves carefully."

Alone once more, Eamon reflected on the gambit he had set into motion. Igor Krakarov, Eagle, would be his eyes and ears, a silent guardian watching Helena's efforts. Whether she succeeded or failed, Eamon would remain the master of the game. Mayhap risking this queen would reveal more significant threats.

Controlling Helena, a task increasingly akin to taming the ocean, and integrating Eagle required finesse. Eamon plotted and planned, his long-term strategy unfurling like dark sails.

The door to his study slid open silently. The man who entered the room was dressed in a dark, tailored suit. "You summoned me, Grandmaster?"

Igor Krakarov did not physically resemble his namesake bird beyond the cold, calculating gaze that seemed to miss nothing, piercing and pale blue. Iron-gray and close-cropped hair screamed long-time military service, and the scar running from his left eyebrow to his high cheekbone completed the look.

"Eagle, your vigilance over Helena is paramount. She teeters on the brink of disobedience, which I cannot tolerate."

Krakarov's rigid posture eased. "Understood."

Eamon circled Krakarov, much like he had with Helena. "You have proven yourself valuable, Eagle. But remember, the Sodality is a realm where the slightest misstep can lead to downfall. Watch her, but more importantly, watch the currents she swims in. We must anticipate, not react."

As Krakarov bowed slightly, Eamon turned away.

In the quiet that followed Krakarov's departure, Eamon considered his existence. He was an ancient being of power and malice. His disdain for the weaknesses of humans and other supernaturals was a mantle he wore as comfortably as his physical guise. Shrouded in the mists of time, his origin was a world where gods and demons played games of power and betrayal. His rise to power had been marked by manipulation and the exploitation of fear and greed.

The Sodality, an offshoot of one of the groups he had spawned centuries ago, had risen in power. He'd presented himself as a sympathetic acolyte. They had been woefully unaware of who or what he was. The world had progressed to a point where consolidation was feasible, so he'd worked his way into the order and ascended through the ranks until he took total control and merged all the disparate pieces into what existed today.

Now, Eamon, ensconced before the monitors in his command center, observed Helena's exit from the Vault with a scrutiny that missed nothing. As she moved through the dimly lit corridors, her stride was purposeful. The set of her shoulders reflected her readiness, yet her posture hinted at the plans swirling through her mind.

As Helena's vehicle disappeared into the night, the screens before Eamon flickered with intelligence from every corner of the world.

The frailties of those around him—their petty squabbles and fleeting lives—were shadows flickering in the light of his indomitable will. He was the last of his kind in this world. The others had all been killed, banished, or forced to flee to other realms.

Eamon's hidden influence on the political world was almost too easy. Authoritarianism was on the rise. Instability fed political and religious extremism. Puppet leaders stoked nationalism under the guise of 'protecting sovereignty' while stripping away rights. The people were too distracted by flashy rhetoric and demagogues to notice the creeping consolidation of power. Protests across major cities were being framed as acts of terrorism, giving governments the excuse they needed to crack down. Soon, there would be more. A few of his other pet projects were nearing fruition.

It was a straightforward equation: create division, exploit fear, and present solutions that only resulted in more control. He had practiced this for centuries across countless regimes, but the current environment was exceptionally fertile. The rise of surveillance states, disguised as a defense against invisible threats, was a tool he could never have imagined a century ago. Now, entire populations relinquished their freedom for the illusion of safety. Privacy diminished, becoming a relic of the past, while trust in institutions eroded with each passing day.

No one questioned why global instability peaked in step with corporate influence over governments. The masses blamed each other, divided along political lines. Even climate disasters were spun for political advantage, each catastrophe amplifying the chaos he thrived on. These were games he played for amusement. They also gave him a huge advantage when other threats arose.

Eamon contemplated one of those emerging threats. Lucian Miller and his allies had somehow found the key to open a Pandora's box. They had captured and manipulated Richard and disappeared. They had bested Helena, not once, but twice. It was time for him to take a more active role in their demise.

A rare smile touched Eamon's lips. The storm was looming, a tempest that would test his mettle and that of his adversaries. "Let the games begin," he whispered to the shadows. Let them see what attacks on Lucian Miller's businesses would reveal.

This was the diversion Eamon had craved, a complex puzzle that would demand all his cunning and power to solve. The players moved inexorably toward a confrontation that would echo through time. And Eamon Vale, Grandmaster of the Sodality of the Thorns, was ready to play.

Part One

One

ANJA STEPPED THROUGH the arched entrance into a chamber she had glimpsed before but never explored. Unlike her wardrobe room, with silks, satins, and corsetry, this one bore a heavy stillness and purpose.

Racks of armor lined the walls, some displayed like sculptures, others hanging on wooden mannequins. Steel, leather, bone, and chain—all were represented here. The sets ranged from full-plate suits of baroque craftsmanship to waxed leather armor, gleaming under ethereal light.

Her inner demon's voice purred in her mind. *"At last, you come here. Don't you tire of charging into danger with only curves and cleverness?"*

"I've managed," Anja said aloud, running her hand across a dark crimson breastplate that felt like it had been carved from crystalline blood.

"Managed, yes. But your delicious body can bleed. Distraction has its uses, but armor has its place. If you intend to challenge Eamon, you need more than seduction and sass."

The demon's words were not scolding, but wry. Amused. There was pride in it, tangled with a hunger.

She moved slowly through the chamber, scanning the various pieces. One glittered with black mirrored scales, spikes worked into the edges of its pauldrons. Another was sleek and serpentine, a liquid sheen of tiny platinum rings. It looked as if it might drink in her soul.

But then she saw it.

Hanging on a simple wooden stand was a set unlike the rest: a deep red cuirass, sleeveless and cupless, shaped to her silhouette and embossed with tiny arcane runes that seemed to shimmer and shift if looked at too long. Matching bracers bore similar sigils, more elegant than brutal. Thigh-high boots with reinforced soles and supple knee guards completed the set.

It was not only about protection, not entirely. It was about presence. Control. Power. It allowed freedom of movement, freedom to weaponize allure, but with enough armor to survive a serious fight.

"Yes," Anja murmured. "This one."

"Try it on," the demon purred.

Anja didn't hesitate. She banished her dress to the wardrobe room and let the change come. Her breathing deepened. Her skin darkened, losing its warm tones to mingle with shadow and night.

Horns curled from her scalp like a crown. Her tail lashed behind her as it grew, the spade-shaped tip twitching with excitement. Her wings unfurled—massive, leathered appendages ending in razor-sharp tips. Talons extended from her fingers.

She called the cuirass over her bare form. It molded to her body like a second skin, hot and snug, as if it had been waiting for her. The runes flared briefly as corset-like armor encased her body. She slid into the boots, then slipped the bracers into place, feeling warding enchantments settle around her.

Her other form, the seductive one, was powerful in its way. This one, however, had a different appeal. Initially, she'd been reluctant to accept that this was also a part of her, so much removed from her previous life and human form. But now…

She flexed her hands and stepped in front of the full-length mirror. The figure that stared back at her looked nothing like the woman she had been only months ago. Not just darker, not just sharper—but truly changed.

Transformed.

Empowered.

Turned on.

"It suits you," the demon said, satisfaction like smoke behind the words. *"Now let them come."*

Anja smiled, all teeth and danger. "Yes. Let them."

The armor sang against her skin. Not with sound, but with

sensation.

It was heat and hunger, coiling in her belly, rising to the curves of her breasts and radiating outward like electricity under the skin. Every rune etched into the cuirass thrummed with dark recognition, like it knew her.

She could feel the bloodlust rising. Not wild. Not yet. But eager. It mingled with the other lust that pulsed more familiarly through her: the ache for skin, for tangled limbs and bitten lips. Her tail curled behind her in anticipation, the motion sinuous.

This dark form was not just stronger—it was harder to rein in. Even now, standing alone, she could taste the blood that would flow in battle. Her fangs pressed against her lower lip. The boots made her taller, more imposing. She didn't want to take them off now. Not ever.

She was still breathing through it when she heard footsteps approaching.

Lucian stepped in first, his jacket open and heavy on one side—his pistol was in his pocket. She could feel it. Not see it, not guess. Sense it. Its weight registered in her mind like a pressure drop in the room.

Zoe followed, less cautious, but her fingers brushed the Glock under her arm out of habit. The weapon sat snug in its holster, black-on-black over a loose shirt knotted just above her navel and faded jeans. Her brows lifted the second she saw Anja, her eyes going wide, then narrowing.

"Okay," Zoe said, hands on her hips. "The armor is new."

Anja turned toward them, the tail flicking. "Like it?" she purred.

Lucian's gaze dipped to her bare chest, where the deep red leather formed a wreath around her breasts. "Well, I approve," he said.

Zoe smacked his shoulder without looking away from Anja. "Uh-huh. Right."

"It distracts," Anja said, a fang catching her lip as she smiled. "But it also protects."

Zoe eyed the runes. "Looks like it bites."

"Only if you deserve it. The armor wakes something up. Or maybe it just gives it permission."

"I like your other form much better. This one still gives me the creeps," Zoe noted. "Do you…"

It's time," Anja said.

The room around them shimmered as the chamber faded away.

They stood beneath a canopy of dark pines, moonlight cutting through the high boughs in slanted silver lines. The scent of moss and loam filled Anja's nose. Lucian shifted beside her, one hand in his jacket, ready. Zoe's hand hovered near her Glock.

The first crunch of a footfall sounded in the distance, between the trees. Then another.

Anja stepped forward, demon form radiant under the moon, and let her tail flick with anticipation, like a cat hunting.

"Shall we?" she asked.

Lucian smirked. "After you."

Zoe sighed and flexed her fingers. "I hate it when you get that look. The one that says someone's going to scream—and not for a fun reason."

The sound of more figures moving through the woods drifted toward them.

Anja's grin widened. "Let's go meet our guests."

The shadows in the trees moved fast—too fast.

Anja dropped into a crouch just as the first figure burst through the underbrush, metal glinting in one hand. She felt Lucian move beside her, a blur of motion and precision. His pistol came up, barked once. The attacker dropped, tumbling into the leaves.

Another charged from the left. Zoe pivoted, arm already up. Two shots—clean, center mass. The body jerked, spun, collapsed. But more kept coming.

Anja's wings spread, massive and bladed, sweeping out behind her in a rush of air. She charged, talons slicing through the dark. She didn't hold back. Not here. Not now. The forest echoed with gunfire and the screams of the dying.

And then Lucian went down.

A blade had caught him in the side, too fast to dodge. He staggered, blood already soaking his white dress shirt, pistol falling.

"Lucian!" Anja roared.

She dove toward him, tearing through two men in her path. One of them got a swing in, blade dragging across her arm. She didn't stop. Couldn't stop.

She reached him just as Zoe cried out.

More figures had slipped through—Zoe fought fiercely, her stance solid, but they overwhelmed her. She fell under two attackers, her gun firing into the air.

Anja screamed—something primal and wordless. A banshee's shriek wrapped in rage and agony.

"Weak," her inner demon hissed. *"You let your heart slow and distract you. They're gone. Finish the fight or join them."*

"No," Anja snarled aloud, wings trembling with fury. "They're not gone. I won't let them be."

"Fool. Attachments chain you. You could be more—pure, clean, untethered."

"They make me human. And without that, I'm just like him—Eamon. I won't become that."

She surged forward, into the last of the enemy ranks. Her whip flared with heat, its razor tip shrieking through the air. Flesh parted. Bones cracked.

"Yessss… Let the rage flow through you!"

Her tail skewered one man into a tree with a sickening thud. She was a blur of dark rage and vengeance.

And then the silence fell.

The clearing was littered with bodies. The blood dripping down her form was warm, though barely discernible against her red armor and darkened skin.

Her breathing ragged, Anja turned, her chest heaving, to where Lucian lay.

He wasn't moving.

Zoe's face was streaked with blood where she was slumped against a tree.

"No," she whispered, stumbling toward them. "Please…"

A hand reached out to her from the ground.

Lucian. His bloodied fingers curled around hers.

Zoe coughed weakly. "You could've just let us sleep in…"

The world melted. The moonlight fractured like a shattered mirror. The trees faded into fog.

Anja bolted upright in bed, her heart hammering.

Next to her, Lucian groaned and turned, his eyes flickering open. Zoe blinked up at the ceiling, still catching her breath.

They were all tangled in sheets, breathless and flushed with adrenaline, sweat glistening in the low light of the room.

Lucian exhaled slowly. "Well. That was…not our usual kind of dream."

Zoe pushed her hair back from her face. "You got stabbed. I shot people. What the hell did you eat before bed?"

Anja lay back down, staring at the ceiling. "It wasn't food."

Lucian turned to her. "You all right?"

She nodded. "I think it was a warning. Or maybe more demon training, like when I was Helena's captive. I dreamed then of battle and learned to call my dark form. Maybe it was a reminder."

Zoe tilted her head. "Of what?"

"That they will come for us. That there is more blood and battle in our future."

Lucian pulled her close. Zoe draped a leg over both of them, sighing into the stillness.

"We should really get better dreams," Zoe muttered, "ones with less blood."

"I'll work on it," Anja murmured. "But I have a feeling I'll need that armor."

But she didn't close her eyes just yet.

She was still wary.

Just in case the dream hadn't ended.

Two

Lucian felt the hush that hung over the group as they gathered around the conference table. It was time to plan. While the respite over the last weeks had allowed rest and healing, waiting for whatever the next crisis would bring was not viable. Anja, Lucian, and Zoe, the heart of this makeshift team, were flanked by their closest allies. Lucian surveyed the faces around him, each bearing the weight of recent events—and dreams—with resilience.

The Sodality's relentless pursuit had taken a toll on all of them, but amidst the scars, there was a spark of something indefinable, a shared resolve forged in the crucible of their battles. None had been more impacted than Anja by her brutal rape as a captive of Helena. He pushed his rage over his own family's murders down again. Now was not the time. It was looking like there would never be a time for that.

Anja's presence was almost ethereal. She was beautiful with a fair complexion and long, flowing burgundy hair, but the weight of her recent ordeals marked her. Her green eyes, usually vibrant, now reflected the depth of her experiences, adding a pensive aspect to her natural grace. She was still recovering, and Lucian and Zoe would help her heal. Until she was not only herself again, but even stronger than before.

She had been forced to kill for the first time, and nothing in her life had prepared her to face that. She had once been a librarian, but was now so much more. That she had enjoyed killing weighed heavily on her heart and the humanity she was desperately trying to retain. The darkness haunted her dreams, as he had experienced firsthand. Or was that secondhand?

Zoe, with her mix of American and South Asian heritage, carried her own blend of resilience and ghosts. Anja was not the only one who'd been forced to kill, and Zoe was holding Anja's hand under the table to share strength. Shoulder-length dark hair framed her face with its expression of focused intent. Her eyes reflected unyielding strength.

To her horror, the guard she had killed in one battle had risen from the dead in the next. That her bullets had failed to stop him the second time continued to haunt her sleep. The images of the shambling corpses bursting into flame amid the storm just topped it all off.

The weight of their shared history and the recent events that had challenged them to their core was ever-present. The unity and strength of their bond were undeniable, a beacon of hope amidst the darkness that sought to envelop them all.

"It's not just about survival anymore," Lucian began. "Every victory against the Sodality, every piece of ancient knowledge we reclaim, brings us one step closer to ending their tyranny."

Anja nodded, her sight fixed somewhere beyond the room's confines as if visualizing their path forward. "The Sodality fears what they can't control. Uncovering the secrets of the past, the lost arts and knowledge… It's how we turn the tide," she said.

Zoe leaned forward. "The Sodality's efforts to find and eradicate us will only intensify. We need an advantage, something they can't anticipate. We can't just sit here and wait for them."

With his unkempt salt-and-pepper hair, Lucian's uncle Howard looked the part as he took up the mantle of wizard, or perhaps sorcerer might be a better moniker. Looking at the others behind his round spectacles, he broke the silence. "The Golden Library," he said. "Legends speak of it as a repository of untold knowledge. It will be difficult to find…"

His words hung in the air, igniting curiosity and hope. It was not the first time he had mentioned it, but now they needed a new objective, no matter how daunting. The Golden Library, a mythical cache of ancient wisdom and artifacts, could hold the key to their success against the Sodality's crusade.

Lucian's gaze lingered on Howard. "Howard, I need you to research it more. Anything that can lead us to the library—rumors, ancient manuscripts, cryptic notes."

Howard nodded. "I'll start with my academic contacts, those not under the Sodality's influence. The Vatican Secret Archive, though rich in secrets, is a fortress currently beyond our reach, especially after...well, you know," he said. A shadow flickered across his lined features. Helena had kidnapped him in Rome while researching ways to counteract blood oaths.

"After what happened, the Vatican, and Rome for that matter, is off-limits," Lucian agreed. "We need to focus on less guarded but equally valuable possibilities. The library you have mentioned would have already been found if it were easy. It won't be."

After discussing the library, the conversation shifted, introducing a lighter note. "We also have a new strength among us," Lucian declared.

Macaria 'Cari' Aguilar, sitting with an ease that belied her readiness, was a drone operator for the Akar Labs security team and had been identified as having otherkin genetic markers. Her presence was unassuming yet distinct. Her long, dark hair was tied back in a no-nonsense ponytail. Her long-sleeved, back-fitted shirt and tactical pants were practical.

Lucian added, "Cari has already proven herself in our recent encounters with the Sodality, and with her abilities now awakened, she brings even more to our collective effort. Carlos has some competition now."

Sitting close to Cari and with a distinctly affectionate look, Carlos clapped her on the back and said, "Definitely." With a square jawline and a neatly trimmed beard, Carlos exuded rugged masculinity. His short, dark hair reflected the same Latin origins as Cari's.

The group responded with murmurs of recognition.

"As we expand our numbers, so too do we expand our ability to challenge the Sodality. Each new member brings new abilities and strengths to our cause," Lucian continued, his gaze sweeping over their faces. "Zoe, Emma, I'd like you to lead the setting up of a new intel and investigation team. We need eyes everywhere, and added to Jonas's resources, I believe you can make significant headway."

Emma's raven-black hair, which could fall in waves past her shoulders, was pulled back in a ponytail. Emma's piercing cat-green eyes revealed her feline otherkin nature as she exchanged a look with Zoe.

"We're on it, boss man," Zoe confirmed. Zoe and Emma were both former FBI agents: Zoe had been a profiler, and Emma had spent significant time undercover. He had no doubt they would get the results they desperately needed. It was past time to formalize some of their evolving roles.

Turning his attention to Ian and Claire, Lucian could almost see her wolf peering out of her amber eyes. She had once been a member of the British Royalty and Protective Service team before becoming one of his bodyguards. Her athletic and toned physique reflected her capabilities. All of his former bodyguards were now full partners in their struggle to end the Sodality.

Ian, formerly Captain Ian MacGregor of the SAS and another former bodyguard turned partner, had a sturdy, muscular build honed by years of rigorous training and military service. His dark, closely cropped hair was peppered with hints of silver at his temples. His blue eyes hinted at tenderness as he watched Claire.

"Ian, Claire, your efforts in England need to be continued. Claire's relatives would be a welcome addition to our ranks if they could be convinced. Your outreach," Lucian continued, "is vital. We're at a tipping point; every new ally strengthens our position. Let's ensure we give them every reason to join us. My jet should be arriving here in a few days. My uncle will be in London, and you're welcome to invite your relatives to the estate. Will that work?"

"Sure, Lucian. We'll do everything we can," Claire said, with Ian adding a silent nod of agreement. "Hiding is not in their nature, and many will respond to the call."

Lucian nodded, then addressed the aerially inclined duo. "Carlos, Cara, your drone and falcon coordination work has been exemplary. Continue refining the integration."

Carlos responded, "Absolutely, Lucian. We've got some new ideas we're eager to test out."

"You'll be working closely with Graham on training and honing your skills."

Graham, who had been silently observing, nodded in agreement. Ian's nephew, another bear otherkin, was also an imposing figure. The family resemblance was striking. The chief of security for the lab was a younger incarnation of his uncle, only with a shaved head and full dark beard, and dressed in tactical gear.

"Mike," Lucian continued, turning to the lab's new chief engineer, "I need you to oversee the safety of our new quarters and coordinate with Graham for any enhancements that could fortify our position."

"Got it, Lucian." Mike was ruggedly built, and though not as tall as Ian or Graham, he could still hold his own.

Finally, Lucian's gaze swept over Elín, Isabelle, Lynn, Dora, and Anja. "We need to enhance our genetic and healing research. Our understanding of otherkin biology is still limited. We need to improve on that. We'll move on to that and let everyone start on their tasks."

Lucian sat at the cluttered table. Recent research papers held the promise of understanding, and laptops, open to databases of genetic codes and medical anomalies, had become the focal point of this smaller, more intimate gathering.

Dr. Elín Þórdís Björnsdóttir, director of Akar Laboratories, moved to the head of the table, her long auburn hair in a bun, held in place with a dragon pin. That pin carried a new meaning now—it had become a symbol of her otherkin identity.

Alongside her sat Dr. Teodora 'Dora' Ziem. She pushed a strand of her strawberry-blonde hair behind an ear as she scanned one of the research papers. Lucian noted it was one on flux receptors, the attempts to link them to their new abilities, and the question of where the energy originated to power them. She sat relaxed but focused as they waited for the others to arrive. Dora had not undergone her awakening ceremony yet, but he hoped she would. Soon.

Dr. Isabelle Sinclair was an elegant five foot nine with eyes that were a brilliant shade of azure. Isabelle's wavy, chestnut-brown hair was pulled into a practical bun much like Elín's. She was visiting from NexGen in Geneva, another of Lucian's biotech corporations, where she was the CEO and led genetic research.

Lynn, more formally known as Dr. Brendalynn Innes, was the chief medical officer here at the lab. Her recent awakening as a unicorn otherkin reflected her healing abilities. Her specialties were internal medicine and rare genetic diseases, and she worked closely with Dora. She was dressed in a lab coat over casual clothes. Her golden-blonde hair fell past her shoulders, and her sky-blue eyes twinkled with smiles.

The room grew silent around the core team tasked with understanding the mysteries of otherkin genetics. In this hush, Lucian leaned forward in his seat next to Anja.

"Let's focus on genetic traits," Lucian began. "We're dealing with about three billion pairs of genetic instructions in human DNA, though we have begun to understand only the two percent that makes up our forty-eight chromosomes."

Elín's gray eyes moved to Lucian. "The human genome is vast and largely uncharted. Let's consider the possibility that the so-called 'junk' DNA—the ninety-eight percent that's been mostly overlooked—contains sequences like the transposons that could be key to activating otherkin capabilities."

Lucian turned his attention to Isabelle, who had been listening. "Isabelle, your genetic makeup has shown few matches for these otherkin traits in our current tests. However, if we can target and manipulate specific transposon sections in the unexplored regions of your DNA, we might activate your flux receptors."

Isabelle allowed a flicker of hope to cross her features. "It's an intriguing hypothesis. We have observed the ability of transposons to move through the genome, activating or deactivating genes. If we can harness this property, we could, in theory, awaken those dormant genetic pathways."

Dora, who had been reviewing some of Anja's notes, chimed in. "Anja's experiences and our observations of other awakenings suggest there's a trigger mechanism. If transposons play a role in this, could we awaken Isabelle and refine our approach to awakening others?"

Although not formally trained in genetics, Anja had had a crash course facilitated by the fast-learning techniques and eidetic memory practices she had unlocked during her own awakening. They'd discovered that the key to the awakenings was a combination of advanced quantum biology and ancient rituals that enabled their transformation. The prototype serum developed by Lucian and Isabelle, which had been used in early and mostly unsuccessful therianthropy experiments, formed the basis for the current regimen they were following now, albeit enhanced by Lucian's unique ability to customize the serum to match an individual's specific genetic coding.

Anja leaned back. "Using our genetic 'dark matter' as a canvas for awakening is electrifying and daunting. If we proceed, we must be cautious. The ethical implications are vast, and the impact on an individual's identity and physiology could be profound."

Lynn pushed a strand of hair behind her ear. "How do we safely test these theories? The risk of unintended consequences is high, and we'll need a controlled environment to monitor any genetic alterations closely."

Lucian's gaze settled on each of his colleagues. "This is new. Our next steps must be carefully planned. Our ultimate goal is to understand what makes us otherkin. This research could redefine our understanding of genetics, identity, and the very nature of our existence." Lucian's focus narrowed on Isabelle, a cornerstone of his early research team. "Isabelle, you've been instrumental in our research, and your contributions have been invaluable, yet you have not experienced awakening. I'm sure you have sometimes felt left behind."

Isabelle's attention was riveted on Lucian.

"We believe there's hidden promise in you," Lucian continued. "Anja has seen something, a spark, that suggests you're capable of undergoing an awakening. But"—he paused, ensuring he had Isabelle's full attention—"you're aware of the risks involved."

The opportunity to join her colleagues and share in their unique bonds and abilities would be tantalizing, Lucian knew. However, he also knew that the scientist in her understood the unpredictability of their proposed methods.

"I've seen the transformations," Isabelle replied. "The possibility for discovery and understanding is immense. So are the risks." She took a deep breath. "Yes, I'd like to try. The chance to awaken—to truly be a part of this world we're uncovering—is worth it. I trust you."

Lucian nodded. “We’ll proceed with the utmost caution,” he assured her. “Your safety is our priority. This step could identify new horizons for our research and for understanding the very nature of our existence. We also don’t want to risk a misstep. You will likely be working from the lab here rather than at NexGen for the foreseeable future. I assume that shouldn’t be a major issue?”

“I can work remotely from here without much trouble, as I have for the last six weeks. The facilities here are top-notch.”

“Good. We’ll make it work. While you’re here, I would like you to oversee the local production of more of the serum. Can you do that?”

“Certainly. I have some thoughts on improvements and additional tailoring based on the results we have seen.”

“Thank you. I’d also like you to explore whether there is a way to adapt the serum for oral administration rather than injection. Also, maybe tailor the serum for wolves and Claire’s relatives. Would that be possible given blood samples from Claire and serum samples I have enhanced?”

“I’ll add that to the list,” she said.

Three

AFTER A PLEASANT evening meal, the group adjourned to the communal warmth of their new dwelling. The space still echoed with the laughter and shared memories of the recent housewarming and Anja's birthday celebration.

"As you may know," Howard began, in lecture mode, "Zoe Palaiologina, or Sophia as she was later known, was the niece of the last Byzantine Emperor, Constantine XI Palaiologos. In 1472, she married Ivan III or Ivan the Great, the Grand Prince of Moscow, and brought a dowry that was more than gold or land."

Anja added, "Yes, she was said to have carried the intellectual flame of the Byzantine Empire to Moscow: vast collections of scrolls, manuscripts, and books. This wasn't only a physical transfer; it was the symbolic passing of the torch of the Orthodox Christian intellectual tradition from the cradle of Byzantium to the burgeoning Moscow."

Howard nodded appreciatively. "Exactly, Anja. The Byzantine Empire was a beacon of intellectual culture in its time, its libraries a repository of centuries of Greek, Roman, and early Christian thought. To avoid confusion, let's refer to Ivan's wife as Sophia," Howard suggested, smiling at Zoe. "It will make our discussions less entertaining, but probably a bit clearer."

Lucian asked, "Uncle, if this library is so valuable, why hasn't anybody looked for it? Or, rather, found it?"

Howard leaned back with a slight smile; he had anticipated the question. "A good question, Lucian. Many *have* searched for it, but its whereabouts have become something of a legend, shrouded in mystery and political maneuvering. The fall of Constantinople, shifting powers in Europe, and even the church's agendas have all played a part in obscuring the true fate of this collection. And," he added with a knowing look, "this is only the tale's beginning. I haven't had a chance to do significant research, only to learn what's generally known."

Howard's light, scholarly tone belied the depth and breadth of the history they were about to explore. He was entirely in professor mode now, drawing his class into rapt engagement.

Howard adjusted his glasses. "Indeed, the question is not why people weren't interested but what challenges obscured its pursuit. Historical upheavals, the shifting of borders, and, not least, the secretive nature of those who might have known its whereabouts have all played a part. The tumultuous events following the fall of Constantinople and, later, the political complexities of Ivan IV's reign have shrouded much of this history in mystery."

Howard added, "As for these texts, it is widely believed they were kept within the walls of the Kremlin. There, they likely seeded the first libraries of Russia, becoming a wellspring of knowledge for the clergy and nobility alike.

"The cultural renaissance that followed saw the infusion of Byzantine art, architecture, and even administrative reforms into Muscovite society. This period was transformative, bridging the gap between East and West and blending cultural and intellectual ideas that defined Russia for centuries."

Zoe couldn't help but interrupt. "The damn Kremlin! How are we supposed to get in there?"

"We'll need to figure that out," Emma agreed. "Maybe Nomad can finally prove his usefulness. He trained in Russia, after all." She turned back to Howard. "But first, I'm sure there's more to this story, right?"

"Indeed, there is. Under Ivan III, Sophia's cultural influence became even more pronounced. Ivan, captivated by her heritage, took significant steps to expand the library, enriching it with additional Slavic, Greek, and Latin manuscripts. The library was more than a collection of books; it was a symbol of Moscow as the 'third Rome,' especially after the fall of Constantinople. Ivan the Great envisioned the city as the new bastion of Orthodox Christian civilization, and the library played a central role in this cultural and spiritual assertion.

"Upon inheriting the library, Vasily the Third continued his father's work and extended its scope by adding works from Western Europe. This reflected the growing interactions between Moscow and the rest of Europe.

"The enhancements made by Vasily were not just about quantity. They represented a diversification of knowledge, encompassing various fields of study and offering a panoramic view of the world's intellectual landscape at the time."

Howard's voice took on a grave tone. "Ivan IV, more commonly known to history as Ivan the Terrible, was deeply influenced by his grandmother Sophia, who fed his voracious curiosity. From a young age, Ivan showed an intense interest in the library, expanding its collection with an array of Eastern and Western works, and even commissioned translations into Russian.

"As Ivan's reign progressed, especially during the oprichnina—the period marked by state terror—the library became a secluded treasure, heavily guarded and shrouded in secrecy," Howard continued. "It's said that Ivan IV moved the library several times to protect it, hiding it in underground chambers and secret rooms within the Kremlin, as his distrust for the boyars, a privileged class of wealthy landowners, intensified. It was rumored that he dabbled in rituals he discovered—even black magic.

"After Ivan the Terrible's death, the whereabouts of the library vanished into the realm of speculation and legend, contributing to the mystique that cloaked his reign. Rumors abound of hidden passages within the Kremlin and other fortresses, of secret societies, sworn to protect the library, and even curses cast upon those who dared to seek it."

Howard's account left the group contemplative, pondering the intricate web of history, myth, and the supernatural that now enshrouded the Golden Library.

Zoe broke the silence. "So, it's more than just a collection of books."

Howard nodded. "Exactly. And uncovering and reclaiming it could change everything for us. But we must proceed carefully, for if even a fraction of the rumors are true, we are not just hunting for a library but uncovering a history that some would prefer to remain buried. I would bet that the Sodality has also had its hand in the tale. I've found no proof of this, but I'm certain it's there."

"So, Howard, are you suggesting we just stroll up to the Kremlin and ask to rummage through its basement?" The sarcasm in Zoe's voice elicited a few stifled chuckles.

Howard's expression turned serious. "We start with clues from the past. I've come across references to revelations by an engineer named Apalos Ivanov that could provide a tantalizing hint. He spoke of the library being within the Kremlin's walls, hidden under a veil of the strictest secrecy. If Ivanov's claims are to be believed, we might have a starting point."

"A back door?" Zoe asked.

"Maybe secret entrances," Anja said. "The historical accounts hint at Ivan the Terrible's interest in dark arts and the occult. He would likely hide those treasures in places of power or significance, possibly related to where he felt most secure or conducted his most secretive work. Probably secret passageways under the Kremlin."

Howard continued, "Ivanov's tale, though filled with the mystique of legends and curses, points us towards looking into the architectural history and any documented renovations or construction projects within the Kremlin across centuries. These could reveal hidden chambers or forgotten passages."

Lucian raised an eyebrow. "We need detailed architectural blueprints or historical records from that era—anything that might have been overlooked or deemed insignificant at the time. Howard, could you also verify the veracity of Ivanov's account?"

"I'll do that," Howard assured him.

Emma added, "We might not need to knock on the Kremlin's doors yet. Nomad's contacts in the underworld and our resources could be key in unearthing forgotten records or oral histories that haven't made it into the public domain. He may even know of alternate entrances that others do not."

"Indeed," Howard replied. "We have many avenues to explore between public archives, private collections, and the darker corners of the market. The key is knowing where to look and whom to ask."

Howard leaned back, his gaze drifting over the expectant faces around him. "Toward the end of his life, Ivan the Terrible became increasingly obsessed with the occult and safeguarding his treasures against perceived threats. This paranoia, fueled by his descent into darkness, led him to make extraordinary efforts to hide his most valued possessions."

"And there's speculation that Bogdan Belsky, one of Ivan's most trusted advisors, played a key role in the final days of the tsar's life," Anja said. "Ivan was not only involved in state affairs but deeply engaged in mysticism, searching for ways to extend his life and power."

Lucian said, "If Belsky was that close to Ivan, he might have known the library's true location or even been instrumental in its final move."

"Yes, Belsky's connection to Ivan and the oprichnina makes him a figure of interest. There are rumors that, fearing the library would fall into the hands of his enemies, Ivan ordered its relocation to a place only a select few would have known."

Zoe's brow furrowed in thought. "So, we're looking for a needle in a historical haystack. Ivan's sudden death was the moment the library vanished."

Emma suggested, "Our research should also focus on the aftermath of Ivan's death and the transition of power. Any turmoil or shift in allegiances could have provided the perfect cover to move the library undetected."

Howard stated, "The key to unlocking the library's location may lie in piecing together the final days of Ivan's reign, his relationship with Belsky, and the tumultuous period that followed. Ivan's death remains shrouded in mystery and controversy. It's claimed that Ivan died suddenly while playing chess with Bogdan Belsky in his private chambers. Given his interest in the occult and his unpredictable behavior, there's much speculation about the cause of his death."

Anja shifted in her seat. "Some accounts suggest that the stress of his reign, marked by fear, betrayal, and loss, culminated in a fatal stroke. Yet the abruptness of his passing, without any apparent illness, fuels theories of poison or other dark interventions."

Lucian leaned forward. "If Belsky was present at his death, it places him at the heart of the Kremlin's secrets."

Howard nodded. "Precisely. The immediate period following Ivan's death was chaotic. The Rurik dynasty was nearing its end, and the power vacuum led to the Time of Troubles. Within this turmoil, the library was lost."

Zoe speculated, "Could Belsky have used the chaos as cover to move the library? If he feared Ivan's successors or rivals might seize or destroy it, hiding it away would ensure its preservation."

Emma added, "If we believe the stories about Ivan's curse on those who sought his treasures, Belsky might have been among the few who dared to act. But what if Belsky wasn't entirely in the loop? Considering Ivan's notorious paranoia, it's plausible he could've misled Belsky intentionally. If Belsky had control of the library, or knowledge about its whereabouts, wouldn't he have used it to his advantage later? The fact that it hasn't been found suggests he didn't know as much as some think."

Howard leaned back, stroking his chin as he pondered Emma's suggestion. "That's a valid point. Ivan IV was not only suspicious of those around him but also cunning in his manipulations. It's entirely possible that in his final years, he devised a scheme to protect his treasures, including the library, that didn't involve Belsky. Perhaps he entrusted its safety to a select few, or even a loyal confidant whose identity has since been lost.

"Or," Howard continued, warming to the theme, "Ivan might have used a decoy strategy. He could have spread false rumors about the library's location, even as he secreted it somewhere unexpected. His obsession with the occult could have led him to employ elaborate measures to conceal its whereabouts, relying on misdirection and mystery to guard it."

"Yeah, and curses… You did mention curses," Zoe added. "And Anja mentioned poison…"

Zoe closed her eyes, her demeanor shifting. Anja gestured to the others to give Zoe a moment to think.

Finally, Zoe leaned forward. "You know, considering the Sodality's long-standing agenda and Ivan's reputed dabbling in the occult, there's a pattern here that might not be coincidental."

Lucian picked up on her trail. "Are you suggesting Ivan's death was not just political or personal, but tied to the Sodality?"

"Exactly. Emma mentioned the peculiar circumstances of Ivan's death. Chess with no witnesses, a sudden demise—it sounds like the perfect setup for a covert assassination. If Ivan was involved in the occult, perhaps he was a threat to someone or something more secretive. The Sodality comes to mind."

Emma leaned in. "That's a leap, but not an unreasonable one. If Ivan had enemies who were aware of his occult practices, they might have used that knowledge against him, employing poison or a curse disguised as a natural death. That does seem to follow."

"There were always rumors about Ivan's court being a nexus for dark arts practitioners," Howard said. "Ivan's obsession with securing his library, along with his forays into the occult, could have made him dangerous in the eyes of the Sodality. They might have decided to intervene, ensuring the tsar and his library vanished."

Zoe nodded, a smile touching her lips. "We might be looking at a centuries-old battle between Ivan and those who sought to control the library. Ivan's death would have been crucial in that shadow war, warning future generations about the dangers of delving too deeply into the forbidden. The Sodality claims to oppose all magic and the supernatural unless, it seems, it's under their control. Helena and the Grandmaster are prime examples."

Anja nodded, leaning forward. "Exactly. Then there's Ashton and his grimoire. His mysterious death pulled me into this world, and soon after, we saw the Sodality's interest spike. They're implicated in Ashton's demise, and we've seen firsthand their ruthlessness with the attempted assassination of Lucian." Lucian's expression darkened at the mention, and Zoe squeezed his hand.

"It's about power," Lucian said, his voice tight but controlled. "Exclusive power. They eliminate what they can't control or understand. Their mission isn't human purity; it's dominance."

Howard shifted in his chair, a thoughtful expression on his face. "Their methods haven't changed, then, from Ivan's era to our own. Secrecy, manipulation, elimination. It's a pattern. If they deemed Ivan's library a threat or a tool they couldn't wield..."

Emma cut in to finish his statement. "Then they'd erase it—from history, from memory—just as they tried with Lucian, Anja, and all of us."

"Which means," Anja concluded, "if we're looking for this library, we're not just fighting history. We're up against the Sodality. They have played this game for millennia. And we need to be smarter."

"Well, fuck," Zoe said. "What was that about the Vatican Secret Archive again?"

"Um, what are the chances of them controlling that, too, or at least infiltrating and having their agents there?" Emma asked.

"I think that has already been demonstrated," Howard grumbled. "What we're seeing is a pattern of power and suppression that extends back through the ages. The Sodality's interest in controlling such knowledge isn't new. They've always sought to dictate the narrative surrounding magic and the supernatural."

Emma proposed, "Our first step should be to dig deeper into the records from Ivan IV's time, looking for anomalies or gaps that might suggest interference. At the same time, we should explore the occult angle and figure out how Ivan's dabbling in the dark arts might have made the library—and him—a target for the Sodality."

Anja suggested, "We should also reach out to our contacts in academia and the black market. Maybe Raymond Archambault in New York. He provided me with clues to Ashton's mystery; he could have information. There might be manuscripts, artifacts, or even whispers of lore that can guide us. The Sodality is thorough, but they're not infallible."

Howard's final thoughts echoed through the room. "Finding the Golden Library is more than an academic venture; it's a battle for the soul of our history and future. We're not just researchers but guardians of knowledge against those who would see it buried."

Four

CLAIRE WAS EXHAUSTED. Yesterday had been chaotic, starting with giving blood samples for Isabelle to create a tailored serum for wolf shifters. Meetings, planning sessions, and calls to her mother had added to her stress, leaving her feeling overwhelmed by events that never seemed to slow down.

Now that Iceland was dwindling into the expanse of sea and sky behind their plane, Claire turned to Ian. "Ian, do you ever wonder if we're making the right choice? Bringing my relatives into this world, exposing them to the dangers of reclaiming their legacy?"

Ian took her hand in his. "Claire, love, I know you're worried, but you've already answered that question, haven't you? The time for hiding, pretending we're less than we are, is past. It's better to be prepared, to embrace all the capabilities at our disposal."

Claire sighed. "I just...I want to protect them, Ian. But you're right. Hiding isn't real protection. Not when we have the chance to be so much more."

Ian smiled. "Exactly. And remember, our session with Anja wasn't just about control. It opened the door to new possibilities, new strengths we hadn't imagined." His eyes sparkled.

"The control I've gained, it's... It's empowering, truly. And the intensity of it all..." Claire paused, her thoughts drifting back to the awakening rituals with Anja. The first one had gone sideways; she had lost control and shifted under the full moon's call, leaving her ability to control her wolf incomplete. The second session had been more intense. She and Ian had agreed to be monogamous, and she identified as straight, but Anja's guidance through that erotic ritual had been mind-bogglingly good.

"It made me wonder what else there is. Anja mentioned she could guide us further and help us discover the mysteries of our legacy. That mind link thing was incredible. It made me question if I'm as straight as I thought I was. But with Anja..."

Ian grinned. "I'm definitely open to another repeat."

"Yeah, you would be. Men."

"Hey, didn't you just...?"

"Okay, okay, we'll see. Let's not get ahead of ourselves."

As they dropped through the clouds, the gray wisps thinned, streaming past to reveal a patchwork quilt of the English countryside. The towering skyline of London loomed in the distance, obscured from time to time as they flew through patches of clouds.

As the plane descended, cutting through veils of early morning mist, Biggin Hill Airport emerged below. The landscape of England, wrapped in the golden embrace of dawn, unfolded like a story.

Geoffrey 'Geoff' Barnes, the steadfast driver of the Miller family, awaited their arrival. "Welcome back to England, Ms. Claire, Mr. Ian."

The drive from the airport to Lucian's family estate was a quiet sojourn through the heart of Kent's countryside. Upon arrival, the estate stood majestically against the morning sky. Emily, the lady's maid, welcomed them with genuine warmth. "Oh, it's so good ter see you both. The estate's missed yer presence, it 'as."

James, the butler, gave a nod of acknowledgment. "Your trip went well, I trust?" His words contained only the trace of an accent.

As they entered the estate, increased security was subtly evident. Claire noticed the discreet cameras and the vigilant eyes of the estate's security personnel. "It seems the estate is more...alert than I remember."

"Necessary precautions, I suppose. I'm glad Edward is taking things seriously," Ian said.

Emily, catching their looks, said, "Aye, the world's filled with shadows now. But 'ere"—she gestured around—"we do our best to keep the light shinin'."

James affirmed, "The Millers have been stewards, protecting those who call it home."

"It's strange," Claire mused as they settled into their room, "returning here." After a thoughtful pause, she said, "I need to let my mother know we're here."

"Mum," Claire began after the call connected, "we've arrived at the Miller estate."

"Claire, it's time then, is it? Simon and I will meet you there. We can discuss who else to call. Best to do that before we shock the rest of the clan."

A knot of worry tightened in Claire's stomach. "I'm just concerned, Mum. This world, our realities…the danger. Is it right to expose them to this?"

"There's always danger in the unknown, darling, but knowledge and unity are our strengths," her mother replied gently. "We'll bring them to the estate. They have a right to know their heritage. Most will take it well enough, though there will be…difficulties with a few. Once I'm there, we can discuss it properly."

"All right, Mum. Thank you."

On her last visit, Claire had revealed her ability to shift, but the visit had been cut short by news of Howard's kidnapping. This was no ordinary family reunion; it was a summons to stand united against the shadows that sought to encroach upon their world. Soon, they would put out the call.

Claire felt the duality of her legacy more intensely than ever. It was both a strength and a burden. Yet, surrounded by those who walked the line between the mundane and the mystical, Claire found the courage to embrace the path ahead. The calling of the Pack was not just an invitation; it was a rallying cry, a reclamation of a legacy that promised to unite them, as it had in times past.

While they waited for her mother and brother's arrival, Ian and Claire wandered the verdant grounds that had, for centuries, witnessed the ebb and flow of fortunes. The rustle of leaves in the breeze provided a tranquil soundtrack to their contemplation. The natural beauty of the surroundings—ancient trees, manicured lawns, and hidden gardens—spoke of an enduring presence, a contrast to the fleeting nature of their current respite and the tumultuous future that awaited them.

Their walk led them to a vantage point where the estate sprawled below. “We are the guardians of this legacy now,” Claire mused, her gaze fixed on the silver thread of a stream winding its way through the estate.

As they wandered through the grounds, a different kind of memory tugged at the edges of her consciousness. The scent of jasmine wrapped around them, carried by a breeze that rustled the leaves—a delicate yet insistent aroma. Claire paused, inhaled deeply, and let the fragrance envelop her. It stirred a deep, visceral response within Claire, a mix of nostalgia and undeniable arousal.

“Ian, do you smell that?” Claire’s voice was soft, almost dreamy. “The jasmine… It reminds me of Anja.”

Ian chuckled, a sound that danced with the light filtering through the trees. “I bet Lucian had the gardeners plant more varieties in the gardens just for her.”

Claire smiled. “It’s strange, isn’t it? How a scent can bring it all back.”

Ian wrapped an arm around her, drawing her close as they walked. “No, not strange at all. It’s not just the jasmine, love. It’s everything we’ve experienced together.”

Standing at the vantage point and looking out over the estate, Claire felt the truth of Ian’s words. With a wistful sigh, Claire said, “We should head back in now. Mum should be arriving soon.”

As the sound of a car engine broke through the tranquil air, Claire’s chest tightened. The modest but well-maintained sedan came down the winding drive, coming to a gentle stop in front of the mansion. The moment the car door opened, Claire’s heart leapt.

“Mum!” Claire exclaimed, rushing forward as Margaret stepped out. She was a woman with timeless grace. Her hair that grazed her shoulders was threaded through with silver, but it still retained a vibrant golden undertone. Her eyes held wisdom and secrets, yet Claire could see her own eyes gazing back at her.

Her brother Simon followed behind her, and his youthful face bore the same amber-hued eyes and golden-brown hair, albeit unruly and windswept.

“Simon!” Claire greeted him warmly, observing how much he had matured since their last meeting.

“It’s good to see you, Claire. And you, Ian,” Simon acknowledged, extending a hand to Ian, who clasped it firmly.

As they entered the estate, Margaret's gaze lingered on Claire and Ian, a blend of motherly affection and the steely resolve of a matriarch who had weathered many storms.

"Shall we go inside and have a word?" Margaret suggested. "We've plenty to discuss, and I daresay a bit of refreshment wouldn't go amiss."

The study's walls were lined with bookshelves and its windows offered a view of the grounds. Emily entered, bearing a tray laden with tea, biscuits, and lighter fare suited for the afternoon's discussions.

Once they were seated, Margaret began. "I've drawn up a list of relatives. Some will be receptive, of course, though others…less so."

"I would really like you to take the lead on organizing the clan, Mum. You know them better than I do. I've been away so much, and I have commitments to Lucian and Anja. You call, and they will come. They will need a leader."

"But…"

"No buts, Mum. It needs to be you."

After a long pause, Margaret nodded. "We shall see."

"Thank you, Mum. This awakening has brought so much into focus. Revealing my wolf to you on my last visit felt like a turning point."

Margaret reached across the table, resting her hand over Claire's. "It was, my love. I've always known our legacy carried power, but watching you embrace it so fully…it's given me hope."

"The others?" Ian inquired. "How will they respond to the call?"

Simon leaned forward, his eyes alight with the spark of excitement that Claire remembered so well. "There will be skepticism, of course. But those stories, the legends we grew up with…they've always been more than just tales to some of us."

"I've already invited your aunt Fiona, of course," Margaret said. "She's my sister—she'd never forgive me if I left her out. She'll be along as soon as the university term ends. She says she can give us the whole summer, and I suspect with her being an anthropology professor, this rather appeals to her curiosity. I'm quite sure she'll be invaluable."

Simon indicated the list. "Cousin Alex, with his environmental law background, could be helpful, but his skepticism towards our heritage… It's a tough call. On the other hand, his daughter, also a lawyer, should be more receptive to the idea. She's been advocating for the return of wolves to England."

Margaret nodded thoughtfully. "Indeed. Alexander's pragmatism cuts both ways. His regard for the family may help him come round, but that cautious streak of his could just as easily get in the way. Perhaps best to invite them together." She made a small mark beside their names.

"Bee's passion for history and that insatiable curiosity of hers might well make her an ally. With a little guidance…" Claire let the thought hang.

Margaret leaned back slightly, intertwining her fingers as she considered Claire's hopeful tone regarding Blevine. "There's also the matter of Bee's boy. She married her professor whilst still at university —predictably enough, that didn't last. Her ex-husband, who's now in New York, has been rather obstructive about the boy learning anything of his heritage. They're divorced now, and their son is with Bee for the summer—perhaps longer now he's turned eighteen."

Simon raised an eyebrow. "Has he shown any interest in our… unique traits?"

Margaret sighed. "He has, actually. Bee said he's started asking questions about wolves—whether the old stories might be true. Seems he's unwittingly tapping into his roots. Perhaps his instincts are nudging him towards what he is."

Ian leaned forward, his strategic mind ticking over. "If he's showing interest, we should consider how best to introduce him to his heritage."

Claire said, "We must be cautious if his father has resisted this part of Blevine's life, dismissing it as myth and fantasy. Introducing him to the truth about himself could complicate things legally and emotionally."

Margaret nodded slowly. "Indeed. Bee asked my advice on how to broach it with him. She's torn—whether to shield him from his father's backlash or start guiding him towards an understanding of himself."

Simon interjected, "Maybe we could help Bee frame this…

revelation as a broader exploration of his ancestry. Make it about discovering his roots in a historical context before we touch on the more...personal aspects."

Margaret inclined her head. "That could work nicely. Ground him first in the family history—keep the...other aspects for later. Ease him in as his curiosity grows."

Claire's face lit up. "Let's invite them both here. It might be safer and more reassuring for her son to explore this part of his life surrounded by family who understand and share his heritage."

Margaret gave a decisive little nod, marking Bee's name. "I'll ring Bee today. And with a bit of care, we can guide her son towards embracing his heritage when the time's right."

"And Sarah?" Claire asked, noting her young niece's creative spirit. "Her self-doubt might be her biggest obstacle."

Margaret sighed. "Sarah's connection to us—and to you, Claire—might just be what she needs to find her strength. She already looks up to you." She added an asterisk beside Sarah's name.

The discussion turned to those marked "wait," like her uncle Michael and his son Rafe. "My brother Michael and his boy Rafe... their reservations come from much the same place," Margaret mused. "Rafe's skepticism and the constant rows between him and my brother mean we'll need to tread carefully. And Michael's a crown prosecutor —could put him in a rather compromised position."

"Oh," Claire said. "I'd forgotten that. What if we're breaking some old, obscure law just by existing? He might have an obligation to report what he witnesses. That would be bad."

"Really bad. Maybe it's best to wait on them and gauge the initial responses from those more receptive—stack the deck, so to speak," Ian said.

"Well, we've a starting point," Margaret said. "I'll make the calls. Depending how the first lot respond, we'll see about the others...once the deck's stacked in our favor."

Five

ANJA ACHED FOR rest as she followed Lucian and Zoe into their shared bedroom. Their discussion about the library had left her drained. This space, a harmonious blend of function and comfort, was more than just a living area. An oversized bed promised rest and renewal, and a lounging couch invited them to unwind. One wall had been painted in a warm coral hue, at Zoe's request, and a throw blanket the color of sunrise had been flung across the end of the bed, already tangled from her antics before dinner.

Lucian had added his own touches in quieter ways: a low table carved from dark mahogany held a weathered conch shell and a pair of sleek silver candle holders that matched nothing but still looked somehow right.

Anja's contribution stood across from the bed—an oversized reading chair upholstered in rich burgundy velvet, flanked by a lamp that cast a honeyed glow. A small bookshelf beside it held some of her treasured books from her apartment in Brooklyn. On a side table rested a loaned volume from Raymond, *Nocturnal Yearnings: An Anthology of Dark Love*. Its sumptuous, deep black cover was adorned with intricate, gold filigree patterns. She and Zoe had both read through it at least once and had shared some of the tales with Lucian, much to his delight.

The gentle hum of the lab whispered through the walls, reminding them of the world outside their doors that never slept. Anja watched Zoe move around the room, shedding her clothes and the weight of her worries. It was a ritual of sorts—Zoe's way of marking the day's end, casting off expectation in exchange for softness, skin, and ease.

Zoe's serene actions signaled a collective sigh among them, a silent acknowledgment that here, in this room, they could let down their guard. Lucian began his nightly routines, his movements deliberate and thoughtful.

Anja felt profound gratitude for this space and the sense of belonging that enveloped her as she watched her companions. There was something comforting about ending the day together, about the unspoken bond that tethered them as lovers and as chosen family.

Here, underground, the longer days of the Icelandic summer could be hidden. Anja crawled into the comfort of the bed, the softness enveloping her, and looked over at Zoe and Lucian, feeling immense gratitude for their presence. The silent promises of support and camaraderie were renewed night after night. The sex was good, too, but she was still coming to terms with the darker corners of herself that she must face.

The room was bathed in the gentle glow of the nightstand lamp as Anja turned to Zoe and Lucian. "Howard's presentation today… It's like we're on the cusp of something monumental," she mused.

Zoe, lying beside her, nodded in agreement. "Absolutely. But"—she paused, turning to face Anja—"it's also a reminder of the dangers we face. The Sodality won't just stand by and watch us uncover the past. The Kremlin…fuck, I'm really not looking forward to a trip to Russia."

Lucian propped himself up on one elbow. "Howard's strategy is solid. We're not going in blind, but we need to be prepared for anything. The Sodality's reach is long, and we've only seen a fraction of their capabilities."

Zoe steered the conversation towards Anja. "And you, Anja? How are you holding up? All this talk of libraries and secrets is fascinating, but we haven't checked in on you. After everything you've been through…"

"I'm…healing," Anja admitted. "Every day feels a bit lighter, though I know there's a long road ahead. If I continue to face what I am, I fear losing my humanity. Being here with you both gives me strength I didn't know I had. It helps me hold on."

Lucian reached out, squeezing her hand. "We're in this together, Anja. Whatever comes, we face it. Your strength is ours, and ours is yours."

The weight of Anja's eyelids grew heavier, and the warmth of the bed more welcoming. Zoe let out a yawn. "As much as I hate to say it, we need to catch some sleep. Tomorrow is another day, and who knows what it will bring. Sweet dreams."

Anja sank deeper under the covers, a sense of peaceful resignation settling over her. "Okay," she murmured, the trials of the day and the emotional toll of their conversation giving way to the primal need for rest.

Lucian switched off the bedside lamp using the app on his phone. Silence enveloped the room, and the darkness wrapped around them. A flicker of unease disrupted her calm. The rhythm of Zoe and Lucian's breathing was soothing in the quiet night, but not enough to ease Anja's inner turmoil. She sensed Zoe tense in response.

"I..." Anja started, barely a whisper. "There's something I haven't shared—about the dreams."

Zoe propped herself up. "Like last night? Anja, what's been happening?"

Lucian turned towards her, alertness returning to his features. "What dreams, Anja?"

Anja took a deep breath. "Not those dreams, Zoe. Since I altered Helena's blood oath, I...I created a link between her and me. A link I thought I could manage. But now, I find myself being pulled toward her dreams."

The revelation hung in the air, a confession that drew a tight line on Lucian's brow and a gasp from Zoe.

"It's not just random dreams," Anja continued. "They're vivid, intense...and I'm afraid. Afraid of what it means, afraid of losing myself to them. I've been resisting, waking myself up, avoiding facing whatever it is that calls to me in those dreams. But I feel...I feel like I'm being pulled to give in, to enter Helena's dreams and confront whatever awaits. To become that succubus, draining life in visits by traveling through the night."

Zoe reached out, her touch a balm to Anja's frayed nerves. "Anja, that sounds...terrifying. But you're not alone in this. We're here for you. Maybe there's a way to shield you or to sever the connection?"

Lucian interjected, "We'll find a solution, Anja. This link was created with a purpose, but perhaps it's grown beyond what you intended. Remember, your darkness was riding you at the time. Was there more to it than you understood at the time? We need to understand it, control it, or break it if we must."

"But I don't want to break it and I've been trying to shield. I've been scared to face it," Anja admitted. "Scared of what it might mean for me—for us. But ignoring it won't make it go away. I must confront this, but I fear what I might find...or become."

In the quiet that followed Anja's confession, the weight of her words settled around them. Lucian and Zoe, each processing the gravity of Anja's situation, shared a look.

Zoe broke the silence first. "You say you don't want to sever this connection entirely. Can you tell us more about that? Why keep this link?"

Anja's gaze drifted into the dim light. "The connection...it wasn't made lightly. My demon guided me through it, believing it could be advantageous. Helena, linked to the Grandmaster through the blood oath, could unknowingly or even willingly become our eyes and ears. It's a tether to the Sodality we otherwise wouldn't have."

Lucian nodded slowly. "An edge, yes, but at what cost, Anja? If this connection is hurting you... We don't fully understand the possible repercussions."

Anja sighed. "I know, Lucian, but if there's a way to control it without losing myself, we could gain so much."

Zoe broke the silence first. "Anja, we've noticed you haven't been taking as much energy from sex with us recently. Could that be what is stirring the connection to Helena?"

Anja lowered her eyes, ashamed. "I'm sorry, I just...I'm afraid of draining you too much, of weakening you both when you need to be strong. You may be right, though. I was taking every chance to feed, and with the awakenings, I had ample opportunity. I fell into that out of fear of getting too hungry and letting the need control me. That could be what is happening now. Since Helena, though...and what I became..."

Lucian reached out and squeezed her hand reassuringly. "Hey, it's okay. Just talk to us."

"It's like...I'm only sipping from you both now," Anja explained.

"Feeding too often or taking too much energy at once could drain you completely. That's my deepest fear—killing you by taking too much."

Zoe's expression softened with understanding. "Oh, Anja..."

"We trust you, Anja," Lucian affirmed. "If you need more, you only have to ask. We're here for you, whatever you need."

"Thank you," Anja whispered. "I don't deserve you both, but I can't bring myself to risk your lives, even if you offer freely."

"There must be another way," Zoe murmured thoughtfully. "Maybe you can feed on some of the others. I'm sure there would be no lack of volunteers. Monogamish, remember? This situation qualifies as meeting your needs with others, and that doesn't put us at risk. Ask around..." With a wicked grin, she added, "They could join us. That has always been quite enjoyable."

Lucian raised another possibility. "How about in your dreams? Could you feed on Helena that way?"

"The legends say yes, but the tales mostly talk of visiting a man in his dream or being there with him while he slept. That was likely a gender bias on the part of the storytellers. Lust is the driving factor, so probably. I've been afraid to try." After hesitating, Anja continued. "I'm also afraid this is like rape. She had me raped and enjoyed it—even participated. It's part of what gave me an opening and drove me, in effect, to rape her mind—ride on her oath with her blood on my hands—talons, claws."

The three sat in contemplative silence, each considering the moral dilemma. Anja nestled between Lucian and Zoe, and the skin-to-skin contact was comforting. Zoe reached out to hug Anja and offered a supportive smile. "Then focus on learning to shield, to give you control over when and how this connection influences you. You and Howard know of the arcane and mystical. You're not without options. Just be careful if you visit her dreams to try and feed."

"Thank you," Anja whispered, the words barely carrying across the room but heavy with meaning. "Together, then. We'll explore this shield, learn to control the connection...and maybe turn the Sodality's weapon against them."

Anja sighed deeply, the weight of their discussion still hanging heavily upon her shoulders. She knew revealing her struggles had been the right decision, but part of her still recoiled at exposing this vulnerability. But this was different. This bond with Helena cut deeper than she wanted to admit, threatening to unleash parts of herself that reveled in the darkness.

She steadied her breathing, visualizing the door she had begun to hide behind, one meant to keep others out…and the darkness in. But tonight, the pulses of light that leaked around the edges were strobing like a heartbeat—Helena's heartbeat. Anja gritted her teeth. Even now, she could feel an insistent pull, the temptation to give in, to let the door swing open, and to allow her darkest desires to come flooding out. She turned away, leaving it shut tight.

Sleep eventually claimed Anja, but her dreams did not bring the solace she would have sought. Instead, they plunged her into a world of shadows and half-formed figures rooted in the link to Helena. Dreams were different now since her first awakening, frequently lucid as if it were just another form of consciousness. Sometimes, she had difficulty distinguishing between dreams and reality. As she drifted, Anja found herself drawn toward that door.

No. She couldn't keep hiding from this. If she was going to take control, she needed to stop running. Stop hiding. Anja's chuckle was low and sultry, vibrating through her body as she flung the door wide.

"Let's go play," her demon said in her thoughts. *"We're hungry."*

When Anja was young, her grandmother Madeline had claimed she was on the cusp of a great destiny that could only be fully realized if she embraced herself and accepted what lived within her. Upon her awakening, she'd recognized herself as a succubus but thought that was all; that she had accepted her sexual nature. Even after reading Madeline's diary and diaries from others in her lineage, she hadn't realized that there was more. It was clear that her family hadn't known the whole of it either.

She'd understood it only when Helena's cruel ministration drove her to her darkest times. She had three forms: human, demonkin succubus—more of a crossbreed human-succubus that was the lighter part—and the full monty: succubus. This was the darkness she had always felt and struggled with, her 'other demon,' she had begun to call it, but it was really herself, just unrestrained. She still wondered if her sanity had left.

She was fighting for her humanity and soul, but the battleground was in her mind. Lucian and Zoe's love and acceptance helped anchor her to them and herself, but she wondered if her love for them would be enough. It would be, she assured herself. It had to be.

"Let's do this," Anja thought. She had to face it.

"Yessss!" came the response.

Together, they—she—flowed along the pulsing thread of emotion leading into the depths of Helena's mind.

In this dream, Helena stood alone, clad in a black silk gown that clung to her figure. Although Anja had not seen this setting before, she took it to be Helena's bedchambers in the castle at Zamec Echo. Anja watched as Helena fought with herself, one part craving Anja, the other recoiling from the chains it represented. A battle waged on many fronts played out before her eyes, one of body, mind, and soul, much like her own internal conflict.

Guided by her demon, Anja stepped from the shadows and materialized before Helena as a glowing apparition. "Helena," she said softly.

Helena gasped as Anja appeared before her, radiant and alluring. Gone were the razor-tipped whip, armor, talons and fangs. Instead, Anja stood nude in her demonkin form, her burgundy hair cascading over her shoulders and down her back. Lustrous green eyes met Helena's gaze. Leathery wings unfurled behind Anja, the same deep red as her mane. A spade-tipped tail twined around one leg, completing the tempting vision.

"Anja…" Helena breathed, eyes raking over the succubus's figure. Her reservations seemed to melt away at the sight, replaced only by the desire shining out of her eyes. She reached out as if to caress Anja's cheek but stopped short.

Anja gave a knowing smile. "I've come for you, Helena," she purred. With a sweep of wings, she closed the distance between them, one hand grasping Helena's wrist. Slowly, she guided Helena's hand to her face, pressing into the touch.

Helena shuddered at the contact. Her thumb reverently stroked Anja's cheekbone. "Are you a dream?" she asked. "But you feel so

Six

The room around Helena transformed. A massive four-poster bed appeared, its silk comforter invitingly rumpled. Plush red fabrics adorned the walls, and the air was thick with the scent of jasmine and sandalwood incense. Anja guided her back toward that bed.

Any resistance she might have felt crumbled like a sandcastle beneath a relentless tide as she fell back onto the downy expanse. This creature of the night moved toward her with predatory grace. Anja leaned over her to gaze into her eyes before kissing her. The succubus's lips were warmer and softer than she had thought possible. Anja's tail coiled around her waist, pulling them impossibly close as their bodies melded together. Helena's self-control fractured, the dam that had held back her desire for these tortured weeks crumbling in the face of such exquisite seduction.

Anja's tongue slipped into Helena's mouth, stealing the last of her breath and reason in a searing kiss. Helena tangled one hand in Anja's hair as she drew her even closer. Tonight, she would have this—would have her, consequences be damned.

Anja's tail tightened around Helena's waist as she deepened the embrace and let her other hand roam over Helena's body. Her fingers left a trail of fire behind as they explored the curve of her hip, squeezing a breast. Their bodies began to move together.

Helena whimpered as Anja's lips trailed down her neck. Anja nipped her collarbone with her teeth. "Anja..." Helena gasped, arching into the demon's touch.

Helena moaned as Anja's lips found her breasts, pulling a nipple into her mouth. Her hips arched involuntarily, craving more contact with this exquisite creature's body. Anja took her time, lavishing attention on one breast before moving to the other, her tail teasing its way between Helena's legs to caress her entrance.

Helena cried out, her head thrown back in ecstasy. The warmth of Anja's mouth combined with the persistent strokes of her tail brought her to the very edge of climax within moments. "Anja!" she panted, nails digging into the sheets beneath her. "Oh…"

Anja cast a knowing glance upward before smirking and lowering herself even further. She teased Helena's center with feather-light kisses.

Helena arched into the touch. "Anja…" she panted. "I…I need…"

Anja chuckled, the sound sending shivers down Helena's spine. "And I will give you what you need, dearest, and take what I need," she purred. "Tonight, you will know what it is to be mine."

Her tail coiled around Helena's thigh, spreading her wantonly as Anja nestled between her legs. Anja's hand continued to explore, dipping lower to find the source of Helena's arousal. Helena cried out at the light touch, her hips thrusting upward.

"So ready for me," Anja purred into her ear before nipping at her lobe. "And all for me."

Helena lay back, watching with heavy-lidded eyes as Anja rose above her, one hand slipping between her thighs to tease herself. The sight of wings spread above them was what she had longed to see.

"You are so beautiful," Helena breathed, a wave of desire pooling in her belly.

Anja smiled, her arousal-slick fingers glistening. "Ah, my dearest," she purred before lowering herself onto Helena's mouth. "Taste me," she commanded, her voice thick.

Helena didn't hesitate before obediently parting her lips, letting Anja's sex rest upon her tongue. She lapped at the succubus's entrance, already addicted to the intoxicating taste of her arousal. The sounds Anja made spurred her on, and she redoubled her efforts, sucking and licking the sensitive nub.

Anja gasped, her fingers digging into Helena's hair. She moved against Helena's face in sync with her ministrations. "Yes…just like that…" She pressed against Helena's mouth. "Helena," she panted.

Helena moaned around a mouthful of slippery flesh, emboldened by Anja's reactions. Her core throbbed in time with Anja's movements.

Helena reluctantly pulled away from Anja's core and looked up at her flushed face. Anja leaned down to capture her lips in another searing kiss. Helena's hands roamed back up to cup Anja's breasts, kneading the soft, full mounds as their tongues dueled hungrily.

Anja broke the kiss, panting as she lowered herself down to scissor between Helena's spread thighs. They moved together in the dreamscape, their bodies grinding against one another in a primal rhythm as they raced toward release. Anja's tail curled around Helena's waist like a lover's embrace, drawing her close as they moved.

Helena felt herself teetering on the edge, her nails digging into the sheets beneath her as she clung on for dear life. She felt Anja's tail release her waist and slide between her breasts to coil around her neck. "Anja...I..." she panted, unable to finish her sentences as the world itself seemed to explode around her.

Anja's tail tightened around her neck as her climax washed over her, stars filling her vision. Anja cried out as she took everything Helena had to offer and fed deeply. The ecstasy of their release and the surge of power brought them again.

As their tremors subsided, they lay together, panting and spent. Anja pulled away, settling down beside Helena with a contented sigh. "You could be more," she said, brushing a stray strand of hair from Helena's damp forehead.

Helena smiled, her heart pounding. "Anja..." she tried, still drunk with desire.

Neither woman could foresee the challenges that awaited them upon waking. However, for now, they were content to stay in their dream world and the afterglow of their passion.

"Anja..." Helena breathed, trying again. "What you've done to me is dangerous. It's like you cast a binding on top of what was already there, but it's much more insidious than the Grandmaster's—Eamon's. I took his oath to gain his trust. I had to. You entwined another within it but laced it with desire for you. I don't want to break it even as I want to be free of Eamon. There's no way I can break free of him short of his death. A death I have longed for. Longer than you would believe."

"Perhaps we can find a way to work around it, and maybe even break it. I had your throat in my talons and could easily have ended you. I wanted to feel your life bleed out, to watch you die and the light in your eyes dull and go dark for what you did to me," Anja said. "But I saw another way. A better future beyond death and hate."

Looking at Anja lying beside her, still flushed from their pleasure, Helena felt the stirrings of something she had never wanted or anticipated. Her life had been filled with thoughts of revenge, hate, and death. It was all she knew or thought she could know, but now...

As if reading her mind, Anja said, "I have seen your powers—that you can animate the dead. Death is not all there is in life. It doesn't need to be that way for you."

A tear leaked from the corner of Helena's eye. "I cannot betray the Sodality. Eamon has seen to that. I can't provide you with information that compromises them...him."

Anja touched that tear, gazed at her with those enchanting green eyes, and offered an alternative: "Perhaps you can let me learn about you. Your life and other things that are not directly tied to your other master. You seem to have some leeway and not be held in total blind obedience. Something in your past may hold the key to your freedom. Think about it." With a throaty chuckle, she added, "Dare to dream."

Helena found herself alone in the opulent dream chamber as Anja disappeared. The scent of jasmine and sandalwood still lingered as she surveyed the lonely splendor around her. Her heart still pounded from their shared passion, but now it was mixed with a new seed of apprehension.

Helena believed Anja's request was reasonable. It wasn't directly defying her oath to Eamon, but it felt like walking on a tightrope over an abyss. Would reliving her past be a betrayal of Eamon? Or would it unearth the painful memories she had buried long ago?

The echoes of Anja's laughter reverberated within her dreams, and Helena sighed. She wanted to be free—free from the shadowy chains of servitude and fear that held her captive, now torn between Eamon and Anja. She had sought revenge and found herself trapped instead. Did she dare hope once more?

Lying on the plush bed, drained but satisfied, she let herself dream of her past—an action she hadn't dared to undertake in years. Too many nightmares lurked in those depths. In this dream world, momentarily shielded from reality's harsh glare, Anja had provided her with a way safe enough to remember.

She considered how different the path she had walked must have been from Anja's. Her childhood had been torn away. Love or lust had never factored into the equation until now—until Anja.

Helena found herself immersed in memories of a time long past. It was as if Anja's offer had unlocked doors within her mind that she had long since locked away.

Meanwhile, somewhere between sleep and wakefulness, Anja watched the unfolding dreamscape with a bittersweet triumph. She now held power over Helena's heart—an intoxicating blend of desire and control. Her demon was pleased with her and now sated as it reveled in the beautiful chaos they'd created.

A part of Anja hoped Helena would find her freedom. It was a strange, poignant wish from a succubus to someone now bound to her.

Helena dreamed of her childhood village nestled among the rugged fjords so long ago. Crisp air filled her lungs, carrying the scent of pine, and she heard the distant echo of laughter. Snowflakes danced around her as she watched children play, their cheeks flushed with joy and cold. Among them was her younger self, a carefree girl named after the shining light of the stars. Life could be cold and harsh, but she was loved and cared for.

Her mother, Astrid, stood at the doorway of their modest home, her eyes warm and wise. She beckoned Helena inside, where the hearth crackled with a fire. Her father, Bjornulf, hummed a familiar tune as he sharpened his tools. Soren, her little brother, tugged at her sleeve, eager to show her a shiny pebble he had found by the shore.

But the serene image shattered like glass. Dark figures emerged from the forest—cloaked men bearing the sigil of the church, their faces stern and unyielding. They had come for the village Völva, her mother. Flames engulfed the village, and smoke choked the sky. Cries of terror and pain filled the air as Astrid and Bjornulf were seized and accused of witchcraft and heresy.

Helena's heart pounded as she relived the horror. She reached out, but her hands passed through the apparitions like mist. She watched, powerless, as her parents were torn away again and her siblings were lost amid the chaos. The bite of hatred replaced the warmth of her home.

The cold seeped into her bones as she trudged through a dense forest, the canopy above blocking the sun while snow fell in clumps from the branches. Shadows clung to her like a second skin. Her brother Soren traveled with her, the only one she had saved from the horror that day.

She recalled her mother's teachings, knowing she was destined to follow in her footsteps one day. She immersed herself in the ancient texts her mother had concealed—a grimoire of necromancy and forbidden knowledge. The runes and incantations became her guides, serving as a means to survive and a weapon to wield. They adhered to the forn siðr—the old way, now known as Ásatrú—honoring the ancient traditions. That was why the Christians had killed them.

Helena found herself standing over the graves of those priests who had wronged her, the ground cracking as she summoned the dead. Faces twisted in fear flashed before her as she exacted her revenge, one by one. Each act carved a deeper scar across her soul.

Then came the night she lost Soren. They had been found despite all her precautions. She remembered their frantic escape, the way his hand slipped from hers as they ran through the darkness, the silence that followed his final scream. An ache pierced her heart—a pain that neither time nor power could dull.

Sea mists washed over her dreams as she stood on the deck of a merchant ship navigating the turbulent waters of the North Sea. The cold, salty wind whipped against her face as she gazed at the receding coastline of her homeland. Turning away from the sight and the pain of loss, she looked across the stormy seas that churned as empty as her heart.

Her first sight of the bustling canals of Amsterdam was unlike anything she had ever encountered. It represented a new opportunity. The air was filled with the scent of spices and the chatter of a dozen languages. Helena navigated the crowded marketplaces, absorbing every detail. She studied Dutch, posing as a trader's assistant, and spent her evenings poring over maps and texts in dimly lit taverns. Here, she first heard the whispers of a secret society manipulating events from the shadows. Perhaps they could offer answers to why the priests had hated her family. All she found were more mysteries, so she moved on.

In the narrow, winding streets of Venice, the masks and revelry of Carnival surrounded her, but Helena was immune to the festivities. The mantles they wore only reminded her of the secrets she sought. She learned to converse in fluent Italian, gleaning information from merchants and nobles alike. Under the guise of a courtesan, she accessed circles where rumors of the supernatural were discussed in hushed tones, and Vivaldi concertos played in the background. She learned to use her beauty and her body as a means of empowerment. Love did not touch her. Her heart had been frozen in the icy forests of her homeland.

Dressed in the finest gowns, Helena blended with the aristocracy in the opulent courts of Versailles in France. She mastered French and the intricate court etiquette while discreetly gathering intelligence. Here, she encountered encrypted correspondences hinting at the organization she sought.

The French Revolution soon overtook the country, and the trail ran cold. Maybe she hunted the wrong prey. The shadows were too dark to search. If she sought out the targets of this hidden organization, she could spot their attacks.

Prague was a nexus of mysticism and science, and Helena immersed herself in both. She frequented coffee houses where intellectuals debated philosophy and the occult. In hidden alcoves, she exchanged knowledge with alchemists and Kabbalists, expanding her understanding of the unseen forces.

As the decades passed, Helena found herself in the industrial heart of London. Smoke billowed from factories, and the clatter of machinery filled the air. Adopting the persona of a scholar, she infiltrated academic societies and attended lectures on emerging sciences. The English language became another tool in her arsenal. Despite the veneer of progress, she witnessed the persistent undercurrent of fear toward the supernatural.

Amidst the backdrop of the Russian revolution, she saw how fear and suspicion could be wielded to control. Speaking Russian fluently, she climbed the complex social hierarchies while searching for links to the elusive society she sought. The chaos of the times mirrored the hidden war she fought from the shadows.

World War II's devastation cast a dark pall over her dreams. Helena moved through war-torn Europe, the landscapes scarred by conflict. The hidden hands guiding events appeared to manipulate opinion to further their agenda. She could clearly see the symbols in Nazi Germany.

Next, scenes from Soviet-occupied Latvia showed the streets of Riga, lined with austere Soviet architecture, and whispers of dissent hung in the air. Here, Helena saw an opportunity. She infiltrated the Zvaigzne Syndicate, a clandestine network established to enforce Soviet control. Using her beauty, charisma, and abilities, she rose through the ranks, eventually seizing control.

In a dimly lit chamber beneath the city, Helena stood before a table covered with documents and maps. The Syndicate now served her purposes—amassing wealth, gathering intelligence, and acquiring artifacts.

Throughout these shifting scenes, Helena remained physically unchanged, her youth preserved by the life forces she absorbed from those who crossed her path. Mirrors and reflective surfaces in her dream showed the same face, untouched by time but carrying the weight of centuries in her eyes.

Yet, as she traveled through her memories, a sense of isolation permeated her dreams. The languages she mastered and the customs she adopted all served a singular purpose but left little room for genuine connection. Faces of those she had known faded into the past, overshadowed by her obsession with uncovering the roots of fear and hatred that had killed her family.

A flicker of doubt crept into her thoughts. Had her relentless pursuit brought her closer to avenging her family? Or had it only entrenched her further in solitude and darkness?

She began to mimic the words spoken against her kind, playing the part of a lone hunter. It was then that Eamon entered her life. His piercing gaze and charismatic words offered her a purpose. She showed him her ambitions for power. All he required was her loyalty sealed with an oath, and he would reveal "secrets unlike any you have known."

In the dream, she stood before Eamon again, his presence imposing and suffocating. "Swear to serve the Sodality," he commanded, his voice echoing in the vast chamber. This was the answer to her search for the truth and a chance to quench the burning rage within her. She agreed. The oath was a chain she had willingly clasped around her own neck, though her quick wit and linguistic acrobatics weakened the vow. It was a risk, but it was her only chance to learn the truth.

Under Eamon's tutelage, Helena became an enforcer for the Sodality—a hunter of those they deemed impure. This was the organization that had decreed her family's deaths. She carried out missions ruthlessly, her actions a dark mirror of the injustices she had suffered. Yet a part of her still sought vengeance and freedom, buried deep beneath the bindings of her oath.

The scene flashed to Zamec Echo's grand dining room. Anja and Helena sat at an ancient oak table, its surface polished to a mirrorlike sheen. She had discussed the possibility of an alliance with Anja while she was captive. The collar around Anja's neck suppressed any abilities she might have. That plan had gone wrong. Her rescuers had come sooner than expected and tripped the magical wards. Helena stood to respond, closing her eyes to call the castle's dead.

Shouts pulled her attention back to the room where a nightmare vision rushed at her—a demon of the night, glorious and fearsome. She had not anticipated what Anja had become, nor that she could somehow defeat the metal band around her neck. Enormous, dark wings with vicious spikes propelled Anja, tail thrashing, her dark form glistening with splashed blood from Helena's men. Before Helena could process the scene and react, she felt a sharp pain as Anja's taloned hand closed around her throat. Blood trickled down her neck where the claws pressed just enough to draw it forth. For the first time in centuries, she faced the real possibility of death.

Instead of tearing out her throat, Anja's gaze pierced into the very fabric of her being. Helena sensed the familiar bindings of Eamon's oath stirring, the chains of compulsion reacting to the intrusion.

Anja's eyes never left hers as she spoke words woven with ancient power. Helena felt a new thread intertwining with the existing oath—a subtle yet unbreakable addition. It was laced with a profound longing, an irresistible allure that burrowed into her mind. The realization struck her: Anja was embedding something in her psyche, something she couldn't unwind or resist.

A metallic tang lingered in the air as Anja tasted the blood trickling down her neck with a serpentine tongue. Those eyes held a complex mixture of emotions—determination, anger, pity, even a hint of sorrow. With a final, deliberate act of will, Anja released her grip. Helena collapsed to her knees, breathless and disoriented. The invasion of her mind left her reeling, her thoughts a tangled web of conflicting loyalties and newfound desires.

"**Remember me, Helena.**" Anja's voice echoed in the vast hall. The demon's words carried a weight that Helena knew would haunt her.

A crash of thunder reverberated in the hall. Helena looked up to see Anja's silhouette against the shattered window, a flash of lightning framing her as she spread her wings. In an instant, Anja had vanished into the storm raging outside, leaving Helena alone amid the remnants of their confrontation and the dead.

She awoke with a jolt. Her memories and dreams blended with echoes of the passion Anja had shared with her. Her hands caressed her body as she sought to recapture the ecstasy of Anja's touch. Yes, she would remember.

"Jasmina!" she called out, summoning her maid.

Shortly, the door to her bedchamber opened, and her servant's eyes were drawn to her on the bed. Those dark eyes and flowing hair were nothing like the glory of Anja, but she was adept at the services she was occasionally invited to perform.

Closing her eyes, Helena imagined Anja once more.

Seven

"ANJA, WAKE UP."

Anja was jolted awake by Zoe's urgent whisper. She blinked her eyes open, disoriented.

"You were freaking me out. After the talk last night, it seemed like you were in some kind of dream or nightmare," Zoe explained.

Anja sat up slowly, unclenching her hands. The encounter with Helena in her dream had brought out her darker side. Her nails were receding to normal. That she had started to change while sleeping was a disturbing development. Lucian was watching the exchange with a worried expression from his side of the bed.

"Zoe, Lucian, I need to tell you something important."

Zoe exchanged a concerned glance with Lucian before nodding for her to continue. Anja took a deep breath, gathering her thoughts. "Last night, I visited Helena in her dreams. I talked with her directly, and then I watched her dream of her past, at my suggestion."

Lucian sat up, his expression shifting from sleepy to attentive. "What did you see?"

Anja hesitated for a moment, choosing her words carefully. "Helena is centuries old. Her family was murdered by the Sodality, just like yours—mother, father, sister, and brother."

Lucian's features clouded over.

Anja related Helena's dreams. It was like an epic tale played in her mind's eye.

Zoe's eyes widened. "So Helena has a similar vendetta against the Sodality. But how could she be a part of it?"

Anja nodded. “Helena is still bound by a blood oath to the Sodality’s Grandmaster, but now she’s also bound to me.”

Lucian frowned, pain from his losses reflected in his eyes. “We’ve always seen Helena as a threat, an enemy. But could there be common ground if she shares our goal of eliminating the Sodality?”

Zoe leaned forward. “It’s possible, but Helena’s allegiance to the Grandmaster means we can’t trust her. She might still prioritize his orders over shared vengeance.”

Anja sighed, the weight of the revelations pressing down on her. “Exactly. While Helena’s motivations may align with ours, her bond with the Sodality complicates any alliance. Trusting her outright would be dangerous, but completely dismissing her might mean losing a valuable opening.”

Lucian rubbed his temples. “If Helena is still under the Grandmaster’s control, how can we be sure she won’t use us to further his agenda? Or, worse, turn against us when it suits her?”

Anja met his gaze. “We need to approach this carefully. Helena might be our best chance to understand the Sodality from the inside. Her centuries of experience give her significant power, and her methods are just as ruthless as the Sodality’s.”

Zoe placed a reassuring hand on Anja’s. “We need to find a way to use this common ground without getting caught in Helena’s web. Perhaps there’s a way to negotiate or find a mutual understanding that benefits both of us. She tried to tell us that before she took you.”

Anja nodded. “I’ll continue to visit Helena’s dreams, see if there are any signs of her true intentions beyond revenge. If she’s genuinely seeking to dismantle the Sodality, there might be a way to align our efforts.”

Zoe gave a small, determined smile. “We’ll figure this out together. Helena’s history with the Sodality might be the key we need.”

Howard’s study held a close, warm light from two lamps. Anja stood behind the table and took in the mess—open books, marked printouts, the map with Howard’s notes in the margins. Hours of work sat in uneven stacks.

Lucian, Zoe, Emma, and Dora had filed in when Howard called. Extra chairs scraped across the rug and settled around the table. Anja watched Howard's hand rest on his notebook, pinning it in place.

She drew their attention. "The legends around the Golden Library always pointed somewhere. We need to find it. Ivanov's account may be our first real lead."

Howard raised his palm. "Unfortunately, I cannot attest to that. It may be a start, but after conducting due diligence, it appears that much of the information related to Ivanov's account may be embellished or based on wishful thinking and adventures he had in his youth. He was just twenty-two and wanted to search for the lost library, probably due to increased popular interest and treasure hunting, rather than a desire for knowledge. In interviews, he claims to have held this secret for over fifty years."

Zoe exhaled. "Great. Now what? Is the library even real?"

"I believe it is, and that it still exists," Howard said. "Searches began not long after Ivan the Terrible's death. Records are vague and blend fact with legend, much like Ivanov's, and untangling them won't be easy.

"Interest rose in the nineteenth century. Historians debated possible contents and locations. Those debates drove speculative probes but no firm discoveries. Ivan Zabelin and Sergei Solovyov helped fuel that wave."

Zoe sighed. "Well, do we have any hope for a place to start?"

"Through the Soviet era, the searches continued, but as you can imagine, records are scarce and shrouded in secrecy. Recently, interest in the library has increased again, with historians, amateur treasure hunters, and even government-backed researchers speculated to have looked for it. Searches often focus on analyzing old maps and documents, as well as employing modern technologies like ground-penetrating radar to explore beneath the Kremlin. Despite all of this, no verified discoveries of the library have been made."

Lucian said, "It looks like it's more about elimination at this point, with the most promising leads already followed."

"I don't believe all hope is lost. With the right skills in Moscow, we may gather more insight by approaching some of those involved with recent excavations or attempts to locate the library. Their primary challenge was the Kremlin's status as a highly secure, operational government complex. Additionally, it's designated a UNESCO World Heritage site, making extensive excavations difficult or impossible. The Kremlin has undergone numerous renovations and reconstructions over the centuries, complicating efforts to find the hiding place of the library."

Emma nodded. "We find where searchers left off or overlooked and pick up the trail."

Dora spoke softly. "And the less savory? Moscow's underworld won't have ignored it."

Zoe said, "The Sodality would have looked, too. If they're involved, the danger is real."

"There's more than the physical hunt," Anja said. "Ivanov hints at other threats."

Howard inclined his head. "He spoke of guardians—not flesh and blood, but spirit and shadow—protectors of the secrets. It's a reminder that the defense may be arcane as well as physical. I also found tales that Sophia was a sorceress who guarded her dowry with a curse she learned from a scroll."

"Remember my caution on Ivanov's tale. In the summer of 1933, Ivanov and a friend supposedly found what they had been searching for—an old tunnel within sight of the Kremlin. This was during Stalin's campaign against religion. Stalin had blown up Christ the Redeemer Cathedral, and this was where the pair made their discovery. Ivanov, an engineer on the site, studied a nineteenth-century church document and noticed dotted lines leaving a room. His director dismissed the lines as a drafting error. Ivanov kept looking.

"He said he tapped the foundation with a metal bar and listened for a hollow. He found one. The next night, he and his friend broke through white stone to a rusted iron door. They pried it open and found steps into darkness."

Emma said, "They went down, of course. What did they find?"

"Several nights later, the two returned with lanterns and, indeed, went down to find a maze of tunnels. They followed a passageway leading toward the Kremlin rather than others toward the Moscow River. They passed several tiny chambers holding skeletons and encountered one holding a crucified skeleton attached to a cross with metal bars."

"Creepy," Dora commented, but motioned for Howard to continue.

"Well, after deciding to continue, they eventually came to a rusted steel door about three hundred meters from the Kremlin that they could not force open. They decided to return and come back the next night with tools to help them get the door open." Howard paused.

Zoe asked, "And when they returned?"

"They didn't. Guards at the ruined cathedral caught them leaving and arrested them. Ivanov's boss got them freed and warned them off. Stalin wanted the secret contained. He surely knew the tunnels and used them. Years later, that same boss was arrested and executed, accused of plotting an underground attack on the Kremlin."

The room fell silent.

"So what became of Ivanov and his friend?" Anja asked.

"His friend, Boris Konoplov, died about five years before Ivanov related his tale. Times had changed under President Gorbachev, and he felt he could finally tell his story. How much is true, I cannot say. Ivanov went blind and soon died of 'domestic ailments,' most likely vodka."

Howard stacked his pages. No one spoke.

Lucian leaned forward. "We bring Nomad in. Moscow is his ground. He may have angles we don't."

"It's time he earned his keep," Emma said. "We need to decide what to do with him."

Nomad stood at the end of the table, shoulders square. Quiet navy jacket, clean beard trim, open collar, light brown hair kept close. Nothing flashy. He waited like a man used to being overlooked.

When Lucian finished the setup, he turned to Nomad. "We're at a crossroads. Your knowledge of the Kremlin's inner workings could guide us where maps and history have failed. We plan to travel to Moscow in search of Ivan the Terrible's lost library. Have you heard of it?"

Nomad's hand came up, thumb brushing the edge of his beard. Brown eyes moved from Lucian to Emma, then to Anja, steady and unreadable. "You're serious," he said. The voice was even, trained, soft. "This is the task where I earn my freedom? If caught, it could mean my death."

Howard shifted a fraction. Anja caught the flick of Nomad's eyes to him, then away again. Howard looked down as if he'd only been studying his notes.

"It would be a worthy test," Anja said. "And yes, there are incentives not to get caught or betray us."

Nomad nodded once. He stood a little taller. Light brown hair kept close. Average in all the ways that let him disappear on command. Still, when he met Anja's eyes, something there held.

"I understand what you're asking," he said. "My past won't change. Give me the chance and I'll prove my worth. I'll put what I know to use for something larger than where I came from."

Howard's pen paused mid-line. Nomad didn't look at him this time. He kept his attention on Lucian, clean and direct, chin still, hands open at his sides.

Anja marked the tells, the careful voice, and the practiced stillness. She decided he'd do.

"A noble goal," Zoe said.

Anja spoke again. "Your past actions can't be undone, but they don't have to define your future. Your respect for the challenges we face, and for us by your side, is your first step towards redemption."

Nomad's gaze stayed on her. "Anja, I've seen what you are and what you're capable of. What you are…shocked me. I had expected to die or be tortured after you captured me. Instead, I've been treated well and with honesty. That is quite the opposite of my treatment at the Sodality's hands."

"Then let's move forward together," Lucian said. "Your experience, Nomad, and our resources will help. In the process, we'll uncover more than lost knowledge—we'll find a path to freedom for us all. That includes you."

Nomad nodded. "The Kremlin," he began, "is more than just the heart of Russia's power. Its walls hold closely guarded secrets. My training was not just about espionage or deception; it was an education in the unseen world that operates in and around the Kremlin and below. There are passages, some forgotten by time but not by those who know where to look. The Moscow underworld is a key to understanding the Kremlin's secrets."

Anja's intuition was honed by her supernatural insight and the grim realities they faced. She regarded Nomad thoughtfully. "Your past, though shadowed, may indeed help us."

Zoe added, "Have you heard about the library and searches for it?"

"Yes, it was somewhat of a game and used in our training. Some of the underground is still in use, like Metro-2, for example…" he began, but was interrupted.

"Metro-2?" Emma asked.

"It's a secret underground railway linking various locations, which important government officials use to avoid scrutiny or for emergencies. There's a long history of Kremlin occupants using the underground levels for many purposes, sometimes for spies to come and go unnoticed. The tunnels would be used to evacuate to shelters, store weapons or treasures, even dispose of bodies."

"Our best hope is to find a new entrance. Have any suggestions, Nomad?" Emma asked.

"During our training, there was an underlying objective beneath the guise of exercises and games—to uncover these forgotten or unknown access points. It was a proactive measure, ensuring vulnerabilities were identified and secured before they could be exploited."

Lucian asked, "Are there any such points we could use? Or a way to uncover new ones if the ones you knew are no longer viable?"

Nomad shook his head with a rueful smile. "I doubt any hidden entrances I knew would be accessible now. Security measures are constantly evolving, and the Kremlin does not take kindly to breaches in its defenses." He paused, considering. "However, if we're seeking new points of entry, the urban explorers of Moscow, sometimes YouTubers or other vloggers who creep into the city's hidden spaces, might have found some. They dare to go where others do not. They might have ways in that have escaped official notice."

"We could monitor these explorers' findings, looking for any hints of access points that skirt the edges of the Kremlin's underground secrets," Emma said.

Anja interjected, "We'll need to be discreet. They may be curious or thrill seekers, but they may not fully understand the risks."

Zoe started typing away at her laptop. After a moment, she looked up and said, "There really are explorers like Nomad mentioned. One unlucky one was recently arrested and sentenced to prison. They may understand the risks but choose to explore anyway, for fame, the chance of discovering treasure, or even political aims. I'll have our new intel team start digging. This will be our priority."

Nomad looked up. "Diggers—Diggerstvo. I believe that the government has co-opted some of the best of them. As Zoe has said, prison is threatened if they do not cooperate. Contacting them would be risky, but maybe with the right incentive, one of them may be useful." He looked at Anja and Lucian.

"That may be our best bet at this point. We'll need to approach likely candidates in person. Until we do that, our plans to explore will only be tentative, pending what we can learn from them." Lucian looked around the room and then at Dora. "Dora, I'd like you to work with Nomad and develop some thoughts on how we can get into Moscow without attracting unwanted attention, and find candidates from these 'diggers.'"

Anja, her eyes flitting between Dora and Nomad, sensed the delicate weave of alliance and skepticism between them. Her instinct understood the precarious nature of the trust being extended.

Zoe, falling back to old habits, tried to lighten the mood. "At least it will be summer in Moscow."

No one laughed.

Eight

Lucian stirred as light seeped through the curtains, illuminating the bedroom. He exhaled slowly, conscious of the looming decisions before them. Their upcoming venture into Russia brought too many unknowns, and he already felt the weight of every choice.

He sensed movement beside him. Zoe and Anja, still lying close on either side, blinked awake. Their eyes found his, and the moment they shared steadied him more than words could have. The connection between the three of them continued to deepen.

They eased into their morning routine. Zoe brushed through Anja's burgundy hair while Anja dabbed on her perfume. The scent of jasmine and sandalwood drifted to Lucian at the other sink.

"Remind me to ask someone to restock the coffee, please," Zoe said over the low hum of Lucian's electric razor.

Anja grinned. "I'll put it on the list right after the part where we avoid international incidents."

Clothed and ready, they made their way to the communal dining area, where breakfast had been arranged and the rest of the team had assembled. The table, laden with a variety of food options and hot beverages, was a delightful sight. Lucian enjoyed his coffee while the others discussed trivial matters. Each conversation helped to lift the weight, if only for a few moments.

When the meal ended, everyone moved to the common area. Claire and Ian's departure to England and their safe arrival were mentioned. The conversation shifted to the realities of covertly entering Russia. Dora outlined possible contacts. Nomad highlighted the risks. Lucian listened, pinching the bridge of his nose as he studied the scattered maps.

Zoe touched his arm. Her voice stayed low enough for only him to hear. "You don't have to carry this alone, Lucian."

Lucian turned to meet her gaze, finding solace in her understanding eyes. "I know, Zoe. It's just..." He paused, searching for the words. "Sometimes the weight feels overwhelming."

Zoe squeezed his arm.

Anja joined them, placing a comforting hand on Lucian's other shoulder. "Lucian, Zoe's right."

He took a deep breath. "Thank you, both of you," he said, managing a small, grateful smile.

The atmosphere in the room felt less daunting now. Lucian looked around at his team. They were more than individuals; they were a unit.

Dora leaned forward, her expression serious, and began outlining their options. "Given my contacts in the Polish underworld, we have a few options. One involves using established smuggling channels that operate in the Baltic states. They're used to moving goods unnoticed; we could be just another 'shipment' they transport. I would suggest starting in Poland. We already have a foothold there with weapons and such." Dora glanced at Anja and Zoe. "Please don't take this wrong, but...ummm, I hate to bring this up..."

"Just spit it out, Dora. We need to consider options, so if you have ideas, please tell us," Zoe said.

Lucian caught the pleading look in Dora's expression as she turned to him. "Go ahead, Dora," he prompted.

"We could use Anja and Zoe as part of a 'shipment'—posing as trafficked women..." The look from Lucian stopped her short.

Before he could respond, a calm flowed from Zoe as she held up a hand to stop him. "Let her continue, Lucian."

Anja had a faraway look for a few moments before she looked at Dora. "Let's not be hasty in dismissing this. I'm sure she has good reasons to propose this." As Anja continued, her eyes softened. "Please. I think I know why this is so hard for you to bring up, and you do not need to explain."

Dora looked down before continuing. "Anja and Zoe are beautiful, and their travel would be otherwise difficult to explain in the current environment of Eastern Europe and Russia. With the war and other hardships, traveling as tourists is out of the question. We considered the methods we used to get into Poland the last time, which will work for the first part, but crossing into a country at war is another thing altogether. The stakes there are much higher." She glanced back up at Anja briefly.

Nomad agreed. "Dora and I discussed this, and she was initially very against the approach. Everything else we thought of would bring too much attention or suspicion. The best approaches we could come up with all involved going underground. Anything else had greater risks. This gets us to where we need to be with the least attention directed our way.

"We'll need to secure fake identities and documents for all of us, but that shouldn't be a problem. Those dealing with transport will not look too closely compared to official scrutiny encountered in other circumstances." Nomad looked at Dora, who nodded in agreement. She still did not look happy.

"Anja? Zoe?" Lucian asked.

"I don't see any better options, but Zoe and I will need to work through the specifics. I think it would be a good idea for us to have another conversation with Dora," Anja said, looking at Zoe and then Dora. "Just the three of us in a more private setting after we're finished here."

Dora could finally meet Anja's gaze and nodded once before looking down again.

"So, how will this work?" Lucian asked.

"Nomad would accompany Anja and Zoe as a 'handler,' escorting them to a 'buyer' in Moscow, one who has specifically contracted for the two of them. We'll pick one of the oligarchs to name-drop. It should be sufficient to avoid further questions," Dora said.

Nomad added, "I know names that will get us in."

Lucian nodded. "And once they're inside Russia?"

"Ideally, they can be transported all the way to Moscow," Nomad replied. "Once there, I have a friend in Moscow who owns a brothel. We can use it as a cover for Anja and Zoe when they arrive. It's possible we could all meet there."

Lucian raised an eyebrow at this new information but kept his thoughts to himself. Zoe's influence helped him stay calm, even though he wanted to punch something. He also knew they had their own abilities to protect themselves, but still…it grated.

"How will we handle the rest of us?" he asked.

Dora spoke up. "We were thinking drug smuggling. A new designer drug that we would like to present directly to a buyer and distributor. One that only we can manufacture. I think we can cook up a few samples before we leave."

Elín gave a brief nod. "That should be relatively easy."

Zoe cut in. "Wait, you're talking about cooking up some new illegal drug to sell in Moscow? What about…"

"Technically, it wouldn't be classified as controlled or illegal. It would be more like a new or experimental treatment," Elín responded.

"That's a really thin technicality," Zoe said.

"It's not like we'll sell it or set up a distribution network. Think of it as a sting to catch those who would."

Zoe blinked. "Oh."

Dora switched back to transportation. "Lucian and I can travel with Mike as a guard to cross into Russia. We'll also have to pick up a local to go with us for their connections. Emma…well, she may sneak along as a kitty…"

She was interrupted by a few chuckles and a hiss from Emma, but Lucian motioned for her to continue.

"Graham could cross into Russia at a remote location as a bear, meet us at a predetermined location, and join us as an additional guard. We're looking at routes and will discuss it." Hesitantly, she added, "I may have a few contacts I can convince to help us."

Lucian listened intently, processing each suggestion. "What about transportation once we get to Moscow? We may need to move quickly or change plans."

Nomad leaned back. "There's an old colleague of mine, now a 'businessman' in Moscow, who could arrange for vehicles. It would cost, but he's reliable."

Dora added, "And I can secure encrypted satellite phones for communication between all team members. We must maintain secure lines of communication, so those will be purchased anonymously."

The team continued to refine their plan, taking into account the added elements of sex and drug trafficking. Lucian couldn't help but feel a sense of unease even with Zoe's help, knowing the danger they would likely face.

"The key," Dora said, "is splitting up and crossing at different points and times. Smaller groups attract less attention. Once inside, we rendezvous at the brothel."

Nomad discussed the accelerated Russian language sessions they had begun. "Understanding the language is essential," he explained. "We need to continue those sessions."

Lucian and Anja were learning quickly. Their eidetic memories gave them a distinct advantage, and Anja's other languages made her a natural. Dora had a basic conversational ability already. Mike and Graham were picking up essential phrases.

"Da," Lucian said. Zoe rolled her eyes.

The conversation transitioned to the logistics of their travel route. Lucian focused the team on the first leg, emphasizing the proposed visit to Raymond, the rare book and antique dealer who was Anja's friend.

"Hopefully, that visit will provide more clues," Lucian explained.

Anja said, "I need to visit him anyway. He's helped me so much already, and I want to make sure he's safe and warn him about what we're planning."

"Right. From there, we'll head to England to meet with Claire's relatives," Lucian continued. "That isn't just about gaining allies. It's about building the personal connections and strategic alliances necessary for our future. Claire and Ian are already laying the groundwork; our presence will solidify those efforts.

"Howard, Anja, Zoe, Emma, and I will head to NYC first. Our visit to Raymond needs to be discreet. I also need to attend to various business matters while there. Troubles have been popping up. The Sodality is trying to stir things up. After New York, we'll return to my Kent estate. Howard will remain there to support Ian and Claire by guiding the awakening ritual," Lucian added, turning to Howard, who nodded in agreement.

"Dora, I want you to go to Poland with Nomad, Mike, and

Graham," Lucian continued. "Get set up and make what arrangements and what preparations you can. Once the rest of us arrive, we'll finalize our plans before we move into Russia. Elín, Lynn, and Isabelle, your work here at the lab is too important to interrupt. The breakthroughs you're making in genetic research could redefine our understanding of otherkin abilities and the ability to awaken them. You must continue.

"Sigri, your oversight and coordination capabilities will ensure that all moving parts remain synchronized. You'll have a bird's-eye view, and we rely on you to keep us on track."

Sigri nodded.

As the meeting drew to a close, Lucian watched Anja and Zoe accompany Dora to have a conversation about sex trafficking. He wanted to punch something—or someone.

Helena stood at the arched window of her bedroom at Zamec Echo, her gaze sweeping over the dense forest surrounding the castle and the lake below. The morning mist clung to the treetops, rendering the world beyond her domain a hazy silhouette. She found comfort in the castle's isolation—a fortress in structure and secrecy.

Remaining at Zamec Echo was a calculated decision. Returning to the Vault would place her squarely under Eamon's watchful eye—and hands.

She shuddered at the memories of her recent ordeal. She preferred to keep a measured distance from the Grandmaster. She suspected he harbored suspicions about her nature; his probing questions during her punishment hinted at more than mere curiosity. He chose not to confront her directly for reasons she could only speculate upon.

He believed her oath held true, and she had presented herself for his punishment. No matter the reason, she intended to stay one step ahead and as far as possible away.

She turned away from the window. Her footsteps echoed against the stone floor as she made her way to her study.

She approached the desk and logged in to her link with the Vault. Reports were awaiting her perusal. Opening up the first one, she scanned the contents—a summary of recent movements within Lucian Miller's corporate circles. Eamon had been applying pressure to Lucian's businesses, subtle manipulations meant to force him into the open.

Lucian will have to respond sooner or later, Helena thought. *No man allows his empire to crumble without a fight.*

She closed that one and opened another—a detailed account of sightings and rumors concerning Anja. Helena felt a familiar stir of frustration. Anja was a variable she couldn't pin down, and their last encounter lingered at the back of her mind.

Focus, she reminded herself. Personal entanglements were a luxury she could ill afford, although this was one she had little control over.

A knock at the door pulled her from her thoughts. "Enter," she commanded.

The door creaked open to reveal Anatol, one of her most trusted lieutenants. His sharp features and keen eyes reflected his efficiency. "Madam, we've received word from our contacts in New York," he reported. "There's been unusual activity at Miller's headquarters office."

Helena arched an eyebrow. "Define 'unusual,' Anatol."

He handed her a slim folder. "Increased security measures, encrypted communications spiking in frequency—it's as if they're preparing for something."

She leafed through the documents. "Interesting. And what of Anja?"

Anatol shook his head. "Nothing that we've detected. She would likely be with Miller."

"Continue monitoring the situation. I want updates on any changes."

"Of course, madam." He hesitated for a moment before adding, "There's also the matter of surveillance around the castle."

"Go on."

"We've identified at least two separate teams attempting to observe the castle from the outskirts of the forest. They're skilled professionals."

"Eamon's spies," she said with a hint of disdain. "He's testing me."

"What are your orders regarding them?"

"Keep them at a distance. Let them see what I wish them to see—nothing more. Let them be content knowing where I am."

Anatol inclined his head. "As you wish." He turned to leave but paused. "Madam, if I may be so bold, do you expect a confrontation with the Grandmaster?"

Helena regarded him for a moment. Trust was a rare commodity, but Anatol had repeatedly proven his loyalty. "Eamon is playing a game," she replied. "As long as I fulfill his assigned tasks, he has no cause to act against me openly."

"And the tasks themselves?"

She allowed a faint smile. "They serve my purposes as well. Finding Lucian and Anja aligns with both our interests—albeit for different reasons."

"Understood. I'll see to the arrangements."

After he departed, Helena returned her attention to the map on the wall. Pins marked locations where Lucian's influence was strongest—London, Kent, Geneva, Dublin, and New York. Connecting threads indicated supply chains, corporate holdings, and residences. If Lucian were to surface, it would likely be in response to threats against his assets.

Eamon applies pressure, and I observe the ripples, she thought. *But to what end?*

Her gaze drifted to a pin marking Geneva—a facility rumored to be one of Lucian's pet projects. Perhaps it was time to orchestrate a more direct approach.

Moving to the desk, she typed instructions for her operatives. They would increase surveillance and intercept communications where possible.

A subtle unease settled over her. Anja's influence weighed upon her thoughts. The bond Anja had woven into her psyche was a constant undercurrent—one that, by its very nature, she did not want to break. It didn't compel her actions overtly, but it stirred unfamiliar emotions—and needs.

"Stay focused," she reminded herself. Personal distractions could jeopardize everything.

Yet, in quiet moments, she couldn't help but wonder about Anja and how long it would be before another nocturnal visit.

The sound of footsteps echoed in the corridor outside. Helena listened until they faded away. The castle was secure, but she would take no chances. Eamon's watchers would find it difficult to penetrate her defenses, but overconfidence was a folly she refused to indulge in again. The last time she had…well, that had not gone well.

She turned out the lights, plunging the study into shadows. For now, she would continue to dance along the edge, balancing her obligations to Eamon on one side and Anja on the other.

"Lucian will emerge," she whispered into the darkness. "And Anja will come again."

Nine

Dora sat stiffly in the sitting area of the trio's bedroom. Her hands were clasped tightly in her lap, at odds with Zoe and Anja's relaxed postures. She swept her strawberry-blonde hair back over her shoulder.

Dora had dreaded the day her secrets would be revealed. She feared the judgment and scorn—or, worse yet, pity. The cause she had committed to joining had brought her back into a shadowy underworld she had thought she had left behind forever.

She had returned to that world to help them obtain the weapons they needed to rescue Howard. In some ways it had been empowering. But as she had feared, that box would not close again once it had cracked open.

Zoe leaned forward, her gaze fixed on Dora with an intensity softened by concern. "Dora, when we discussed the routes into Russia, you were...particularly uncomfortable with the idea of using the sex trafficking networks, even just as a cover. There's more to it, isn't there?"

Anja added, "I've found that sharing past secrets has a profoundly liberating effect. You take control back by facing and understanding how they make you stronger in the here and now. When they're no longer ghosts in your past."

"We all have pasts with shadows. Secrets we don't want to share for fear of being judged." Zoe focused on her, making Dora want to turn away, but she could feel an easing of tension and confidence that it would be okay. "Go ahead, Dora, we're here for you."

Dora looked away, a storm of memories darkening her expression. She took a deep breath and felt the weight of her past pressing down. "Yes, I...I have reasons," she started, her voice a mere whisper. "My past—before I became a scientist, before all of this—involved that dark world."

Anja reached out, placing a gentle hand on Dora's. "You're among friends, Dora. Whatever it is, you're safe here," she said.

"When I lost my parents, I was left alone, vulnerable. I ended up on the streets and, eventually, in the grip of a syndicate. They...used me, first as a young and pretty prostitute, then later in their labs." The words pained her, each a reminder of the scars on her soul.

This story of her early life was one she had locked away and sworn never to revisit or reveal.

"Those years were marked by hardship and pain," Dora began, her voice distant, as if relating someone else's life. "My mother struggled with a genetic disease, a condition that drove her to self-medicate with whatever substances she could find. It was a battle she lost when I was just twelve, leaving me and my father to fend for ourselves."

She paused, collecting her thoughts. "My father, devastated by my mother's death, sank into drinking and gambling. It wasn't long before his debts to the local underworld were more than he would never be able to repay. On his last day, I overheard an argument. They wanted to take me as payment. He refused, but they said he had no choice. I don't know how the fire in the house started, whether he did it or they did. I almost believed it would have been better if I had died in that fire with him. Sometimes I wished I had." Dora's voice faltered slightly. "But I survived. Utterly alone. I don't know how I survived."

Dora's memory of her vulnerability after the fire was still vivid. "I found myself on the streets without protection or guidance. My appearance...it made me a target for exploitation. I was forced into prostitution. Those men collected their payment."

Zoe's eyes were filled with unshed tears. She reached out to cover Dora's hand.

"Before my mother's illness, she had encouraged a love of science. The syndicate I was entangled with recognized my interest and trained me in their drug labs. They nurtured my aptitude for chemistry and biology. It was a far cry from the groping hands of old men. Talented lab help was harder to find than young girls for sex. They taught me the skills for their drug-making operations. It was a harrowing time, but I learned a lot. It was a much better arrangement." She paused, reflecting again before she continued.

"As I gained skill, respect, and trust, the syndicate trained me in weapons to provide unexpected backup for sales or purchases. I was their go-to chemical expert who looked innocent and could test for purity or verify substances, but was also useful in situations that went awry."

She glanced up to see them listening intently. "There was a fire—an explosion in one of the labs—not my doing. I was out on another deal. I had considered arranging something like that, but this was an unexpected opportunity. In the chaos that followed, I saw my chance to run. I took nothing but the large sum of money I'd skimmed and hidden away from the syndicate, money I used to make a new life for myself."

With a deep breath, Dora continued. "I changed my identity with the help of a few contacts, for a price—sex and some of the money I had stolen. I was able to disappear and move away to enroll in university, where I studied biotechnology thanks to what I had learned working for the syndicate.

"Of course, access to lab equipment and chemicals brought other attention. Word spread that I knew my way around synthesis. At first, it was classmates begging for study aids. Then, men I didn't know asked for small 'custom runs' off the books. It was a risk, but it let me stretch tuition and keep the lights on.

"I was driven to make something useful of my life, to keep others from suffering the way my mother had. That's what pulled me toward genetics."

"My work, especially in regenerative medicine, is personal. It's not just about advancing science but about healing—both myself and others—and for my mother, who I was too late to save. My past, with its manipulation and exploitation, drove my research fiercely. Eventually, Elín recruited me for the lab here. It was a dream come true."

When Dora concluded her story, a profound silence settled. Anja was the first to break the quiet.

"Thank you for trusting us with your story, Dora," Anja said, squeezing her hand. "You showed incredible strength, and your presence here, with us, is a part of that."

Zoe nodded in agreement. "You're not just a survivor, Dora; you're an inspiration. We're here for you, always."

A weight lifted from Dora's shoulders. The bonds with her new allies were strengthened by vulnerability and mutual respect. The judgment, the pity that she had feared, was nowhere to be seen. The pain of her past would always be a part of her, but now, she had friends who understood and supported her. She was ready to face whatever lay ahead.

Zoe's brow furrowed. "Dora, what you suffered was horrific. I'm so sorry you had to endure that. But here, now, you control your story. You control your life."

Dora nodded. "I know. I fought hard to get here. My involvement in those networks, even superficially, is too close to the past I left behind. That's why I was afraid. I still am, but less now. Thank you."

Zoe took advantage of the conversation's lull and glanced at Anja, who appeared lost in her thoughts.

"Anja," Zoe began, her voice breaking through the silence. "I know you've…well, you've been reluctant to feed on Lucian and me. This option to get to Moscow could provide a prime opportunity to sate that need." She glanced at Dora, who looked startled.

"Oh! My fears blinded me, and I didn't consider that angle. Now I think I understand why you would enter willingly into this." Dora shuddered.

Anja looked up from her reverie and offered a small half smile. "Yes," she replied. "I do have certain advantages by being what I am. A wolf in sheep's clothing doesn't quite seem like the right metaphor."

"Understatement," Zoe said, then added, "And I have certain… protections as well. I'm gaining more emotional influence over others and am certain I can control any situations that arise. I've always leaned into sexual pleasure. Anja has called me a hussy. I didn't correct her, but I lean more toward 'slut.' Now I'm awakened, that has only grown more pronounced."

Anja chucked and nodded at that. "If the men we encounter want to use us...well, it won't be without payment in kind."

As Anja explained how she could use this to her advantage in trafficking circles, Dora shivered; it was too close to the world she had escaped from. But there was a distinction here—Anja wasn't merely surviving as she had been forced to do; Anja was using her abilities purposefully and strategically, maybe even eagerly. The shiver turned into a shudder.

"Dora, we're not like those women who are taken unwillingly into that horrific trade." Zoe's hands curled tightly into fists at the very thought of it. "We have plans and protections. We may even be able to bring some justice for and to those we encounter along the way."

At that, Dora noticed a predatory gleam in Anja's eyes. Zoe looked at Anja intently, and Anja looked down at her hands, curling like claws. Something must have transpired between them, but Dora was afraid to ask.

Dora took a deep breath and closed her eyes briefly before beginning to speak again. The memories were painful but necessary; she needed to prepare them. "In these circles, they'll judge you by your appearance, the way you speak, move, or even breathe," Dora said in a steady voice. She had relived these moments countless times in her nightmares. "Each room will be a battlefield; each encounter is a danger."

When Dora finished her overview of what to expect, Anja broached another topic. "You're strong, Dora, and you could be even stronger. It's deep within you, waiting to be awakened." She sought reassurance from Zoe with a glance.

Dora's pulse quickened. Her otherkin nature was still a mystery, an unexplored part of her existence. "Howard and the others talked to me about it while you were a captive, but I wasn't ready. I don't know if I am now, either. What...what do you mean by 'awakening?'" Dora's voice was a mere whisper.

"Your otherkin nature is connected to who you are. But it's more. For those who inherit a genetic legacy, it's intrinsic—a deep part of your being." Anja paused. "Awakening brings the genetic legacy you have out of its hibernation, so to speak. You've seen the epigenetic changes it brings—the flux receptors are switched on, enabling us to tap into unique capabilities. For some, it enables the ability to shape change. For you, I believe any changes will be mostly internal, more like an amplification of who you already are. Physically stronger and more resilient, harder to injure and faster to heal, maybe even to the point of regenerating lost limbs. Your escape from the fire that killed your father was probably a manifestation of it. It's also why I fear revealing too much. You could rely on it too much and take foolish risks."

Zoe said, "Think of it as a Jungian shadow self. Although Jung and Freud had no empirical evidence to back up or explain their theories, we now have tangible proof there's more to it than psychology, at least for some of us—and you."

Their descriptions fit, stirring memories and feelings that seemed distant and familiar, like echoes of nightmares or fragments of old fairy tales.

"It's a part of yourself that has been mostly dormant," Anja continued, her eyes sympathetic. "Of course, it may not be easy because"—she paused and glanced at Zoe before returning to Dora—"because of your past. You've heard that my guidance tends toward the sexual, and that's probably the cause of your reluctance."

"I haven't since…you know," Dora admitted, her gaze falling to her hands clasped in her lap. Her words were heavy, laden with pain and vulnerability.

Anja reached out, her hands enveloping Dora's. "This could be your liberation, Dora, or it could bring difficult memories to the surface. Only you can decide if it's a path you're ready to walk." Her touch was comforting.

Zoe added, "We'll be here with you every step of the way, no matter your choice."

Dora nodded, acknowledging the enormity of the decision before her. The conversation had opened the door to a path filled with pain and healing, and while the prospect was daunting, their support provided a beacon of hope. As they continued to discuss the awakening ritual, which included elements that would be erotic and profoundly transformative, Dora felt a cautious readiness to explore the depths of her being.

Dora was quiet for a long minute, staring at their intertwined hands. "I trust you," she whispered, finally lifting her gaze back to Anja's. That was the truth—she trusted Anja and Zoe, and now she had to learn to trust herself.

"Thank you," Anja said.

Zoe placed her hand on top of theirs—a tangible warmth. The serenity that blanketed the room was broken only by the ticking of a clock, its metronomic rhythm soothing Dora's anxious heart.

"I'll let Lucian know," Zoe said.

Ten

Dora watched as Zoe leaned back on the sofa rather than leaving to fetch Lucian. Then the realization hit her. She had sensed something unspoken between Zoe and Anja earlier, a connection that seemed to transcend the usual bounds of communication.

Curiosity and astonishment tinged her voice as she asked Anja, "Wait, did she really just use telepathy or something to call Lucian?" The idea was like something out of fantasy, yet somehow, they made it seem mundane.

Zoe smiled. "Yes, in a way. It's related to my talents and part of the triad connection that I share with Lucian and Anja. We can communicate emotions and even thoughts. It developed over time, deepening our bond through our otherkin natures. It's like messaging in a private chat room."

Dora listened, fascinated by the concept of such intimate and immediate communication. The idea was alien yet intriguing. She pondered the implications of such a bond, the level of trust and understanding it required, and the vulnerability involved.

"It's quite special," Anja added, her voice warm with affection. "It's not just about the practicality of quick communication. We're connected on a level that's...well, indescribable."

"That's incredible," Dora said in awe. "It must be comforting to know you're never really alone and can reach out and find each other."

Zoe and Anja shared a look, a silent acknowledgment of Dora's words. "It is," Zoe agreed. "It's a reminder of how our strengths can complement each other. And terrifying if it's cut off."

When Lucian entered the room, Dora could feel the atmosphere shift. The air seemed infused with an energy that had been absent: tense yet hopeful, uncertain yet determined. She noticed him observing their joined hands.

Lucian prepared the serum under their watchful eyes.

Anja explained, "Lucian is using his powers to analyze your genetics and adjust the serum. The base serum is tailored to seek out and bind to specific epigenetic markers, unlocking protein pathways that would generate a recurring supply of flux." This was their fundamental discovery and what made magic possible for them. "Watch the glow," Anja said.

When Lucian was ready, he approached, and she felt his intense gaze. It was almost as if he were looking at her innermost self. Perhaps he was. As he drew a measured amount into the syringe, the clear liquid glowed with a flickering orange light before settling into a gentle red hue, barely perceptible.

After administering the shot, Lucian turned to leave, glancing back at Anja and Zoe with a fleeting smile.

"How do you feel?" Anja asked.

"Tingly, but it's not unpleasant. Relaxed and strangely calm," Dora replied.

"Perfect," Anja stated, glancing at Zoe, who had begun undressing. Zoe looked more at ease than she ever did while clothed.

The door shut behind Lucian, leaving the trio alone in silence.

Dora's eyes fluttered as she took a deep breath. The scent of jasmine, sandalwood, and femininity floated around her. She looked around for the first time since the serum took hold, truly observing her surroundings. A king-sized bed dominated the space on the other side of the room, covered in plush sheets and pillows.

Her heart skipped a beat when she saw Zoe standing nude, one shoulder resting against the wall as she watched Dora with heavy-lidded eyes.

Anja stood beside Zoe, her body fully revealed, every enticing detail on display. Dora's arms tingled with goosebumps at the sight before her eyes; she'd never realized such beauty was possible.

"Anja," Zoe requested, "show her your form. Show her what's

possible." Suddenly, an even more startling change began to happen.

Dora's heart began to pound with fear as Anja's form started to morph before her eyes. She recalled her terror as the dead attacked that stormy night in Poland, in the shadow of Zamec Echo castle—a night filled with horror, when lightning flashed through the storms, and futile gunshots echoed until flames finally consumed the undead figures. Anja had been a dark and fearsome presence among them then: horns atop her head; taloned claws extended; a wickedly sharp tail slashing through the chaos; spiked wings flashing in terrible beauty; blood cascading down her body in the rain—a demon from hell itself come alive.

But this was different. The metamorphosis was seamless, a dance of biology and magic intertwined. Dora watched as Anja's height increased slightly, her body curving and expanding in areas that blended power with pure sex appeal. It was mesmerizing. It was ethereal. A lighter version that was as alluring as Anja's dark form had been terrifying. Burgundy bat wings sprang from her back, almost matching her hair color, unfurling majestically to span the space around her. Two delicate horns emerged through her hair, and a sleek tail ending with a spade-shaped tip danced back and forth. This tail was not sharp and dangerous but softer, supple, and...

"Oh!" Dora exclaimed.

Zoe chuckled and said, "I've heard tales," grinning wickedly at her pun. The tip certainly appeared more phallic than menacing, at least in the usual sense.

This was nothing like that terrible night—the sight before Dora was one of pure sexual power. Anja's burgundy wings spread behind her like a supple cape, casting shadows across the room.

Anja approached Dora cautiously, her hands outstretched in offering as if to say, "Trust me." Dora nodded and let Anja help take off the rest of her clothes until they both stood naked together. Dora's skin was pale and smooth like porcelain, and her strawberry-blonde hair was much lighter than Anja's burgundy. Zoe's darker skin contrasted with theirs, her silky black hair cascading to her shoulders. The change in Zoe was more subtle but no less alluring; she just seemed...more, like nothing Dora could have imagined.

Dora climbed onto the bed and leaned against the pillows as Anja and Zoe joined her. Zoe lay on her stomach at Dora's side while Anja settled on the other side.

Anja's voice was gentle as she instructed Dora to breathe deeply, massaging her shoulders with skilled hands while gazing into her eyes. Anja had deep, beautiful, hypnotic green eyes. "You're doing so well, Dora. Just breathe."

As Dora inhaled deeply, she felt Zoe's warm hands caressing her legs, kneading away tension. Soft touches sent shivers down her spine and settled between her thighs; she could feel herself starting to get wet, arousal unlike anything she had ever felt before. Her nipples hardened unbidden under Anja's heated gaze, and the sight of those burgundy wings spread above them added to the unreality of the moment.

"That's it," Anja purred in a sultry voice that curled around Dora like smoke. "Let your guard down."

Dora closed her eyes, trusting these women with her very core. She arched back, presenting herself to Anja, who wasted no time taking a taut nipple between her lips, teasing sensitive skin between tongue and teeth while reaching lower to slip her hand between Dora's legs.

Zoe's mouth found Dora's other breast, sucking and teasing it. Her tongue swirled around the stiff peak before she suckled hard enough to leave a mark on Dora's breast.

Dora moaned as pleasure coursed through her, more potent than anything she had experienced in the past. Ever. Her hips bucked against the dueling sensations of Anja's fingers and their mouths.

Anja pulled away from her breast, trailing a path of kisses down Dora's stomach, pausing only to tease her belly button. She then settled between Dora's thighs, inhaling deeply before running her tongue along Dora's opening.

Dora gasped as Anja lapped at her clit while Zoe sucked a nipple into her mouth once more. The contrasting sensations sent electric shockwaves up and down her spine.

"Oh...yes, I..." Her moans were cut short when Anja's tail plunged into her wet core, stretching her walls while Zoe continued suckling on her breasts.

As their tongues and fingers danced across every sensitive inch of her body, she felt herself unraveling: mind, body, and soul. Pleasure like she had never known before coiled low in her abdomen, tightening her muscles as she teetered on the edge of release. She was only vaguely aware of her moans echoing in the room and her nails digging into the sheets.

Anja sensed her building orgasm and intensified her ministrations, thrusting her tail in tandem with the suckling of her clit. Zoe moved to one side, taking hold of Dora's hand and guiding it to her groin. "Touch me," she whispered, her voice thick.

Dora obeyed without thinking, slipping her fingers between Zoe's wet folds as Anja continued to pleasure her mercilessly.

Her mind seemed to open to vast vistas where flames danced in sync with words and tones she could not grasp. The flames rose, and embers fell like ashes, forming a map around her. Anja's chants echoed in her mind, rather than in her ears. Beneath the unusual melody was a pounding bass beat that accompanied the movement of Anja's tail.

The combination was overwhelming; Dora couldn't take it any longer. Her orgasm crashed over her like a tidal wave, ripping a cry from her lips that was muffled by Zoe's mouth covering hers. Sparks and lightning flashed in her vision, swirling down into darkness.

She wasn't sure how much time had passed before her eyes fluttered open. She could feel her body thrumming and reverberating from what had been the most explosive orgasm of her life, not that she'd had many before. What she saw was not something she could have imagined.

Anja and Zoe knelt on either side of her. They were kissing passionately in one another's embrace. Anja's tail curled around Zoe and slipped between her legs. Dora could see the tip sliding in and out very clearly.

Zoe gave Anja room to maneuver while Anja straddled Dora's face, positioning herself above her mouth. "My turn," Anja said with a wicked grin.

Dora looked at Anja, desire clouding her vision. She opened her mouth eagerly as Anja ground against her face. The tangy sweetness of arousal mixed with the musky scent of sex.

Anja moaned loudly above her, rocking her hips in time with Dora's ministrations. "Yes…just like that…don't stop," she gasped, her fingers tangling in Dora's hair. Zoe lay on Dora's heated body, one leg propped up, watching the show as Anja's tail continued its dance.

Dora enthusiastically lapped at Anja's folds, sucking and teasing the swollen bud while moans spurred her on. That she could return the pleasure she had received reinforced her newfound confidence.

"Oh, fuck, Dora. Yes, right there," Anja cried out, her body tensing as her climax drew near. "I'm going to come!" With a long, drawn-out scream, Anja shattered apart above Dora.

Zoe let out a cry and shuddered, quaking as she lay over her. It seemed they were all of one mind and body at that moment. The sensation of Anja's tail inside her echoed in Dora's memory and mind so strongly that it was as if she was experiencing both of their orgasms now. Another orgasm tore through her. Was it hers, Zoe's or Anja's? She didn't know or care.

After a while, she lay nestled between Zoe and Anja, a sense of profound transformation coursing through her. The room was quiet; the only sound was soft, rhythmic breathing. The awakening had been intense—more so than anticipated—leaving her with strength and clarity still settling into her bones.

"How do you feel, Dora?" Anja adjusted her position slightly, turning to face Dora with a gentle expression.

Dora paused, her mind and body still vibrating. She admitted to herself that it was overwhelming, but in a good way. She felt stronger and more complete somehow.

"Whole."

Zoe smiled warmly beside her, and her hand found Dora's. The reassuring squeeze brought comfort.

The conversation drifted to their upcoming trip to Poland. Now more grounded, Dora felt a responsibility that extended beyond her healing. She was ready to discuss her role—a task that had filled her with dread before her time with them and her awakening.

"I've been thinking about our plan to infiltrate the trafficking network," Dora began with newfound confidence. She realized that Anja and Zoe would be able to take care of themselves and that she might assist in introducing Zoe and Anja into that world.

Eleven

As Lucian's private jet prepared to land at Teterboro in the bright morning light, Anja observed the dense landscape of New York and New Jersey sprawled beneath them. The city was stirring awake. They had done as much planning as they could in Iceland. Now it was time to put those plans into action.

Lucian leaned over the table. "Once we land, Emma and I will deal with the complications at Coruscant's headquarters in Manhattan. It seems the Sodality's been meddling more than we anticipated."

Emma nodded, her face set in a determined expression. "I've arranged for enhanced security measures."

"We'll visit Raymond at his antique store in Brooklyn and meet you later at the penthouse," Anja said.

The jet touched down smoothly, and the team gathered their belongings, ready to begin.

Lucian and Emma departed for Manhattan in the SUV as Thomas, Lucian's NYC driver, held the door to the Rolls. "Good to see you again, Miss Anja, Miss Zoe," he greeted as they reach the car.

"This is Howard," Anja introduced. "Lucian's uncle."

"A pleasure," Thomas said. "The antique shop?"

"Yes, please, Thomas," Anja replied.

Soon, they were crossing the Hudson into Brooklyn.

The drive to Raymond's shop was quiet. Upon their arrival, the familiar sign of Archambault Antiquities greeted them, its intricate script a promise of the mysteries held within. The bell above the green door jingled as they entered.

As they stepped through the doorway, Anja led the way, with Howard a step behind, absorbing the sight of the eclectic shop for the first time. The air was filled with the scent of aged paper—the many treasures Raymond had collected over the years.

"Raymond, it's good to see you again," Anja greeted warmly as the elderly shopkeeper emerged from behind a pile of books. She turned to Howard, introducing him with a smile. "This is Howard, a first-time visitor to your wonderful shop."

Raymond's eyes twinkled behind his glasses as he extended a hand to Howard. "Any friend of Anja's is a friend of mine. Welcome, Howard. I hope you find the assortment fascinating."

After the introductions, Anja pulled a carefully wrapped book from her bag. "Raymond, I've brought back the book you sent with Zoe. *Nocturnal Yearnings*. It was as entertaining as you promised." She handed it over.

Raymond accepted the book, his fingers brushing the cover. "Ah, thank you, Anja. I was growing a bit worried about you. You hadn't been back in a while, and given the nature of your pursuits, one does worry, even as Zoe here and her friend Emma assured me you were okay. She promised me that you would return the loan in person, as you have." He cast a grateful smile at Zoe, who smiled in return.

"It's been a challenging time, but here I am. We've been quite busy."

"Busy? Anything in particular that's brought you to my humble shop today? Perhaps borrowing another volume?"

"Not this time, Raymond. We're going to search for the lost library of Ivan the Terrible—the Golden Library."

Raymond's eyebrows rose. "The Golden Library? Many have speculated about its existence."

"Yes, and it's a long shot," Anja conceded, "but we believe there are pieces of history we need to understand not just the past but also the forces we're dealing with today. We're gathering all the information we can before we head out to search for it."

Raymond nodded, his expression turning thoughtful. "I see."

As the conversation about the possible locations of the Golden Library continued, Howard steered the discussion towards a specific figure from the past. "Raymond, we've come across mentions of

Bogdan Belsky in some of our preliminary research. He was close to Ivan the Terrible. Do you think he could have known about the library?"

Raymond shook his head. "Bogdan Belsky, while influential, is a bit of a red herring in the tale of the Golden Library, I fear. He was a prominent figure, but if he had known where the library was, I believe it would have surfaced by now, either through historical documents or the family line. His descendants have been well-documented, and none have hinted at possessing such knowledge."

"Are you aware of Apalos Ivanov's account?" Howard asked.

"An interesting tale, that."

"Ivanov claims extensive knowledge about secret chambers and pathways beneath the Kremlin. Do you think there's any merit to it?"

Raymond considered. "His accounts are fascinating, certainly, but they've led to dead ends. His claims were broad, and while they spurred many to search, nothing concrete has ever been found. His tales seem to be steeped in as much imagination as fact."

"What about the possibility that Ivan the Terrible might have sought to move the library out of the Kremlin, perhaps to the east?" Howard asked. "I came across references to his dealings with the Stroganov family."

"That's a promising angle. The Stroganov family had extensive influence and resources. If Ivan sought a safer location for the library, leveraging the Stroganovs' networks and territories would have been an option. Siberia was very remote at that time."

"So, pursuing the Stroganov lead could be worthwhile?" Anja asked.

"It wouldn't be far-fetched to consider they might have helped in hiding or preserving something as valuable as the Golden Library. But then again, if that was the case, it seems that too would have come to light in the centuries since."

"This could mean expanding our search beyond the immediate vicinity of Moscow. Great. Let's just tour Russia. Siberia? Wonderful," Zoe grumbled.

"Indeed," Raymond agreed. "And remember, while the Golden Library is a significant piece of your puzzle, there will likely be other histories and secrets to be found."

As the team prepared to leave, Raymond extended his hand, his expression mingling regret with support. "I must apologize," he said. "I don't have any documents, books, or even letters that could directly assist you with your search. My collections have primarily been sourced from Europe. However, if you come across any leads or items that require verification, please don't hesitate to bring them to my attention. I'm always here to help with authentication."

Anja nodded. "Thank you, Raymond. We appreciate all the guidance you've given us today. It's reaffirmed some of the paths we were considering."

Zoe added, "We'll certainly take you up on that offer. Who knows what pieces we might stumble upon that need your expert eye?"

"Well," Raymond said, "if there's anything you need to know, you know where to find me. Safe travels, and may you find what you are looking for."

As they turned to leave, Anja gave Raymond a grateful nod. "We'll keep you updated, Raymond. And hopefully, we'll return with stories to rival even your most fantastic tales."

With final handshakes and promises to return with anything they found, they left Raymond's shop, the bell chiming behind them as the door closed.

Lucian stepped out of the elevator into his penthouse, the familiar scent of polished wood and leather greeting him. Emma walked beside him, as watchful as ever. Ahead, Ava Mitchell, his personal secretary, rose from her desk to meet them.

Ava's high heels made her slightly taller than Emma, and her slender frame radiated elegance. Her skin had a soft tone that complemented her deep brown eyes and dark brown hair. Those expressive and intelligent eyes met his with a hint of warmth as she smiled.

"Welcome back, Mr. Miller," Ava said.

"Good to be back," Lucian replied. "I wish I could be here more, but things have escalated."

"Of course," she said, holding a tablet. "As you requested, Jonas

Richter, Daniel Reynolds, and Charles Montgomery are waiting for you in the conference room."

"Excellent." He accepted the tablet, glancing over the latest reports. "I see we've had some unwelcome attention."

"There have been a significant number of concerning incidents. As per Jonas, security protocols have been tightened across all departments."

Emma leaned in slightly. "Looks like you have some fires to put out."

Natural light poured into the space through the expansive windows overlooking the city, illuminating the polished mahogany table. Jonas, his head of corporate security, rose to greet them. He was a solidly built man in his late forties with short black hair and vigilant eyes. "Welcome back, Lucian," he said, offering a firm handshake.

"Good to see you, Jonas," Lucian replied. He nodded to the others. "Charles, Dan."

Charles, his corporate lawyer, acknowledged him with a slight nod. He stood taller than Lucian, and his physique suggested he didn't skip gym sessions—a carryover from his military days, Lucian presumed. Charles' salt-and-pepper hair was neatly trimmed, framing a face with high cheekbones and a strong jawline. Deep blue eyes peeked over tasteful designer glasses, and his tailored charcoal suit was impeccable.

Dan offered a brief smile. He was in his early forties, and his rugged appearance hinted at years of field experience. He also had a military background and had been a private detective investigating Lucian's family's murders. Lucian had poached him out from under Horace Reed, his very capable defense attorney.

Dan was tall and lean, and his wiry build spoke of an active lifestyle. He had firsthand experience dealing with agents of the Sodality.

Lucian took his seat at the head of the table, and Emma sat beside him. "Zoe couldn't join us," he said. "She's out with Anja but will be available later if we need her input."

Ava distributed documents to everyone before taking her seat. Lucian glanced around the table. "I've been updated on the situation. There have been odd stock purchases, multiple lawsuits, and negative press from unnamed sources. Someone's applying pressure."

Jonas leaned forward. "We've noticed these moves are sophisticated. Whoever is behind them knows how to cover their tracks."

"Agreed," Charles added. "The coordination suggests significant resources and intent."

Dan tapped his fingers on the table. "It's possible they're trying to draw you out, Lucian. Force you back into the open."

Lucian met his gaze. "The Sodality's intent, I'm sure."

Emma looked up. "It wouldn't be surprising."

"Then we need a strategy," Lucian said. "One that addresses these threats without exposing us further."

"We're trying to trace stock purchases and sources of the mudslinging. Both are proving difficult. There are several similarities to the rumors and videos from last time. The tabloids are running with whatever they get their grubby hands on," Jonas said.

Ava blushed at the mention of the deepfake incident. A very capable operative had created some hardcore videos of Lucian and Vanessa, a high-end escort. The effort had failed, but the sting was still fresh. Ava had been involved in coordinating the response to those photos and videos. Watching them with her boss in the starring role must have been…awkward.

Charles interjected. "We've gone the same route as last time, issuing takedown orders, filing defamation suits, and all the usual responses, but it's like playing whack-a-mole."

"Get a bigger mallet. Any other issues?" Lucian asked.

"Unfortunately, yes. There have been rumblings of opposition to genetic research efforts to go along with the anti-vax movement. There's a Senate bill sitting in committee. The Human-Animal Chimera Prohibition Act of 2023 is similar to the ones defeated in 2007 and 2021. It's related to Republicans blocking IVF protections."

"I wonder if any of the sponsors can be traced back to the Sodality or their influence," Lucian said.

"Yeah, no doubt. I wouldn't put it past them. There's a lot of dark money floating around. The political situation is getting scary," Emma added.

"Let's keep monitoring, but keep our heads down on this issue. We have enough other fights as it is." Lucian changed the subject. "Dan. Any indications of activity at the office we tracked Richard to?"

Dan shook his head. "No, it's been completely abandoned. I went in myself. The place is empty."

"What about the electronics?" Emma asked.

"All electronics were non-functional," Dan replied. "Looks like they wiped everything clean. Probably a security measure to destroy any evidence."

Lucian sighed. "So the trail has gone cold."

"Unfortunately, yes," Dan confirmed. "We've got nothing to go on at this point."

"Any sightings of Raven?" Lucian's tone was edged with frustration. "Nomad claimed she was responsible for the deepfakes and tabloid leaks."

"None," Dan said. "She's vanished without a trace. Again. But it appears she may be in on the effort."

Dan had tailed her once while providing security for Anja. He had been spotted and cut in an altercation with the woman.

Jonas crossed his arms. "They're making calculated moves to pressure us."

Charles adjusted his glasses. "It's clear they're trying to draw you out, Lucian. Force you into the open."

Emma glanced around the table. "We need a new angle. Maybe focus on their weaknesses."

Lucian considered. "Ava, can we dig deeper into any financial anomalies that might link back to the Sodality? Shell companies? Can we find any information that may provide hints on their financial operations?"

"I'll coordinate with the CFO to get records of recent stock purchases," Ava replied, her stylus moving across her tablet. "I'll pass them on to Jonas."

Dan leaned back. "In the meantime, we should assume they're monitoring our responses."

"Agreed," Lucian said. "Try to stay one step ahead. Keep all communication secure and need-to-know." Lucian focused on Jonas. "Let's talk about your priorities. How's the workload?"

"The regular security angles are well covered," Jonas said. "But the new tasks from Zoe and Emma on the Russian front are suffering due to our lack of experience and manpower. With new problems cropping up almost daily, we're getting stretched too thin. Is there anything we can cut back on?"

"We can shift focus off Helena," Lucian replied. "We seem to have a handle on that front, at least for now."

Emma spoke up. "Nomad mentioned that he was recruited into the Sodality by an SVR officer named Igor Krakarov. Can you see what you can dig up on that angle?"

"Okay, but…" Jonas hesitated.

Lucian paused, tapping his fingers on the table. "Jonas, how quickly can we find someone suitable to help you?"

Jonas considered. "If we rush, we might be able to secure someone sooner rather than later. Expanding our search could help."

"If they happen to be in England, that's fine," Lucian said. "We're planning to stop there next."

Emma nodded. "That works. Zoe and I can vet whoever you find before they come on board."

"Perfect," Lucian agreed. "Jonas, reach out to your contacts. Maybe consult Ian as well—he might have some leads on former operatives."

"Will do," Jonas replied. "But just to clarify, what's our top priority here?"

"We need someone with expertise on Russia," Lucian said. "Given that I'll be heading there soon, we must bolster that angle."

"Understood," Jonas said. "I'll get on it."

As the meeting concluded, Lucian watched Jonas, Charles, and Dan exit the conference room. He turned to Ava. "Could you arrange a room for Howard? The others should be arriving soon."

"Certainly," Ava replied, making a note. "And Zoe and Anja will be staying in your suite?"

"That's right." Lucian glanced at Emma. "You've settled into your room?"

Emma leaned casually against the table. "All moved in. Though I was considering joining you, Anja, and Zoe tonight. Could be fun."

He rolled his eyes, a smirk tugging at the corner of his mouth. "They're rubbing off on you, aren't they?"

"They can…"

"Stop right there." Lucian scowled.

Ava suppressed a chuckle, her cheeks tinting pink. "After that last incident, I'm sure the tabloids would have plenty to say." Realizing she'd spoken aloud, she covered her mouth. "Sorry, that just slipped out."

Lucian laughed. "No need to apologize."

Emma grinned. "See? Even Ava thinks it's a good idea."

Ava's blush deepened. "I didn't mean it that way."

"Hey, you could even record it. No deepfake needed." Emma laughed.

Ava covered her face with her tablet.

He shook his head, amusement crinkling his eyes. "All right, stop torturing her, Emma. I don't want to scare away my secretary."

He headed toward the door without further ado, leaving the two women behind him. He wasn't sure that was a good idea either.

Twelve

Anja gazed out the window as the jet descended toward Biggin Hill Airport. Below, the English countryside stretched—a mosaic of rolling hills and quaint villages. The skyscrapers of London loomed in the distance.

The jet touched down smoothly, and soon, they descended the steps onto the tarmac. Geoffrey stood beside a sleek black limousine, his posture impeccably straight. "Welcome back, Mr. Miller," he said with a courteous nod.

"Thank you, Geoffrey," Lucian replied. "It's good to be back."

Anja exchanged a warm glance with Geoffrey. "Always a pleasure to see you."

He tipped his cap. "The pleasure is mine, Miss Anja."

They settled into the limo's luxurious interior. As Geoffrey pulled away from the airport, Anja turned to Lucian. "I'm looking forward to meeting Claire's relatives—seeing what they're like."

"I'm sure Claire and her mother chose wisely," Lucian said. "Ian mentioned that not everyone made the cut for this first introduction. I'm hopeful everything will go smoothly. We should be able to trust this initial group, at least."

Howard, seated across from them, adjusted his glasses. "I've been meaning to discuss my role at the estate. Staying here to help the wolves embrace their heritage is quite the undertaking."

Anja nodded. "Your knowledge will guide their awakenings and help them establish a social structure."

Lucian leaned back comfortably. "You'll be working closely with

Claire's mother. She mentioned that one of Claire's cousins is a history teacher. Collaborating with them should ease the process."

Howard smiled. "A shared passion for history could bridge any gaps. I'm eager to meet them."

Anja glanced out the window as they passed through a charming village, its cobblestone streets lined with centuries-old cottages. "Lucian, you mentioned a batch of serum being delivered?"

"Yes," Lucian confirmed. "Isabelle developed a new formulation based on Claire's bloodwork, both in her human form and as an otherkin wolf, and my tailored enhancements. Since it's intended for her relatives and their lineage, it should activate the flux receptors just as effectively. We also formulated it to be taken orally rather than as an injection. With Howard guiding the ritual, it should work effectively."

Howard's eyes lit up with curiosity. "I've read through Anja's notes and have my own awakening as a guide. I hope that will be enough."

Lucian nodded. "Claire can assist in guiding the new wolves through their transformations after you complete the ritual with them."

"So I won't be the one initiating them?" Anja raised an eyebrow, playfully teasing.

Lucian chuckled. "Yes. Asking you to handle all of them would be rather awkward, not to mention a bit unfair. We don't have time for you to give them your usual individualized attention."

Anja pouted. "I'm guessing sex with the lot might cause a stir. Regardless, Claire will be an excellent mentor for them. I'm sure you will do fine, Howard."

Howard cleared his throat, a hint of embarrassment in his eyes. "Diversifying the process should make things smoother for everyone involved."

Geoffrey's voice came over the intercom. "We'll be arriving shortly."

The limo soon turned onto a long, tree-lined drive leading to the Miller estate. The manor house emerged from behind a grove of oaks.

Lucian glanced at Anja and Howard. "Once we've settled in, we can review the plans in more detail. There's still much to prepare. We should meet with Claire's mother, Margaret, before the others to discuss the approach."

Howard nodded. "I agree."

As they pulled up to the entrance, staff members came out to greet them.

Anja stepped out of the limo, the crisp air carrying the scent of blooming jasmine from the estate gardens. Claire stood at the entrance, her golden hair catching the afternoon light. Beside her was a woman with a warm smile—Anja could see the resemblance.

"Hi," Claire said. "Anja, I'd like you to meet my mother, Margaret."

Anja extended her hand. "It's a pleasure to meet you."

Margaret shook her hand. "I've heard so much about you."

Geoffrey approached them. "I'll have your luggage delivered promptly," he informed Lucian.

Turning to the staff, Lucian instructed, "Anja's and Zoe's belongings to the master suite with mine, Emma's to the adjacent room, Howard's to the room he used during the funeral." Lucian glanced at James, who had just appeared at the doorway. "Could you bring some refreshments to the library?"

"Of course, sir," James replied. "I'll have everything prepared shortly."

"Shall we go in?" Lucian suggested. "We have much to discuss."

They walked through the grand foyer, the polished marble floors reflecting the glow of chandeliers. Anja found herself walking beside Margaret.

"It's wonderful to meet you finally," Margaret said. "Claire speaks very highly of you."

"She's been a great friend," Anja replied. "I'm looking forward to getting to know you and your family."

Emma leaned in from the other side. "I could use a drink."

Claire chuckled. "I'm sure they can find something to your liking."

They entered the library, a room lined with towering bookshelves and filled with the rich scent of aged paper. Lucian gestured toward the comfortable seating arranged around a large table. "Please, make yourselves at home," he said.

James arrived with a tray of refreshments—an assortment of teas, coffees, and light snacks. He placed it on a side table and quietly exited the room.

Anja settled into one of the leather armchairs in the library, the scent of old books mingling with the aroma of fresh coffee. Ian entered, carrying a tray of glasses of Guinness.

"Thought there might be a few takers." He grinned.

Emma reached for a glass. "You're a lifesaver, Ian."

Howard accepted one as well. "Don't mind if I do."

Lucian stood near the fireplace, a list of names in his hand. "Let's revisit the invitations," he began. "Margaret, any updates?"

Margaret adjusted her glasses. "I've only invited those we trust implicitly. Fiona, for one—she'll be here in a few days."

Claire leaned forward. "And Bee—Blevine Musgrave. She's already arrived. With some guidance, she might overcome her fears. Both hers and for her son, Dillon."

Margaret continued. "He's only just turned eighteen and is here for the summer. Bee tells me he's been asking questions already—about wolves, and the old family stories."

Anja sat up straighter. "Dillon? He wouldn't be from New York, would he?"

Margaret regarded her curiously. "It's possible. Bee's ex-husband's in New York, and Dillon was with him up until recently."

Anja exchanged a glance with Lucian. "I met a young man named Dillon at the Morgan in New York. He was exploring concepts like otherkin. He's why I picked up on that. He was like a trigger of sorts."

Emma raised an eyebrow. "Small world."

Anja felt a mix of surprise and intrigue. "If it's the same Dillon..."

Margaret smiled. "Perhaps your paths were meant to cross."

Lucian nodded. "Your previous connection could help ease his introduction to his heritage."

Anja considered this as she looked off into the distance. "It's him," she said after a moment.

Claire added, "We ought to tread carefully. Bee's ex has always been difficult about Dillon knowing anything of the family. No point making it messy. But...he's eighteen now. That choice is his to make."

"I'll go get them," Margaret said.

Anja watched as Margaret left the room, her mind racing. The possibility of seeing Dillon again filled her with a curious blend of excitement and apprehension. She hadn't expected their paths to cross so soon. Here, of all places.

As they waited, the murmur of conversations faded into the background. Anja recalled Dillon's earnest questions at the library, the way his eyes lit up when discussing his feelings and his affinity for wolves and the moon.

The click of the door opening snapped her attention back. Margaret entered, followed by Bee and Dillon. Dillon scanned the room, and the moment he spotted Anja, his eyes widened in surprise.

"Anja?" he exclaimed, a mix of disbelief and joy.

She stood, a warm smile spreading across her face. "Hello, Dillon. It's good to see you again."

He crossed the room quickly. "I can't believe you're here! How do you know everyone? What..."

Before she could answer, Bee approached with a gentle smile. Margaret touched her arm. "Bee, it seems Anja and Dillon have already met."

Bee looked between them, curiosity evident. "I can see that. How?"

Anja nodded. "We met at the Morgan Library in New York. Dillon was exploring some...unique topics."

Dillon laughed. "You could say that. Anja was helping me understand things I couldn't quite put into words."

Margaret said to Bee, "Seems Dillon had already begun to suspect something."

Bee's eyes softened. "Well then...so be it."

Anja gestured to the seating area. "Why don't we all sit? There's much to discuss."

Dillon glanced around, still taking in the grandeur of the library. "This place is incredible."

Lucian stepped forward. "Welcome, Dillon. We're glad you could join us."

Dillon offered a polite nod. "Thank you, Mr....Miller?"

"Just Lucian is fine," Lucian replied with a reassuring smile.

As they settled into chairs, Dillon turned to Anja. "I have so many questions. After our talks in New York, I started noticing...more things."

She met his gaze. "You're not alone. Everyone here understands more than you might imagine."

Bee squeezed her son's hand. "Margaret brought us here to speak about the future…and the past. About our family's heritage—our legacy."

Claire added, "This is a safe place to explore who you are. That's what we'll be doing in the coming days and weeks."

Dillon looked around the room, a mixture of relief and anticipation on his face. "I always felt different, like there was something more beneath the surface."

Anja placed a comforting hand on his arm. "It seems there was—is. We'll help you with whatever comes next."

He took a deep breath. "So, all the legends, the stories about wolves…they're real?"

"Many myths have roots in truth," Howard said from his chair. "History is rich with tales that explain much of what you might be feeling."

Bee offered Anja a grateful smile. "I'm glad you're here. I'd imagined this would be a bit more…gradual, but Dillon clearly trusts you, and you've already spoken with him. Thank you."

Anja returned the smile. "I'm happy to help."

Lucian leaned forward. "You and your family have a unique heritage, Dillon. Embracing it is a personal choice, and we're here to support you."

Dillon looked thoughtful. "I've been searching for answers for so long. If I really could be part wolf or whatever, there is no choice. I need to know."

Anja felt a swell of empathy. "You're exactly where you need to be."

Emma, lounging on a nearby sofa, winked at him. "And trust me, things are about to get much more interesting."

He chuckled nervously. "I can only imagine."

Margaret stood. "Why don't we give Dillon and Anja a moment? Bee, shall we take a turn around the gardens?"

Bee rose, chuckling. "That sounds lovely. So much for the slow and gentle approach…"

As the others began to disperse, Anja and Dillon remained seated. The room grew quieter, the crackling of the fireplace filling the comfortable silence.

He turned to her, eyes earnest. "I had a feeling there was more to you than met the eye. Back at the library, you seemed to understand what I was going through, even when I didn't get it myself."

"I recognized something familiar in you," she admitted. "A kindred spirit, perhaps."

He hesitated before asking, "So, are you…like me?"

Anja considered her response. "In some ways, yes. Many have a heritage or a legacy that was lost long ago. That's another tale for later. Claire, Ian, and the others will be able to explain."

He looked relieved. "That makes me feel less…alone. It's a lot to take in, but I feel ready. Will you be there to guide me?"

"Ummm, not directly, but I'll be back to see you again. I promise. We need to search for more information. We'll be traveling for a while."

A comfortable silence settled between them. The weight of unanswered questions lingered, but so did the promise of discovery.

"Thank you, Anja," he said. "For everything."

She shook her head. "You don't need to thank me. We're all connected in this."

He smiled, the uncertainty in his eyes giving way to hope. "I'm starting to see that."

The door opened, and Claire peeked in. "Dinner will be ready soon. Thought you might like to know."

Anja glanced at Dillon. "Hungry?"

He stood up with a grin. "Starving, actually."

She laughed. "Come on, then. Let's see what culinary delights await."

Anja stirred awake as the first light of dawn filtered through the curtains. Nestled between Lucian and Zoe, she listened to the sounds of the manor coming to life. A knock sounded at the door.

"Come in," Zoe called out.

James and Emily entered the master suite. James pushed a cart laden with an enticing breakfast spread. "Good morning," he greeted them.

Lucian sat up slightly. "Just set it up on the table in the sitting area, if you would."

Emily's accent added a rustic charm. "Would ye like some help gettin' dressed this mornin', Miss Zoe?"

Zoe waved her off with a friendly smile, slipping out of bed. "No, thank you. We'll get dressed after we eat." She moved to assist James with arranging the dishes. Catching the aroma of freshly brewed coffee, she glanced at him appreciatively. "Thank you for the coffee, James."

He focused on setting out the silverware, consciously trying to keep his eyes averted. Anja rose from the bed as well and followed to the table.

Lucian exchanged a subtle look with James, then shrugged. "Let's see what you've brought us this morning."

Emily busied herself by adjusting the curtains, her cheeks slightly flushed. "Is there anythin' else ye'll be needin'?" she asked.

"That will be all for now," Lucian replied. "Thank you both."

James and Emily bowed before exiting the room, closing the door behind them.

Anja poured herself a cup of coffee and inhaled its rich scent. "They seemed a bit flustered," she remarked with a hint of amusement.

Zoe chuckled. "Emily didn't seem to mind on our last visit. It must have been the sight of Lord Charming here."

Lucian took a seat at the table. "If we spend more time here, I think they'll get used to it..." He certainly enjoyed the view. It could be a distraction at times, but it was worth it.

Anja smiled, taking a sip from her cup. "Well, they keep everything running smoothly."

Zoe began filling her plate with fresh fruit and pastries. "Let's enjoy this lovely breakfast before the day's chaos begins. The spook we're interviewing should be arriving soon. Damn. I guess I need to get dressed for that."

"We wouldn't want to scare him away before he starts," Lucian said.

"Hey! Scare?"

"Um, maybe I should have said he should be focused on our questions, not on the gorgeous scenery."

"Nice save, Lord Charming."

Anja adjusted the collar of her blouse as she walked alongside Lucian and Zoe toward the study. Zoe had dressed after threatening not to out of spite. The morning sun filtered through the manor's windows, highlighting the rich textures of the hallway. Emma joined them, a curious glint in her eye.

"Ready to meet our former spook?" Zoe quipped.

"Sure," Emma replied.

They entered the study to find a man examining a painting on the wall. He turned as they approached, revealing sharp gray-blue eyes and a scar above his left eyebrow.

"Mr. Sebastian Harper, I presume?" Lucian extended his hand.

"Call me Ash," he said, clasping the offered hand in a firm, no-nonsense grip. "Though I've been called 'the bastard' more than once, if we're being honest." His mouth quirked into a dry smile. "Usually by people who lived to regret it."

Lucian smirked. "Lucian Miller. Do you know anything about me?"

Ash gave a nod. "Coruscant Biotech. Endless web of subsidiaries. The Miller family fortune. Oh, and your whole clan got itself slaughtered recently, didn't it?"

Lucian's expression remained steady. "You've done your homework."

Ash cast a glance at the others. "And this lot are who, exactly?"

"Anja, research librarian and soon-to-be covert operative." Lucian gestured. "Zoe and Emma, both former FBI."

Ash gave a short, wry nod. "Charmed, I'm sure."

Emma leaned against the edge of a desk. "So, Ash, before we get into details, do you have any questions?"

Ash tilted his head, eyeing the room. "Only what you're actually hiring me for. A man does like to know what sort of shit he's wading into. Is this about your dead family? And where does Moscow come into it?"

Lucian met his gaze. "Your expertise with Russia and clandestine work is what we need."

Ash crossed his arms, his lip curling slightly. "Right. Well. You've got my attention."

Zoe leaned against a bookshelf, her eyes fixed on Ash. Anja knew she would get a feel for his emotions and gently encourage honesty and openness, not that he wasn't rather blunt already. Anja sat nearby, arms crossed, silently assessing.

Lucian took a measured breath. "Before we proceed further, I need your assurance of absolute confidentiality. Whatever you learn of us and our secrets cannot be revealed to anyone outside our circle. You will also learn some extraordinary things that will change your view of the world as you know it. You will likely not believe some things until you see them with your own eyes. It is especially those secrets that you must protect at all costs. Do you agree?"

Ash eyed them each in turn, as though weighing just how mad they all were. "Right. Sounds barking."

"Barking? That isn't the half of it. Your life is about to get very interesting. Do you still wish to go on? Can you keep our secrets?"

Anja could sense his internal debate and struggle to understand what could be so world-changing. He had to find out. She sent to Zoe and Lucian, *"He's hooked."*

"I give you my word of honor."

Zoe gave Lucian a slight nod, more for Ash's benefit than for Lucian.

"Very well," Lucian said. "We've uncovered a secretive organization responsible for my family's murder. While they have deep connections to Russia, they're not strictly a Russian entity. Their influence stretches across the globe."

Ash's interest sharpened. "Now you're speaking my language. And you think my expertise can help you crack it open?"

"Yes," Lucian replied. "We've captured and turned one of their operatives, known as Nomad. He was trained as an SVR illegal. He was not involved with the murders but knew firsthand the assassin who was. That assassin is dead now, but the organization remains."

"You turned an SVR illegal? Bloody hell. You don't do things by halves, do you?"

Emma stepped forward. "It's true. You'll have the opportunity to debrief him yourself."

Zoe added, "We need someone with your skills to focus on intelligence gathering and to guide our covert operations in Russia."

Ash glanced between them. “This organization—do you have a name?”

“They call themselves the Sodality of the Thorns,” Lucian said. “But we need to learn more. You’ll get a full briefing on what we do know or suspect. They cover their tracks meticulously, but we’ve learned some.”

“Can’t say I’ve ever heard of them, at least not by that name. And if they’re as big as you claim, I think I should have.”

Anja spoke softly. “Perhaps by other names, or maybe individuals you’ve encountered in different roles. We suspect they’re manipulating events worldwide, but we have little proof and few details.”

Ash blew out a breath. “Right. Well then. If half of what you’re saying holds water, this could be big.”

“That’s why we need the best,” Emma said. “Are you interested?”

He looked at Lucian squarely. “Assuming the terms are decent and you don’t try to fob me off with a rubbish budget, aye. I’m in.”

Lucian extended his hand. “Welcome aboard, Ash.”

Ash shook it firmly. “When do we kick off?”

“Now,” Lucian replied.

“Knew you’d say that. So, I’m staying here at the estate then?”

Lucian nodded. “At least for now. Howard, my uncle, can bring you up to speed on the Sodality’s history and what we have learned so far. You’ll also meet Ian and Claire; they’re part of our circle and staying here for reasons you’ll soon learn.”

“Smashing. And the immediate?”

“We need your input on our upcoming plans to get into Moscow,” Lucian said.

Ash’s brow furrowed. “And just how do you lot think you’re going to manage that? There’s a bloody war on, in case you missed it. You do realise Russia isn’t exactly rolling out the welcome mat, don’t you? This isn’t a weekend in Paris.”

Emma smirked. “We’ve faced tough situations before.”

He shook his head. “Russia’s another beast entirely. CCTV on every corner. FSB sniffing around. One misstep and it’s a gulag—or a ditch.”

Zoe exchanged a glance with Emma before responding. “We’ll be splitting into two teams and reconnecting once we’re in Moscow. One using drug trafficking channels, the other, um, sex trafficking."

Anja added, "We have some assets on the ground who have contacts and experience in each. Nomad will be going in with Zoe and me with a 'special buyer' he intends to sell us to."

Ash blinked at her. "You're serious?"

Zoe stepped forward, stretched languorously, and subtly enhanced her appearance. "You don't think we would make good merchandise, Ash?"

"I do... I mean... Uhhh..."

"Stop teasing him, Zoe," Anja chided. "Ash, we have capabilities and protections, and know what we'll be getting into. It's our choice. Our options are limited without spending time we don't have."

Lucian met his gaze steadily. "We need someone to help with intel and guidance once en route. That will be your focus. You'll understand more once you have a chance to talk with Ian, Claire, and Howard. Before we go off the grid, you'll have only a few days to communicate with Nomad via a secure link. Ian will be able to arrange for anything you need after that."

Ash exhaled through his nose. "All right, all right."

Emma leaned back. "Knew you'd come around."

He gave her a sharp, humorless grin. "Oh, don't get cocky. Somebody's got to keep you amateurs alive. And I've got a feeling this is going to be very bloody interesting."

Thirteen

Zoe felt the jet begin to descend for their stopover. Vienna's sprawling lights twinkled far below, but her mind was elsewhere, flipping through a mental checklist of everything they needed to pull off.

Her counterfeit Polish passport was tucked safely in her carry-on, and she trusted Dora and Nomad enough to assume they'd pass without issue. Still, her nerves hummed. A lot was riding on this.

"Are you okay?" Lucian asked from across the cabin, his eyes catching hers.

Zoe flashed him a half smile. "Fine. Just thinking about Poland, Dora, and what comes next."

Lucian nodded, leaning back in his seat, one hand resting casually on his armrest. "Polish citizenship suits you," he said dryly. "Zofia Aleksandrowicz. It has a nice ring to it."

Zoe snorted, then glanced over at Anja, who was absorbed in her thoughts, her fingers tracing the edge of her forged passport. Anja's burgundy hair caught the dim cabin light, casting a glow on her features. Zoe knew Anja was worried.

"Don't worry, Anja," Zoe said with a teasing smile. "We've got this. If things get tricky, we'll pull out those Jedi mind tricks you're so good at now. I mean, we got past those officials in Iceland with Nomad and the Controller without even breaking a sweat. You're basically a Jedi Master at this point."

Anja's lips twitched at the reference to their Star Wars movie night when Zoe had introduced her to the Force. "I'll take that as a compliment," Anja murmured, a small smile breaking through her worry.

Zoe looked back at Lucian and considered the trip ahead. They would be split up, and things could go wrong. He would have capable people with him, including Emma, who was watching their banter with amusement.

The monogamish triad Zoe, Anja, and Lucian shared was flexible enough to accommodate their needs. Perhaps now would be a good time to broach the subject.

"Emma," Zoe started, catching their attention. "If things are tense, and an opportunity arises, you and Lucian have our blessing to take the edge off." She gave a lopsided smile. "I'd rather you both come back slightly smug than be tightly wound and end up dead. Right, Anja?"

"He can and should if it comes up," she replied with a grin.

"Take care of the boss man, okay?"

"If you insist," Emma said, her green eyes sparkling.

Lucian looked like he was about to say something, but remained silent. Smart man.

"Dora will meet us at the airport, right?" Emma asked, changing the subject.

Zoe nodded. "Yeah. She'll help us get through smoothly. Having Polish citizenship is one thing, but she knows the customs and quirks. She's been on the other side of this before."

Anja sighed. "It's strange to think how much Dora's been through. She was trafficked as a kid. She was taken to Łódź after her father was killed. Now she's taking us there."

Zoe felt a flicker of sadness for Dora. Her past was brutal, but it had become an asset in this twisted mission. "She can face it on her terms now," Zoe offered.

Emma stretched. "That's true."

"Exactly. Modlin's a smaller airfield with less traffic. Fewer eyes," Lucian confirmed. They had discussed the route—Biggin Hill, Vienna, then Modlin—making sure to avoid high-profile airports and minimize their exposure. It wasn't foolproof, but it was the best plan they had.

"Dora said she grew up in a small town outside Łódź before

everything fell apart. That's where her childhood ended, and her time in the underground began," Anja murmured. "We're headed right back into the place that took everything from her."

Zoe felt a chill settle over the cabin. The reality of what they were about to do sank in. They would be walking into Dora's past—the same streets and shadows that had nearly swallowed her whole. The same syndicate that had trafficked her was now their key to infiltrating this world. In effect, they would be taking her place.

To ease some of the stress, Zoe volunteered her confusion with Polish names. "When Dora pointed out 'Woodge' on the map, I almost had a fit. I hadn't been able to find it! How the hell do you get that out of 'Łódź?' Now I understand all the Polish jokes."

Lucian smiled, and Anja covered her mouth to hide a grin. That was the reaction Zoe had hoped for. She didn't want to lose her touch.

"Zoe! That's not very PC of you," Anja replied, trying not to laugh. "But, yeah, I can see your point."

The plane gave a jolt as it came in on its final approach, and Zoe glanced at her watch, still grinning. Soon, they'd be on the way to Poland, meeting Dora. Then, it would be on to 'Woodge,' to the underground, and deeper into that dark, hidden world.

But for now, Zoe pushed those thoughts aside. She'd need all her wits about her later. It was enough for the moment to focus on the immediate—arriving safely, slipping past any suspicions, and getting to Nomad's van without a hitch.

"Almost there," Lucian said. "We'll be fine."

Zoe nodded, but in the back of her mind, she knew that 'fine' could change in an instant.

The van rattled down the uneven road as the group headed toward Łódź. Zoe shifted uncomfortably, trying to find a spot that wasn't pressing against something hard or making her legs cramp. The small vehicle wasn't designed for comfort, especially not with all of them packed in like this. Dora had apologized for the van, a Lublin, she said. It struck Zoe as odd that there was a driver's seat and a kind of bench seat for two passengers up front and a rickety seat for three in back.

Nomad drove while Dora and Emma sat side by side on the passenger side.

"Mike arrived yesterday," Dora began. "He's holed up with Graham at the inn—it's quiet, out of the way. We decided two bodyguards would be best, just in case things get messy, and Graham has more security experience. Having him cross as a bear didn't seem like the best plan. We'll go over the details later."

Lucian nodded. Next to him, Anja leaned back, her hair tumbling over the seat behind her, listening intently. Zoe sat on Lucian's other side, her expression neutral.

"We've collected the weapons from our last visit," Dora continued, "and enough cash for bribes. Mike brought a few samples cooked up at Akar Labs to establish legitimacy in case we have to demonstrate... you know."

Zoe exchanged a glance with Lucian. The samples were supposed to be potent, and showing them off might draw more attention than they wanted. But it wasn't like they had many other options.

"We'll be meeting with the drug smuggler after we get Nomad set up with Anja and Zoe," Dora added, her gaze shifting apologetically to them. "I'm sorry...I know this part isn't easy."

Anja gave Dora a reassuring smile. "It's how we want to do it, Dora. We've got this."

Zoe shot her a sideways look. She couldn't help but feel a knot of anxiety coiling in her gut, though she buried it beneath a layer of forced casualness. She liked sex—a lot—but still...

Nomad, silent until now, glanced at the rearview mirror, catching Zoe's eye. "I've been talking with Ash," he said, his voice gruff. "Filling him in on everything we're walking into. He's got some contacts that might help smooth things out. Some names to drop if nothing else."

Zoe raised an eyebrow. "Might?"

Nomad shrugged, his eyes back on the road ahead. "It's always 'might' in situations like this. However, if he comes through, it could give us a slight advantage. If not...we're back to plan A."

Zoe sighed and leaned her head against the window, watching the scenery slide past. The van's suspension groaned over another bump, and she couldn't help but smirk at the absurdity of it all. They were heading deeper into a dangerous underground world, squeezed into a rickety van.

"Plan A," Zoe muttered, "always the fun one."

Anja turned to her with a grin. "Just think of it as another adventure."

Zoe snorted. "If by 'adventure,' you mean pretending to be a sex slave, then sure."

Zoe thought she heard a low growl from Lucian as the vehicle continued to bump its way toward Łódź, but it might have been the grinding of the axle. His emotions were roiling, so it was probably a growl.

The van's tires rumbled as they entered the city, the gritty industrial sights rising around them. They passed crumbling factories and derelict warehouses. Once a booming textile hub, the city now had an air of abandonment, its past glory lost to decades of decline. Shadows stretched across the streets, where rusted metal and cracked concrete spoke of neglect, and abandoned machines sat like relics of a bygone era. It was a far cry from their last visit to Poland. Better than zombies, she guessed.

Yet, amidst the decay, there were pockets of new life—modern renovations that seemed out of place against the backdrop of urban decline. Glass-fronted buildings reflected the grim outlines of old factories. The duality of it all—the façade of normalcy hiding a much darker undercurrent—felt palpable here. The city wore its scars and modern mask in equal measure.

They passed through narrow streets where people bustled about, seemingly oblivious to the decay. But Zoe knew better. Beneath the everyday motions of life, there were darker dealings, a thriving underground where black markets and syndicates flourished. This place felt on the edge of something—an uneasy balance between progress and corruption, hope and despair.

The van turned a corner and pulled up to the inn. The inn had likely once been a grander establishment, but time had stripped it down to functional simplicity. It had an air of discretion, a place where people came to disappear for a while.

Zoe climbed out, stretching her legs as she glanced at the inn's weathered stone walls. There was nothing flashy about it, but that was the point.

Inside, the air was stale but warm. The dark wood paneling gave it a heavy, oppressive feel, and the scent of cigarettes and old leather hung in the air. The inn was quiet, save for the murmur of a few guests at a far table. Zoe followed the others through the narrow hall to a room where Graham and Mike were waiting.

When they entered, Graham stood, his figure towering. Sitting with his arms crossed, Mike nodded, though his face looked tense, as if he were already bracing for what would come.

"Glad you made it," Graham said, his voice low and serious. "Everything's in place."

Dora stepped forward. "Nomad, Zoe, Anja, you're with me. Let's stop in my room first to get ready, then we'll head out. The rest of you, stand by."

Zoe took a deep breath. The reality of their plan was sinking in fast, and she thought it was like ripping a bandage off. Just get it over with. She could feel Anja tensing beside her, though her face remained calm. Lucian gave Zoe a steady look.

Zoe took one of Lucian's hands, Anja the other, and they opened their link to him.

"It will be okay, Lucian," Zoe said.

"Zoe and I will take care of each other," Anja said.

"You don't want to know what I'll do if you don't make it through," Lucian sent.

"Love you, too."

It was a silent exchange, but the feelings were clear.

The group split, and Dora led the way out.

In a small, dimly lit room, Dora pulled out a plastic bag filled with clothes that barely qualified as decent. She distributed the items: a cheap, short minidress for each, along with underwear, high heels, and some basic, locally sourced makeup.

"This is all you'll have for now," Dora said. "Anything else will be taken or stolen anyway, so don't get attached."

"Don't have to worry about that," Zoe grumbled.

"You left your cell phones and such in England?"

"Yeah, we all did," Zoe answered. She held a dress up, raising an eyebrow. "This is it? I've seen better outfits in a dollar store."

Dora smirked. “Likely. You’re not here for a fashion show. It’s all about blending in. You two need to look like you’ve been through hell.”

Anja ran a hand through her long burgundy hair. “What about this?” she asked with a wry smile. “I’m kind of stuck with this color.”

Dora eyed her. “Yeah, that’s gonna stand out.”

Anja exchanged a glance with Zoe. “We’ve been practicing with Lucian. Shifting, I mean. We can modify our appearance a bit, making ourselves look younger and less developed. Lucian can do more, but we’ve tried to keep that very secret.”

Dora crossed her arms. “Well, let’s see what you can do.”

Anja and Zoe stripped down, tossing their clothes aside. Anja stood tall, her deep green eyes fixed on a point across the room as she let the familiar hum of her powers wash over her. Her body began to change; her face smoothed, and her features softened. Her curves became more subtle, her entire form assuming a more youthful, innocent appearance. Her burgundy hair seemed less striking, almost a muted shade of red.

Zoe followed suit. Her skin tone deepened to a rich, warm brown, and her features softened slightly, adopting a more distinctly South Asian appearance. She remained beautiful yet looked younger.

Nomad watched from his spot near the door, his gaze appraising but without any hint of heat. He was merely judging the changes.

“It’ll do,” Dora said as they dressed in the skimpy outfits. “Remember, the point is to look the role—to blend in, not stand out. Much.”

Zoe slipped into the dress, grimacing slightly at the feel of the cheap fabric against her skin. “This thing might fall apart before we even get there.”

“That’s the idea,” Dora replied dryly, handing them the makeup kits. “Now, some makeup. Don’t overdo it. Just enough to look like you’ve had a rough few days and are trying to hide it.”

Zoe dabbed on the makeup while Dora went over a few more basics. “When we meet the trafficker, don’t speak unless spoken to. You two are merchandise now. Nomad and I will do all the talking. He’s more like an owner, but the endgame is selling you in Moscow. Nomad has the name of the person you’re supposed to go to. They don't care about anything except how much you're worth and what their share is."

"Also, they may wish to view the wares. You may be touched, fondled, or grabbed. I may even need to touch you," Nomad said.

"Is that your way of getting permission?" Zoe asked.

Nomad remained silent.

"We know the role, Nomad," Anja said. "We won't hold it against you."

"Don't resist, or you will likely be beaten. You can play up the role if you wish, but know what will come."

Anja smiled. "I hope so," she said and received an elbow from Zoe.

Zoe slipped on the uncomfortable heels. She exchanged a glance with Anja, knowing what they were walking into but determined to see it through, although Anja almost seemed eager.

Dora gave them a final once-over. "All right, let's go," she said.

The narrow street where the three-story house stood was quiet, lined with modest, unremarkable buildings. It seemed an odd place for the kind of business they were about to conduct, but Zoe knew these kinds of transactions thrived in plain sight, blending into the everyday.

Nomad led the way, his steps deliberate and unhurried. Anja followed, her heels clicking against the cracked stone steps, and Zoe trailed just behind, her stomach tight with anticipation. Dora walked behind them, her expression unreadable. Zoe could feel the swirl of emotions her face tried to hide.

Nomad knocked on the door, the sound sharp in the stillness of the street. A few moments passed before it creaked open, revealing a hulking brute of a man. He filled the doorway, his eyes cold and predatory as he glanced over the group. Nomad spoke a name in Russian, barely above a whisper, but the brute nodded, his gaze lingering on Zoe and Anja.

The brute stepped aside, motioning for them to enter. Zoe's skin prickled as she crossed the threshold, the air inside thick with the musk of old perfume, sweat, and something darker that she didn't want to linger on. The interior was as grim as she'd expected: faded wallpaper, sagging furniture, and a pervasive sense of neglect. The house had long since lost any pretense of being a home.

They moved through a narrow hallway, the floor creaking beneath their feet, into a dimly lit sitting room. Zoe's eyes swept the room, and she noted the threadbare rug and the low table cluttered with vodka bottles and overflowing ashtrays. The smell of smoke clung to everything.

As they waited, another man appeared at the top of a staircase. He descended slowly, like a man used to having others wait on him. His suit was too good for this place—clean and well-tailored—and his dark hair was slicked back, though the sheen of oil on his skin betrayed the veneer of style.

This was the trafficker. His eyes swept over them, assessing each. He and Nomad exchanged a few clipped words in Russian. The facilitator's gaze shifted to Zoe, and she instinctively reached out to Anja using their link. *"I don't like this."*

"Zofia," Nomad said, using the alias from her counterfeit passport, his tone flat.

"Think undercover work. You can do this."

Zoe held the man's gaze, her body tense. His eyes roamed over her, calculating, like a butcher appraising fresh meat. He didn't need to touch her to convey his dominance; the power dynamic was clear. She dropped her eyes.

He turned to Anja next, his expression unchanged. Nomad said, "Adela." Anja's posture differed from Zoe's—slightly more relaxed, almost eager, though still playing the part of an obedient captive. There was a faint smile on Anja's lips, though Zoe caught the tension in her jaw. She felt Anja's succubus stirring beneath her human skin.

The trafficker's eyes narrowed slightly as he took in Anja's appearance, clearly noting her youth. He glanced at Nomad, then back at Dora, who had remained silent, standing at the back of the group.

"Tovar vyglyadit khorosho," the trafficker said. "Tsena, kotoruyu ty ozhidayesh' ot svoego pokupatelya, kazhetsya vysokoy." Anja translated for Zoe through their link. "The price you expect from your buyer seems high." He waved a hand toward one of the closed doors in the hallway. "Leave them there. You need to prove them before the deal is confirmed."

Nomad spoke in Russian, but it was relayed in her mind. "I have to accompany them to get my commission. I found them, trained them, and found a buyer for them. Remember that. He won't be happy if the deal is broken."

"We'll see."

Nomad gave a curt nod, but Zoe caught how his hands flexed slightly at his sides. He didn't like this, but they all knew the plan. They had to play the part, no matter how far it went.

Dora turned to leave after whispering in Nomad's ear.

The man barked after her in Polish with the first smile they had seen. "You're training girls now, Kasia. You must have learned well while in my houses."

Zoe could feel the flare of emotions from Dora and knew she was suppressing tears...and rage. It was tearing her up to leave them like this. The brute by the door leered after her as she went out into the streets. Zoe knew Dora would be okay, but would soon face more of her past demons.

The trafficker motioned toward another man who had appeared from a side room, his eyes dull but watchful. He approached Zoe and Anja, gesturing for them to go through the door.

As they moved, Zoe's heart raced, her mind cycling through everything that lay ahead. They were walking deeper into the belly of the beast, and there was no turning back now.

Fourteen

As Anja entered the dimly lit room, she smelled the reek of stale cigarette smoke and sex, overlaying a scent of fear.

There was a bed against one wall, a chair in the corner, and a small dresser with a basin and pitcher on top. A single bulb cast sharp shadows. Nomad had followed them in and leaned against the wall with a bored expression.

The man closed the door behind them. "Razdevaysya!" the man barked in Russian.

Anja complied but with downcast eyes. She silently translated and saw Zoe swallow. Usually, she was happy to get naked at the slightest pretext, but this was different. She had no choice. Dora had told them to expect this.

Zoe glanced at Anja. They had no choice but to comply. Anja gave Zoe a slight, reassuring nod and a silent message. *"We can do this."*

They put their clothes neatly on the chair, standing naked under his leering gaze.

The man's eyes swept over their naked forms, scrutinizing every detail. Zoe clenched her fists as she struggled to maintain her composure. Beside her, Anja was a model of silent compliance, her expression calm.

After what felt like an eternity, the man stepped in front of Zoe. He reached out, his fingers brushing against her cheek as he tilted her head back, examining her face. Zoe closed her eyes.

Anja watched as he grabbed a breast and squeezed. They were high and firm. He fondled them briefly before dipping his hand between her legs. Abruptly, he turned to Anja and repeated his rough inspection, only this time, his hand lingered between her legs. She was already slick and anticipating what she knew would soon follow. Her demon, mostly silent since her dreams with Helena, stirred in her awareness. *"Feeding time? Can we drain him?"*

"Not completely, but we'll see."

His eyes lingered on Anja's youthful curves before he motioned to the bed. She could feel his lust building.

Anja took a deep breath, her eyes meeting Zoe's briefly. She gave her a small, encouraging smile before facing the man. With a grace that belied the tension in the room, she climbed onto the bed, lying back on the stained and rumpled sheets, and spread her legs. Zoe joined her, and she could feel Zoe's revulsion.

Zoe clenched her hands into fists. *"I'm not so sure this was a good idea."*

Anja translated for Zoe. *"The white one is much better trained. She's wet already. The dark one, not so much. Tell them to get each other ready. Give us a show."*

Nomad said, "Do it."

"Let's have some fun. Make the best of it. I'll handle the man when the time comes," Anja sent.

Anja reached out to Zoe, who hesitated for a moment before allowing herself to be drawn closer. Their lips met in a tentative kiss, and Zoe's body began to relax. They broke the kiss and gazed into each other's eyes, communicating silently.

The man watched as Anja and Zoe continued to explore each other's bodies, their hands and mouths working.

As they continued to touch and kiss each other, Anja's demon stirred again. She could feel its energy building within her, knowing it was hungry. She could control it so far, but knew she needed to feed it soon. She glanced over at the man watching them with rapt attention. He was almost drooling at the sight of them. Despite the lust in his eyes, he was practically limp and likely to take it out on them. Nomad appeared to be studying his fingernails.

Anja's hand slid up Zoe's thigh, her fingers brushing against her now slick folds. Zoe released a trembling breath. Their lips met in a kiss filled with urgency and need. Zoe arched her body into Anja's, their breasts pressing together as hard nipples met sensitive flesh.

With an encouraging nod from Anja to continue, Zoe parted her legs slightly, inviting Anja to explore further. She didn't hesitate, her fingers tracing circles around Zoe's clit before dipping into her center. Zoe gasped at the sensation, feeling both vulnerable and aroused under the touch.

The man watched with hungry eyes as they pleasured one another. As Anja continued to tease Zoe's sensitive nub, she felt the telltale stirrings of her demon within her. Its hunger was aroused as it sipped from the potent energy in the room.

Removing her hand from between Zoe's legs, Anja licked her fingers clean before reaching out to rub the front of the man's pants. The man let out a low growl as she teased him through his clothing before unzipping his pants and freeing his still-flaccid member.

Anja seductively ran her fingers over her body. She could feel the energy building within her and knew what to do. She rolled over to the edge of the bed next to him. He eagerly began to touch her. As his lust grew, so did Anja's hunger. She could feel it coursing through her veins.

He growled, "You better be good."

With a sly smile, Anja whispered in his ear, "Oh, I'll be better than good."

The man's eyes widened as Anja's fingers closed around him, and he felt a sudden surge of arousal. He gasped, his body responding in a way it had not while he was watching. Her demon would not let a little impotence get in the way of feeding.

His limp form swelled. She could tell that Zoe was watching and, despite the situation, was enjoying the show. Zoe leaned back and started to masturbate. Her lineage and affinity with sex were coming to the forefront now.

Anja could feel her demon pulsing within her, actively striving to fan the flames of lust in the man and Zoe.

Anja leaned in close and whispered seductively in his ear, "I promise you'll never forget this." At her words, she felt a surge of energy from her demon that sent powerful shudders of lust through him.

Anja took the man into her mouth, swirling her tongue around his head before taking him in deeper. She could taste him on her tongue —a mixture of saltiness and musk. The man's moans grew louder as she continued, each sound fueling her demonic lust even more.

As Anja bobbed her head. Zoe was now consumed with her self-pleasure, each stroke of her fingers drawing them both closer to orgasm.

Anja could feel the man nearing his peak, his body tensing as his grip tightened in her hair. With a final thrust, he released hot spurts of seed she felt in the back of her throat. Anja drank it down as she greedily fed on his energy—and his life force.

Zoe reached her climax, a powerful wave of pleasure washing over both women as the man fell limp onto the bed.

Anja turned to Zoe, who was caught up in their shared orgasm. The mutual feedback from their link was bouncing back and forth.

"Enough," she said to her demon.

"Why?" it responded with what seemed like genuine curiosity.

"Because," Zoe said in their still-open link. *"Wait, what the fuck is going on? Why am I talking to, er, thinking at your demon?"*

"Welcome to the club. See why I thought I was going crazy?"

Anja and Zoe exchanged a look as the demon's presence faded, both still panting and covered in sweat. She had shared some of the stolen power with Zoe, as she had shared power with Lucian when he needed it to heal Richard. The bond with Lucian and Zoe made that give and take possible.

Nomad asked, "Is he alive?"

"I think so," Anja replied. "He may be out of it for a while, though."

"It would be bad if he died," Nomad said, his eyes flicking over to the unconscious man. "This won't be the last of it."

Both of them understood what he meant. They still had to get to Moscow.

"I'm still not sure this was such a good idea," Zoe said out loud.

"We'll both be stronger for it. It was the best option we had. Maybe the only option," Anja said, then added silently, *"I've never been able to feed that way with you or Lucian. You can see that, can't you?"*

"I guess so…" Zoe replied to both the statement and the unspoken question.

Anja's pulse still thundered in her ears, and she could feel Zoe's mind brushing against hers, the last remnants of their shared experience crackling in the background of their thoughts. Their bodies were slick with sweat, hearts still racing from the strange power exchange. She glanced at Zoe, whose brow furrowed as she tried to pull herself back from the mental link with Anja.

"No, leave it open, Zoe. I can keep translating for you, and it's getting easier to share this way."

They barely had time to collect themselves when the door burst open. The trafficker stormed in, his expression darkening as he took in the sight of the man unconscious on the bed.

"What the hell is going on here?" he barked, his voice sharp with suspicion. His gaze darted between Anja and Zoe and then to Nomad, who stood against the far wall, watching the entire situation with detached interest.

The trafficker stalked over to the bed and kicked the unconscious man's legs. The limp body shifted but did not wake. With a growl, the trafficker crouched down and slapped the man's face a couple of times, trying to rouse him. The man stirred, mumbling.

Anja smiled sweetly, batting her lashes at the trafficker as he glared at her. "We showed him the best time of his life," she said, her voice like honey. "It must have been too much for him to handle."

The trafficker narrowed his eyes at her, then back at the tester, who was slowly coming around, still dazed and confused. He leaned in closer, muttering harsh words in Polish to the man, who jolted awake, his eyes wide. The trafficker pulled him upright and shook him, demanding answers.

"I...I have to buy them," the man stammered, his words slurred but insistent. "I must buy them. They...they're worth..."

Anja's smile widened as she exchanged a glance with Zoe. Zoe shrugged slightly, the corners of her lips twitching upward.

Nomad, standing off to the side, let out a scoffing laugh. He pushed away from the wall, arms crossed over his chest as he stepped closer to the man. "You?" Nomad said, his voice laced with contempt. "You can't afford them. They're already spoken for. Far too valuable for the likes of you."

The trafficker's face twisted in frustration as he glanced between Nomad, Anja, and Zoe.

The tester still had a look of disbelief, like he wasn't entirely sure what had just happened, but his eager insistence was hard to ignore.

"They…seem to be worth what you said," the trafficker finally admitted, though his voice was strained. He didn't want to make that concession. "But this…this is unusual. We need to renegotiate."

Nomad shook his head. "There's no need for renegotiation. You've seen what they can do. They're worth more than you realize. The price is set. You'll get your commission when they're sold in Moscow."

The trafficker's lips curled into a hard line as Nomad's words hung in the air. "Maybe you didn't hear me," he growled, his voice low and dangerous. "I said we need to renegotiate. This isn't just transport anymore. They're valuable—but that means more risk."

Nomad's expression remained icy. "The risk is why you'll be well compensated," he said. "But don't try to strong-arm us. The price is set. When they're delivered, you'll get what you're due in Moscow."

The trafficker's eyes darkened, his hands balling into fists at his sides. "That's not good enough," he spat. "These two are trouble, and we both know it. I'm not sending some lackeys to babysit them all the way to Moscow. No, I'll be going with you. And that means the price for transport just went up."

Zoe shifted beside Anja, tension radiating from her as she eyed the trafficker. Zoe's unease mirrored her own, but they both remained silent, waiting for Nomad's response.

Nomad's eyes flicked to the trafficker, his lips curving into a dangerous smile. "You think traveling with us will change the deal? It won't. You'll get paid when we arrive in Moscow and not a second before."

The trafficker let out a bitter laugh, shaking his head. "That's not how this works, friend. Transporting them means keeping them safe, and I'm not sticking my neck out for nothing. They'll earn their keep if you can't pay more upfront."

A cold silence fell over the room as the implications of his words sank in. Zoe's gaze sharpened, her jaw tightened, and her eyes flashed with barely contained anger. Anja's muscles tensed, and the demon within her stirred with the promise of violence, but she kept it in check for now.

"Let it go, Zoe."

Aloud, she said, "I'm sure you two can come to an agreement," putting some energy into the suggestion.

The trafficker's eyes gleamed. "There are a few stops on the way to Moscow," he said smoothly, as though he hadn't insulted them. "Places where I do business. Houses I run. We'll stay there, and they can...work for their transport. Earn their keep."

Anja took a deep breath, suppressing the dark laughter she could hear echoing in her mind. She caught Zoe's eye, the briefest exchange of understanding passing between them. This was part of the game.

Nomad stepped closer to the trafficker, his face like stone. "You've already been paid a substantial sum for transport," he said, his voice dripping with menace. "They won't be 'working' for you on this trip. They're spoken for, and their value is far beyond what your customers could afford."

The trafficker narrowed his eyes, his bravado faltering momentarily. But he recovered, crossing his arms over his chest. "Then you'd better come up with more cash if you don't want them earning it another way. I've got expenses."

Nomad's eyes darkened, and for a split second, Anja thought he might lash out, his calm finally cracking. But instead, he took a deep breath and smiled, though it was anything but friendly.

"We'll see about that," Nomad said, his voice barely above a whisper, yet it carried the weight of a threat.

The trafficker's smirk faltered for a fraction of a second, but he covered it with a sneer. "You don't scare me," he said, though his voice held a trace of uncertainty.

Nomad took a step back, his smile never wavering. "It's time to get moving."

The trafficker took a deep breath, turning his gaze back to the girls. "Fine," he grumbled. "I'll get everything ready for the trip. But know this—if anything goes wrong, you'll regret it."

He gestured toward the tester, who was struggling to regain his composure. "Get him out of here," he snapped at one of the other men waiting by the door. The man rushed forward, hoisting the tester to his feet and pulling him out of the room.

"Get ready. We leave soon." The trafficker gave them one last glare before storming out of the room, barking orders to his men as he went, leaving the door ajar behind him.

As soon as he was gone, the tension in the room lifted, and Anja let out a sigh of relief.

"That could have gone worse," Zoe muttered, her eyes flicking to Nomad.

"It's not over yet," Nomad replied. "We have a long way to Moscow and plenty of time for things to go wrong."

"Great. Way to give a pep talk," Zoe said before turning to Anja with a raised eyebrow. "Best time of his life?" she asked, amusement lacing her voice.

Anja grinned. "Obviously."

Zoe rolled her eyes, but there was a smile on her lips. *"Next time, a little warning before I talk to your demon would be nice."*

"Awww." Anja chuckled softly, then sobered. *"At this point, I don't think it works that way. She's part of me now. Maybe* is *me, if that makes sense. Maybe I'm crazy."*

Nomad watched them both as they finished dressing, his face unreadable, but there was the faintest flicker of something in his eyes. "Let's get going."

Fifteen

DORA DESCENDED THE steps of the house, her heartbeat pounding in her ears. The echo of the man's taunt still clung to her skin like the stench of the place, impossible to shake. *You must have learned well while in my houses.* Her jaw clenched so tightly it hurt, but she didn't dare look back, not at the leering brute by the door, not at Nomad, and definitely not at Zoe and Anja.

As soon as her feet hit the cracked pavement, she felt the tight grip of control slipping away. Her breath came in ragged bursts, each carrying the weight of memories and faces she had long since buried in the recesses of her mind. The shadows swallowed her as she hurried to the Lublin parked under a dim streetlight. The air felt heavy, thick, and suffocating. It tasted of smoke and decay.

The door to the van creaked as she yanked it open and slid inside. The cold vinyl seat did little to abate the heat of her anger. The door slammed shut, and the moment it did, the last of her composure crumbled. Her hands tightened around the steering wheel as a wave of fury tore through her.

She had whispered a threat to Nomad, and she meant it. If this went wrong, if something happened to Zoe and Anja, she would make sure Nomad paid for it—slowly. He would never taste the freedom he sought. But beneath the anger was the gnawing fear that it might not be enough. She had to trust him—them.

Her chest tightened as the tears she had fought so hard to suppress finally spilled over, running down her cheeks in hot, angry streams. She slammed her fists against the steering wheel, a muffled scream of frustration escaping. How had it come to this? How had she, once a victim of this world, now found herself playing its twisted game again? The faces of the men who had owned her flashed in her mind, and she recoiled at the thought of Zoe and Anja having to face what she had endured.

The tears kept coming, and Dora let them, just for now. It wasn't weakness—it was survival. But the raw edges of her emotions cut deep, and she wasn't sure if she could stitch herself back together this time if Anja and Zoe didn't make it through.

Finally, after what felt like hours but was only minutes, she inhaled deeply, forcing herself to gather what strength remained. She wiped away the tears, leaving her face blotchy. She couldn't afford to break, not now. Not when so much was at stake.

Dora checked the rearview mirror. Her reflection was barely visible in the dim light. Her eyes were red, swollen from the tears, but they were hers—no longer the hollow, empty eyes she had once worn in the houses. She was in control now, and she needed to remember that. No one would take that from her again.

The engine rumbled to life with a low growl that matched the storm raging within. With one last glance at the house, she shifted the car into gear and pulled out onto the street. As she drove through the narrow streets of Łódź, the once-familiar landscape flowed past, but it now felt foreign, like an old enemy she was forced to confront again.

She headed back to the inn, where the others were waiting. They needed her to hold it together, to focus on the plan, but her mind was spinning. If anything happened to Zoe or Anja, she would burn this city to the ground, regardless of the consequences. Somehow, she knew she could.

The night air slipped through the cracked window, drying the last remnants of her tears. Dora clenched the steering wheel again, her anger now a glowing ember instead of a raging fire. She would be strong. She had to be. For them. For herself.

As the inn's lights came into view, she took another deep breath, forcing calm back into her body. It was time to face the other demons waiting for her. But they would find she was no longer the girl they had once known.

Dora pushed open the door to her room, the tension still clinging to her like a second skin. The rest of the group was crowded inside. Lucian's dark eyes flicked up to meet hers, scanning her face for signs of distress, but to his credit, he didn't comment. He didn't need to. His lips pressed into a thin line, and his only question was a clipped, "Are they in?"

It was clear who he referred to. The weight of the situation pressed on all of them, and Lucian's disapproval of the arrangement lingered in the air.

Dora nodded. "They're in. It's our turn now. Emma, here's your costume," she said as she pulled out a black collar.

"What the fuck is that? You can't expect..."

"It has a microphone and transmitter embedded in it. This was Nomad's suggestion, seeing as your grasp of Russian and Polish seems minimal. Good at sneaking but not so good at reporting what you hear."

"Oh."

"Care to try it on?"

With a scorching look, Emma started to undress. "You'll be carrying my clothes, I presume?"

"Yes, but you probably won't need them until we reach Moscow."

Emma sat on the sofa and closed her eyes. Dora was still in awe of the ability as she shrank and curled up. Her long black hair receded as her body formed a shorter fur of the same color. Soon, Emma looked up with green cat eyes.

Dora leaned in with the collar, and Emma hissed before issuing a rather menacing growl. "I think you should do the honors, Lucian."

Lucian took it and showed it to Emma, letting her sniff it. "It could be worse. I hear flea collars smell awful."

Another hiss, but she flattened her ears back and stared at him as he eased it on.

"There, *purrfect* fit. We'll test it out later to make sure we can record."

Dora retrieved a set of sleek, unassuming cell phones and wireless earbuds from her bag, distributing them to each. "Jonas had these specially acquired for us with guidance from Ash and Nomad," she said. "They have satellite capability, so they can be used and stay off the local cell networks. The hardware to do that has been introduced into most recent models, but not activated—these have been."

Mike turned the device over in his hand. "They look ordinary enough."

"That's the point," Dora replied. "But they have a few hidden features. Encrypted messaging and secure connections that can't be easily traced. Nomad walked me through the specs, and Ash provided additional instructions and tests to ensure they're up to the task."

Graham raised an eyebrow. "And we're confident these are secure?"

"Better than what I had in mind," she admitted. "We can communicate covertly without raising any red flags. It's best to leave them in airplane mode or off and use them only when needed."

Emma leapt down from the sofa, her eyes glinting with curiosity as she padded over to inspect the phone in Mike's hand. Dora chuckle. "Even in cat form, you're nosy. Remember what they say about curiosity and cats..."

Emma's hiss drew a chuckle from Lucian.

Dora reached into her bag and pulled out a small plastic pouch containing a bloodstained rag. She tossed it to Lucian, who caught it with a sharp look. Next, she handed him a stolen passport. It was worn with frayed edges, but it would serve its purpose.

"You said you could mimic someone if you had their DNA," Dora said. "Time to see if that's true."

Lucian's eyes darkened as he looked at the bloodied cloth. She had seen him use his powers a few times to shift and heal, but this? He'd said he had experimented a little, but this was why the secrecy. It was a novel form of identity theft. Anja had even hinted that he might be able to become a woman, saying it would do him good to experience what they experienced.

He held the rag, his expression hardening with focus. "This should work," he muttered, more to himself than anyone else.

Emma returned to the sofa and curled up again, watching with half-closed eyes. The sight sent a slight shiver down Dora's spine. She couldn't shake the old superstitions about black cats being bad omens, but she had to remind herself that Emma was far from unlucky. If anything, Emma's presence was their secret weapon. She would likely be more good luck than bad. Or so Dora hoped.

Now entirely focused, Lucian laid the bloodstained cloth on the small table and inhaled deeply, preparing himself. The air in the room seemed to shift as he tapped into his abilities. His body tensed, his muscles tightening as he assumed the form of the man whose DNA lingered on the rag. It was subtle at first—his features shifting, his skin taking on a different tone—but it soon became unmistakable. The transformation was almost seamless, his body mimicking the exact appearance of the man whose identity he was about to steal.

Watching him change, Dora marveled at the ease with which he did it. The man standing before them now was not Lucian—not on the outside, at least.

"Impressive," she muttered, stepping back slightly as she took in the transformation.

Lucian glanced at his reflection in the small mirror on the wall, flexing his fingers and examining his new face. "Ugly cuss," he said, his voice not quite his own. It was deeper now.

Dora nodded. It was impressive and a little scary. No, a lot scary. "You'll need to act the part, too. The man you're replacing was supposed to meet the trafficker tomorrow. He's a Russian chemist who has been in and out of the operation for years. They'll expect you to be…familiar, but you shouldn't have to talk much. I can do most of the talking, but I hope you remember your Russian lessons from Nomad."

Lucian gave a slight nod. "Da." This was no ordinary deception. They weren't just infiltrating a network—he was stepping into another man's life.

"You know the plan. Convince them that they can make a substantial profit and establish some new connections within Russia, and we're the ones to make that happen if they agree to get us there. One issue is that they know me from before. Let me handle that part. I know how they think."

"Are you sure about this?" Lucian asked.

"Mostly," Dora said, glancing at Graham and Mike. "We have the weapons from our last foray into my lovely home country if things get out of hand. We have enough cash to grease palms, and I have the samples. It should be enough. This is our best shot, but I still think this whole thing is crazy."

Lucian stepped away from the mirror. "It may be," he said grimly. He adjusted his jacket, checking the pockets for his weapon.

They had prepared as much as they could. As she watched Lucian, now a ghost of the man he was about to impersonate, Dora knew this was when everything would either come together—or fall apart spectacularly.

With one last deep breath, she turned back to the door. "Just me and Lucian for the first meet. We'll be back. Let's get this done."

The vehicle's headlights revealed the industrial wasteland sprawled before them. It was a shell of what it had once been. Dora led the way after they exited the Lada. Her boots crunched over the shattered glass that sparkled in the light from the bare bulb above the door to the dilapidated warehouse. Like many others in this forgotten corner of Łódź, the building had been abandoned years ago, left to rot as the factories shut down and the city's lifeblood drained away. It smelled of rust and mildew.

Dora pushed the door open as they reached the entrance. The heavy metal groaned as she did so, revealing the cavernous interior. Rusted machines sat dormant in the shadows, and stacks of old crates littered the floor. It was dark, save for a few low-hanging lights, casting the space in a dull, yellowish glow. The distant hum of a generator reverberated through the walls.

Several figures waited in the dim light. Unlike their surroundings, the weapons they aimed at them were not decrepit. As Dora stepped in, the group straightened, recognizing her. One man, broad-shouldered and scarred, stepped forward. His eyes glinted in the faint light.

"Well, well, look who's back," he said. "And here I thought you'd blown up with the lab, Kasia."

The name hung in the air for a moment—Kasia. Lucian's eyes flicked toward her, but she didn't flinch. She stood tall, her expression cold and unreadable, despite the use of a name that was long dead to her.

"I didn't blow it up, Yakov," Kasia—Dora—replied, her voice steady. "You know I wasn't there. Lab work was a bit too dangerous for my taste. I learned a lot after I left."

The scarred man chuckled darkly, crossing his arms over his chest. "Learned a lot, huh? Disappeared without a trace after the explosion. You're not the only one who learned something, Kasia."

Another figure stepped forward, a woman with short, choppy hair and a sneer. "You owe us an explanation, Kasia. The lab went to hell after you left. What makes you think you can just walk back in here?"

"I'm not here to dig up the past. I've got something far more valuable than apologies."

The man with the scar raised an eyebrow. "You? Valuable? You've got nerve coming here after all this time."

Dora reached into her bag and pulled out a small vial, holding it up for them to see. The liquid inside was an iridescent blue. "This," she said coolly, "is a new designer drug. It's powerful. It's addictive. And it's undetectable in any of the current drug tests."

The room went silent, and the figures around her became far more interested.

"It's also safe," Dora continued. "Relatively speaking. Much safer than fentanyl. The formula is worth millions. More. We want to sell it to a contact in Moscow."

Yakov frowned, stepping closer. His eyes darted between the vial and Dora's face. "You're telling me you came back after all this time, not to give us the formula, but to pass through?"

Dora slipped the vial back into her bag. "You can't afford it," she said bluntly. "But I might be willing to facilitate some distribution for you at a discount. And provide you with samples to test out."

The group broke into murmurs as they processed the offer.

"You're talking big numbers, Kasia," the woman with the short hair said, her voice laced with suspicion. "We're not exactly flush with cash, but we can find a way to afford it."

Dora shook her head. "I'm not selling the secret here. I'm not that stupid. I won't let it disappear into your pockets. But I need something from you—transport. You've got routes into Russia. I need someone to get us through those routes and into Moscow. Do that, and I'll make sure you're on the ground floor when the product hits distribution."

The scarred man looked at his crew, clearly weighing his options. He turned back to Dora, his jaw tight. "And what's in it for us, exactly? You get to Moscow, make your deal, and we're left with what? Some discounted batches, if we're lucky?"

Dora's eyes narrowed, and her voice lowered to a dangerous tone. "You'll get what you've always wanted—a foothold in the Russian market. And if you can't see the value in that, then maybe you're not as smart as I thought you were."

Yakov's face twisted into a scowl as he turned his attention to Lucian, sizing up the man who had remained silent up to this point.

"And what about you, Lev?" Yakov asked. "Is this what you wanted to meet about? What's your part in all this? Kasia's the brains behind the formula, but you… What are you bringing to the table?"

Lucian—Lev—lifted his gaze. His voice, low and grave, was carefully crafted, a tone he'd been practicing with Dora on the ride over. "I'm helping to scale up the manufacture and production."

Yakov's smile faded a fraction as he listened, waiting for more.

Lucian's lips quirked slightly, but the gesture had no warmth. "I've been refining the process, making sure we avoid…complications. You know, fire, fumes—explosions. Those sorts of things aren't exactly good for business."

Yakov's face clouded over before he gave a short, gruff laugh, his eyes flicking to Dora. "Yeah, we've had our fair share of those," he said, his voice dropping a notch. "You're saying you can handle that? Keep things from going up in flames?"

"I've already run through several iterations of the process. Streamlined it. No excess fumes, no risk of flammability. Everything controlled, safe…predictable."

Yakov crossed his arms, his gaze never leaving Lucian's. "You've got some nerve. But I like it. Explosions, after all, *are* bad for business." He paused, stroking his face. "And bad for my skin."

Lucian replied in an equally dry tone. "I'm here to ensure you keep what's left of that intact."

The scarred man exchanged a glance with the others and then gave a slow nod. "All right, Kasia," he said, his voice grudging. "You've got our attention. We'll facilitate the passage. But we expect to be heavily compensated once the deal is done. And the transport will not be free."

Kasia's lips curled into a cold smile. "You'll be compensated. Don't worry. What do you have to lose?"

The group shifted, clearly unhappy but willing to comply.

"I say how and what routes," Yakov stated. "If anything goes wrong, I'll take it out of your hide."

They had cleared the first hurdle.

"Good," Dora said, stepping back. "Then we have a deal. When do we leave?"

The early morning air was heavy with mist as Dora stepped out of the van and into the desolate street. Two Mercedes vans idled near the warehouse's loading bay, their engines humming. They were in better shape and more comfortable than the battered Lada. The sun was just rising, and the light of dawn cast long shadows over the crumbling industrial landscape.

Yakov was already there, leaning against the side of one van, smoking some foul cigarette. Three others stood nearby, looking more alert than their leader. Yakov wasn't coming with them, but the three were there to guide the group through the backchannels and ensure payment was received for their assistance.

Dora could hear the shuffle of movement behind her as Lucian—still in his assumed form as Lev with Emma perched on his shoulder—Graham and Mike trailed behind them. The morning was cold, and the smell of diesel hung thick in the air, mixing with the metallic scent of the industrial ruins around them.

Yakov flicked his cigarette to the ground, crushing it underfoot as he approached. He scanned over the group. "What the fuck is that?"

Lev said, "My good-luck charm. She has a keen instinct for trouble and has kept me out of more than one bad situation. She likes to ride up here," he said, giving her an affectionate scratch. "It would not be good to cross me. Might bring you bad luck, yes?"

One of the men spat three times to his side.

"These guys will get you through Brest and on to Minsk," Yakov said, gesturing to the three men beside him. "From there, you'll have a clearer shot into Russia. No visa needed for Polish citizens between Poland and Belarus." He glanced over at Dora and Lucian. "Crossing into Russia is trickier, but you know how things work there. Bribes are as good as a passport." He chucked at his own joke.

Dora nodded, knowing that part was risky, but the route made sense. Minsk was a common stop for smugglers, traffickers, and those who wanted to go unnoticed between the two nations. The border crossing into Russia was their biggest hurdle, but as Yakov said, money greased the wheels. She hoped they had enough to avoid any unwanted complications.

Yakov pushed off the van and exhaled, the morning fog swallowing his breath. "From here to Brest, you're looking at about five hours. If all goes well, another three or four to Minsk. You'll need to rest somewhere, but don't linger. Once you hit Minsk, you'll want to head straight for the Russian border. You should be able to make it across by nightfall with the right bribes. The whole trip should take you no more than two days."

Lucian nodded thoughtfully, taking in the information as though considering his options, though he already knew the stakes. He glanced at the vans. They needed to move quickly but with enough subtlety to avoid undue attention.

The three men guiding them exchanged words with Yakov, their expressions hard and unreadable. They looked like the type who knew their way around—muscle, with just enough intelligence to make things run smoothly. But even muscle had its limits.

Yakov clapped one of them on the shoulder before turning back to Dora. "You're in good hands with these guys. Just make sure everything's sorted by the time you get to Moscow. I'll be expecting a tidy sum once the deal's made."

Dora gave him a thin smile, knowing this deal was more precarious than anyone was letting on. There was no deal, but they would put on a show. "You'll get your cut, Yakov. Don't worry."

He grinned, his teeth flashing in the dull light. "I'm not worried. Just make sure you don't screw this up or fuck me over."

The three men began loading supplies into the second vehicle.

There was no turning back now.

Sixteen

EAMON SAT ALONE in his command center—a modern space with cutting-edge technology. It was a far cry from Eridu, both in time and distance. The walls of this circular chamber were lined with sleek, dark panels that integrated new high-definition displays.

At the center of the room stood a large, curved workstation made of tempered glass and carbon fiber. A new holographic screen floated above it, displaying a myriad of data streams: surveillance feeds, real-time tracking maps, and his network of influence. Eamon's fingers moved over a virtual keyboard projected onto the desk's surface. He had no need of a huge staff. In effect, the governments of the world unknowingly filled that need. He just pulled the levers of power from here.

He called up a three-dimensional map of the world dotted with pulsating markers indicating Sodality operations. A cluster of activity centered around Europe and North America. With a slight gesture, he zoomed in on the northeastern United States, where a pair of red icons blinked over New York City.

The first alert was about an article concerning Krasnov. He dismissed the report, which was based on unsubstantiated claims from a former Soviet intelligence officer. It was one of many that had been largely ignored. The idiot was facing numerous legal issues. He cared little either way. Managing that issue was not his concern. Any resulting speculation served to divide and cast doubt, which created fertile ground for a more authoritarian world.

Eamon tapped on the second icon and accessed Helena's latest communiqué, which appeared before him as a translucent document. He began to read her report.

According to Helena, Lucian Miller had resurfaced in New York City, arriving at his corporate headquarters accompanied by Emma Turner, one of his trusted bodyguards. Anja and Zoe Ananda were also observed entering the building later, though their specific activities remained unknown. Notably, Lucian's other three bodyguards were absent—a deviation from his usual pattern.

Helena noted that Lucian's private jet had departed for England the following day, following his customary route to his family estate. However, he'd left the estate again the next day, and his jet's destination shifted unexpectedly to Geneva.

"Geneva," Eamon muttered, his voice barely audible in the quiet room. He summoned additional data on the city, overlaying it onto the holographic map. NexGen Pharmaceuticals, one of Lucian's enterprises, was headquartered there. Helena proposed more direct action against the company—sabotage, industrial espionage, anything that might force Lucian into the open or cripple his operations.

Eamon leaned back in his chair, the leather molding to his form as he contemplated the information. Helena's report was thorough, yet he sensed she was withholding something.

He minimized Helena's report with a swipe of his hand and accessed another file labeled 'Eagle.' It contained observations from his operatives stationed near Zamec Echo, Helena's secluded castle. The high-resolution images and encrypted notes confirmed that Helena remained at the castle rather than returning to the Vault. Officially, she claimed it was to better focus on tracking Lucian and his associates. Eamon suspected that she might be avoiding his direct oversight.

Eagle's report noted that Helena was making it difficult for them to monitor her activities closely. Additionally, Eagle mentioned his need to return to Moscow to attend to his duties within the SVR and review official reports for additional information. His men would stay in place and continue their watch.

Eamon tapped his fingers against the smooth surface of his desk. He gestured toward a corner of his desk, and a small holographic avatar of an imp appeared—his digital assistant, a test of this new technology. The imp bowed slightly. This new technology was like magic without the expenditure of his own power. It amused him. The AI was excellent at handling routine tasks without interacting with less trustworthy humans.

"Yes, Grandmaster?" the imp inquired.

"Dispatch a directive to our operatives in Geneva," Eamon ordered. "I require comprehensive intelligence on NexGen Pharmaceuticals—facility layouts, security protocols, and key personnel profiles. Also, activate our sleeper agent within the company. I want inside information."

"Understood," the AI imp responded. "Initiating."

As the imp disappeared in a flash of holographic fire, Eamon returned his focus to the global map. With a few swift motions, he overlaid data streams showing Lucian's known travel patterns, financial transactions, and communication logs. Since Richard's failure, Lucian had been obscuring his movements.

"You're cautious, Lucian," Eamon mused. "But are you cautious enough?"

He considered Helena's suggestion for direct action against NexGen. While sabotage could be effective, he decided that a more nuanced approach was necessary—one that combined misdirection with strategic pressure.

Eamon accessed a secure channel and recorded a message to Helena. "Helena, proceed with caution regarding NexGen Pharmaceuticals. Prioritize intelligence gathering over direct action for the time being. Our objective is to understand Lucian's strategy before we disrupt it. Continue to monitor his movements and report any significant developments." He encrypted the message, which would then be sent through the usual channels.

Leaning back, Eamon considered his options. Despite Helena's apparent compliance, he remained wary. Direct surveillance was proving difficult, but Eamon had other resources. He would watch the watchers until he could locate Lucian and his circle. It would be the same at NexGen. He would compare his findings to hers.

A chime alerted him to an incoming communication. He accepted the transmission, and a new holographic screen materialized, revealing the face of Shade, one of the Sodality's most skilled operatives in covert activities. After Nomad disappeared, Eamon had begun requiring an oath of allegiance from all but the most junior and compartmentalized members. Shade was now bound. Independent thinking and actions had become less important when weighed against the possibility of betrayal. There were signs that Nomad had been turned, and that risk could no longer be taken with others.

"Grandmaster."

"Report."

"Preliminary investigations suggest that Helena may be concealing aspects of her activities," Shade informed him. "She is communicating with unidentified parties in her syndicate. While she continues to provide valuable intelligence, some discrepancies warrant concern."

Eamon's eyes narrowed. "Can you identify her contacts?"

"Not at this time. Their encryption methods are sophisticated, and she uses her systems, not those provided by the Sodality."

"Keep looking," Eamon ordered. "I want definitive proof of any disloyalty." She knew anything she did on her 'official' systems could be monitored. She had access to that system as an enforcer and surely suspected other safeguards were in place.

"As you command," Shade acknowledged before terminating the communication.

Eamon felt vindicated. His instincts about Helena were proving accurate. While she remained a valuable asset, the threat of her divergence could not be ignored.

"So, Helena," Eamon murmured, "you're playing your own game."

He reviewed his file on Anja Kinsey and Zoe Ananda. Anja's abilities were particularly concerning; her aptitude for manipulating metaphysical energies posed a significant risk. What she had accomplished with Richard was unexpected. While she hadn't been able to free him of his oath, the ability to alter or implant memories was alarming. Eamon accessed his collection of scanned ancient texts and records for entities with similar capabilities, seeking methods to counteract her influence. Had she somehow succeeded with Helena where she had failed with Richard? He knew of no methods to break such an oath short of death. Was this something new? Those were questions that demanded answers.

Eamon considered his options. Confronting Helena directly might prompt her to flee or retaliate. A better approach would be to set a trap, using her machinations against her. He began outlining a plan to feed her false information, thereby flushing out her allies. He still needed to find them if she was somehow cooperating with Anja against him.

He also called up his files on Helena. As Eamon reviewed the dossier, unease began to settle in. The profile was impeccable—perhaps too good. The details were thorough, but upon closer inspection, they lacked the depth expected from someone of Helena's stature. Her past hardships seemed almost textbook, a narrative designed to elicit sympathy and explain her drive without revealing vulnerabilities, but the depth of her anger when relating the deaths of her parents while she was still young rang true.

He instructed the imp to cross-reference the data with external sources, accessing global databases and records. Public records confirmed the deaths of her parents, Viktor and Katarina Petrova, as well as her aunt and guardian, Olga Ivanova. Property records showed the transfer of substantial assets to Helena. Everything appeared legitimate. She had changed her name to Dröger, and when he asked her why, she claimed she wanted a name that fit her position. He had accepted the explanation then, but Eamon couldn't shake the feeling that Helena's history was a carefully constructed façade. The technological means existed to fabricate such records, especially for someone with significant resources, and the bureaucratic transition from the USSR to an independent Latvia added additional barriers to accessing complete records.

Her supposed disdain for the occult could also be a deliberate misdirection, a way to mask her true intentions. Was it to attract the Sodality's attention? Was she playing the game that deep?

He instructed the imp to analyze the documents' metadata and cross-verify timestamps, geolocation data, and other forensic details.

"Analyzing," the imp intoned. "No discrepancies detected in archival records from the Latvian registry. Metadata is consistent with the original scans. However, there are gaps in records and inconsistencies."

"Highlight."

The holographic display illuminated sections of documents,

including dates that didn't align and signatures that differed upon close examination.

"Helena, who are you really?" he murmured.

He expanded the search parameters, searching historical records of the Petrova family. References to their lineage dating back to Viking traders were sparse and based on anecdotal accounts rather than verifiable evidence.

Eamon's mind raced. If Helena had fabricated her history, then her origins were a mystery. This deception could mean she harbored motives counter to his objectives.

He recalled her efficiency in taking over the Zvaigzne Syndicate and how ruthlessly she had consolidated power. It now appeared that she might have other abilities or prior experience—experience that could not be accounted for in her supposed thirtysomething years of life. "Could she be older than she claims?"

"I cannot determine that with the data available," the imp replied.

He swiped the display, banishing it in irritation. "Obviously, rhetorical questions are not your forte."

The implications were significant. If Helena possessed supernatural abilities, as he was beginning to believe, it would explain many things.

The imp appeared again. "Grandmaster, you requested a follow-up."

"What?"

"The report detailing the March inspection of the decommissioned submarine reactors is complete. The placement of the muon detectors underneath the cement containment structures captured clear images of the reactors and detected no deterioration. The Estonian government is considering additional long-term waste storage there."

The reactors in the submarine simulators had provided training for Soviet crews. His 'arrangement' with the government allowed them access to the long hall that housed the now-decommissioned simulators. That arrangement also provided additional security personnel who had no idea what else they were guarding. His additions, including a small reactor hidden in new chambers directly below, used the storage area as cover. Aerial, satellite, or even local detectors would only see what they expected—residual radiation.

"Keep monitoring. I want to know about future inspections or storage additions."

"Yes, Grandmaster," the imp said before vanishing.

The actual facility and his headquarters remained hidden. It was the perfect lair.

Part Two

Seventeen

THE AFTERNOON SUN bathed the study of the Miller estate in a warm glow, streaming through the tall windows and illuminating rows of leather-bound books while casting intricate shadows on the polished wooden floor. Claire leaned against the edge of the grand mahogany desk, while Howard sat in a high-backed chair, a centuries-old manuscript open on the table before him. Ian stood nearby, gazing at the gardens below.

The door swung open, and Ash stepped inside. He held a thin dossier in one hand.

Claire straightened. "Ash, glad you could join us. You mentioned having an enlightening conversation with Nomad before they had to go dark. What's your assessment of him?"

Ash exhaled through his nose and dropped into a chair opposite Howard, loosening his tie slightly. "Legit. No question about it. The lad's a proper ex-SVR illegal. Knows his tradecraft, his protocols, all of it checks out."

Ian shifted his focus from the map spread out on the table. "Did he give you anything useful?"

Ash gave a thin smile, almost apologetic. "Not as much as I'd have bloody liked. Sodality runs tight on compartmentalization—need-to-know and nothing more. He only ever got his little corner of the bigger picture. Still..." Ash opened the file, flipped a page, and tapped it. "He did drop one name I know well enough to wake me up. Igor Mikhailovich Krakarov. Goes by the codename Eagle in their little club."

"You don't look happy," Claire said.

Ash barked a laugh with no humor in it. "That'd be because I'm not. Krakarov's top brass at the SVR—runs the Special Operations Training Division. Mid-fifties. Don't let the years fool you. Still sharp enough to cut your throat before you know it. Nasty piece of work."

Ian leaned forward. "What can you tell us about him?"

Ash leaned back, eyes narrowing. "Been on MI6's radar. On paper he trains Russia's best and brightest. Off the record? Holes all over his file. Months, even years where no one knows what he was really up to. And his methods…brutal. Breaks agents down and rebuilds them to his liking. The ones who survive come out very, very good."

Claire felt a chill as she listened. The description matched disturbingly well with what they had uncovered so far.

"He's ruthless," Ash went on. "Cunning as they come. Looks patriotic enough on the surface, but you never know with men like him. And if he's involved with the Sodality, you've got yourselves a proper nest of vipers. His reach inside Russia is long. Very long. Your team heading there better be bloody careful. If he wants you to disappear, you will."

Ian crossed his arms, his expression grim. "So Nomad was recruited by Krakarov himself?"

Ash nodded once. "So he says. Makes sense, too. Krakarov's style is to pluck talent, fake their deaths, and tuck them into his stable where no one's watching. He's done it before."

Ian's gaze hardened. "That fits."

Claire took a deep breath, trying to steady herself. "We need to be careful. With someone like Krakarov pulling strings, we can't afford mistakes."

Ash met her eyes, deadpan. "Spot on, love. Margin for error's not just thin, it's non-existent."

Ian unfolded his arms and stepped closer to the group. "So, what's our next move?"

Ash leaned forward, steepling his fingers. "I dig into Krakarov. Hard. See if there's anything we can use. Weak points, dirty little secrets, the lot. You'd better assume he already knows about Nomad turning. I don't have access to the Service's files anymore, but there are other avenues. Private intelligence shops have decent databases.

Not cheap, mind you."

"I don't think cost is an issue," Ian said. "We can check with Jonas to see what corporate arrangements they already have. If you need more, I'll approve it, and Jonas can arrange it."

"We'll need to coordinate our efforts carefully," Claire said. "And keep this information tightly secured."

Ash gave a curt nod. "Understood. I'll start compiling everything I have on Krakarov and see how it intersects with Nomad's intel." He set the dossier down. "Nomad's intel lines up with what you lot have been saying. Hard to dismiss the Sodality now I've heard it from his lips."

Claire folded her arms. "That brings us to why we wanted to meet with you today. You need to know more about the Sodality's history and influence over time."

Howard adjusted his glasses, directing his gaze toward Ash. "Their roots stretch back to ancient Sumerian civilization. Over millennia, they've woven themselves into the fabric of societies, manipulating events to steer the course of history to their liking."

Ash raised an eyebrow, a dry note in his voice. "That's quite the bloody claim. Got any receipts?"

Howard leaned forward. "Consider the Inquisition. Under the guise of religious fervor, countless individuals were persecuted or even tortured to death, many of whom possessed unique heritages or knowledge the Sodality deemed a threat. In more recent history, look at the rise of the Nazis. The appropriation of symbols and their obsession with occult artifacts aligns with the Sodality's patterns of control and elimination. And now, there are indications they're involved in the current conflict between Russia and Ukraine. You've surely seen photos of the Z on the side of Russian armored vehicles without the bar through it."

Ash frowned at that, his humor evaporating.

Howard opened his notebook, which displayed an array of symbols. "The bar 'Z' represents the Wolfsangel sigil, a symbol historically associated with oppression and extremist ideologies. It's based on a trap for wolves—a nasty one. It's not just a coincidence. The Sodality has a penchant for repurposing symbols, embedding their influence subtly yet pervasively."

Ash took a moment to process the information. “Those examples are all separate instances. Are you saying they’re all connected? You’ve left out quite a bit. Ancient civilizations to now? How could they have kept their secrets so long?”

“Yes, they are connected. The Sodality has worked very hard and gone to extraordinary lengths to remain hidden. They have always operated to influence, if not directly control, other organizations under many names. If you look closely, you can find the subtle indications. I can show you the connections later if you have time.”

“I’ll take your word for it…for now. What’s their endgame?” Ash’s tone was flat but edged with curiosity.

Claire met his gaze. “Control. Eradication of those they consider a threat—people like us with unique heritages.”

Ash studied her, his brow lowering as he weighed her words. “You keep saying ‘heritage.’ You want to spell that out in plain English?”

She took a steadying breath. “I come from a line of wolf otherkin. We possess abilities that the Sodality fears and seeks to eliminate.”

He blinked, searching her face for any hint of jest, but found none. “You’re serious.”

“Very,” Claire affirmed. “Our abilities have been passed down through generations. It’s part of who we are.”

Ash gave a sharp exhale. “Bloody hell. Wolf…otherkin? That’s what you call it? What, like bloody werewolves?”

“Something like that,” Claire allowed, the corners of her mouth twitching. “That’s a much longer conversation.”

Howard interjected. “The Sodality has hunted families like Claire’s for centuries. They fear what they cannot control. It’s as simple as that.”

Ash’s eyes narrowed as he processed. Then he leaned back, folded his arms and let out a low whistle. “Well. This is a bit of a turn-up. Lucian did say there’d be things I’d have to see to believe…and I suppose this counts.”

“It does,” Ian said earnestly. “We understand it could be difficult to believe.”

Ash rubbed at his temple with his thumb and forefinger, lips quirked in a sardonic smile. “Wolves, eh? All right. Assuming I humor you and buy into all of this…what’s it got to do with me? You want me to help infiltrate Moscow to find Ivan the Terrible's lost library because you reckon it's hiding something that'll help you fight back?"

Claire nodded. "That is the hope. The library may contain knowledge or artifacts that can level the playing field."

Howard tapped his notebook. "There are references to texts and items of power that have been lost to history—things the Sodality doesn't want us to find."

Ash looked around the room. "Well, I've always believed that where there's smoke, there's fire. And given what I've seen and heard so far, I'm inclined to keep an open mind."

Claire offered a slight smile. "That's all we ask."

Ash sighed, a hint of wry humor returning. "Besides, it's not the strangest thing I've encountered in my line of work."

Ian chuckled. "It will probably top that list soon. Trust me, it's about to get even more interesting."

Ash glanced at the symbols in the open book. "Tell me more about this Sodality. If we're up against an organization that's been manipulating events for millennia..."

Howard moved to sit beside Ash, his worn notes between them. "We'll start with our earliest records and work our way forward."

Claire left the study as Howard described the Sodality's history to Ash. She needed to prepare for the evening meal, aware that the pack members who had arrived would gather to reconnect. It was an opportunity for them to bond and start understanding their legacy. After dinner, they would listen to stories about their history and determine what it all meant for them.

The meal was simple yet hearty, filled with introductions and light conversation. Ash observed quietly, absorbing the atmosphere and perhaps the gravity of what he was becoming a part of. Dillon sat nearby, his eyes curious.

As twilight settled, they moved to a spacious sitting room. A fire crackled in the hearth, casting warm shadows that danced across the walls. The servants had been dismissed for the evening, granting them privacy. Claire caught her mother's eye.

“Mum,” Claire began, taking a seat beside her. “Would you tell us the tale your grandmother Edith passed down? The one about Isobel?”

Margaret leaned back in her chair, her gaze sweeping the room thoughtfully. “Of course,” she said. “It’s a story from a time when fear and superstition hung over the land like a fog. The early to mid-seventeenth century was a turbulent age—plague ravaged the cities, and the English Civil War tore the country apart. King Charles’s forces clashed with Parliament’s armies in Devon. The Siege of Exeter brought hardship to our very doorstep, and fear crept into even the most secluded corners of Dartmoor.”

The room grew quiet as everyone leaned in to listen. Dillon’s eyes were wide, his attention fully captured.

“She was known as Isobel,” Margaret continued, her voice rich with emotion. “The last of our line to walk freely in the wolf’s guise. In those days, the moors and dense forests of Dartmoor were not just our home but our dominion. Isobel was magnificent, embodying the spirit of our ancestors with grace and power as natural to her as the air we breathe.”

Claire felt a shiver run through her. She could imagine Isobel moving through the misty woods, the moonlight glinting off her silvery fur.

“Isobel’s ability to shift into a wolf was not seen as a curse but as the highest embodiment of our clan’s heritage. As a gift that allowed them to protect their territory and all who dwelt there. But as the years passed, the winds of change brought a storm of fear and superstition.” Margaret’s gaze drifted to the flames dancing in the hearth. “Across Europe, the witch hunts were in full force. The infamous witch trials in Salem were still decades away, but here, in our land, Matthew Hopkins, the self-proclaimed Witchfinder General, was spreading terror. Tales of sorcery and dealings with the Devil sowed seeds of distrust among the people.

“It wasn’t long before those whispers reached our lands,” she continued. “Stories of werewolf hunts in neighboring regions began to surface. Reports of trials, tortures, and executions painted a grim future for those who bore the ancient gift. Isobel, whose very essence was intertwined with the wolf, faced an agonizing decision—a choice to remain or flee into hiding for the survival of her kind and the preservation of our legacy."

Dillon clenched his hands.

"With a heavy heart, Isobel chose to conceal her true nature. Our nature," Margaret said, her eyes misting. "She knew that to continue revealing herself, to embrace the wolf openly, would not only invite peril upon her head but endanger the entire clan. It was a sacrifice—a sealing away of her most sacred gift—to ensure the safety and continuation of our family.

"In the dead of night," Margaret recounted, "under the witness of the same moon and stars that guide us today, Isobel gathered the clan—called the pack. She declared their new path—hiding, concealing the wolf within, and living in the shadows to safeguard future generations from the fate that had befallen so many others during those dark times."

The room was silent except for the crackling of the fire. Claire felt tears prick at the corners of her eyes. The enormity of Isobel's sacrifice touched her.

"And so," Margaret concluded, "the wolves of the moors became but whispers—a legend fading into the mists of time to be replaced by tales of monsters: lycanthropes and werewolves. Isobel lived out her days in the guise of an ordinary woman, but those who knew…they saw. The wild still lived in her eyes. Most of the pack scattered to take up new lives elsewhere, but she remained on the moor to keep watch, even in exile. A dozen generations have passed since then. The tales passed down through the centuries, like this one, were our only ties to the past. The ability to shift was lost."

Claire glanced around the room. Ash appeared thoughtful.

Listening to her mother's words, Claire felt a profound connection to Isobel—a lineage of strength and sacrifice flowing through her veins. In Isobel's choice, she recognized not just echoes of their past but a guiding light for their future. It was a reminder of their kind's resilience and the enduring spirit of the wolf that, even in hiding, had never truly gone dark.

Claire finally spoke, her voice low. "We carry her legacy in our blood. It's ours to honor…or squander."

Her mother nodded, a smile touching her lips. "Indeed, my dear.

Our choices will shape the path for those who come after us."

Dillon looked up, his voice barely above a whisper. "Is it possible? Do you think Isobel would approve of us embracing the wolf again if it were?"

Margaret reached over to squeeze his hand. "I believe she would. Isobel made her sacrifice out of love and protection. It's time to honor her by living fully, even if we must remain hidden. For now."

"We owe it to her," Claire said, meeting the eyes of those gathered. "To ourselves and future generations. Let's honor Isobel's legacy and ensure that the spirit of the wolf thrives once more."

The crackling of the fire was the only sound. Claire glanced around, observing the thoughtful expressions on the faces of those gathered. Bee was the first to break the silence.

"That was a moving story," Bee said, her eyes reflecting the flickering flames. "But how do you propose to restore that legacy? Margaret has hinted that it's possible, and Anja said as much. How can this be true?"

Claire met Bee's eyes. "Howard will help awaken each clan member who decides to join us in this fight. That's why we're here."

Simon leaned forward. "I've seen. Seeing is believing," he remarked. "Perhaps you could show them, Claire?"

"I suppose that's the most direct approach," she agreed. Rising from her seat, she moved to the center of the room. The eyes of everyone followed her.

She began to unbutton her blouse with steady hands. Noticing Dillon's flushed cheeks and averted gaze, she smiled. "No need to be embarrassed, Dillon. You'll get used to it."

Dillon managed an awkward nod, his eyes fixed on the floor. Bee placed a reassuring hand on her son's shoulder.

Claire continued until she stood naked and unashamed, the soft glow of the fire casting warm hues across her skin. She took a deep breath, centering herself. The familiar sensation of transformation began to flow through her—a ripple of energy that started at her core and extended to every limb.

Closing her eyes, she embraced the change. When she opened them again, her amber eyes reflected the light with an otherworldly sheen. Her form shifted seamlessly, altering until she stood on four paws instead of two feet. Thick fur, the color of her golden hair, covered her now lupine body.

A collective gasp echoed in the room. Claire's heightened senses picked up the rapid heartbeats of those present, the scent of astonishment mingling with the wood smoke. And fear.

Ash shot to his feet, eyes wide. "What on earth..."

Ian placed a hand on Ash's arm. "Easy now," he cautioned. "No sudden movements."

Ash's shock was evident, but his eyes showed a keen analytical mind already processing this new reality. His gaze met hers, and for a moment, they regarded each other—man and wolf—as the scent of fear faded. She could hear the shift in his breathing as the initial alarm in his eyes gave way to curiosity.

Dillon, on the other hand, was entranced. "It's real," he whispered in awe. "My dreams... It's all real."

Bee's expression softened as she watched her son. "Yes, it is."

Claire took a few steps toward Ash, her movements fluid and unthreatening. She tilted her head slightly, observing him with intelligent eyes. The myriad scents and sounds of the room enveloped her—the trace of cologne, the rustle of clothing, the heartbeat of each person present.

Ash slowly lowered himself back into his chair, his eyes fixed on her. "Bloody remarkable," he murmured. "Didn't really think you'd pull it off. Wouldn't have believed it if I hadn't seen it with my own eyes."

Claire retreated a few steps. She moved among them, giving each a chance to touch her fur. To feel the strength beneath. To acquaint themselves with the reality of the change. She could sense her relatives' longing to reclaim what had been hidden for generations. Bee, who had been so afraid of what it might mean for her son, relaxed. Now that they had all seen it, none could turn away and forget.

"Now you understand," Margaret said. "This is the legacy we've inherited. This is the gift that has been hidden for so long."

Ash ran a hand through his hair, still processing. "I can see why the Sodality would consider you a threat. Hell, a lot of people would see it as a threat."

"Exactly," Howard interjected. "They fear what they cannot control or comprehend."

Dillon sat on the carpet next to Claire, his eyes bright. "Can I...will I be able to do that?"

Howard smiled warmly at him. "If you choose to embrace it."

Bee looked between her son and Claire. "What does this mean for us—for our safety?"

"It means we must stand together," Margaret replied. "To protect ourselves and each other. Howard will guide you through the awakening process, but it must be a choice each of you makes willingly."

Simon folded his arms. "I'll do it. Whatever it takes. The pack deserves to live again."

Ash gave a whistle. "Bloody hell. Pack, eh? You weren't kidding." He sat back in his chair, his eyes still on Claire. "If the bastards come for you...well. At least now I know what they're up against. Puts me in a slightly better mood about your odds."

Ian gave him a dry smile. "Don't get too comfortable just yet."

Claire hopped up into Ian's lap and flopped down.

"Ooof, aren't you a bit big to be a lap dog?" Ian teased.

The growl that escaped her throat elicited chuckles from around the room.

"I'll probably pay for that later," Ian said as Claire laid her muzzle on his arm.

Eighteen

THE OLD HOUSE in Łódź creaked with age. Zoe caught Anja's determined gaze as they descended to the main floor.

The trafficker, whom they now knew as Marek, barked orders to his men in rapid Polish. His sharp features and cold gray eyes conveyed an air of authority that demanded obedience. Standing beside him was his driver, Tomasz, a stout man with a stoic expression.

"Time to move," Marek announced, his gaze lingering on Zoe and Anja a moment longer than necessary. "Remember, you're under my watch now. No trouble."

Nomad stepped forward. "They'll follow instructions," he assured Marek. "Zofia and Adela know what's expected of them."

Zoe suppressed a shudder at the use of her alias, Zofia, although it reminded her of Zoe Palaiologina, who became Sophia. It felt oddly appropriate considering their goal. She glanced at Anja—Adela—who maintained a façade of indifference.

They were herded toward a dirty white van parked outside. The streets were quiet at this time of day.

Tomasz opened the van's side door, gesturing for them to enter. "Get in," he said.

Zoe did, settling onto one of the worn seats. Anja slid in beside her, and Nomad took a position behind the driver. Marek entered last, taking the front passenger seat. The door slammed shut, enclosing them in a tense silence.

As the van drove off, Zoe looked out the window, watching the cityscape disappear. She couldn't help but think about what was coming next.

The hum of the engine and the rhythmic motion of the vehicle created a lulling effect, but Zoe remained alert. Marek's other men were seated in the back row.

After just a few hours, they were driving through the streets of Warsaw. The van navigated busy roads and finally stopped in front of a house in the entertainment district. It was a much nicer place than the one they had just left, though the neighbors were a bit noisy. It wasn't far from flashy signs advertising sex shows and discotheques.

Zoe adjusted the strap of her dress, the fabric clinging. The lights of Warsaw shimmered outside the bordello's windows, casting a warm glow over the bustling streets. Inside, the atmosphere was thick with laughter, music, and the clinking of glasses. The establishment was one of Marek's most prosperous ventures, so he had claimed—a lavish venue that catered to the city's elite and travelers seeking discreet indulgences. Marek had insisted on the stopover, citing necessary arrangements.

As they entered the grand foyer, Zoe took in the opulent surroundings—crystal chandeliers casting prisms of light, velvet drapes in rich hues, and artwork that spoke of old-world elegance. Scantily clad women moved among patrons, their laughter a practiced melody. The air was perfumed with a blend of exotic scents. *Yep,* she thought. *No doubt about what happens here.*

Marek exchanged a few hushed words with an older woman who stood and greeted him, the establishment's matron. He gestured subtly toward Zoe and Anja before turning back to Nomad.

"They'll be in good hands here," Marek assured him. "But as we discussed, they must contribute for their stay."

Nomad's eyes narrowed. "That wasn't part of our agreement. We've paid you generously for safe passage to Moscow."

The woman interjected, her tone diplomatic. "It's customary for guests to partake in the evening's activities. However, exceptions can be made for a price."

Anja placed a hand on Nomad's arm. "It's all right," she said, her gaze steady. "We can manage for a night."

Zoe shot her a sharp look. "Adela..."

"It's fine," Anja insisted. *"We need to keep up appearances,"* she sent.

Nomad hesitated before giving a curt nod. "I'll be nearby."

The woman smiled. "Excellent. I'll have someone show you to your room. They will also find you some attire better suited for the customers here. After you freshen up, please join the fun down here."

As they followed a young woman through the richly adorned corridors, Zoe leaned closer to Anja. "You didn't have to agree to this," she murmured.

Anja met her gaze with quiet determination. *"Yes, I did. We need to maintain our cover. Besides, it's just mingling…mostly."* Then she said aloud, "We'll be fine."

The girl opened a door and ushered them inside. "I think there are some dresses in the closet that should fit. You both look to be the same size as Moria was. Don't take too long. It would cause trouble."

Anja thumbed through the hangers, many pieces barely more than a suggestion of fabric and shimmer. Silk and lace caught the light, gauzy and delicate, in shades of black, red, and a soft champagne. She lifted one slip of a dress only to realize it was more air than material. Zoe leaned in, eyebrows lifting in amusement as she inspected a mesh bodysuit with cutouts that left nothing to the imagination.

"These make our rags look like nuns' habits," Zoe muttered, sifting through a few other choices. "You'd think a simple little black dress was out of fashion."

Anja paused, pulling out a red leather corset set that looked like the most modest option available. "This would look good on you. Leather's…practical, right?" She held it out, grinning as Zoe took it, eyeing the structured piece.

After a moment's wrestling and a few half-joking curses about the physics of lingerie, they were more or less dressed. Anja had decided to go with the naked dress trend. The shimmering fabric flowed and hugged her figure. The effect was enticing.

"Kinda like we've swapped roles," Anja said. "You're the one usually running around naked, and look at you! All dark and dangerous."

Zoe ran her hands down the front of her corset. "I feel like armored garnish."

Anja chuckled, adjusting a strap as they prepared to leave. "At least it's high quality. Beats the rags."

"True," Zoe quipped, giving a little strut as they headed out the door. "Not sure if I'm more ready for a cocktail party or a conquest, but hey, why not both?"

Entering the main lounge, they were greeted by a scene of subdued revelry. Patrons reclined on plush sofas, sipping expensive liquors as soft jazz played in the background. The lighting was dim, casting a golden hue over everything.

Zoe took a deep breath, composing herself. "All right," she conceded. "Let's make the best of it."

"That's the spirit."

They moved through the crowd, drawing admiring glances. When approached, Zoe engaged in light conversation, her demeanor cordial yet distant. Anja mirrored her approach, and their unspoken coordination kept aspiring suitors at bay.

A well-dressed businessman approached them, his eyes alight with curiosity. He was staring at Anja's nipples that were quite visible through the sheer fabric. "Good evening, ladies," he greeted with a charming smile. "I haven't seen you here before."

"Just passing through," Anja replied.

"Then I'm fortunate to have crossed paths with you tonight," he said. "May I offer you a drink?"

Anja smiled politely. "Maybe another time. We're actually just about to take a break."

He raised his glass in a gesture of understanding. "Another time, then."

As he moved away, Zoe exhaled. "Letch. He couldn't take his eyes off your tits."

Anja chuckled. "He seemed harmless enough."

"Yeah, right."

Hours passed in a similar fashion, with the two navigating conversations and declining offers. Their synergy was seamless, each supporting the other without missing a beat. Their silent conversations helped immensely with that coordination.

Later in the evening, a distinguished gentleman caught their attention. He was older, with silver streaks in his dark hair and an air of quiet confidence. Dressed in an impeccably tailored suit, he exuded wealth and sophistication.

He approached them with a respectful greeting. "Good evening. I hope I'm not intruding."

"Not at all," Anja replied, her eyes flickering with interest. "We were just enjoying the atmosphere."

He smiled. "As am I. Allow me to introduce myself—I'm Leonid Morozov, visiting from St. Petersburg. Leo."

"Zofia," Zoe said, offering her hand, which he took with a light touch. "And this is Adela."

"A pleasure," he said. "It's rare to find such captivating company."

"Flattery will get you everywhere," Anja teased.

He chuckled. "In that case, may I entice one of you to join me for a private conversation? I promise to make it worth your while."

Zoe exchanged a glance with Anja.

"We don't usually entertain individually," Anja said. "But could we make an arrangement for both of us?"

Leo's eyes sparkled. "I would be most agreeable to that."

"Very well," Anja said with a slight tilt of her head. "Lead the way."

He guided them to a secluded alcove, away from the main lounge's prying eyes. As they settled into the comfortable seating, a server appeared with a bottle of champagne at Leo's request.

"To serendipitous encounters," he toasted, raising his glass.

"To new acquaintances," Anja replied, clinking her glass against his.

They engaged in light-hearted banter, the conversation flowing. Leo was attentive without being overbearing, his wit matching theirs at every turn. "You both have an air of sophistication not commonly found in establishments like this."

Anja smiled coyly. "Perhaps we're full of surprises."

"I have no doubt." Leo leaned forward slightly. "I must admit, spending time with both of you has been the highlight of my evening. I would be honored if we could continue this conversation in a more private setting."

"Are you sure you can handle the two of us?"

"I assure you, I'm quite capable."

Anja's eyes glinted with mischief. "Then we can accommodate your wish."

"Excellent," Leo said with a satisfied smile.

They rose from the alcove, and he offered his arms to both of them.

As they walked toward the private suites, Zoe caught Nomad's eye from across the room. He gave a barely perceptible nod, indicating his awareness and readiness should they need him.

Once they were inside a room much finer than theirs and obviously reserved for the most affluent patrons, the door closed behind them, muting the noise of the lounge.

Leo gestured for them to sit on the plush sofa. He poured three glasses of wine from an exquisite decanter and handed them each a glass. "To new...adventures," he toasted, his eyes lingering on Zoe's cleavage.

They sipped the rich, fruity wine in silence before Anja placed her glass down, and with a sinuous arch of her back, she straddled Leo's lap. "Oh, I do hope you know what you've gotten yourself into," she purred in his ear as she deftly began to undo his shirt buttons.

Zoe watched them with hooded eyes, sipping her wine. She could feel the sexual tension in the air, thick and heady like incense. Her empathic powers buzzed to life, drinking in the raw lust emanating from Anja and Leo. She set her glass down and stood before sauntering over to them.

"Enough teasing," she said, brushing a finger down Anja's bare back. "Let's see if he's as 'able' as he claims." Zoe unbuckled her corset and let it fall to the floor, revealing her gorgeous naked body beneath. Her breasts were high and pert, nipples hardening in anticipation.

Leo's eyes practically bulged out of his head as he took in the sight of both women before him. "Damn," he muttered under his breath, then chuckled nervously. "Ladies, I am yours to command."

Anja smirked and leaned in for a deep, hungry kiss while Zoe knelt before him, taking his rock-hard member into her mouth. Leo groaned, his eyes rolling back in his head as they went to work on him. Anja's tongue danced over his lips, her teeth grazing his lower lip just enough to send shivers down his spine, while Zoe's expert mouth and hands teased and caressed every inch of him.

As he moaned into Anja's mouth, Zoe looked up at her lover, their eyes meeting in a silent communion. Both of them knew how to push a man to the edge without sending him over. They could do this dance all night if they wanted to, but this was just part of the game.

Slowly, Zoe released Leo with a wet pop. Anja slid over and

mounted him. Zoe reached around Anja to between her legs and rubbed just where and how she wanted. Leo cupped her breasts from behind as Anja rode him on the sofa, facing out. Zoe moved to Anja, her tongue lapping at her clit as Leo watched in the mirror, transfixed.

"You said you had dealings in Moscow? We'll be traveling to another house there. Perhaps we can meet again," Anja said.

Leo gripped the sofa cushions as Anja rode him, her moans of pleasure mingling with Zoe's teasing licks. He looked into Anja's eyes in the mirror, his own glazed over with desire, and nodded. "Yes," he managed to gasp. "I…I'd be… Yes, I'll give you my card."

Zoe lifted her head from between Anja's legs, her lips swollen and glistening, and smiled. She traded places with Anja and began to move slowly.

"Excellent," Anja purred, running a finger along Leo's jawline. "We'll be in touch then. Please be sure to tip the house here generously. We'll keep your payment directly," Anja added before taking Zoe's place. Zoe could feel the compulsion that accompanied the suggestion. *Jedi mind tricks again.*

Zoe felt herself nearing climax. Anja's tongue continued to torment her sensitive clit, driving until she cried out, her body shuddering around Leo's hard length. He groaned, his hips bucking up into her as he, too, found release. She could feel Anja feed, but not too deeply, and the return of energy stretched her orgasm out and she clenched hard around Leo's member.

Their breathing ragged, they collapsed against the sofa, their bodies in a sticky tangle. Leo was the first to speak, catching his breath. "Ladies, that was…beyond compare. I must say, though, you've worn me out completely."

Anja smiled lazily, running a hand down Zoe's damp back. "We aim to please." She winked at Leo.

Zoe and Anja made their way back to their room. The corridors were empty. The bordello's patrons were either enjoying their own adventures or had departed. Zoe carried the corset under her arm, not bothering to tie herself back into it.

Anja stretched her arms, a contented sigh escaping her lips. "Well, that was…fun."

Zoe chuckled. "He's certainly an interesting man."

As they entered their room, Nomad was waiting. "Everything all right?"

"Better than expected," Zoe assured him. "Our friend was quite the gentleman."

Anja nodded. "And generous."

Nomad raised an eyebrow. "Did you learn anything useful?"

"Maybe," Zoe said, lowering her voice. "He's connected—mentioned dealings in Moscow. Could be advantageous."

"Good," Nomad said. "We'll discuss it more later."

Anja glanced at the clock on the wall. "We should rest. Marek said we'll be leaving in a few hours."

Zoe agreed. "A brief sleep is better than none."

As they settled in, the events of the night lingered in Zoe's mind. Tonight had provided a taste of another life. The energy that Anja had taken would offset lost sleep.

As she relaxed in the bed and curled up next to Anja, the connection they shared was open. It had once taken effort to maintain. Now, it was almost effortless and always there. Their time with Leo had been pleasant and left them both well-satiated. Anja, though, seemed to always want more. Zoe caught a glimpse of Anja's dream as she visited Lucian before drifting off to sleep.

Morning came swiftly. They gathered their belongings and met in the foyer, where Marek and Tomasz were waiting for them. Marek appeared pleased, his demeanor more accommodating than it had been the previous day.

"I trust your stay was comfortable," he said.

"Quite," Zoe replied.

"Excellent. The trip to Moscow should be straightforward from here."

Nomad eyed him. "No more unscheduled stops?"

Marek held up his hands. "Only one in Minsk. I need to drop off a girl there. We can stay overnight and move on to Moscow tomorrow morning."

They exited the bordello, the city stirring to life around them. As they settled into the van, Zoe caught sight of Leo standing at a distance, watching them with an inscrutable expression. He raised a hand in a farewell, which she returned with a slight nod.

“Do you think we’ll see him again?” Zoe asked.

“Possibly,” Anja said. “The world’s smaller than it seems.”

The older woman who ran the business for Marek ushered a young girl to the van and spat a few curses at her as she climbed in. Zoe motioned for the girl to sit between her and Anja.

The van pulled away, merging into the flow of morning traffic. The road ahead was long, but they were one step closer to their destination.

Nineteen

LUCIAN ADJUSTED EMMA'S position on his shoulder as he approached the idling vans. The early morning mist clung to the industrial outskirts of Łódź, shrouding the dilapidated warehouses and casting everything in a muted gray. He glanced over his shoulder to ensure that Graham and Mike were close behind, their expressions stoic as they presented the guise of bodyguards. Emma wrapped her tail around his neck and watched the men loading the van.

One of the men muttered something under his breath, but Yakov waved it off. "Superstitions," he chuckled.

Dora stepped up beside Lucian, her coat pulled tight against the chill. "Long drive ahead," she said.

"Right," Yakov agreed. "Sergei will drive the lead van with you and Lev," he said, using Lucian's assumed name. "Viktor and Alexei will follow with your associates."

Graham and Mike exchanged a glance before climbing into the second van.

As Lucian settled into the passenger seat beside Sergei, Dora took her place in the back. Emma leapt from his shoulder to curl up on the dashboard, her tail twitching slightly. Sergei eyed the cat but said nothing, starting the engine with a low rumble.

The convoy pulled away from the warehouse district, the cityscape gradually giving way to open countryside. Fields stretched out on either side of the road.

Lucian gazed out the window. The route to Brest was straightforward, but border crossings always carried risks. He glanced at Emma perched on the dash—they were not entirely without advantages.

Hours passed with the hum of the engine and the rhythmic pattern of the road beneath them. Conversation was sparse. Sergei seemed content to focus on driving, his eyes fixed ahead. Dora occasionally checked her phone, scanning for any updates or warnings.

They made their first stop at a small service station nestled among towering pines. The air was crisp, carrying the scent of resin and damp earth. Sergei announced a brief break to refuel and stretch their legs.

Lucian stepped out of the van, the cool air refreshing against his face. Emma hopped down beside him. He knew she would use the opportunity to observe discreetly. Her microphone would be recorded on Dora's phone.

Graham and Mike emerged from the second van. They stood a short distance away, surveying the area while remaining within earshot.

Sergei and his companions spoke quietly near the fuel pumps. Lucian noticed the tension in their postures but detected no immediate threat. Still, he remained cautious. They would need to review that conversation later.

After a few minutes, Emma slipped unnoticed back to Lucian's side. She brushed against his leg.

They resumed their travel, winding through dense forests and scattered villages. The conversation inside the van remained minimal, but Lucian took the opportunity to study Sergei more closely. The driver exhibited the demeanor of a man accustomed to such trips—efficient, detached, and possibly dangerous if crossed.

As they approached the Belarusian border, the atmosphere inside the van grew taut. Lucian felt the familiar tightening in his chest. The border crossing at Terespol was known for its unpredictability. It was one of the primary crossings.

"Documents ready?" Sergei asked without turning his head.

"All in order," Lucian replied, tapping the pocket where his stolen passport rested.

They crossed a river marking the border and followed the highway to the inspection station. The queue was mercifully short. Trucks and cars idled ahead of them in what seemed from the inside like a long tunnel with several lanes. Drivers tapped their fingers on steering wheels. A mother stood with a toddler beside their car, taking advantage of time to stretch. This was not what he had imagined. He was too used to luxury air travel.

When it was their turn, an image of their license plate flashed on a screen, indicating the booth to approach. They were instructed to step out. Sergei handed over a bundle of passports with a practiced smile.

"Destination?" the inspector asked.

"Business trip to Minsk," Sergei answered. "Transporting equipment."

The guard's gaze shifted to Lucian. "Nationality?"

"Polish," Lucian said.

"Purpose of your visit?"

"Accompanying our shipment to ensure a smooth transaction," Lucian replied truthfully.

The guard examined the passports as a handler walked a dog around the vehicle. Lucian noticed the other van in the next lane undergoing the same procedure.

"Everything seems to be in order," the guard finally said, handing back the documents. "Safe travels."

Lucian inclined his head in thanks as they got back in. The van moved forward, and he allowed himself a measured breath of relief. This would have been a very bad place for things to have gone wrong.

Once they cleared the crossing, Sergei remarked, "Not bad. Sometimes, they like to ask more questions. Mornings and evenings are worse."

"Good timing," Lucian said.

Sergei merely grunted in response.

They continued toward Brest. He could see the city seemingly split to the north and south by a parklike area along the river dotted with clusters of birch trees. On either side, the buildings were primarily tall, gray apartment complexes. Closer to the river, the buildings were newer, with more glass. Further back, the apartments had a distinctly Soviet feel. These gave way to a suburb with single-family homes.

On the other side of Brest, Sergei suggested a stop at a local eatery. "Good place here," he said. "We can rest before continuing."

The restaurant was a modest establishment with a faded sign and flower boxes under the windows. Inside was filled with the comforting aromas of hearty stews and fresh bread.

They took a table near the back. Emma remained outside, disappearing into the shadows.

Graham and Mike sat at a neighboring table with Viktor and Alexei. The two guides spoke in low tones, occasionally glancing at Lucian's group.

Their meals arrived—bowls of rich borscht and plates of potato pancakes. Lucian ate methodically.

After finishing their meal, they set out again. The road to Minsk stretched ahead, the afternoon light casting long shadows across the pavement.

As dusk approached, they made a brief stop at a roadside rest area. Sergei announced the need to check the vehicles and advised everyone to take the opportunity to stretch.

Lucian stepped out, the cool air invigorating after the confines of the van. Emma padded up to him silently.

"Anything?" he murmured under his breath.

She looked up, her green eyes conveying caution.

"Noted," he said.

Graham approached, his expression unreadable. "All clear so far," he said.

Lucian nodded. "Stay sharp. We're not through yet."

They continued on, the cityscape of Minsk gradually coming into view—a mix of Soviet-era buildings and modern structures reaching toward the darkening sky.

Sergei eventually pulled into a quiet neighborhood. "This is where we'll spend the night," he announced. "We have accommodations arranged."

They disembarked in front of an unremarkable building. The front was worn, but the windows were intact, and the area seemed quiet.

Inside, the apartments were sparsely furnished but clean. Sergei handed over a set of keys. "We'll depart early tomorrow. Rest while you can."

"Appreciated," Lucian said.

Once Sergei and his companions departed, Lucian gathered the group in the main living area of the sparse apartment. He settled onto a worn sofa, and Emma—still in her feline form—leapt into his lap. He reached up to slip off the small collar around her neck, a device discreetly embedded with recording capabilities.

As soon as the collar was removed, Emma transformed back into her human form, the shift enveloped in a brief shimmer of light. She remained seated comfortably in his lap, unbothered by her lack of clothing.

She grinned mischievously at him. "I guess you want me to move now?"

Lucian raised an eyebrow, a smile tugging at the corner of his mouth. "It would be easier to talk that way."

She sighed theatrically. "Awww, you're no fun."

Emma moved over next to him and accepted some food Dora had picked up for her. "I suppose this is better than cat food," she said and began to eat.

"Don't think I wasn't tempted," Dora said. "Want your clothes?"

"Nah, If they come back to check on us, I'll need to change quick."

"Likely story. Anyway, they're sticking to the plan so far, but they're cautious—possibly hiding something. It could also be just the tension of crossing into Russia. Let's listen to what Emma picked up."

She pulled out her phone and tapped on an app linked to the collar's recordings. The screen displayed a series of audio files with timestamps.

Lucian leaned forward, his attention focused. "I'll do my best to translate," he offered.

Dora set her phone to speaker to ensure everyone could hear clearly. She selected the most recent recording, and muffled sounds of footsteps and distant conversations played. After a few moments, voices emerged more distinctly—Sergei speaking in Russian.

Lucian listened intently as the conversation played out.

"Yakov wants an update," Sergei's voice said.

"Tell him we're on schedule," Viktor replied.

There was a pause, followed by the sound of a phone dialing and connecting.

"Yes?" Yakov's voice came through, gruff and impatient.

"We're in Minsk," Sergei reported. "Everything is proceeding."

"Good," Yakov responded. "But I need you to delay them there."

"Delay?" Sergei sounded uncertain. "Why?"

"I have some associates interested in your passengers," Yakov explained. "They require more information before proceeding."

Viktor interjected, "That wasn't part of the agreement. We were to take them to Moscow and be done."

"Consider it a new opportunity," Yakov countered. "There's more money in it for you if you cooperate."

Alexei hesitated. "And if they become suspicious?"

"Keep them comfortable," Yakov instructed. "Tell them there's trouble at the Russian border—anything to buy time."

The call ended abruptly.

Lucian translated the exchange, his voice steady but edged with concern. As he finished, a silence settled over the group.

Graham clenched his jaw. "So they're planning to stall us."

Mike shook his head. "Shit. Not good."

Dora crossed her arms, her gaze distant as she processed the information. "We need to decide our next move. If they intend to delay us, they're likely setting up a trap."

Emma nodded. "Agreed."

Lucian considered their options. "We have a few choices. We could directly confront Sergei and his men, which might escalate the situation. I bet they won't do anything until we're in Russia. Once we're in, it would be much easier to make it to Moscow on our own. Failing that, we could wait until Nomad arrives, and he could arrange to pick us up."

Graham raised a hand. "If we disappear now, they'll know we're onto them. Could make things more complicated down the line."

Mike added, "But if we wait too long, whatever Yakov is planning could catch up to us."

Dora sighed. "It's a delicate balance. We need to stay ahead without tipping our hand."

Emma leaned forward. "Perhaps we can use their plan against them. If we act as though we're unaware, we might gather more information—or at least control the timing."

Lucian agreed. "Yes. We maintain the appearance of compliance while preparing for contingencies. We should set watches tonight and ensure we're ready to move at a moment's notice."

Dora looked at Graham and Mike. "Can you two handle the first shifts?"

Graham nodded. "Yeah. I'll go first."

Mike checked his sidearm discreetly. "No problem."

Lucian stood. "Dora, can you send a message detailing our situation to Ash? He may be able to track down who Yakov is dealing with. He might be trying to sell us out. It would need to be somebody who could take advantage of a new drug formula."

Lucian watched from the dimly lit living area as Dora stepped out onto the small patio adjoining their apartment. The cool night air carried the distant hum of Minsk, but here, it was quiet enough to hear the rustling of leaves. She held her phone aloft, tilting it toward the sky in search of a satellite signal. The glow of the screen illuminated her face, etched with concentration.

After a few moments, Dora's phone pinged. She began typing, her fingers moving swiftly over the keys. Lucian knew she was sending an encrypted message. They needed guidance—Sergei's sudden delay had made that clear.

Dora reentered the room, closing the door behind her. "Message sent," she announced, her voice low to avoid echoing in the sparse space.

"Any response?" Lucian asked.

"Not yet," she said, taking a seat.

They waited in a tense silence. Mike and Graham busied themselves with checking their gear.

After about five minutes, Dora went back out and checked her phone. "Reply from Ash," she said. "He says he'll look into it but needs more information. He's also contacting Jonas to see if he can help."

"Good," Lucian replied. "Send him our approximate location and intended crossing point. Keep the details minimal but sufficient. Maybe we can use this delay to see what we can get from our escorts."

She nodded, composing the follow-up message carefully before returning to the patio to hit send. "Done."

"I'm going to get some sleep. You too, Dora, Emma. Mike, wake me up when you're done with your watch."

"Okay, boss."

"Only two bedrooms," Emma noted. "Mind if I join you, boss?"

"I do need sleep, though, Emma."

"Sure."

They picked one of the bedrooms while Dora went to the other.

Once the door was closed, Lucian stripped and climbed into bed next to Emma, who was already there.

"Remember, Anja and Zoe said it would be good if we had the opportunity to take the edge off," she said.

"I know. I think they're rubbing off on you."

"They can…"

"Yeah, I know," he interrupted. "Let's get some sleep."

"I guess I can wait. You're not as pretty as Lev."

"Hmph."

Emma curled in next to him as he tried to relax. Eventually, he drifted off to sleep—and to dream.

Lucian dreamed of a dimly lit room, the air thick with a heady, musky scent that seemed to penetrate his very core. The walls were adorned with lush tapestries, the figures on them moving and writhing in a sensual dance. In the center of the chamber, Anja reclined on a plush chaise, naked and glistening with a sheen of perspiration. Her eyes, those mesmerizing emerald orbs, locked onto his.

"Lucian," she purred.

His body moved of its own accord. He sank to his knees before her, unable to tear his gaze away from hers. Her scent filled his nostrils, intoxicating and potent. Jasmine.

"Do you want me, Lucian?" she breathed, running her fingers down her curves teasingly.

"Always."

Anja laughed throatily.

"I want…I want to feel you," he managed as he reached out to cup her breasts.

"Then take me, Lucian," she purred. "Make me yours again."

In his dreams, Lucian lost himself in Anja's embrace, their bodies entwining. Her skin was like silk against his, and her moans of pleasure spurred him on to the heights of passion. He explored every inch of her supple form, leaving nothing untouched.

In the real world, however, Emma felt the brunt of his pent-up desires. She moaned, her body arching towards his hungry touches and caresses. The line between dream and reality blurred further still as Lucian plunged himself into her. Emma's legs wrapped around him, drawing him deeper inside as she met his thrusts with equal fervor.

Their shared passion built like a storm, feverish and consuming. Anja's face melded with Emma's; their moans became one euphoric chorus that filled the room. Every touch, every kiss, every gasp for air fed the fire within him until he couldn't bear it any longer.

With a final roar, Lucian felt himself go. The world around them seemed to shatter and reform, the dimly lit chamber replaced by the reality of the apartment bed. His breath came in ragged pants as he opened his eyes, disoriented for a moment before reality came flooding back to him.

Emma lay beside him, her chest heaving in tandem with his own, her skin flushed and damp with their exertion. A contented smile played on her lips as she propped herself up on one elbow and gazed into his eyes. "Well, boss…that was…unexpected," she panted, a mischievous glint in her eyes.

"I-I'm sorry, Emma…I didn't mean…it was just a dream…" he stammered, at a loss for words.

She placed a finger on his lips, silencing him. "It's okay, Lucian." A knowing smile tugged at her lips. "I know it wasn't me you were with tonight." Her gaze softened as she caressed his cheek tenderly. "But I want you to know that I don't mind."

Lucian swallowed hard. It wasn't guilt he felt. He knew Anja's intention, but it was still shocking. It wasn't his first time with Emma. That time, Anja and Zoe had been there. He pulled her close, wrapping his arms around her and burying his face in the crook of her neck. "Thank you," he whispered hoarsely.

"Shh," she soothed, running her fingers through his sweat-dampened hair. "I know they have your heart. If I can share in that sometimes, it's enough."

Reluctantly, he released her from his embrace and looked into her eyes, searching for any sign of deception or hurt. Instead, he found only acceptance shining back at him.

As they lay there, the last vestiges of the dream faded away.

"Your Lev skin is gone, so you'll have to shift back in the morning. I'll take it as a high compliment that you lost control. It's something to keep in mind."

Morning arrived with a pale light filtering through the thin curtains. The group gathered again as they prepared for the day, with Lucian back as Lev. There was a knock at the door, and Graham peered through the peephole before opening it cautiously.

Sergei stood in the hallway, his expression unreadable. "Good morning," he greeted. "There's been a development."

Dora stepped forward. "What sort of development?"

Sergei shifted slightly. "We've received word that there are issues at the Russian border—heightened security measures. It would be unwise to attempt crossing today."

Dora feigned concern. "Do you know how long the delay might be?"

"Hard to say," Sergei replied. "Perhaps another day or two."

Lucian exchanged a glance with Emma. "That's unfortunate," he said.

Sergei seemed relieved by their acceptance. "Indeed. In the meantime, we can ensure you're comfortable here."

"Thank you," Lucian said. "Can you bring us some food, or should we venture out and get it?"

"No need, we'll bring you something."

As Sergei departed, closing the door behind him, Mike exhaled. "Well, that's confirmation."

Dora frowned. "They're stalling, just as Yakov instructed."

"Okay, Emma, time for you to earn your catnip," Lucian said as he set her out on the patio.

Twenty

Claire stood at the edge of an old grove beyond the manicured gardens; the moon cast a silvery glow over the estate's sprawling grounds. The moon was not quite full, but that was not a requirement. She remembered the full moon shining for her first shift. The call had been too strong to resist before the ritual was complete and had resulted in a wildness that was difficult to control. She didn't want to repeat that experience with her relatives.

The scent of the earth and blooming flowers filled the air, mingling with the aroma of burning sage from the ritual space Howard had prepared. Tonight, her family would begin to reclaim a legacy long hidden.

Howard moved methodically within the circle of stones, arranging candles and carefully inscribed talismans. He held a small case containing vials of the new serum—a formula tailored for their wolf lineage.

"Who would like to go first?" Howard said.

Dillon stepped forward, his youthful face reflecting excitement and nervous anticipation. "I'm ready," he replied, glancing at Claire for reassurance.

She gave him an encouraging nod. "You'll do great."

Howard handed him one of the small vials. "This will initiate your awakening," he explained. "Drink it all, and then when we start, listen to my chants. Let the sounds guide you."

Dillon accepted the vial, peering at the shimmering liquid inside. "Looks…different than I expected," he murmured. "Kinda plain, not sparkly or magical."

"What does it smell like?" Simon asked.

Dillon uncorked the vial and sniffed tentatively. "Kind of metallic, like…copper? But there's something else too, like mint."

Bee stepped closer. "Are you sure this is safe?"

"Trust me, Dillon will be fine," Claire said.

Taking a deep breath, Dillon raised the vial. "Well, here's to new beginnings." He tilted his head back and drank the serum in one swift motion. He grimaced. "Oh, that's…interesting."

Simon leaned in. "What does it taste like?"

Dillon licked his lips. "It's got a metallic tang, kind of like sucking on a penny. There's a bitter edge, too, like tea. And it's a bit thick—more like syrup than water." He paused, a shiver running through him. "Now there's this warmth spreading in my chest and a tingling sensation. It's not unpleasant, just…weird."

Simon took his vial and drank.

Once he collected the empty vials, Howard gestured for the two prospective wolves to gather around the circle. "Before we begin, you must remove any barriers between yourselves and the natural world," he instructed, glancing at Dillon.

"Besides, when did you last see a wolf in a hoodie?" Claire asked.

Dillon chuckled nervously.

Claire began to undress, folding her clothes and placing them aside. Even though the ceremony was not for her, she would be there for them. Simon followed suit, but Dillon hesitated, glancing around. His cheeks flushed as he saw Claire and Simon standing unabashedly.

Claire noticed his discomfort and offered a reassuring smile. "It's natural," she said. "There's nothing to be embarrassed about. Like I said…"

"You'll get used to it," Simon finished for her with a wink. "Besides, it's more practical this way."

Dillon took a deep breath and nodded, beginning to undress. Once they were all prepared, Howard motioned for them to enter the circle.

"Sit comfortably," Howard instructed. "Close your eyes and listen to my voice. Let the chants guide you. Feel the connection to your ancestors, the earth beneath you, and the moon above. Close your eyes. Focus on the sensations. Let the serum awaken what's within you."

He began to chant in a low, rhythmic tone, the ancient words resonating in the still night air. The tones and syllables were foreign yet seemed familiar.

The chant Anja had used with Claire echoed in her memory and harmonized with Howard's. Claire closed her eyes and let the sound wash over her. The serum would flow through their veins, a warm current awakening dormant senses. The world around her faded until only the cadence of Howard's voice remained.

A tingling sensation spread across her skin, and she felt the familiar pull of transformation. Bones and muscles shifted seamlessly, fur sprouting where skin had been. She welcomed her wolf anew.

Dillon sat with his eyes closed, his expression a mix of concentration and wonder. Simon appeared focused but tense, with a furrow between his brows.

Howard's chants continued, bridging the gap between the physical and the spiritual. Claire sensed Dillon's transformation beginning. His form shimmered, outline blurring as his body adapted to its new shape.

In moments, a young wolf with rich auburn fur stood where Dillon had been. He opened his eyes, golden and luminous, meeting Claire's gaze. She could sense his exhilaration and offered an encouraging nod.

Simon, however, was struggling. His muscles twitched, and his breathing grew ragged.

"Stay with the rhythm," Howard urged. "Let go of resistance. Let it flow and embrace what lies within."

Claire approached Simon slowly, her presence meant to reassure him. She nudged his hand with her muzzle.

Simon opened his eyes, meeting her gaze. The tension in his features eased, and he took a deep breath. Gradually, his form began to shift. It was a more arduous process, his body resisting the change, but eventually, a large wolf stood with them.

He looked around, disoriented. Claire sensed his confusion and fear. She moved beside him, pressing against his side, offering silent comfort.

"You're not alone," she tried to project through their shared sibling

connection. *"I'm here."*

Simon steadied, his posture relaxing as he acclimated to his new form.

Dillon bounded over and nudged Simon. Simon responded tentatively at first, then with growing confidence.

Howard watched them with a satisfied smile. "Well done," he said.

Claire led the two younger wolves into the woods. They moved through the forest with increasing ease, each step building their confidence. The night was alive with the sounds of wildlife, the rustling of leaves, and the distant call of an owl.

After some time, they returned to the circle. Howard awaited them, along with Margaret and Bee, who were next to undergo the ritual.

Claire remained in wolf form, standing as a silent sentinel. Dillon shifted back to human form, a grin spreading across his face.

"That was incredible!" he exclaimed, reaching for the clothes he had set aside earlier. "I wish Anja had been here to see this."

Simon attempted to shift back but found it challenging. He looked to Claire, uncertainty in his eyes. She approached him, touching her muzzle to his.

"Focus on your breathing," Howard guided. "Remember how it felt when you transformed. Let the change flow naturally."

Simon closed his eyes, concentrating. Slowly, his form began to shift back. It was a struggle, but with Claire's support, he managed to return to his human self.

"Thank you," he whispered, meeting her gaze with gratitude.

She nodded and licked his cheek, her eyes conveying understanding.

Margaret stepped forward next. She undressed gracefully, unperturbed by the ritual's requirements. Howard handed her a vial of serum. She drank it, her eyes reflecting the moonlight.

"Listen to the chants," Howard reminded her. "Let them guide you."

As he resumed the ancient melody, Margaret closed her eyes. Her transformation was smooth and graceful, demonstrating her acceptance and inner harmony. A dignified wolf with silver-streaked fur and watchful amber eyes emerged. Claire felt a deep connection to her mother in that moment.

Bee was the last for the evening. She embraced the change readily.

Throughout it all, Claire remained in her wolf form, providing support and reassurance.

Howard concluded the ceremonies. "You've all taken a significant step tonight," he announced. "Embrace this gift and the responsibilities that come with it."

Margaret addressed the newly gathered pack. "Tonight was just the beginning. The dangers we hid from throughout the centuries are still there, and we must face them. We have returned to the forest as Isobel once did. She led us into hiding to wait until we had a chance to fight back. Now, we must prepare for that fight."

Claire took in the sight of her family, stronger now, connected in ways they hadn't been before. Finally, she, too, shifted back, feeling a deep sense of fulfillment.

"Tonight, we reclaimed our legacy," she said, her voice filled with emotion. "But this is just the beginning."

As they made their way back to the manor, the first rays of sunlight peeked over the horizon. Despite the obstacles ahead, she knew they would stand strong, united as a pack, bound by blood.

The sun hung low in the sky, casting a golden hue over the estate as more of Claire's relatives arrived. Heather Bennett stepped out of her car, adjusting her glasses as she took in the grandeur of the manor. "Aunt Claire," she called out, a smile spreading across her face.

"Heather, it's so good to see you," Claire replied, pulling her into a hug. "I'm glad you could make it."

"Wouldn't have missed it for the world," Heather said with a grin. "Though I'll admit, your mother's message was…well, let's just say it was a tad cryptic."

Claire smiled enigmatically. "All will be explained."

Next to arrive was Alice Warren, her eyes alight with excitement. "Claire! It's been ages!"

"Alice, welcome," Claire greeted her. "I'm glad you came. I've heard about your efforts to reintroduce wolves. I have a few ideas for you."

Alice tilted her head. "Now you've piqued my interest. I could use a fresh perspective. The environment secretary dug his heels in, and frankly, he's scuppered any progress we were making. Even north of the border, there's still stiff resistance."

Last to arrive for the day was her aunt Fiona Bradley. The resemblance to her mother was striking. "Claire, my dear," she said warmly. "Your mother was most insistent I come and stay for a while. Haven't the faintest idea why, mind you. But I must say, this is a rather splendid setting for a family gathering."

Claire chuckled. "It is, Aunt Fiona. Come inside; Mum's looking forward to seeing you."

They gathered in the grand dining hall, now transformed into a meeting space. They had had a light meal, but it was apparent that everyone was anxious to learn what had brought them here. A large oak table dominated the center, surrounded by high-backed chairs. Howard stood at one end, arranging notes and texts. Margaret was beside him, her hands folded calmly, and the space beside her set aside for Fiona.

The previous arrivals were also present, with the only exception being Ash. He was busy researching something about a possible trap or double-cross for Lucian and his group. Nomad had reported no significant problems on their route, but they were traveling at a slower pace than he had hoped.

As everyone settled, Claire stood and addressed the group. "Thank you all for coming. We have much to discuss. Our family is at a crossroads."

Heather adjusted her glasses. "This sounds rather serious. What exactly is going on?"

"I'm calling the pack," Margaret declared. "Some of you may think that's merely an old-fashioned turn of phrase from our family stories and traditions. But you'll soon understand the true weight of those words."

Fiona held up a hand. "I thought this was to be a family gathering. Who are these others?"

Claire sat back down and motioned to her mother.

"Ian MacGregor of Clan MacGregor is not blood, but his people share a similar history. He knows of our legacy, and I have welcomed him here. He is also Claire's…mate."

"MacGregor, is it? That name was proscribed at one time, was it not?" Fiona asked.

Ian nodded. "Aye. The clan was declared forfeit about the same time your own family went to ground. We kept the name alive but buried the truth of what it meant, much as your lot did. There's still reason enough for secrecy even now—as you'll soon see."

Fiona looked at Howard inquiringly.

Before she could speak, Claire supplied, "Howard Miller—one of the Millers. This is his family's estate."

Howard cleared his throat. "Allow me to provide some context. Your family lineage is rich with history that intertwines with the mystical and the occult. For generations, you've possessed abilities. Connections to the natural world that have remained dormant, suppressed by necessity at first, and then faded over time."

Fiona leaned forward, her eyes keen. "Are you referring to the old legends?"

Margaret nodded. "Yes, Fiona. The legends are true."

A murmur rippled through the room. Alice's eyes widened as she looked from Margaret to Claire. "You can't be serious. Can you?"

Claire met her gaze steadily. "Yes. But with this gift comes great responsibility."

"Margaret, is this one of your elaborate little games? Trying to liven up a family gathering? Wouldn't put it past you."

"No, dear sister. This is no game."

Silence.

Claire sighed and shot her mother a look. "I told Mum you'd all want proof before you'd believe a word of it. She thought to save it for later. But clearly, we'll get nowhere otherwise."

"What are you talking about?" Alice asked.

"You'll see," Dillon whispered, earning a hush from his mother.

Claire took a deep breath as she stood and stepped back from the table. Her family regarded her with skeptical gazes. She could sense the disbelief of new arrivals. Dillon watched with a knowing smile, barely containing his excitement.

She slipped off her jacket and handed it to Ian, who folded it neatly and placed it on her chair. Claire began to unbutton her blouse.

"Claire, what the devil are you doing?" Fiona demanded.

"Just trust me," Claire replied. She continued to disrobe, removing her shoes and setting them aside. As she took off her blouse and unfastened her bra, Alice's eyes widened.

"Oh, for heaven's sake—is this really necessary?" Alice questioned, her cheeks flushing.

Claire offered a reassuring smile. "Clothes don't tend to fare well during the transformation. Easier this way, trust me."

Heather leaned forward. "Transformation? You mean actually changing…like into a wolf?"

Claire nodded. "Yes."

Margaret placed a comforting hand on Fiona's arm. "Just watch, dear sister."

Stripping down, Claire tossed her folded clothes to Ian without a hint of embarrassment, letting the glow of the fire warm her bare skin. She closed her eyes for a brief moment, centering herself, feeling that familiar, powerful pull deep within her core.

Her body shifted before their eyes—her frame lowering, muscles and tendons tightening and reshaping as bones realigned. Golden-brown fur spread in a shimmer across her skin, her face elongating into a sleek muzzle, her ears sharpening to points. Where Claire had stood moments before, a magnificent wolf now stood, her coat glinting in the firelight.

Fiona gripped Margaret's hand. "Good heavens!"

Alice's hand flew to her mouth. "This can't be real…but I'm seeing it."

Heather's eyes were wide with a mix of shock and awe. "Incredible," she whispered. "Absolutely incredible."

The wolf that was Claire stepped forward slowly, her movements deliberate and unthreatening. She sat on her haunches, her gaze soft as she looked at each of them.

Ian spoke gently. "You see now why secrecy is paramount. This is the legacy you've inherited."

Fiona shook her head, trying to reconcile what she'd just witnessed. "I always thought the old stories were just myths…tales to frighten or amuse children…"

Margaret's smile was gentle, faintly triumphant. "No, Fiona. They were never just stories. This"—she gestured to Claire—"is the truth."

Alice's expression shifted from shock to delight. "You know," she began, unable to suppress a giggle. "You know my project to reintroduce wolves into England? Little did I know there were already some among us. I guess you were serious when you said you had some ideas for me."

Claire tilted her head, a playful glint in her eyes. A soft chuffing sound escaped her muzzle.

Heather found her voice again. "So, this is what you meant by abilities. It's…astonishing."

Bee nodded. "It explains so much about our family."

Dillon could no longer contain his excitement. "Isn't it amazing? I went through the ritual myself. It's like discovering a whole new part of yourself."

Fiona looked over at Dillon, eyes wide. "You too?"

He grinned. "Yep! And it's the most exhilarating feeling."

Alice stood up slowly and approached Claire with cautious steps. "May I?" she asked, reaching out a tentative hand.

Claire nodded, allowing Alice to place a hand on her head. Alice's fingers sank into the soft fur, and she laughed. "I can't believe this. All this time, I've been advocating for wolves without knowing…"

Claire leaned into the touch briefly before stepping back. She let the wolf melt away, the change rippling through her in reverse. Bones and muscle shifted, fur retreating, until she stood once more on two legs, naked but unbothered. She retrieved her clothes from Ian, set them on the table, and flopped into a chair with a huff of exhaustion.

"Don't you think you ought to get dressed, dear?" Fiona asked.

Claire gave her an unapologetic look. "Shifting takes it out of you. Shifting back even more. At the moment, I'm tired and, frankly, I don't care. You'd best all get used to it—nudity comes with the territory, I'm afraid."

"You mean that we all can do this?" Alice asked.

"Yes," Claire said simply. "Mum can. Bee, Dillon, Simon—they all can, and the rest of you could too. There's a ritual to awaken it properly…with, as Howard likes to say, a bit of 'scientific magic' mixed in. We'll cover all that later.

"Howard will act as a guide. Ian can shift, too—just not wolf. The MacGregors are bears. He can be quite the bear in the morning, too."

Ian gave a good-natured shrug. "Guilty as charged," he said with a wry smile.

"Now you understand why we need to establish rules," Claire said, her voice steady. "Our abilities are a gift, but they also come with risks and responsibilities—both to ourselves and others."

"We must also protect our secret. As Claire and Ian have informed us," Margaret said, "there's a growing threat to our family—the Sodality. They are an ancient organization with intentions that will jeopardize not only our legacy but our very lives."

A hush fell over the room. Claire could sense the weight of her mother's words settling in. She knew this was a lot for them to take in, but it was necessary.

"Lucian Miller is aware and supportive of our situation," Margaret continued. "He offered his estate for us to use in the interim. It's a safe haven where we can gather and plan our next steps."

Fiona raised an eyebrow. "Lucian Miller, the biotech magnate? How is he involved in all of this?"

Claire exchanged a glance with Ian before answering. "Lucian has been directly affected by the Sodality's actions. They tried to murder him, but instead killed his family: his mother and father, as well as his sister and brother. His serum formulation enabled our faded lineage to reemerge. We believe they moved to stop that discovery. They missed him and only accelerated his progress. You can understand why he won't rest until the Sodality is ended."

Fiona exhaled slowly. "This changes everything," she mused. "We need to reconsider…well, everything."

Alice nodded. "If we embrace this part of ourselves, we must be cautious," she said. "The world isn't exactly welcoming of the unknown. Just look at the resistance to reintroducing natural wolves. I don't think the world is ready for this."

Claire felt a pang of empathy. She understood their fears; she had grappled with them herself. "That's why we're bringing everyone together," she explained. "To harness our collective strengths and to support one another. They'll come for us to finish what they started so long ago. We either hide and fade away or make sure we're ready for them when that time comes."

A thoughtful silence settled over the room. Fiona appeared deep in thought, her fingers lightly on the armrest. Alice was pensively staring into the fire, while Heather looked energized, ideas clearly forming in her mind.

Breaking the silence, Fiona looked up. "What exactly do we know about this Sodality's intentions?"

Claire met her gaze. "They seek to eliminate those they consider a threat to their vision of human purity," she explained. "That includes individuals like us with unique heritages. They've been operating from the shadows for centuries. Millennia."

Howard added, "Their influence is far-reaching. They've manipulated events throughout history. More recently, think of the Inquisition, witch hunts, even modern conflicts."

Ian crossed his arms. "They won't stop unless we stand against them."

Alice sighed. "But how can we possibly fight an organization that powerful?"

Claire straightened her shoulders. "By uniting," she said firmly. "By reclaiming our heritage and supporting each other. We have abilities they fear—it's time we use them."

Heather leaned forward. "We should also consider forming alliances with others like us," she suggested. "If there are other clans or groups facing the same threat, we could be stronger together."

Claire nodded thoughtfully and glanced at Ian. "Very true, but we need to secure our own foundations first."

Margaret looked around the room, her gaze softening. "This is a pivotal moment for our family," she said. "We have the chance to define our future. To reclaim what is ours. I've tasted the night under the moon. I will not go back."

Fiona's expression shifted from skepticism to resolve. "Then we need a plan," she stated.

"Quite," Claire agreed, leaning forward. "We can draw on all our strengths. Heather, your legal mind will be invaluable. Alice, your expertise in wildlife and conservation can help us understand our nature, ground it in something tangible. Aunt Fiona, your anthropological insight could give us perspective on the legacy we're part of."

Fiona stood, smoothing her skirt. "Well, it seems we have much work to do," she declared.

"Agreed," Alice said, rising as well. "Let's set tomorrow for our first proper planning session."

As the family began to disperse, Claire felt a hand on her arm. She turned to see Margaret's smile. "You handled that beautifully," her mother said.

"I couldn't have done it without your support."

Margaret squeezed her arm. "Your decision to embrace what we are…I'm so proud of you."

Claire looked around the room as her relatives engaged in quiet conversations. "I just want us all to be safe," she admitted. "To have a future."

"And we will," Margaret assured her. "Because we have each other."

Twenty-One

Anja sat in the van as it rattled along the roads leading away from Warsaw. The early morning light filtered through the grimy windows, casting long shadows across the worn upholstery. Marek, the trafficker facilitating their travel to Moscow, was slumped in the front passenger seat, his head tilted back as he snored softly. Tomasz, the driver, focused on the road ahead.

Between Anja and Zoe sat the young girl, her slight frame tucked into the oversized jacket she wore. She looked younger than Zoe and Anja, with their artificially enhanced youthfulness, and was just barely in her teens. Strands of her chestnut hair fell over her face, partially hiding her red-rimmed eyes that stared blankly at the floor. Every so often, a quiet sniff escaped her, and she hurriedly wiped away a tear with the back of her hand.

Anja exchanged a concerned glance with Zoe. Through their connection, they communicated silently.

"We need to find out what's happening with her," Anja projected.

Zoe gave a subtle nod. *"Agreed. But carefully."*

Anja leaned slightly toward the girl, keeping her tone soft and unobtrusive. "Przepraszam, mówisz po polsku czy rosyjsku?" she asked gently.

Karolina sniffled again and gave the barest shrug. "Trochę," she said, her voice hoarse. "Ale… I speak English also. We learn in school." Her accent was unmistakably Ukrainian—rounded vowels and a touch of musical cadence.

Zoe offered Karolina a warm smile. "That's really good English," she said gently. "Better than my Polish."

Karolina's mouth tugged upward for the first time. Just barely. "Thank you," she said, still hugging her knees. "We had lessons from the third year. My teacher said it was important… in case we had to leave."

Anja's heart gave a slow ache at that phrasing.

"I'm Adela," she whispered, using her alias for the mission. "This is Zofia. What's your name?"

The girl hesitated, her gaze flickering up briefly before returning to her lap. "Karolina," she murmured.

"That's a beautiful name," Zoe said softly. "Are you alright?"

Karolina shrugged, her shoulders tensing. "Only tired," she said softly.

Anja placed a reassuring hand on Karolina's arm. "We understand. Traveling like this can be hard. How old are you?"

"Fourteen." Karolina swallowed, eyes shiny with new tears. "I don't know even where they take me," she said. "They said I didn't… work with them enough."

Anja felt a surge of simmering anger toward Marek and his operation. "Do you have family waiting for you?" she asked gently.

Karolina shook her head. "No. They say there is job, but it was lie. Now I just…taken place to place."

Zoe leaned in closer. "We're heading to Moscow. Maybe we can help each other."

Karolina looked between them, a flicker of hope in her eyes. "How?"

Anja glanced toward the front of the van; Marek was still asleep, and Tomasz seemed uninterested in their conversation. She lowered her voice with a glance toward Nomad. "We have connections there. Perhaps we can find a way to improve your situation."

Karolina's lips trembled. "Why you want help me?"

"Because no one should have to go through this," Zoe replied firmly.

"But…you same like me. How you help?"

Anja sensed the weight of the girl's despair. Through her link with Zoe, she conveyed her thoughts. *"We can't save everyone, but maybe we can save her. One more starfish saved."*

"What... Starfish? Never mind," Zoe responded. *"Okay. How can we save her?"*

Anja considered their options. *"Perhaps we can convince Marek to let us take responsibility for her. If we offer to include her in our 'package' for the buyer in Moscow, he might agree."*

"It's worth a try," Zoe conceded. *"But then what?"*

Returning her attention to Karolina, Anja squeezed her hand gently. "Rest for now. We'll figure something out."

Karolina gave a faint nod, exhaustion overtaking her as she leaned back against the seat. Within minutes, her breathing steadied as she drifted into a fitful sleep.

Anja watched her for a moment before looking back at Zoe. "We have to help her," she whispered.

"We will."

Anja glanced up at Nomad, who was eyeing them warily, but he remained silent.

Hours passed as the landscape outside changed from urban sprawl to the more subdued hues of the countryside. The van stopped intermittently for fuel and brief rest breaks, during which Marek kept a watchful eye on all of them. He seemed oblivious to the earlier conversation, more preoccupied with his own thoughts.

As they drew closer to the Belarusian border, Marek stirred from his slumber. Stretching, he glanced back at the trio. "Everyone holding up?" he asked, his tone devoid of genuine concern.

"Just eager to reach Moscow," Anja replied smoothly.

Marek grunted in acknowledgment. His gaze lingered on Karolina. "She been any trouble?"

"Not at all," Anja replied. "In fact, we were thinking. Our buyer in Moscow is always interested in new...young talents. Perhaps we could include Karolina in our arrangement."

Marek raised an eyebrow. "Is that so?"

"Yes," Anja said, turning to look at Nomad.

Merik scratched his chin thoughtfully. "Interesting. She's been more trouble than she's worth. If he's willing to take her off my hands, I might consider it. For the right price."

"We can discuss the details later," Nomad said. Our buyer is generous when it comes to quality, and she is very pretty."

Marek's eyes narrowed slightly. "Fine. But until then, she's still mine."

Nomad nodded, then scowled at Anja.

With a curt nod, Marek turned back to face the front.

As evening approached, the van crossed into Belarus without incident, thanks to Marek's connections, which smoothed over any complications at the border. It seemed he had done this many times, and the official seemed bored, but there seemed to be an understanding. She wondered if he might be a customer. His eyes lingered on them.

"Creep," Zoe sent.

The cityscape of Minsk eventually came into view—a blend of Soviet-era architecture and modern developments, tinged with the golden hues of sunset.

The van drove through a maze of streets, eventually pulling into a rundown section of the city. The buildings here bore the marks of neglect—cracked façades, faded paint, and dimly lit alleyways.

"Welcome to our accommodations for the night," Marek announced dryly. "Not much, but it serves its purpose."

Tomasz parked the van beside a dilapidated building with boarded-up windows. As they disembarked, Anja noted the absence of bystanders—a stark contrast to the bustling areas they'd passed earlier.

"Stay close," Marek instructed, his gaze stern. "This isn't the safest neighborhood."

Anja suppressed a bitter smile. As if he cares about our safety... Well, only so far as his payment was concerned.

Inside, the building was marginally better than its exterior suggested. The interior was sparse but clean enough. Marek led them to a modest room with a few cots and minimal furnishings.

"You'll stay here tonight," he said. "We leave at dawn."

"What about meals?" Zoe inquired.

"I'll have something brought up," he replied curtly before exiting the room.

Once alone, Karolina sank onto one of the cots, her expression weary. "Is this where they'll keep me?" she asked quietly.

Anja sat beside her. "No. Remember, we're taking you with us to

Moscow."

Karolina looked down. "And then what? Sold to someone else?"

Zoe crouched in front of her, eyes softening. "We're not going to let that happen. We have friends who can help."

Karolina's eyes searched theirs for sincerity. "Why are you doing this?"

"Because we can," Anja said simply. "And because it's the right thing to do."

A faint spark of hope flickered in Karolina's gaze before it faded. "Thank you."

The door creaked open, and Nomad slipped inside, closing it quietly behind him. "We need to talk," he said, his tone urgent.

Anja stood. "What's wrong?"

"I overheard Marek speaking with someone on the phone," Nomad explained. "He's planning to hand Karolina over to a local contact tonight."

Karolina's face paled. "No…"

"Did he say when?" Zoe asked.

"Soon," Nomad replied. "We need to move quickly if we're going to get her out of here."

Anja nodded, determination settling in. "What's the plan?"

Zoe glanced at Karolina, then back at Anja. "We need to convince Marek to let us spend the night with Karolina," she whispered. "You could want to have your last night with the three of us."

Anja considered this. "But Marek isn't likely to agree without something in return."

A sly smile tugged at the corner of Zoe's mouth. "I have some cash hidden," she said, lowering her voice further. "Leo was generous. We can use it to persuade Marek."

Anja raised an eyebrow. "You kept it hidden this whole time?"

"Always be prepared," Zoe replied with a wink. "Nomad will give the money to Marek. Tell him you want to 'use' us for the night before selling us off in Moscow. It would allow you to 'train' Karolina and perhaps increase her value."

Karolina looked between them, confused. "Again I get used?"

Anja placed a reassuring hand on her shoulder. "No, that is only a story to tell that ugly man."

Nomad frowned, his skepticism evident. "Even if Marek agrees for the night, he's expecting to sell her. How do you plan to handle that?"

Anja exchanged a knowing glance with Zoe. "We should be able to handle him," she said carefully. "We might be able to make Marek believe he's already been paid."

Nomad crossed his arms. "You're talking about manipulating his mind?"

"Yeah," Zoe admitted. "He deserves it. It makes me want to mete out justice myself when nobody seems to care."

He hesitated. "I've seen what you can do, but Marek."

Anja's gaze was steady. "We don't have many options. Will you help us?"

After a moment, Nomad sighed. "Alright. I'll take the cash to Marek and propose the idea. But be prepared—if this goes sideways, we'll need to act fast."

"Understood," Anja said.

Zoe retrieved the stash of bills from under her skirt and thong and handed them to Nomad. "This should be enough to convince him."

Nomad took the money, slipping it into his jacket. "I'll be back soon."

As he left the room, Anja turned to Karolina. "Do you trust us?"

Karolina nodded slowly. "I don't really have choice… But yes."

"Good," Anja said softly. "Stay close to us, and we'll do everything we can to help."

Minutes ticked by as they waited for Nomad's return. Anja could feel the tension in the air, each second stretching longer than the last. She glanced at Zoe, who was pacing lightly, her mind clearly racing through possible scenarios.

Finally, the door opened, and Nomad stepped inside, his expression guarded.

"Well?" Zoe asked.

"Marek agreed," Nomad replied. "But he made it clear that the cash covers only one night. He expects a significant payment for Karolina when we reach Moscow."

Anja exhaled. "That's a start."

Nomad eyed them critically. "I still don't see how you're going to pull this off."

"We'll find a way," Anja assured him. "But we need to ensure he doesn't suspect anything tonight."

Nomad nodded reluctantly. "He's occupied with other matters right now."

"Thank you," Zoe said.

"I'll leave you for now, but be careful."

"No, you'll need to stay here. You need to stay with us girls for the night. And pretend you had a good time," Zoe said.

"We could even make that true, Nomad. Maybe not Karolina, but Zoe and I could."

"Stop teasing him Anja," Zoe said. *"I think he's gay, and it would probably mess him up big time."*

"Oh! Well, that explains a lot."

"It already caused him issues when he saw your succubus form when you captured him. Besides, do you really think showing him a good time in front of Karolina would be a good idea? Hasn't she suffered enough?"

"Fuck."

"No, not fuck. That's the point."

"Okay, I see your point. Both of them. I'm sure Karolina is not a virgin…"

"Anja! Fourteen, remember?"

"Okay, okay, I get it."

Karolina sat down on the edge of one of the cots, her hands clasped tightly in her lap. "So… what you do?" she asked quietly.

Anja sat beside her. "We have abilities that can influence people," she explained gently. "It's hard to explain, but we believe we can make Marek think he's already received his payment for you."

Karolina's eyes widened. "You… can do this?"

Zoe offered a reassuring smile. "We've done similar things before. It doesn't always work perfectly, but we're improving."

Anja placed a hand on Karolina's shoulder. "But we need you to stay calm and trust us. Can you do that?"

Karolina took a deep breath, then nodded. "I will try, okay?"

"Yes, good," Anja said. "Now, let's prepare."

They spent the next hour discussing the plan in detail. Anja and Zoe would need to get close enough to Marek to use their abilities without raising suspicion and do it in private. The challenge was to create an opportunity where Marek would be receptive to their influence.

Anja awoke to the soft glow of dawn filtering through the thin curtains of their modest room. The air was crisp, carrying the faint scent of morning dew and distant city life. She stretched quietly, mindful not to disturb Karolina, who was still asleep on the cot beside her. Zoe was already up, as was Nomad, who was making arrangements with Marek. Her gaze focused out the window as she sipped from a chipped ceramic cup.

"Morning," Anja whispered, moving to join Zoe.

"Morning," Zoe replied, offering a slight smile. "Ready for the final leg?"

Anja nodded. "As ready as we'll ever be. How's Karolina?"

"Exhausted, but hopeful," Zoe said softly. "She slept through the night."

The door opened, interrupting their conversation. Nomad stepped in, his expression composed yet carrying a hint of satisfaction.

"Time to go," he announced quietly. "I've spoken with Marek. Everything is in place."

Anja arched an eyebrow. "How did it go?"

Nomad allowed a brief smile. "He believes I had a splendid time with the three of you. I've convinced him that I'll miss the company but intend to use my earnings to enjoy similar…experiences in the future."

Zoe exchanged a glance with Anja. "Good," she remarked. "He's none the wiser?"

"Seems that way," Nomad confirmed.

Karolina stirred, rubbing sleep from her eyes. "Is it time?" she asked hesitantly.

"Yes," Anja replied gently. "We're heading to Moscow today."

As they descended the creaky staircase to the building's entrance, Marek was waiting by the van, his demeanor unusually amiable.

"Good morning," he greeted with a satisfied grin. "Ready for the big city?"

"Yes," Nomad replied, matching his tone. "Looking forward to finalizing our business."

Marek chuckled. "I must say, you know how to make the most of an arrangement. Maybe we'll do more deals in the future."

"Maybe," Nomad said noncommittally.

They boarded the van, with Tomasz once again at the wheel. Anja and Zoe sat on either side of Karolina. Marek settled into the front passenger seat, humming an old tune as the engine roared to life.

The landscape shifted from the worn outskirts of Minsk to the open roads leading toward Moscow. Fields gave way to forests, and eventually, the hints of urban sprawl began to appear on the horizon.

As they approached the Russian border, Nomad turned to Marek. "Any concerns about crossing over?"

Marek shook his head confidently. "All arrangements have been made. Smooth sailing from here."

True to his word, the border crossing was uneventful. Marek's paperwork and some relaxing vibes from Zoe seemed sufficient for the guards, who waved them through with minimal scrutiny.

Once in Russia, the atmosphere inside the van grew tenser. The enormity of Moscow loomed ahead—a city teeming with possibilities and dangers alike.

"You will never find a more wretched hive of scum and villainy. We must be cautious." Zoe quoted, causing Anja to stifle a giggle.

"Do you have that whole movie memorized?"

"Pretty much," Zoe admitted.

"Not long now," Marek commented a few quiet hours later, glancing at the sprawling skyline.

Nomad leaned forward. "We'll be heading to a specific location. An establishment near the city center. Our buyer prefers to conduct transactions in familiar territory."

"Smart," Marek acknowledged. "Less chance of unwelcome surprises."

Anja listened, observing Marek's reactions. He seemed at ease, his earlier suspicions quelled. Through her link with Zoe, she conveyed a sense of guarded optimism.

"So far, so good."

"Let's hope it stays that way," Zoe responded mentally.

Navigating the bustling streets of Moscow, Tomasz followed Nomad's directions. The city pulsed with energy—pedestrians hurried along sidewalks, cars honked impatiently, and the cacophony of urban life enveloped them.

They arrived at an elegant building nestled among high-end boutiques and cafés. The exterior was unassuming, but a discerning eye would note the subtle signs of security and exclusivity.

"Here we are," Nomad announced.

Marek surveyed the location appreciatively. "Impressive. Tomasz, wait nearby. I'll call you or send a message when we're done."

They exited the van, and a doorman approached, nodding respectfully to Nomad. "Welcome back, sir."

"Thank you," Nomad replied.

Anja felt some tension ease as they entered the foyer. The interior exuded sophistication—marble floors, tasteful artwork, and soft lighting that created an atmosphere of privacy and luxury.

Anja recognized Katya based on Nomad's description as she descended a grand staircase to greet them. A striking woman, she extended her hand to Nomad. "It's been a while," she said warmly.

"Too long," Nomad agreed, kissing her cheek in a familiar gesture.

Katya's gaze swept over Anja, Zoe, and Karolina. "Welcome," she said graciously.

Marek stepped forward, offering a polite smile. "Marek. A pleasure to meet you."

"Charmed," Katya replied smoothly, though her eyes lingered on him with subtle assessment. "I've prepared a suite where you can all refresh yourselves."

"Thank you," Nomad said.

They followed Katya up the staircase and down a quiet corridor adorned with ornate fixtures and plush carpets. She opened the door to an expansive room featuring a sitting area, elegant furnishings, and large windows overlooking the city.

"Please make yourselves comfortable," Katya said. "If you require anything, simply ask."

"Thank you," Anja said sincerely.

Katya nodded before excusing herself. "I'll leave you to settle in."

Once alone, Marek glanced around appreciatively. "Your buyer certainly has good taste."

Nomad smiled enigmatically. "Only the best."

Anja took a seat by the window, gazing out at the cityscape. The sun was beginning to set, casting a warm glow over the rooftops. Saint Basil's Cathedral and the Kremlin were barely visible beyond other buildings. This was their target.

Karolina joined her nervously.

"Is beautiful," she whispered.

"Yes, it is," Anja agreed softly.

Nomad checked his watch. "I'll need to step out to make final arrangements with our buyer. It shouldn't take long."

Marek nodded, settling into a comfortable chair. "We'll be here."

Anja stood. "Would you like anything while we wait? Vodka?"

Marek waved a hand. "Alright."

Anja poured the clear liquid into a tumbler for him.

As Nomad exited the room, Anja felt a subtle shift in the atmosphere. Marek appeared relaxed, but there was a watchfulness in his eyes. She exchanged a brief glance with Zoe.

"Quite the view," Marek commented, directing his gaze toward the window. "Moscow has history, doesn't it?"

"Yes," Anja replied, maintaining a casual tone. "It's a city full of possibilities."

He chuckled lightly. "Opportunities abound for those who know where to look."

Karolina shifted uncomfortably, and Anja placed a reassuring hand on her arm. "Why don't we explore the suite?" she suggested. "It looks like there's a balcony."

Marek leaned back. "You girls go ahead. I'll rest here."

Anja and Zoe guided Karolina toward the adjoining room, which opened onto a spacious balcony overlooking the city. The cool evening breeze carried the distant sounds of Moscow's vibrant life.

"Here is safe…?" she asked softly.

"Safer than before," Anja assured her and glanced back toward the main room. "We have a bit of time before Nomad returns. Let's take care of Marek. Karolina, why don't you stay out here for a bit?"

Karolina nodded. "Okay."

Her demon stirred. *"Playtime?"*

Twenty-Two

IGOR KRAKAROV SAT in his spacious office in the Kremlin. The room was adorned with dark wooden panels, heavy drapes, and shelves lined with volumes on history and politics. A large desk dominated the space, its surface neatly organized with folders, two telephones, and a state-of-the-art computer—a concession to modernity amid the traditional décor. The glow of a lamp cast long shadows, giving the room an air of gravitas befitting a man of his position.

As one of the senior operatives in the SVR, Russia's Foreign Intelligence Service, Igor was accustomed to juggling multiple layers of intrigue. His official duties often intertwined with the clandestine activities of the Sodality. He provided guidance and spies for many of the Grandmaster's operations to influence world politics. The fact that the majority of those operatives were unaware of the Sodality and the role they served was by design, and personally satisfying.

A chime from his computer drew his attention. A secure message had arrived from the Sodality's controller for Eastern Europe—a man known as the Broker. Igor clicked to open the encrypted communication and scanned the text.

"Opportunity for acquisition heading to Moscow," the message read. "New drug formulation en route. Potentially lucrative. Current handlers have a buyer but the intermediary seeks a larger profit. Details attached. Possible to intercept and negotiate for greater gain."

Igor leaned back in his leather chair, considering the information. The Sodality's operations in Russia often required substantial funding, and illicit activities such as drug trafficking had become a convenient revenue stream. Personal gain was also an enticing prospect; a successful interception could line his own pockets without conflicting with his official duties in either role.

He opened the attached file containing preliminary details about the individuals transporting the drug. The intermediary was a Polish smuggler named Yakov, who claimed to have stalled the couriers in Minsk. The couriers were described as a man named Lev Kuznetsov, a woman called Kasia Nowak, and two bodyguards whose identities were unknown.

Igor's fingers tapped on the desk as he contemplated. The name Kuznetsov seemed familiar. He accessed the SVR database, entering their names to retrieve any available information.

Lev Kuznetsov: A chemist by profession, Russian-born but holding Polish citizenship. Known to have connections with underground laboratories specializing in synthetic drugs. Intelligence suggests he has been active in the black market for years, supplying various Eastern European syndicates.

Kasia Nowak: A Polish national who disappeared from official records years ago. Before vanishing, she was implicated in activities related to drug trafficking and had associations with a syndicate operating across Eastern Europe.

The two bodyguards accompanying them were described but had no matching records in the database. Likely hired muscle or possibly new players in the field.

Igor concluded these individuals were not directly connected to Lucian Miller or Helena. Lucian was believed to be in Geneva, where he was involved with his company's operations. Helena remained at her castle, Zamec Echo, pursuing her interests. This drug shipment appeared to be a fortuitous opportunity.

He typed a response to the Broker: "Acknowledged. Asset acquisition aligns with current objectives. Request direct contact with Yakov's team to facilitate interception and negotiation. Prepared to assist in ensuring passage into Moscow in exchange for favorable terms."

Within minutes, a reply arrived with contact information for Sergei, one of Yakov's men currently in Minsk.

Igor picked up the telephone, dialing the number provided. After a few rings, a gruff voice answered. "Da?"

"Sergei, this is Igor Krakarov," he began, his tone measured and authoritative. "I understand you're managing the transport of a valuable commodity into Moscow."

There was a brief pause before Sergei replied, "That's correct. Yakov mentioned someone might reach out."

"I believe we can be of mutual assistance. I've reviewed the situation and can ensure your group's passage across the Russian border without complications. In return, we can discuss a more profitable arrangement for all parties involved."

Sergei sounded cautious. "What exactly are you proposing?"

"I have the means to expedite your crossing and provide safe passage to Moscow. Once there, we can facilitate a new buyer who is willing to offer a higher price for your goods. Naturally, this would mean adjusting the original agreement you have in place."

Sergei hesitated. "The sellers won't be pleased if we divert the shipment."

Igor smiled slightly, though Sergei couldn't see it. "Compensation will be sufficient to address any...inconveniences. And let's be frank—the profits from this new arrangement will far exceed what was promised. Yakov has agreed."

There was a muffled conversation on the other end—Sergei likely conferring with his associates. Finally, he responded, "All right. We're interested. What do you need from us?"

"First, maintain the appearance of your original plan. Do not alert your passengers to any changes. I will provide you with a route that will avoid unnecessary scrutiny. My contacts will handle any border issues."

"Understood," Sergei said. "We're currently in Minsk. The passengers are starting to question the delays."

"Tell them that the border situation is resolving and you will proceed as planned. I will send you the route details shortly." Before ending the call, Igor added, "One more thing—provide me with any additional information you have on your passengers. Descriptions, behaviors, anything that might be relevant."

Sergei obliged. "Lev is mid-thirties, average build, dark hair. Speaks Russian. Carries himself like someone educated, but is trying to keep a low profile. Kasia is maybe thirtysomething, with dull red hair, sharp-eyed. She seems familiar with the routes and protocols. The bodyguards are physically imposing but haven't caused any trouble. One's a tall, muscular man with a military bearing; the other's a bit stouter but moves like he knows how to handle himself."

"Armed?"

"All of them."

"Thank you. Keep me informed of any developments."

After hanging up, Igor leaned back, contemplating the situation. The descriptions matched the profiles he had viewed earlier. Lev and Kasia were likely seasoned operators in the drug trade, making them valuable assets or formidable adversaries, depending on how the encounter unfolded.

He began drafting instructions for his contacts along the proposed route. Ensuring their passage into Russia would require coordination with border officials who were amenable to certain incentives. He reached out to Yakov again to get license plates and vehicle descriptions. It was a delicate balance—too much interference might alert the couriers, but too little could risk losing them altogether.

Igor picked up the phone again, dialing a secure number. "Colonel Popov, I need a favor," he said when the call connected. "There's a group crossing near Smolensk tomorrow. I need them to pass without inspection." He provided names and vehicle descriptions.

Popov grunted in acknowledgment. "Consider it done. Do you require any additional assistance?"

"Not at this time. Don't make it look too easy, but let them through."

As he hung up, Igor felt a sense of satisfaction. While this operation wasn't directly related to his primary tasks of monitoring Helena or tracking Lucian, it was an opportunity for significant profit. It could bolster his and the Sodality's resources in Russia.

He returned his attention to the files. The faces of Lev and Kasia stared back at him from the photos. He wondered about their motivations. Were they merely smugglers seeking fortune, or was there something more?

Igor reminded himself that overthinking could lead to hesitation. In his line of work, decisiveness was essential.

As the evening shadows lengthened, he stood and walked to the window. The Kremlin's fortified walls and the spires of nearby cathedrals were silhouetted against the darkening sky. Lights flickered on across Moscow.

His gaze drifted southward as if he could see all the way to Minsk and the players moving unwittingly into his grasp.

Igor turned away from the window and reached for his coat. There was more to be done, and he preferred to handle certain matters personally. As he exited his office, he nodded to Elena, his efficient assistant.

"Hold my calls for the rest of the evening," he instructed.

"Yes, sir," she replied, her eyes reflecting curiosity before she returned to her work.

Igor made his way through the corridors, his footsteps echoing on the polished floors. He relished these moments—the quiet before a carefully orchestrated operation reached its crescendo.

In the back of his mind, he acknowledged that while this venture was opportunistic, it also carried risk. He thrived on it.

As he stepped out into the cool night air, he pulled his coat tighter and set off with purposeful strides. The city awaited, and with it, the next move in a game only he knew was being played.

Emma moved silently along the narrow ledge outside the apartment building. Her green eyes flickered as she leapt effortlessly from one balcony to the next. This form definitely had its advantages.

Sergei and his two associates, Viktor and Alexei, had taken up residence in an apartment across the street from the unit they had been put in. Earlier, she had watched them enter their building.

Perching on the windowsill outside their apartment, she found that the window was slightly ajar. The air that wafted from inside carried the scent of tobacco and the murmur of voices. Flattening herself against the frame, Emma peered inside.

The room was modestly furnished—a worn sofa, a small table strewn with maps, and a flickering television casting a pale glow. Sergei sat at the table, fingers drumming on the wooden surface.

Viktor slumped on the sofa, staring at the television.

Their conversation had been sparse, punctuated by long silences. Emma noted the tension. Despite not understanding Russian, she was adept at reading body language, a skill honed through training and undercover assignments. This was a whole new level of undercover.

Minutes stretched into hours with little of note occurring. Emma contemplated returning to inform Lucian that their guides appeared restless but unchanged in demeanor. Just as she was about to depart, Sergei's phone vibrated on the table. He glanced at the screen, his expression sharpening as he answered.

Sergei spoke in hushed tones, the timbre of his voice low and measured. Viktor and Alexei turned their attention to him, their postures alert. Emma strained to catch any nuances, her ears twitching in anticipation.

Though the words were incomprehensible to her, she observed the shift in the atmosphere. Sergei's gaze grew focused, his free hand gesturing subtly as he spoke. Viktor moved closer, his eyes narrowing, while Alexei retrieved a notepad, jotting down something.

Sergei's tone and demeanor suggested communication with someone of importance.

After a hushed conversation with Viktor and Alexei, Sergei ended the call. He placed the phone down and addressed his companions. The ensuing discussion was brisk, marked by nods and affirmations. Alexei unfolded a map on the table, and the three men leaned over it, tracing a route with their fingers.

Emma shifted slightly to get a better view. The map displayed the region between Minsk and Moscow. They seemed to be altering their original plan, indicating a new path that diverged from the main routes. Viktor pointed to a specific area near Moscow, tapping it emphatically.

As they continued their discussion, Emma noticed a fleeting expression of concern cross Sergei's face. He spoke more animatedly, his gestures conveying a mix of urgency and apprehension. Alexei responded with a dismissive wave, while Viktor nodded thoughtfully.

Recognizing that they were finalizing a new course of action, Emma knew she needed to report back to Lucian. Carefully, she backed away from the window, ensuring her movements remained silent. With a final glance to confirm that the men were still engrossed in their plans, she descended the building with feline agility.

Emma returned to their apartment building via alleys and side streets. Upon reaching the patio door of their ground-floor unit, she paused, scanning the surroundings to ensure she hadn't been noticed.

She scratched at the glass door, her claws making a barely audible sound against the pane. Moments later, the curtain shifted, and Lucian appeared. He opened the door, a question in his eyes.

Emma entered, her tail twitching. Lucian closed the door behind her, locking it.

"Did you find anything?" he asked.

Emma moved to the center of the room and squirmed to kick off her collar. Dora and the others looked up from the table where they had been reviewing maps and notes.

With a brief shimmer, Emma resumed her human form. Her eyes met Lucian's. "They received a call. I couldn't understand the language, but it was clear that whoever was on the other end was giving them new instructions."

Lucian gestured for her to join them at the table. "Tell us."

Emma recounted the details—the tension in Sergei's voice, the way Viktor and Alexei had reacted, the map, and the route they'd traced.

"They seemed to be changing our path to Moscow," she concluded. "I think they plan to take us through a different border crossing."

Dora frowned. "That could complicate things. If they're altering the route..."

Graham leaned forward. "Did you notice any markings on the map? Landmarks, town names?"

Emma shook her head. "It was difficult to see specifics from that distance. But the collar should have picked up the conversation." She pointed to it on the floor.

Lucian retrieved the collar and handed it to Dora. The waveform of the audio recording was soon displayed on her phone. She tapped the play button, and the room filled with the muffled sounds of the conversation. She scanned ahead to about twenty minutes from the end, where Emma thought the call should be.

Sergei's voice spoke first. "Da." Lucian listened intently, his Russian lessons paying off, allowing him to translate.

The voice on the phone was too muffled to make out what was said.

Sergei replied, "That's correct. Yakov mentioned someone might reach out."

After a pause, Sergei asked, "What exactly are you proposing?"

This time, there was a longer pause before Sergei said, "The sellers won't be pleased if we divert the shipment."

Shortly, they heard the three discuss what the person on the line had said.

"Yakov said someone would call, and we should take his offer. He said his name was Igor Krakarov. He wants us…"

Dora hit pause. "Fuck."

"You can say that again," Lucian said dryly.

"Fuck. Fuck."

"That was the name of the man Nomad said recruited him to the Sodality. What the hell? How did he get involved? Do they know about us?" Emma asked.

"Let's listen to the rest," Lucian said.

Dora hit play.

"Understood," Sergei said. "We're currently in Minsk. The passengers are starting to question the delays." Then, "Very well."

Sergei relayed their descriptions and the names Kasia and Lev, but nothing else was said before the call ended.

Lucian translated what Sergei said to the others. "Krakarov said he would ease our crossing and provided a route to avoid checkpoints. We'll cross and then hit the back roads after Smolensk. Krakarov said we would be stopped near Moscow and to cooperate with the men he was sending to escort us the rest of the way. Sergei's men would receive their bonuses from them."

"Can't they see they are going to be double-crossed?" Emma asked. "Kind of ironic."

There were sounds of laughter and clinking glasses before they faded. Dora hit stop.

"We need to get the hell out," Graham said.

"Let's not panic yet. We know what's coming and have a few surprises for them. It seems like they only have our descriptions and aliases. It's unlikely they would link any of us to me as Lucian. It takes us to Russia and near Moscow. It's not what we planned, but continuing on for a little while will be better than striking out on our own this far away. I don't want to delay while Anja and Zoe wait, turning tricks. Dora, can you send the audio to Ash? He might be able to get the other side of the conversation."

"Sorry, the satellite link will only do text. I'd have to use wi-fi or cellular. Want to risk that?"

"No. We probably wouldn't get much else that we can't guess. Just let him know what we heard."

"Okay, will do."

A knock on the door startled them. Emma's eyes widened. "It's Sergei," she whispered.

Without hesitation, she darted back into the bedroom to avoid being seen in her human form. She closed the door, pressing her ear against it to listen.

She heard the apartment door open.

"Evening," Sergei greeted. "I wanted to update you all. We'll be departing early tomorrow morning."

"That's good news," Lucian replied. "Any particular reason for the change?"

"We've received information about a better route—less traffic, easier crossing into Russia. It should make the trip safer," Sergei said.

"About time," Dora said. "Our buyer expects us soon. Delays aren't good for business."

"I understand. We'll ensure there are no further setbacks," Sergei said.

"Very well," Lucian said. "We'll be ready."

"Excellent," Sergei replied. "Get some rest. We'll leave at dawn."

She heard Sergei leave, waited a moment, and went back out to join the others.

"They must think we're oblivious," Emma said.

Graham smirked. "Their mistake."

Lucian addressed the group. "We need to stay one step ahead. We'll go along with their plan."

Mike checked his watch. "We should rest in shifts. Can't afford to be caught off guard."

"Agreed," Lucian said. "Let's get some rest. Emma will head out and keep an eye on them. Keep an ear out for her; she can sleep on the way."

Twenty-Three

CLAIRE STOOD NEAR the tall windows of the great hall, her hands clasped behind her back as she took in the commotion around her. The room smelled of wood polish, fresh tea, and the wildness that clung to awakened wolves. In the last week alone, Fiona, Heather, and Alice had all undergone their awakenings under Howard's guidance, each emerging dazed but alight with the spark of their shared heritage. The newest arrivals—Ben Clarke, Diana Forester, Conall Lawson, and Natalie Wright—had followed soon after, their rituals completed only two days ago.

It had been a whirlwind. Howard and Claire had barely paused, moving from one awakening to the next, guiding each through the raw edges of their first shifts, managing nerves, and calming the inevitable frictions. She had tried to keep her composure as more and more family members arrived at the manor, but there were moments when the sheer weight of it all pressed down on her chest like a stone. Too many lives changed, too many decisions ahead, too many counting on her strength.

At least Ian had been there. Her rock. Whenever she faltered, his steadiness grounded her again—his hand warm at her back, his voice low and sure in her ear. *You're not alone in this, Claire,* he'd told her last night as she collapsed onto the bed in exhaustion. *You never will be.*

Claire scanned the room, taking in the latest faces—Ben, leaning forward in conversation with Heather; Diana fidgeting with a notebook in her lap, her wide eyes drinking everything in; Conall, standing apart but watching everything; Natalie, her easy smile belying the nerves evident in her posture.

These were her people now. Her pack. And whether she felt ready or not, she would help shape what they would become.

Her family settled into their seats. Heather wasted no time. “Right, let’s crack on. Fiona, Howard, and I have drafted a foundational set of laws and a governance structure for the pack. Today, we’d like your thoughts on it.”

Howard added, “The aim’s straightforward—fairness and unity. A council of elders, chosen for their wisdom and experience, will guide the pack without all the power resting in one person’s hands.”

Heather gave a brisk nod. “We propose nominating Margaret, Fiona, and Blevine to the council to start.”

Bee raised a hand. “What about Ian and Howard? Neither’s kin. Where do they fit in?”

Howard replied, “I’ll remain in an advisory role, nothing more. My loyalty is with my nephew Lucian’s circle, but I’m happy to lend a hand here for as long as I’m needed. As for Ian, he represents Clan MacGregor—our allies in Scotland. Together, we’ll stand strong against anything thrown our way.”

Margaret’s lips curved into a faint smile. “Dartmoor Pack. Yes, that does have rather a nice ring to it.”

Howard continued. “The circle’s what we call the lot at the heart of this business—Lucian, Anja, Zoe, and the others committed to bringing down the Sodality. Ian, Claire, and I work closely with them.”

Heather pressed on. “We’ve also sketched out key roles and advisory circles, to be led by whoever’s best suited. Diana, with your background in psychology, you’d be spot on for wellness. Ben, given your knack for organisation, resource management seems the right fit. Conall’s skills make him a natural choice for communications. Natalie, your veterinary experience will bolster our physical health and safety nicely.”

Diana nodded shyly. “I’d be honored to help.”

Ian proposed forming a security advisory circle to prepare for Sodality threats, which he agreed to lead. Conall raised a concern about aggression during transformations. Claire admitted the process wasn't perfect but stressed that control came with practice and clear rules.

Heather summarised the draft principles: consensus-based decisions, mediation to resolve disputes, non-aggression, rotational leadership, mutual support, secrecy about abilities, and respect for all bonds and families equally. Natalie raised a question about combat training. Ian answered simply: "Better to be prepared than left wishing you had been."

Margaret's voice carried into the pause after Ian's answer. "We were hunted once. Not again. Never again."

Heather wrapped things up. "We'll have the vote after the break, then."

Claire looked around at the sight of her family debating respectfully, new bonds knitting themselves together. When the vote was finally called, every hand in the room went up without hesitation.

Heather allowed herself a small, satisfied smile. "Unanimous. We have our laws—and our name."

Margaret rose then, her voice warm. "Our ancestors would be proud tonight. Isobel most of all."

Claire met her mother's gaze, steady and sure. "Let's honor them properly, then."

As the room hummed with quiet conversations and fresh plans, Ian leaned in close, murmuring at her side. "They're coming together, love."

"They are," Claire said softly, her eyes sweeping the room. "And it's only the beginning."

Claire stood at the edge of their improvised training field. It reminded her of their first sessions in New York when it was just Lucian, Anja, and the bodyguards. They had come a long way from there and then.

The estate's expansive grounds provided ample space for the pack's exercises, but as she watched her family struggle through the drills, a knot of concern tightened in her stomach. They were learning in human form at the moment. As wolves, the basics of bite, tear, run, and pounce seemed to be instinctual. As humans, it could be a lot more complicated, hence the drills.

"Keep your guard up, Ben!" Ian called out. Ben, breathing heavily, attempted to mimic Ian's defensive stance but stumbled, wiping sweat from his brow.

Claire sighed. None of them had any formal combat training or experience. The only ones who seemed to be adapting quickly were Simon and Dillon. Simon moved with natural athleticism, and his years of hiking and outdoor activities gave him an advantage. Youthful and eager, Dillon learned fast, his enthusiasm pushing him forward.

"You're doing great, Dillon," Claire called, offering him an encouraging smile.

He grinned back. "Thanks! This is starting to feel...right, you know?"

She nodded, but her gaze drifted back to the others. The realization had been settling in over the past few days: training the pack would not be fast. It might take months or even years to reach the level of proficiency they would need. She and Ian were improvising, trying to impart decades of experience in a matter of days.

Ian approached her, his expression mirroring her concerns. "They're trying hard," he said quietly.

"I know," she replied. "But I worry it's not enough. We're out of our depth here."

He rested a reassuring hand on her shoulder. "We'll find a way. For now, we focus on the basics."

A yelp drew their attention. Natalie had tripped during a drill, twisting her ankle. She sat on the ground, wincing in pain.

Claire hurried over. "Are you okay?"

Natalie nodded, though her face was pale. "I think I just landed wrong."

"Let me have a look," Claire said. Examining the ankle, she could see it was already swelling. "It's sprained."

Natalie sighed. "Brilliant."

"Remember what we discovered," Claire reminded her. "Shifting can help heal injuries."

Natalie looked hesitant. "Yeah, I know. Just...leaves me knackered after."

"I'll stay with you," Claire offered. "We can take it slow. Here, let me help you get your sweats off."

Natalie glanced at the others, then gave a small shrug and peeled off her shirt. Claire crouched to help ease her sweatpants carefully over her ankle, mindful not to jostle it more than necessary.

"All right. Take your time. Focus." Claire's voice stayed calm as Natalie closed her eyes and concentrated.

The shift came slowly, shakier than usual, but as her wolf form took shape the angry swelling of her ankle subsided.

Natalie-the-wolf lowered her head onto the grass, panting.

"Just rest for a while and watch. You'll be okay." Claire stroked a hand through her soft fur, feeling her leg and paw for any lingering tenderness. "No more swelling. That's it. You're going to be okay now." She gave Natalie's fur an affectionate ruffle. "Just rest and watch for a bit. Take it easy for the rest of the day."

As she walked back toward the others, Claire couldn't shake the growing worry. There had been several injuries over the past days—nothing severe, but enough to highlight the risks. They had learned that their otherkin abilities allowed for faster healing, and shifting was almost miraculous, but the cost was significant fatigue.

"Perhaps we should adjust the training," Ian suggested when she rejoined him. "Focus more on control and less on combat for now."

Claire considered it. "You might be right. Pushing them too hard could do more harm than good."

Just then, Margaret approached them, her expression troubled. "Claire, Ian, may I speak with you?"

"Of course," Claire replied. "Is everything all right?"

Margaret glanced around before lowering her voice. "It's Michael. He rang earlier, and he's…well, demanding to know what's going on."

Claire's brow furrowed. "Uncle Michael? I thought we agreed to wait before bringing him into this."

"We did." Margaret sighed. "But he's been trying to reach Fiona. When she didn't pick up, he started calling me. He finally rang my mobile. I've not been home to take his calls, and now he's getting suspicious."

Ian folded his arms, thoughtful. "What does he think's going on?"

"He didn't say outright. But you know Michael. He's concerned, and now he's insisting on meeting face to face."

Claire exchanged a glance with Ian, tension tightening in her chest. "This complicates things."

Margaret nodded. "I don't know what to tell him. We can't keep him in the dark forever...but bringing him in now, when things are still so unsettled..."

Claire drew a steadying breath. "Perhaps it's better if we speak with him. If we brush him off, he could start digging on his own. That could expose us by accident."

Ian gave a slow nod. "He's your family. From what you've told me, he's got integrity."

Margaret's lips pressed together. "But he's not ready. He always dismissed the old stories. He wants to meet tomorrow. I could have him come here."

"That's probably best," Claire agreed. "We can control the setting, keep it private."

Margaret exhaled, a touch of relief softening her shoulders. "Thank you. I'll ring him back and set it up." As she moved away to make the call, she muttered under her breath, "Could go either way, this."

Ian allowed himself a crooked smile. "Not as though we've many choices, is it?"

Claire's lips quirked. "Apparently not." She glanced out across the grounds, watching the pack as they began gathering up their things. "We'd best call it a day."

They strolled back to the group, and Claire clapped her hands to get their attention. "All right, that's enough for today. Well done, all of you."

There were murmurs and a few weary smiles. Dillon bounded over, still brimming with energy. "Think we could have a proper sparring match next time?"

Claire gave a low laugh. "Don't get ahead of yourself."

As the group began dispersing, Ian leaned in. "See? You just need a bit of patience."

"I know," she replied. "But time's hardly on our side."

Ian gave a small shrug. "Aye. Then we make the most of what we've got. Just like old times."

They headed back toward the manor, the sun beginning to dip toward the horizon. The scent of dinner wafted from the kitchen, and Claire's stomach reminded her she hadn't eaten since morning.

"Let's grab a bite, then we can sort out how to handle tomorrow," she suggested.

"Sounds like a plan. Work out how best to approach Michael," he said.

"Yeah," she murmured, a sigh escaping.

Later that evening, Claire sat in the library, a cup of tea cradled in her hands. The room was quiet, the glow of lamplight casting long shadows among the shelves of old books. She had spread out notes on the table—training plans, schedules, and now, a page dedicated to her uncle Michael.

She heard footsteps and looked up to see Margaret entering, her expression weary.

"I spoke with Michael," her mother said, settling into the chair opposite Claire.

"How did it go?" Claire asked.

"He wanted answers, of course. But I persuaded him to come here tomorrow afternoon. He's still suspicious—especially after I told him I wouldn't discuss it over the phone. I think that's what finally convinced him."

Claire nodded. "That's something. We'll just have to be careful how much we reveal."

Margaret let out a sigh. "I do hope we're making the right choice."

"We can't put him off forever," Claire said gently. "And who knows—he might surprise us."

"Perhaps," Margaret murmured, sipping her tea. "Your father always said Michael had a more open mind than he let on."

A faint smile curved Claire's lips. "Then maybe he'll understand."

They sat in companionable silence for a few moments before Margaret spoke again. "How are you holding up?"

Claire considered the question. "It's been overwhelming," she admitted. "Training everyone, preparing for threats, and now this...I feel like I'm in over my head."

Margaret reached across the table, placing her hand over Claire's. "You're doing wonderfully. None of this is easy, but you're not alone."

"I know," Claire said, squeezing her mother's hand. "Thank you."

The door creaked open, and Ian poked his head in. "Hope I'm not interrupting."

"Not at all," Margaret said, standing up. "I was just about to head to bed."

"Goodnight, Mum," Claire said.

"Goodnight, dear." Margaret gave them both a hug before leaving the room.

Ian's voice was calm. "We'll handle it. One way or another."

She gave a faint smile, though her brow was still creased. "I suppose we can't plan for everything."

His lips quirked into a grin. "That's life, love. Keeps you on your toes."

She let out a laugh. "That's certainly one way to see it. I think that's enough for tonight," she said, stifling a yawn.

"Aye, for now." Ian stood, offering her a hand. "Mostly."

She took his hand, rising from her seat. She arched a brow at him and smiled. "Mostly? Cheeky."

Twenty-Four

ANJA CLOSED THE balcony door behind Zoe as they returned to the adjoining room where Marek was waiting. He seemed pensive but not overly concerned.

"How long before your man returns?" he asked.

"He should be back soon. We thought perhaps we could finalize arrangements now," Anja said. "Ensure that everyone gets what they deserve."

Marek swirled his drink. His expression softened, his eyes becoming unfocused. "You? Finalize…arrangements," he repeated.

Zoe joined with her power to relax his anxiety. "Yes. You've been well compensated for your efforts. We're all pleased with how things have turned out."

Marek blinked, a flicker of confusion crossing his features before they settled into a relaxed smile. "Yes, of course. Everything has gone well."

It was starting to work.

"We appreciate your help," she continued. "And we're glad to have settled accounts amicably."

He nodded absently. "Naturally. Always happy to do good business. Wait…is there something in this?" He held up the tumbler to the light. "Something doesn't seem right."

"His suspicion is peaking, and I can't fix it. What now?" Zoe sent.

"Looks like we've got ourselves a player," Anja purred, her voice dropping to a sultry, husky whisper that could make even the coldest man shiver with anticipation. "Maybe we could offer you a different kind of payment, say in the currency of raw, untamed pleasure?"

With a smile on her lips, Anja started teasingly peeling off her clothes, each layer revealing more of her flawless skin. Simultaneously, Zoe stoked the fires of his desire, using their combined energy as an aphrodisiac. But Marek seemed immune.

"Why the hell should I accept that as payment? I can take whatever the fuck I want. Two little girls like you won't stop me," he retorted, his eyes flickering with anger.

"Anja?"

"I can sure as hell stop you," Anja said, her voice echoing in the dimly lit room. "Your days of selling women and children end right here, right now."

With those words, Anja began to transform. It was her darker, more dangerous form that took hold. She blossomed like a night-blooming flower, no longer hiding behind the guise of an innocent young girl.

Her breasts swelled with a dangerously attractive fullness. Horns spiraled out from her forehead. A pair of spiked wings spread wide behind her, their intimidating span nearly filling the confined space of the room with a promise of frightening power.

A wicked grin curled on her lips, revealing razor-sharp teeth. Somehow, even in her monstrous form, she radiated a carnal magnetism. Anja felt his jolt of desire despite the danger she emanated.

Her tail swung back and forth in a hypnotic rhythm. Its tip pointed towards him as though beckoning him closer. Each finger was tipped with razor-sharp talons that promised both pleasure and pain. Anja could feel his body yearning for her touch, eager to dance along the edge of ecstasy and agony.

Marek was frozen, unable to utter a sound for a moment before he squeaked, "What are you?"

"Your worst nightmare come to life."

"You're not going to kill him, are you? Anja?" Zoe asked.

"Probably not, but he deserves it for all the pain and suffering he's caused," she thought to Zoe, then said aloud, **"Remember Kasia?"**

Marek's face went white as he turned to flee. Zoe tripped him on his way toward the door.

Anja was on him in an instant. She lifted him by the neck so his feet kicked in the air.

"You're not going to ask him about the transmissions he intercepted, are you?" Zoe asked wryly.

Anja's demon said, *"That sounds like a fun game."*

Anja's grip on Marek's neck tightened. **"Marek, let's discuss those transmissions you intercepted,"** she purred in his ear. Sweat beaded on his brow as he gasped for air, his eyes bulging in fear.

Zoe rolled her eyes.

"I…I…I don't…know what you're talking about," he sputtered. Anja's expression darkened further, if that were possible.

"Oh, but I think you do," she hissed. **"And I'm sure you'd like to continue breathing, wouldn't you?"**

Marek's eyes darted from Anja to Zoe and back again. His face was mottled as if trying to decide on purple or white.

Anja's eyes blazed with an otherworldly light as she tightened her grip on Marek's neck. The razor-sharp talons at her fingertips extended ever so slightly, just enough to nick the skin beneath his jawline. A trickle of blood began to weave its way down his neck, warm against her fingers.

She could feel the pulse of his fear, each rapid heartbeat echoing through her senses. Her demon stirred within, guiding her with an uncanny familiarity. She leaned in, and her long tongue flicked out to taste the crimson trail. The metallic tang ignited a surge of power coursing through her veins, amplifying her connection to the forces she now commanded.

"Please…let me go," Marek gasped, barely more than a strangled whisper.

Anja's gaze pierced into his, her pupils dilated and rimmed with a red glow. **"You will remember this only in your nightmares,"** she intoned, her voice layered with an eerie resonance. **"You were never here. Speak of our dealings to no one, or I will return to finish what I've started. I will come to you in the night and end you."**

As she spoke, Anja channeled her will into a binding spell. She visualized tendrils of shadow weaving around Marek's consciousness, anchoring her commands deep within his psyche, much like she had done with Helena—only this time, her shadowy chains were the only ones. Her demon guided her through the intricate mental pathways, showing her where to implant the compulsions that would ensure his silence.

Marek's struggles subsided as the spell took hold. His eyes glazed over, a distant look overtaking his features. Anja could sense the turmoil within him—the conflicting emotions of fear, confusion, and an inexplicable desire toward her. They wound around him and then set in.

She rummaged around in his memories, noting names and places, businesses and arrangements, government and police officials on the take. It was more extensive than she had anticipated.

She felt a surge of lust emanating from him, a raw emotion that her demon recognized. Feeding off his helpless fascination, she absorbed the essence of his surrender. The process was intoxicating, a melding of wills that left him utterly at her mercy.

"Sleep now," she commanded. **"Forget this encounter, but remember the warning."**

Marek's eyelids fluttered as he struggled to stay conscious. The binding was complete, his mind now clouded. Anja dropped him to the floor.

Zoe stepped forward, her expression a mixture of concern and awe. "Is it done?" she asked.

Anja nodded. "He won't trouble us anymore. The spell will keep him from recalling the details, and fear will deter him from seeking answers."

Zoe glanced down at Marek's inert form. "Let's hope it holds. You need to change back. I know it's you, but it's still terrifying."

Anja looked into Zoe's wide eyes and saw the fear—and the longing. *"Love you, too."*

Anja flexed her fingers as her talons retracted. The remnants of her demonic transformation faded, leaving her appearing as her younger self. As Adela. She felt a residual hum of energy but pushed it aside while she gathered her clothes from where they had dropped and slipped them on.

Karolina peeked from behind a partition, her eyes wide with apprehension. "Is he…?"

"He's just unconscious," Zoe reassured her. "He won't remember what happened."

Karolina hesitated before stepping forward. "Thank you," she murmured.

Anja offered a faint smile.

Nomad reentered the room, his gaze taking in the scene. "Everything all right?"

"Yes," Zoe answered. "It went mostly to plan, but we need to get him out of here. Is everything set on your end?"

He nodded. "Transportation is ready. Katya told his driver he indulged in too much vodka, and the deal was done."

Anja glanced back at Marek. "He won't be a problem anymore."

"I hope so," Nomad said as he lifted the limp form over his shoulder.

Leaving Karolina and Zoe behind in the suite, Anja helped carry Marek as they approached the back entrance. His weight pressed heavily against her and Nomad. To any observer, they appeared as nothing more than friends assisting a companion who had indulged a bit too much.

Katya nodded toward the alley where Tomasz had just parked in the van. The vehicle's headlights cast long shadows against the brick walls, illuminating the narrow street. As they drew closer, Tomasz stepped out of the driver's seat, concern etched on his usually stoic face.

"What happened to him?" Tomasz asked, eyeing Marek's limp form.

Nomad offered a wry smile. "Your boss decided to celebrate early. Couldn't handle the vodka," he said with a shrug. "But he's quite pleased with how everything turned out."

Anja glanced at Tomasz. "He mentioned wanting to head straight back to Poland. Said there was pressing business to attend to."

Tomasz looked skeptical. "That doesn't sound like Marek."

Anja reached out with her mind, weaving threads of influence into Tomasz's thoughts. She projected an aura of reassurance, encouraging him to accept their explanation without further questioning. "He was quite insistent," she said. "Perhaps you could help him fulfill that wish."

Tomasz's expression softened, the lines of worry easing from his forehead. "If that's what he wants," he murmured. "I suppose it's best to get him back home."

"Exactly," Nomad agreed, guiding Marek toward the van. "He'll appreciate your help in getting him there safely."

Together, they eased Marek into the backseat. Anja could feel the resistance in Tomasz's mind fading, her mental suggestion taking hold. "Safe travels," she said, stepping back onto the curb.

Tomasz nodded, closing the van door. "Thank you. I'll make sure he gets back all right."

As the van pulled away, its taillights disappearing into the flow of Moscow traffic, Anja released a sigh. The first hurdle was behind them.

Nomad touched her shoulder. "Good work," he said. "Let's get back inside."

They reentered and returned to the suite where Zoe was seated on a plush sofa, speaking softly with Karolina, who looked anxious and relieved upon their return. "Is everything okay?" Karolina asked.

"Yes," Anja assured her. "Marek and Tomasz are on their way back to Poland. They won't be bothering us anymore."

Karolina's shoulders relaxed. "Thank you. I think…I was very worried."

"I'm going to update our contacts," Nomad said, already typing a message on his cellphone to send via satellite.

Anja joined Zoe and Karolina, taking a seat beside them. "How are you holding up?" she asked the girl.

"I…I fine…I guess," she murmured.

"You're safe here. We'll figure out the next steps together," Zoe said.

Nomad returned, his expression thoughtful. "I've informed Ian and Ash of our arrival," he reported. "They acknowledged receipt and said to stand by. Lucian and Dora have been delayed and might be facing some complications."

Anja frowned. "Do we have any details?"

"Not yet," Nomad replied. "But they're monitoring the situation. We're to remain here until further notice."

Zoe nodded. "Then we'll make the most of our time."

Karolina looked between them. "And me? What happen now?"

Anja reached out to take her hand. "You'll stay with us for now," she said reassuringly. "When Lucian and Dora arrive, we'll figure things out."

"They…be angry with me?" Karolina asked.

"No," Zoe answered with a smile. "They're good people. They'll want to help."

After a knock, Katya entered the suite, carrying a tray with a steaming teapot and delicate cups. "I thought you might like some refreshment," she said, setting the tray on the coffee table.

"Thank you," Anja said. "You've been very kind."

Katya glanced at Nomad and waved a hand. "It's the least I can do. Your friend has been a valuable acquaintance over the years." She glanced at Karolina, her eyes assessing but not unkind. "And any friend of his is welcome here."

Karolina offered a shy smile. "Thank you."

Katya poured the tea, and the fragrant aroma filled the room. "If there's anything else you need, don't hesitate to ask," she said before excusing herself.

They sat silently for a few moments, sipping the soothing brew. The warmth spread through Anja, easing some of the tension built up over the past few days.

"What do you think happened with Lucian and Dora?" Zoe mused aloud.

Nomad shook his head. "Hard to say. They're capable, but Russia can be unpredictable."

"Should we link with him?" Zoe asked.

Anja considered but shook her head. "No. Let him contact us if he needs help. I wouldn't want to distract him at the wrong moment."

"Okay. We should be prepared in case they need assistance, though."

"Agreed," Nomad said. "But until we hear otherwise, we should lie low."

Karolina set her cup down carefully. "I don't want…you have problem…with me."

"We don't," Anja assured her. "We're all in this together."

Zoe leaned forward, her expression earnest. "Tell us more about yourself, Karolina. Is there anyone you want us to contact? Family, friends?"

Karolina hesitated. "I…no have much family. Mama, Papa…died…

when I was little. Then I live with aunt, but it was hard." She looked down at her hands. "That's how they take me."

"I'm sorry," Anja said.

Karolina met her gaze. "It okay. Maybe chance to new start."

"It is," Anja affirmed. "We can help you find a safe place."

Karolina nodded slowly. "I would like. Yes."

The conversation shifted to lighter topics as they spent the next hour getting to know one another better. Anja found herself impressed by Karolina's resilience and determined spirit.

Karolina shifted in her seat. "I can help something?"

Anja smiled at her. "For now, just focus on resting and taking care of yourself."

"Actually," Zoe interjected, "perhaps you could assist us with some simple tasks. It might help take your mind off things."

Karolina brightened slightly. "Okay."

As night settled over Moscow, the city's vibrant energy pulsed outside their windows. Anja stood on the balcony, gazing at the illuminated skyline. The cool air carried the sounds of traffic, the murmur of urban life, and the occasional wail of a siren.

Zoe joined her, leaning against the railing. "Penny for your thoughts," she said.

Anja sighed. "Just thinking about how quickly things can change. A few days ago, we were strangers to Karolina."

Zoe nodded. "We can't save everyone, but when we can make a difference, it matters."

"Yes," Anja agreed. "I just hope we're making the right choices."

Zoe gave her a reassuring smile. "What else could we have done?"

Anja returned the smile, feeling a surge of gratitude for her friend's unwavering support. "Thank you."

They stood in comfortable silence for a while longer before rejoining Nomad and Karolina inside.

"Get some rest," Nomad advised. "I'll take the first watch."

Anja didn't argue. The day's events had taken their toll, and she knew she needed to recharge. "Wake us if anything changes."

"Will do," he promised.

Twenty-Five

IAN STOOD BY the large window in Ash's suite, gazing out over the sprawling grounds of the estate. The evening sun cast long shadows across the meticulously maintained gardens, but his thoughts were far from the serene landscape. Ash's suite had been transformed into a sophisticated command center, filled with state-of-the-art equipment—monitors displaying data streams and maps pinned with notes and markers.

Ash sat at his desk, hammering the keyboard. The glow from a bank of screens caught the glint in his eyes. "Just had an update from Nomad," he called, not bothering to look up.

Ian turned from the window. "Go on."

"They've arrived in Moscow. Holed up at a knocking shop run by one of Nomad's mates—a woman called Katya. Apparently it was all planned, gives 'em cover."

Ian raised a brow. "A bordello? Really? You think that's wise?"

Ash smirked, just a flicker at the corner of his mouth. "Best idea I've heard all week, mate. In Moscow, the dodgier the better, sometimes. Katya keeps things nice and discreet, from what I can dig up. Bit of baksheesh here and there, but nothing too bent. Nomad reckons she's solid, and that's good enough for me."

"Fine," Ian said, moving to stand by him. "We can't have anything cocking this up now."

"Too bloody right," Ash said, his tone tightening. He clicked open another window. "That said, there's something else we need to chew over."

"What is it?"

Ash leaned back in his chair, arms folded, gaze sharp. "Got word through Dora from Lucian. Name came up—Igor Krakarov."

Ian's expression darkened. "The SVR operative and associate of the Sodality? Eagle?"

Ash nodded once. "That's the one. Crafty bastard's laying a trap for 'Lev and Kasia.' The names Lucian and Dora are using on the ground."

"Does Krakarov know he's targeting Lucian?"

"There are no indications of that," Ash said. "It seems he believes he's intercepting a valuable drug shipment. There's no reason for him to suspect that Lev is actually Lucian."

Ian exhaled slowly. "That means Krakarov won't be prepared for what Lucian is capable of—or the others."

"True, but we can't underestimate Krakarov either," Ash cautioned. "He's resourceful and has considerable assets at his disposal."

"What are Lucian's plans?"

Ash tapped one of the screens, bringing up a secure message. "According to this, Lucian intends to turn the tables—let Krakarov's lot come to him, then give them a right bloody nose. Plans to confront them directly."

Ian's brow furrowed. "That's risky. Krakarov's team will be trained, disciplined, armed to the teeth."

"You're telling me," Ash muttered, leaning back in his chair. "Bloke's likely to send one of his 'special' units after them. Nasty pieces of work. Not the sort of lads you want knocking at your door after dark."

Ian crossed his arms, thinking. "We need to back them somehow. Can we get additional resources to them quietly?"

Ash snorted. "Not bloody likely. Moscow's tighter than a nun's... well, you know. Surveillance everywhere. Anything overt and we risk tipping Krakarov off. If Lucian's going to pull this off, he'll have to rely on what he's already got in-country. Best we can do is keep our ears to the ground and stand ready to advise if it all goes pear-shaped."

"What about Nomad or his friend Katya? Could they provide any local support?"

"Possibly," Ash replied, swivelling slightly in his chair. "But get them too involved and we risk burning the bordello as a safe house.

That sort of attention's not something Katya's likely to thank us for."

Ian rubbed his chin thoughtfully. "You're right. We can't risk blowing that cover."

"I'll make a few discreet enquiries, nothing daft. But if we drag them into a gunfight, we're bloody well asking for trouble."

"Fine. We need to stay focused on the bigger picture anyway. Let's talk contingencies."

"Thought you'd never ask," Ash muttered, pulling up a detailed satellite map of Moscow and its outskirts on one of the larger monitors. Red markers blinked along key roads and city blocks. "Now then. Based on our intel, Krakarov's lot will probably try and intercept here." He jabbed at a remote stretch of road, hemmed in by thick woodland.

Ian leaned in, studying the terrain. "If Lucian's clued into that spot, he can be prepared. But he'll need to be ready to move, and quick. I wouldn't put it past Krakarov to have backup teams in play."

"You're catching on," Ash said, smirking. "That's exactly what I'd expect from him. He doesn't half-arse these things."

"Draft a message to Lucian highlighting these points," Ian said, straightening.

Ash hesitated just a beat. "There's another wrinkle we need to think about."

Ian's eyes narrowed. "Go on."

"At the moment, Krakarov thinks he's after some smuggler moving product. But if this goes tits up and he clocks that 'Lev' is actually Lucian...well, let's just say the whole thing goes from bad to bloody catastrophic."

Ian's jaw tightened. "Lucian and the others would become high-priority targets overnight."

"Bang on," Ash confirmed. "He'd throw every resource he's got at them, and you can be damned sure the Kremlin wouldn't sit on its hands either. So whatever we do, we'd best make sure our boy doesn't end up on anyone's radar beyond what's already inevitable."

Ian exhaled slowly, eyes back on the map. "Then we'd better get this right."

"That," Ash said dryly, "is the understatement of the bloody week. Which brings me to another niggle," he went on, leaning back in his chair. "Should we tell Lucian to steer clear of a punch-up altogether?"

Ian considered that, rubbing his jaw. "That may not be possible. Lucian and the others can handle themselves. And if it can be managed, he should try to take one of Krakarov's men alive for questioning. We might learn more about his operations, maybe even the Sodality's ties."

Ash snorted. "Right. And then what? That's a non-starter."

Ian inclined his head slightly. "Fair point. Scratch that." Pacing to the far side of the room, Ian added, "We also need to consider the wider implications. Whatever happens out there could ripple back here."

Ash tapped a finger against the desk, eyes narrowing. "Helena might have a bead on what Krakarov's really up to. Maybe Anja could have a word in her ear. I'll be honest, mate, this whole thing's bending my brain. I've been doing this job for decades, and you lot have me rethinking every bit of standard tradecraft. You did say it'd be interesting, but bleeding hell."

Ian allowed the faintest smirk. "Not boring, though, is it? But no, asking Helena directly is too risky. Her loyalties are still…murky."

"Aye, fair enough," Ash said, already turning back to his screen. "We'll stick to what's in our lane, then." He finished typing, the keyboard clacking, before he leaned back. "Message sent. Bounced through a few satellites—slower than the usual kit, but it'll get there."

Ian stopped his pacing, arms folding. "Good. Anything else we can do from here?"

"Not a ruddy lot," Ash replied, checking another monitor. "I'll keep an eye on comms and fire updates as soon as they come through, but for now we're passengers."

"I trust your judgment," Ian said simply.

Ash checked his watch and blew out a breath. "I'll ping Nomad as well. Tell him to give Zoe and Anja a nudge. If nothing else, they'll be ready to lend a hand if it all goes sideways."

"Good," Ian said, moving to the door before pausing. He looked back over his shoulder. "And Ash…make sure you actually get some rest. You've been at this for hours."

Ash barked a laugh. "Rest? That's rich, coming from you, MacGregor. I'll kip when I'm dead. Or when the world stops spinning.

Whichever comes first."

"Ash," Ian said more firmly.

Ash finally looked up, meeting his gaze. "All right, all right. I promise. After I finish this sweep, I'll turn in."

Ian held his stare a beat longer, then gave a small nod. "Fine. Just don't burn yourself out. We'll need you sharp when it counts."

Ash smirked, a glint of his usual irreverence in his eyes. "I appreciate the concern, MacGregor, but you ought to know by now—I bloody live for this."

Ian allowed himself the barest hint of a smile before stepping out. The door clicked shut behind him, leaving Ash bathed in the dim, shifting glow of his monitors.

The estate's corridors stretched before Ian, quiet and still, the heavy carpets muffling his boots. Lamps cast warm pools of light against the dark paneling, and murmurs of conversation from a distant sitting room drifted through the hush.

But he couldn't shake the weight gathering in his chest. The stakes were rising, and the intricate web of alliances and enmities felt more tangled by the hour.

As he descended the stairs, the cool air of the lower hall settled over him like a warning.

Lucian was waiting on the sofa with Emma in his lap as the first light of morning filtered through the curtains. A knock signaled Sergei's arrival.

"Morning," Sergei greeted as Dora opened the door. "The vans are ready."

Lucian nodded. "We're all set."

They followed Sergei out to the waiting vans idling by the curb. The vehicles looked the same, but the undercurrent of tension hadn't been so apparent. Viktor and Alexei motioned for Mike and Graham to get in with them. They had been terse and not very talkative before. This was another level of unease.

Lucian settled into the van's passenger seat as they pulled away from the curb, the early morning sun casting a golden hue over the cityscape of Minsk. Emma perched on the dashboard, her green eyes scanning the road ahead. Her tail flicked intermittently. Lucian reached out and stroked her back.

The convoy moved through the waking city, merging onto the route Sergei had assured them would be better. The landscape began to change as they left Minsk behind, but the true nature of the path ahead remained hidden.

Inside the van, the conversation was minimal. Dora sat behind them, her expression composed. Sergei drove in silence, his eyes fixed on the road, while the hum of the engine filled the quiet space.

The city gradually gave way to open fields and stretches of dense forest. The van merged onto the M1 highway, the asphalt ribbon cutting through the Belarusian countryside. They passed the M1 Casino, its garish lights still flickering in the daylight—a stark contrast to the muted tones of the surrounding landscape.

As they approached the Belarus-Russia border, a sense of unease settled over the group. Lucian exchanged a glance with Emma, whose ears perked at the distant sight of the border crossing. Sergei slowed the van as they joined the queue of vehicles waiting to pass through.

“Routine,” Sergei said, breaking the silence. “Shouldn’t take long.”

They inched forward until it was their turn. A stern-faced border guard approached. Sergei rolled down the window, offering a polite greeting in Russian.

“Purpose of your visit?” the guard asked.

“Transporting goods to Moscow,” Sergei replied. “Here are the documents.”

The guard examined the papers, his gaze shifting to the passengers. Lucian maintained a neutral expression, Lev’s passport ready if needed. After a moment, the guard handed back the documents.

“Step out of the vehicle,” he instructed Sergei.

“Of course,” Sergei replied, giving a reassuring nod to Lucian and Dora. “Won’t be a minute.”

Lucian watched as Sergei and the guard moved a few paces away, engaging in a low conversation. The guard’s demeanor softened when Sergei discreetly slipped him a folded bill. After a brief exchange, Sergei returned to the van.

“All set,” he announced. “Just a formality.”

The guard signaled for them to proceed, and the van rolled forward. Behind them, the second van carrying Graham and Mike followed.

Once they were clear of the crossing, Sergei accelerated, taking an exit that led onto a narrower road flanked by towering pines.

"Taking the back roads from here," Sergei explained. "Less traffic, and we avoid the common checkpoints."

"Fine by me," Dora said, flipping a page in her notebook. "We really don't need any problems."

Lucian gazed out the window, the dense forest casting elongated shadows across the road. The isolation of the route was apparent, each mile pulling them deeper into a landscape where assistance would be scarce if needed.

Hours passed with little change in scenery. The overcast sky cast a gray pallor over the terrain, and the radio played a static-laden broadcast in Russian. Emma remained vigilant, occasionally shifting her position on the dashboard. Lucian sensed her restlessness.

At one point, Sergei slowed as they made a series of sharp bends. An old sign indicated a detour ahead due to road construction.

"Unexpected," Sergei muttered. "Must be recent."

"Are we still on schedule?" Lucian inquired.

"Yes," Sergei assured him. "This route will connect us back to the main road soon."

Lucian nodded but made a mental note of the deviation.

As dusk began to settle, Sergei spoke again. "Not much longer now. We'll reach the outskirts of Moscow soon."

"Good," Dora replied. "Our contact will be waiting."

Sergei glanced at Lucian. "You can relax now. The hardest part is behind us."

Lucian offered a faint smile. He turned slightly in his seat, catching Dora's eye. With a subtle gesture, he signaled her to be alert. Reaching over, Lucian ruffled Emma's fur. "Time to wake up," he murmured.

Emma stretched and leapt into his lap, her body warm against his. He slipped her collar off while Sergei was watching the road ahead. She looked up at him, her eyes conveying understanding. He subtly set his gun on the floor of the van, and Emma jumped down and covered it with her body.

Just then, the van rounded a bend in the road. Ahead, the path was obstructed by a makeshift roadblock—two black SUVs parked diagonally across the road, their hazard lights flashing. A group of armed men stood in front, faces obscured by shadows and the brims of their caps.

Sergei's hands tightened on the steering wheel. "Ah, seems we have a small complication," he said.

Lucian's senses sharpened. "What's this about?" he asked.

"Probably just a routine check," Sergei replied, though his tone was flat.

Behind them, the second van came to a stop as well. Lucian glanced in the side mirror.

The lead armed man stepped forward, signaling for them to halt. Sergei brought the van to a complete stop and killed the engine.

"Stay here," he instructed, reaching for the door handle.

"Allow me," Lucian said.

"No need. I'll handle it."

"I'd prefer to speak with them myself."

Before Sergei could protest, two of the armed men approached.

"Everyone out of the vehicle," one of them ordered in Russian.

"Is there a problem?" Lucian asked, stepping out with his hands visible.

"Routine inspection," the man replied curtly. "Papers, please."

Dora exited the van following Lucian, her expression composed but eyes alert. Emma remained inside, crouched low on the floor of the van.

Sergei stood off to the side, his posture stiff. "Let's cooperate," he said, though he avoided meeting Lucian's eyes.

Lucian handed over his passport, noting the man's scrutinizing gaze. The atmosphere was thick with unspoken tension.

From the corner of his eye, Lucian saw Graham and Mike stepping out of the second van, positioning themselves.

The lead man spoke into a radio clipped to his vest. "Subjects secured. Awaiting further instructions."

Lucian's suspicions were confirmed. This was the trap they had expected.

"Mind telling us what this is really about?" Lucian asked.

The man regarded him coldly. "Stand by and keep your hands where we can see them."

Sergei shifted uncomfortably. "It's just a misunderstanding," he muttered.

Lucian glanced at him. "Indeed." He caught Dora's eye once more. The time for subtlety was over.

Lucian stood beside the van, the tension winding higher as the armed men faced them. Sergei shifted uneasily, clearly caught off guard by the escalation. The leader of the roadblock team barked orders in Russian, his weapon trained on Lucian.

"Keep your hands where we can see them," the man repeated.

Lucian met Sergei's eyes. "It seems there *has* been a misunderstanding."

Sergei forced a strained smile. "It's nothing we can't sort out."

"The misunderstanding," Lucian continued, his voice edged with steel, "is on your part. You've been set up, Sergei. Krakarov has no intention of paying you—only of disposing of loose ends."

Sergei's eyes widened. "What are you talking about? How do you know...?"

Lucian took a deliberate step closer. "Think about it. Why send you on a route through the middle of nowhere? Did you think it was to hand us over? You're expendable to him now."

Viktor and Alexei exchanged wary glances. The armed men at the roadblock shifted, concern flickering across their faces. Their leader glanced at Sergei. "What did he say?"

Sergei hesitated. "He's trying to cause doubt. Ignore him."

But that doubt had already taken root. Alexei tightened his grip on his weapon. "Sergei, is there something you're not telling us?"

The leader of the armed men stepped forward. "We don't have time for this. They come with us, and no one gets hurt."

Dora moved behind the open van door, scanning the scene. Mike and Graham edged apart.

Lucian spoke again, his tone steely, eyes locked on Sergei. "If you value your life, you'll listen. Krakarov's men aren't here to make a deal—they're here to eliminate witnesses."

For a beat, silence held. Then the tension snapped.

Viktor's expression twisted as he swung his weapon toward the men in black. "Is that true?" he demanded, voice cracking with fear and fury.

The leader of Krakarov's team snarled, no longer bothering to mask his contempt. "Enough of this shit!" he barked, raising his rifle.

Before he could fire, chaos erupted.

Mike's eyes narrowed, his power surging as he focused on the first SUV. A deafening boom split the night as its fuel tank ignited. The fireball hurled men and shrapnel into the air, washing the scene in searing light and heat. Screams pierced the smoke as the blast wave caught the brush at the side of the road on fire.

Graham was already moving, drawing his sidearm and diving behind the van for cover. He fired two quick shots, striking one of the black-clad soldiers squarely in the chest. The man dropped, but others rallied, ducking behind the remaining SUV and firing back in controlled bursts.

The first man who had dropped rolled over coughing. "Shit, bulletproof vests!" Graham called out over the din.

Viktor and Alexei froze, then panicked. Torn between conflicting orders and terrified by the explosion, they fired wildly at everyone. Their rounds tore through the night, one bullet sparking off the edge of the van just inches from Lucian's head.

Inside the van, Emma's eyes flared as she shifted back into her human form. Without a word, she grabbed the pistol Lucian had stashed there and flung the door open. She stepped out naked, her sudden appearance cutting through the din. Several of the attackers stared in confusion, their hesitation costing them dearly.

But not enough.

The other SUV's doors burst open, and two more of Krakarov's men emerged—one hefting an RPK machine gun. He swept the roadway with a brutal spray of rounds, forcing Lucian and Dora to hit the ground behind the van as bullets shredded the air around them.

Lucian snarled under his breath, scanning for a weakness. He spotted it—a momentary gap as a gunman paused to reload.

He surged forward, crossing the open space in three powerful strides. A rifle butt swung toward his ribs, but he twisted under it, grabbed the barrel, and wrenched it free. The man stumbled, and

Lucian drove his elbow into his temple with bone-cracking force.

Beside him, Dora rolled to a crouch, firing. Two more attackers went down, but the RPK gunner still held his ground, spitting fire at Graham and Emma as they flanked him.

Mike's eyes flashed. He raised a hand toward the second SUV. It detonated in a thunderous roar. This time, the fireball engulfed two more of Krakarov's men as they tried to retreat. They were screaming as they rolled to the side of the road, trying to extinguish flames. All that did was catch more grass on fire.

Still, the RPK kept roaring. Graham was pinned, bullets chewing up the dirt inches from his boots.

Then Emma moved.

Inhumanly fast, she darted low, her bare skin smeared with soot and dust. Before the gunner could adjust, she slammed into him, knocking the weapon aside, and shot him in the face.

Silence fell in jagged pieces as the echoes of gunfire faded. Smoke curled off the twisted wrecks, and the acrid smell of fuel and blood clung to the air.

Lucian straightened, scanning the scene. His breath came hard, controlled, his thigh throbbing where a stray round had grazed him. Around them lay the bodies of Sergei, Viktor, Alexei, and Krakarov's men—crumpled on the scorched road like discarded marionettes.

Dora lowered her weapon, her dark eyes meeting his. "Not as clean as we'd hoped," she muttered.

Lucian's jaw tightened. "No. But it's done."

Emma exhaled, and her eyes met Lucian's. "We need to move," she urged.

"Agreed," Lucian replied, glancing at her. "Need clothes?"

"Why bother now?"

"Your clothes are in my bag, Emma," Dora said. "We don't know where we're going to end up."

He turned to the others. "Gather any IDs and documents. We can use them to mislead anyone who comes looking. Might as well grab a few weapons and some ammunition, too."

He chose one of Krakarov's team members, a man who seemed to be about his height and build, and searched for ID. He found a pocket knife and cut a piece of cloth that wasn't too bloody from his clothes.

Another identity might be useful.

They worked swiftly. Lucian retrieved his forged passport—Lev's—and placed it on Alexei's body. "This should help throw them off our trail," he said. "For a little while anyway."

Dora nodded, collecting items from the fallen men. "We might want these," she said, pocketing a few phones and wallets.

Graham was already behind the wheel of Sergei's van, engine running. "Let's go!" he called out.

They piled into the vehicle, Lucian taking the front passenger seat. Emma slid into the back. Mike and Dora secured the doors as Graham accelerated away from the scene.

"Dora, turn off the phones you collected. We don't know if they can be tracked," Graham said.

"Got it."

"Any pursuit?" Mike asked, glancing back.

"Not yet," Lucian replied, scanning the side mirrors. "But we shouldn't assume we're in the clear."

Dora was already working on her phone. "I'll try to get a fix on our location and send a secure message to Ash," she said. "He needs to know what's happened."

Lucian nodded. "Good. Inform him that we confirmed Krakarov is involved and that our cover identities may be compromised."

Emma leaned forward. "We need a safe place to regroup," she suggested. "Somewhere off the main roads."

"Side road coming up," Graham said, eyes focused on the road ahead. "Looks like an old service route that runs parallel to the highway."

"Take it," Lucian agreed.

As they sped along the back roads, Dora tapped into the van's GPS. "I've sent our coordinates to Ash," she reported. "Also included details about the confrontation."

"Let's hope he has some ideas," Mike said.

Lucian considered their options. "We must assume that Krakarov will realize his plan failed once his men don't report in. He may send others."

They drove in tense silence under a fading sky. The Russian countryside stretched out on either side.

After an hour, Graham pulled off onto a narrow dirt road, slowing the van as they approached an abandoned farmhouse. "This should give us some cover," he said.

They exited the vehicle and surveyed the area. Satisfied that it was deserted, they gathered inside the dilapidated structure.

Dora spread out the collected IDs and devices on a rickety table. "We have passports, security badges, and some phones," she said, surveying the clutter with her phone's flashlight.

Lucian rubbed his temples. "Can't do much with them now," he remarked.

Dora's phone pinged with an incoming message. She glanced at the screen. "It's Ash. He's received our message and is working on extracting us. He advises us to stay low until he can provide further instructions."

Lucian felt a measure of relief. "At least we're not completely cut off."

Graham checked his watch. "We'll set up a watch rotation. I'll take the first shift."

"Fine," Lucian said. "We should rest while we can. I'll put my old face on. Lev might be at the top of their wanted list if someone spots us."

Twenty-Six

Claire stood on the grand terrace of Lucian Miller's estate, her gaze fixed on the long, tree-lined drive that wound its way toward the manor. The afternoon sun bathed the meticulously kept gardens in a warm glow, but despite the serene surroundings, a knot of anxiety tightened in her stomach. Her uncle Michael was due to arrive any minute, and she wasn't entirely sure what would happen.

"He's running a bit late," Fiona remarked, joining Claire on the terrace. "Typical Michael, always keeping us waiting."

Margaret appeared beside them. "Let's be patient. He probably got stuck in traffic out of London."

Claire glanced at her mother. "I just hope he's in a receptive mood. We need to handle this delicately, especially considering his position."

Fiona nodded. "Yes, crown prosecutor. He's bound by certain obligations. We need to tread carefully."

A sleek silver car appeared at the end of the drive, making its way toward them. Claire straightened. "He's here."

After parking the car in the drive, Michael stepped out, adjusting his jacket and casting an appraising eye over the estate. His short-cropped hair was neatly combed, and his keen hazel eyes held a glint of curiosity mixed with irritation.

"Well, this is a fine place you've picked," he called out. "Didn't realize we were cozy with the upper crust."

Margaret descended the steps to greet him. "Hello, Michael. Good to see you, too."

He accepted her brief hug but pulled back, his gaze sharp. "Care to explain why I've been kept in the dark? I've been ringing you all for days."

Fiona offered a peck on the cheek. "We didn't mean to worry you. Things have been…unsettled."

"Unsettled?" he echoed, eyebrows raised. "And whose estate is this? Last I checked, none of us owned a mansion."

Claire joined them. "We're guests here. It belongs to a friend—Lucian Miller."

Michael's eyes narrowed. "Lucian Miller? The biotech mogul? Since when are we hobnobbing with the likes of him?"

"It's a long story," Claire said. "Shall we go inside?"

He looked between them, skepticism evident. "Fine. But I expect some answers."

They led him through the grand foyer into a spacious sitting room adorned with antique furniture and large windows overlooking the gardens. A tea service awaited on a low table.

"Please, do take a seat," Claire offered.

Michael lowered himself into a leather armchair, his eyes sweeping the grand room. "Right then—what's all this about?" he asked, resting one ankle over his knee.

Margaret busied herself at the tea service, pouring into fine porcelain cups. "We've been…rather caught up in family matters," she said.

He accepted the cup she handed him, though his brow remained furrowed. "Family matters requiring clandestine meetings? This is starting to sound like a bad thriller."

Fiona sat opposite, legs crossed. "It's to do with the old family stories—the legends we all grew up hearing."

Michael gave a groan, pinching the bridge of his nose. "Oh, not this again. Surely you don't expect me to indulge that nonsense?"

Claire took a deep breath. "I understand why you're skeptical, Uncle Michael. I was, too. But…there's more to the stories than we were ever told."

He sipped his tea. "And what, pray tell, would that be? Go on, then."

"For now," Claire said, "just consider the possibility that some parts of the legends might hold water."

He set his cup down with a clink. "I can't quite believe you're seriously asking me to reconsider this after all these years."

Fiona leaned forward, her voice lower. "Purely hypothetical, Michael. But if there were truth to the old stories, would it present a conflict for you in your role? As a crown prosecutor, I mean."

He frowned at her, leaning back. "Hypothetically? Unless there's an actual breach of the law, I hardly see why it should concern me."

Margaret's lips curved in a wry smile. "So then, if someone really could transform into a wolf—hypothetically speaking—you wouldn't feel compelled to report them to be dragged off and burned at the stake? You do realise that's exactly what drove our family into hiding in the first place."

Michael's jaw tightened almost imperceptibly as he glanced between them, his expression caught somewhere between incredulity and professional detachment.

"Still just an old wives' tale, if you ask me. But no." He rubbed his chin thoughtfully. "You're thinking of the Witchcraft Acts. Most of them were repealed mid-twentieth century. The last hold-out, if memory serves, was the Fraudulent Mediums Act 1951, which itself was superseded decades ago."

Claire inclined her head. "Exactly. But we wanted to be sure—hypothetically—that nothing still on the books could…complicate things for us."

Michael shot her a dry look. "Hypothetically speaking, if someone were daft enough to believe they could work magic or had supernatural powers?"

"Something along those lines," she admitted.

He gave a shrug. "Well, under current law, unless someone's actually causing harm or conning people out of money, there's nothing criminal in it. The law's concerned with conduct, not whatever peculiar notions people might have about themselves."

Claire exchanged a glance with Margaret. "That's what we needed to hear. We just didn't want to put you in an awkward position if—if there was any truth to the old stories."

Michael studied them all in turn. "You're all being remarkably coy. Let's dispense with the 'ifs' and 'buts,' shall we? Whatever it is you're dancing around—out with it."

Fiona exhaled sharply. "We'd hoped to avoid an argument, but perhaps blunt is best."

"Blunt usually is. I'm listening."

Claire rose to her feet. "Uncle Michael...what if I told you the legends weren't just stories? That there's more to them—more to us—than you've ever realised?"

He folded his arms, his tone dry as sandpaper. "I'd say you've lost your marbles. But do carry on."

"Would you believe me if I showed you? If you saw it for yourself?"

Margaret's lips pressed into a thin line. "We'd hoped to take this more slowly."

Claire gave her a smile. "You said the same with the others, Mum. But it never worked out that way."

Michael's brow furrowed. "'Others?' What others?"

"We'll get to that," Claire assured him. "For now—just keep an open mind, as you always said you could."

He leaned back in his chair, arms still folded, and let out a short, humorless laugh. "Did I say that? Well then, this had better be cracking."

He watched as she began to remove her cardigan, folding it. She slipped off her shoes.

Michael's scowl deepened. "Claire! What on earth do you think you're doing?"

"Trust me," she said.

Margaret's tone was calm but firm. "It's necessary, Michael."

He gave a shake of his head and turned his gaze to the ceiling as Claire began to undress. "For pity's sake—this is highly inappropriate."

Fiona's dry voice cut through. "Oh, do stop clutching your pearls, Michael. She's only your niece, not some stranger off the street. You need to watch."

Claire met his eyes briefly before closing her own, focusing inward. Heat coiled through her limbs as muscle and bone shifted. Silken fur rippled across her skin, and within moments, she stood on four paws—a sleek, amber-eyed wolf. The shift was becoming almost second nature now. Still, she thought ruefully, she was starting to feel like a sideshow act.

Michael's teacup slipped from his fingers, shattering on the hearthstone. "What in God's name—"

Fiona didn't even flinch. "Michael, sit down and stay calm."

He staggered to his feet instead, wide-eyed. "Is this some sort of trick? A hallucination? What the bloody hell did you put in my tea?"

Margaret rose and placed a steadying hand on his arm. "Nothing, Michael. This is real. All of it."

Michael backed up a step, hands raised as though she might leap at him. "Real? Don't be daft, Margaret. People don't just sprout fur and prance about on four legs like a bloody Labrador!"

Fiona gave a derisive snort. "For heaven's sake, Michael. Pull yourself together. You've cross-examined murderers and terrorists, but one wolf in the sitting room's too much for you?"

Michael shot her a glare, though his color was high and his ears red. "That was in a courtroom, Fiona. With rules and barristers and no one spontaneously turning into a wolf before my eyes!"

Margaret's voice stayed level, though her fingers tightened on his arm. "Michael. Breathe. You saw what you saw. You can reason it away if you like, but you can't deny it."

He huffed, sinking heavily back into his chair and rubbing his temple. "Oh, bloody hell. What am I supposed to do with this?"

Claire took a measured step toward him, her tail low, ears pricked.

"Stay back!" he barked, his voice cracking slightly. "Do you lot even realise the legal ramifications of this? As a crown prosecutor, I can't just turn a blind eye..."

Fiona's tone was flat. "We went over that earlier, Michael."

Margaret held up her hands. "Please, Michael. It's not us who are the threat here. We're the ones at risk."

He shook his head hard, as though trying to dislodge the thought. "I have a duty to report anything that poses a danger to the public. That is my job."

Claire shifted back into her human form, lowering herself to sit cross-legged on the carpet. "Uncle Michael, we're still the same people we've always been. None of us have eaten anyone, if that's what you're worried about."

"Well, that's terribly reassuring," he muttered. "How long has this been going on?"

Claire glanced at her mother before answering. "Not long. Only recently. We meant to tell you, but…we weren't sure how you'd take it. And, well…"

He pressed two fingers to his temple, rubbing as though a headache was coming on. "This is…this is a lot to take in, Claire." He looked up at her. "You do understand the position you've put me in, don't you? If it ever came out I'd known about this and said nothing…"

Margaret's voice was quiet, but firm. "But you won't say anything, will you?"

His sigh was long and heavy, shoulders slumping. His eyes met hers, still clouded with conflict. "This is…unprecedented."

Margaret gave a nod. "In more ways than you realise."

He sank back into the chair, shaking his head. "I can't…I still can't quite believe it. What else haven't you told me?"

Margaret hesitated a beat. "Others in the family have embraced this as well."

His head snapped up. "Others? How many?"

Fiona cut in. "Several."

He let out a low breath and dragged a hand down his face. "Unbelievable," he muttered again, almost under his breath.

Claire offered him a tentative smile. "You could, too…if you chose to."

He regarded her for a long, silent moment before replying. "No. No…I'll need time to think. This rather flies in the face of everything I know."

"Take all the time you need," Margaret said.

His eyes drifted to the shattered teacup on the carpet. "You're absolutely certain you didn't doctor my tea?"

Fiona let out a chuckle. "Just the usual, Michael."

He looked up at her then, a faint smile tugging at his mouth. "Right. Well, promise me you'll all be careful. The world isn't ready for this…whatever this is."

"Understatement of the year," Claire muttered. "No, it's not."

Michael's eyes swept back to her, his brow furrowing. "And Claire… do us all a favor and put something on, would you?"

She inclined her head, amused. "If I must."

He got to his feet with a groan. "I need some air."

They guided him out onto the terrace. The cool evening breeze seemed to steady him; his shoulders loosened as he breathed in.

After a few moments, Claire joined him, now dressed.

"So," he began at last, "what does all this mean, going forward?"

"We continue to learn. To adapt," Claire replied.

He gave a small nod, still staring out into the garden. "This family never ceases to surprise me."

Claire let out a laugh. "Keeps things interesting, doesn't it?"

His gaze flicked to her, sharp again. "You're sure no one's been harmed? No laws broken?"

"No one," Claire assured him. "And by your own words, the ability to shift into a wolf isn't a criminal offence."

Michael ran a hand through his hair, letting out a long breath. "All right. And Claire—next time you decide to…demonstrate—perhaps give a fellow a bit of warning, hmmm?"

She colored slightly, managing a rueful smile. "Sorry, Uncle. But honestly? No amount of warning would've prepared you. You wouldn't have believed me anyway."

He gave a dry chuckle, shaking his head. "You've got me there. This is going to take some getting used to. And I've no doubt you've still not told me everything." His expression darkened slightly as he turned back to her. "You mentioned something about being in danger. Go on, then—what's that all about?"

The glow of the fireplace painted the estate study in muted golds and reds. After a long dinner filled with guarded conversation, Claire sat opposite her uncle Michael, feeling the weight of everything they'd already revealed pressing in.

Michael broke the silence at last, brow furrowed. "So. You're telling me Lucian Miller's entire family were murdered? That's how he came to inherit all this"—he gestured vaguely at the room—"and his family's businesses?"

"Yes. It was a devastating event. It set everything else in motion."

Michael's gaze swept over the opulent paneling, the bookshelves lined with leather bindings, as though seeing it all with new eyes.

"And you and Ian...you were brought in as bodyguards after?"

"That's right," Ian confirmed from his place at her side. "Along with two others. He needed proper protection—there were more attempts on his life even after the murders."

Michael leaned forward, elbows on his knees, his expression sharp. "But why? Why target him and his family in the first place? And how in God's name does that connect to...whatever this business is with your abilities?"

Howard closed the book he'd been leafing through, stepping closer. "It's a tangled web," he admitted. "Lucian had reached the limits of conventional science and began searching elsewhere. His goal was simple enough: to unlock human potential. At the same time, Anja Kinsey—a research librarian with a penchant for esoteric history—was investigating a very old book and the strange death of its author. She reached out to me for help. Together we began piecing together some rather...troubling truths."

Michael looked between them. "And what's any of that got to do with Lucian?"

Claire took a measured breath. "They met during the investigation. It's a long story, but they discovered a connection between ancient mysticism and modern genetics."

Michael's eyebrows rose. "Genetics?"

"Aye," Ian cut in. "They found evidence that certain people carry dormant traits—legacies from a much older time—that can be awakened. Abilities that history has all but forgotten except in legend and old stories like those of your family."

Michael gave her a long, incredulous look. "And that's what you've done? Awakened...whatever this is?"

Claire nodded once. "Exactly. That research is how I'm able to shift."

He ran a hand down his face, visibly struggling to take it in. "This is all a bit much. But still—what's the link to his family being slaughtered?"

Howard glanced at her before answering. "We uncovered evidence of a secret society calling itself the Sodality of the Thorns. We believe they were behind the author's death...and they've been quietly engineering events like that for centuries."

Michael sat up a little straighter. "The Sodality of the Thorns? Sounds like something out of a John le Carré novel."

"Unfortunately, they're all too real," Ian said grimly. "An ancient outfit, single-minded in its purpose: to eliminate anything—or anyone—they deem less than 'pure.'"

Michael's jaw tightened. "You mean people like us."

"Yes," Claire said simply. "They believe any deviation from their idea of normality undermines humanity. Lucian became a target because his research threatened their hold. It's not just about suppressing knowledge—it's about maintaining their control. Their leader won't tolerate anything that could challenge him."

Michael shook his head. "So this Sodality had Lucian's family killed just to bury his discoveries?"

"Aye," Howard put in. "And now, with more of us awakening our abilities, we're even more of a thorn in their side."

A heavy silence followed as Michael processed the scope of it. He finally spoke. "This is far more dangerous than I'd imagined."

"They already know we're active," Ian added. "We've managed to keep out of sight so far, but as we grow stronger, that cloak of protection will only thin. They'll come again."

Michael's eyes found Claire. "And no one thought to tell me this before?"

"We wanted to," Claire said. "But we had to be sure of you first. And we didn't want to put you in an impossible position, given your office."

Michael exhaled slowly, rubbing his chin. "I appreciate the thought. But if my family's in the firing line, I ought to know."

Fiona stepped in then. "That's precisely why you're being told now."

Michael looked around at them, brow furrowed. "I don't see how I can be much use against a bloody secret society."

"You've got contacts," Ian pointed out. "Access to information, and ways of working the system we can't. You could be invaluable."

Michael leaned back in his chair, clearly thinking it through. "Perhaps," he conceded. "But tread carefully. If this Sodality has tendrils inside institutions—and it sounds like they do—we can't go blundering about trusting just anyone."

"They do," Claire confirmed.

Michael straightened. "Pardon? Who? How far does it go?"

"One of ours—a former FBI agent who's now part of our circle—was investigating Lucian's case when she ran into pressure to shut it down. The pressure came from higher up, almost certainly tied to the Sodality. She refused, resigned, and joined us instead."

Michael let out a low whistle. "Well. That rather speaks for itself, doesn't it?" He fixed Claire with a level stare. "And Lucian and this Anja? Where are they now?"

"They're away at present," she explained. "Chasing down leads on the Sodality. Their absence…hasn't made things any easier."

"So you're essentially playing chess without your strongest pieces in play."

"That's one way of putting it," Ian allowed dryly.

Michael rose, paced a circle by the hearth. "And the rest of the family? How many of you have…what did you call it? Awakened?"

"A fair few of your kin," Howard answered. "A dozen wolves to date—Claire and her brother Simon, your sisters Margaret and Fiona, Blevine Musgrave and her lad Dillon, Ben Clarke, Diana Forester, Conall Lawson, Natalie Wright, Alice Warren, Heather Bennett. That lot, thus far. But beyond Claire, none of them has seen so much as a scrap of real combat. Ian's SAS background is invaluable, but the others have a long way to go."

Michael's eyes flicked to Fiona, then Margaret. Both nodded in confirmation.

Claire spoke up. "We're doing what we can, but progress is slow. We've already had a few minor injuries during training. Nothing catastrophic, but it's shown us just how unprepared we really are."

Michael stopped pacing, his expression tight with concern. "Injuries? What sort?"

"Sprains. A fractured ankle. Cuts and bruises," Ian replied. "We heal quickly, but even so, it takes it out of them."

Michael exhaled sharply through his nose, a grim set to his jaw. "This is more serious than I gave it credit for. If this Sodality moves against you in earnest, the family's sitting ducks."

"Which is why we're at it day and night," Ian said. "Building their resilience, sharpening what little edge we've got."

Michael returned to his chair and sat with a tug at his jacket, his demeanor firming into resolve. "Right then. We need more than just drills and wishful thinking. You need a proper plan. Something proactive."

Claire's brow lifted, a flicker of hope in her voice. "You've got something in mind?"

Michael gave a single, measured nod. "For starters, we need to establish exactly where you stand legally. Your…abilities may not be illegal, strictly speaking, but should you injure anyone—Sodality or no—you could end up in the dock. Self-defense? At the very least, you'll want statements drafted and contingencies in place. If something goes pear-shaped, we want you protected."

Ian arched an eyebrow. "I rather think once the shooting starts, the finer points of the law will go out the window."

"Perhaps," Michael conceded, "but until then, I'd rather not hand them a weapon to use against you in court." He leaned back, steepling his fingers. "And you ought to think about moving this operation to a more defensible position. This house is lovely, yes—but it's not a fortress."

Claire caught Howard's eye. "We've considered it, but for now this estate is the most secure place we have."

Michael gave a short, dry laugh. "It's Lucian's property, isn't it? But if he's gone, can you honestly say it's safe? They've already gone after him once. What's to stop them coming back?"

Ian nodded once. "We've thought of that. Security here is tight—layers of it. Cameras, gates, and more than a few tricks. And we've a former MI6 man in residence. You'll meet Ash soon enough."

Michael let out a long breath, rubbing the back of his neck. "Even so, you'd be fools not to have contingencies. Other sites, fallback plans. Don't put all your eggs in this basket."

"We'll see to it," Ian agreed without hesitation.

Fiona cleared her throat delicately. "The family farm in Dartmoor National Park's still mine, you know. Much too big for just me these days, but I couldn't bring myself to sell it. It's been in the family since Isobel's time, if you can believe it. I could open it up as a safe haven, if needs be. Close enough for me to carry on at the university as well."

Michael's brow arched. "Isobel…aye, I vaguely remember that tale. Seems that particular bit of family folklore's taken on new weight now."

Margaret chimed in. "There's also my cottage. Tiny for a group this size, but if we ever needed to split up, it'd serve."

Michael turned his gaze back to Claire, his expression softening. "And you, Claire—are you truly certain of this? Of pulling the family into something so…dangerous?"

She held his eyes without wavering. "I am. The threat is real, and burying our heads in the sand won't make it vanish. This time we stand together. We protect our own."

A reluctant smile ghosted across his lips. "Well then. You've got grit, I'll give you that. Very well—I'll do what I can to help."

"Thank you," she said, and meant it.

He shifted his attention to Ian. "Is there any way to reach Lucian and Anja, then? Surely they ought to know what's going on here."

Ian shook his head. "They're in deep cover. Contact is kept minimal on purpose, to keep them from being traced."

Michael rubbed his temples and muttered, "Right. Then we crack on with what we've got."

Claire leaned forward, her tone gentle. "Earlier you mentioned possible conflicts with your role. Are you comfortable continuing with us?"

He met her gaze, his own thoughtful. "So long as no laws are being broken, and no innocents are at risk, I can stand by it. My job's to protect the public, and my instinct's to protect my family. I suppose that's why I dug my heels in at first—but now…"

She smiled, soft and genuine. "That means more than I can say."

Michael returned her smile before his expression sobered again. "We ought also to consider leaning on a few trusted allies—people I've worked with before who…specialise in unconventional matters."

Ian tilted his head. "You've contacts in that line of work?"

Michael gave a modest shrug. "Over the years, you come across cases that don't fit neatly into a charge sheet. I've made it a point to know a handful of discreet professionals who can deal with sensitive situations without fuss."

Howard's brow lifted. "That could prove useful. But there's a trust question, of course. You'll appreciate that better now."

"Quite," Michael agreed. "We'll need to tread very carefully."

Claire gave a small nod. “It’s a start.”

He stood then, smoothing his jacket. “I’ll make a few enquiries. In the meantime, we’d do well to make sure everyone here understands the risks and knows what to do if it all goes pear-shaped.”

“Agreed,” Ian said. “We’ll call a briefing tomorrow.”

Michael inclined his head. “Good. And if you’ll have me, I can lend a hand with strategy and coordination. I’m no soldier, but I know how to plan.”

Claire’s face brightened. “We’d appreciate that.”

A smile tugged at his lips. “Well then—family looks out for each other, eh?”

“Always,” she replied.

As the evening wore on, they continued sketching plans. Claire felt a weight ease from her shoulders; having him onside made the whole affair feel that bit more manageable.

Eventually, Howard glanced at the clock. “It’s getting late. We should pick this up again in the morning.”

“Agreed,” Michael said with a short nod. “I’ll need to get some kip before diving any deeper into this.”

Claire stood, stretching. “I’ll walk you to your room.”

They made their way through the corridors of the estate, the soft lighting casting shadows across the old carpets. At his door, Michael paused and turned to her, his tone softer.

“Claire…I know we’ve not always seen eye to eye when it comes to family folklore and all that rot. But you’ve done bloody well tonight. I’m proud of how you’re handling yourself.”

Warmth bloomed in her chest as she smiled. “Thank you, Uncle Michael. That really does mean a lot.”

He gave her a brisk nod. “Right then. Let’s get some shut-eye.”

Just then, Ash emerged from his room down the hall, looking… well…ashen.

Ian caught up to them at the same time. “What’s happened?”

Ash glanced from Michael to Claire, then back to Ian, his brow furrowed.

Claire stepped in. “Ash, this is my uncle, Michael. Michael, Mr. Sebastian Harper. He’s part of our circle now. So, please, Ash—what’s the situation?”

Ash rubbed at his jaw. “A team sent by Krakarov made contact with Lucian and his lot. Bit of a cock-up all round, but Lucian’s group managed to slip away. They’ve holed up in some abandoned farmhouse outside Moscow. Proper mess.”

Michael’s eyes widened. “Good God. You said they were in deep cover—but inside Russia? Have they lost their bloody minds?”

Ash snorted. “Asked myself the same. Settled on: probably. Long story.”

Michael gave a tight shake of his head. “Plenty of those about, by the looks of it. Were there any injuries?”

Ash’s expression eased. “Nothing major. They’re all in one piece. Nomad’s fully briefed, and they’re figuring out the next step—best way into Moscow proper to rendezvous with Anja and Zoe.”

Claire glanced at Michael. “Howard will fill you in more on what we’re up against. We can talk again in the morning. Ash, let’s go and take a look.”

Twenty-Seven

Zoe lay back against the soft pillows, the glow of the city lights filtering through the curtains of their suite. The sounds of Moscow's nightlife were a distant murmur, muted by the walls of Katya's establishment. She and Anja had shed the layers of the day's tensions along with their clothes, seeking comfort in the warmth of each other.

Anja nestled beside her, resting her head on Zoe's shoulder. Her fingers traced patterns on Zoe's arm, a soothing motion that helped ease the remnants of anxiety. "It's been quite a day," Anja whispered, her breath a caress against Zoe's skin.

"That's an understatement," Zoe replied with a chuckle. She turned her head to press a tender kiss on Anja's cheek. "But at least we made it, safe for the moment."

Anja turned to face her. "Thank you for being by my side through all of this."

Zoe smiled, brushing a strand of hair away from Anja's face. "There's no one else I'd rather be with. I miss Lucian, though."

They shared a quiet moment, their surroundings fading as they focused solely on each other. The connection between them went beyond words. Zoe leaned in, their lips meeting in a kiss that quickly became more passionate.

As their touches and explorations of each other's bodies turned more intimate, a familiar sensation tugged at the edges of Zoe's consciousness. It was the unmistakable feeling of their psychic link activating. Anja's eyes met hers, confirming that she felt it, too.

"Lucian," Zoe murmured.

Anja nodded, closing her eyes briefly as she opened her mind to the link. Zoe did the same, allowing the mental connection to solidify. A moment later, Lucian's presence filled their thoughts, a steady anchor amidst the swirling uncertainties.

"Glad to find you both awake." Lucian's voice echoed in their minds, tinged with a hint of amusement.

Zoe exchanged a glance with Anja, a smile playing on her lips. *"Just trying to get some rest,"* she replied.

"I'd love to watch to see where that 'resting' would lead, but we've had an unexpected encounter."

Anja's expression grew more serious. *"What happened?"*

"We ran into Krakarov's men," Lucian explained. *"They set up a roadblock just outside of Moscow. It was an ambush."*

Zoe felt a ripple of concern. *"Is everyone all right?"*

"Yes, on our side," Lucian assured them. *"On theirs, not so much. We managed to turn the tables. We're all lying low at an abandoned farmhouse."*

Anja sighed. *"I'm glad you're safe. Did they know it was you?"*

"Unlikely," Lucian replied. *"They were expecting Lev and Kasia. But we can't be sure how much they know. Their entire team and those trying to smuggle us in are all dead."*

Zoe considered this. *Crap. "What's the plan now?"*

"We've updated Ash on the situation. He's coordinating with Ian to devise a strategy for us to enter Moscow without drawing attention."

Anja's brow furrowed. *"Do you need any assistance from our end?"*

"For now, stay where you are. It's best if we don't risk exposing any more of our team. Once we have a clear path, we'll make our way to you."

Zoe glanced at Anja before responding. *"Okay. We'll be ready to help if needed."*

"Good," Lucian affirmed. *"Also, who's the new addition with you? Ash mentioned someone named Karolina."*

Anja smiled. *"A young woman we encountered along the way. She was caught up in Marek's trafficking ring. We couldn't leave her behind."*

"I see," Lucian said.

"She's been through a lot, but she's eager to start anew. We thought we might be able to help her find a safe place," Zoe said.

"All right," Lucian agreed. *"Just be wary. These are precarious times."*

"We will," Anja promised.

"Rest while you can. We'll contact you when we have more information."

"Stay safe," Zoe said.

"You too," Lucian replied, his presence fading as the link diminished.

Anja opened her eyes. "Well, that complicates things," she murmured.

Zoe nodded, her expression pensive. "At least they're all okay. But Krakarov's involvement is concerning."

Anja leaned back against the pillows, her gaze drifting to the ceiling. "Do you think he suspects who Lucian really is?"

"It's hard to say," Zoe admitted. "But we should prepare for the possibility that our enemies are becoming more aware of our movements."

Anja sighed. "I suppose we'll be staying here a bit longer."

"Seems that way," Zoe agreed. She turned onto her side to face Anja fully. "How are you holding up?"

Anja offered a smile. "Better. Now, where were we?"

Zoe returned the smile, shifting closer to Anja. "I believe we were trying to relax," she said. "Hussy."

"Slut."

"Yep, now let's continue," Zoe said as her hand slid down Anja's body to the curls that fascinated her.

A knock interrupted them. Zoe sighed, glancing toward the door. "Looks like *rest* will have to wait."

Anja nodded, pulling the sheet up. "Come in," she called out.

The door opened to reveal Nomad. "Sorry to disturb you both," he began, stepping inside. "But I've just received an update from Ash."

Zoe sat up slightly, alert. "Lucian?"

Nomad closed the door behind him. "Ash and Ian have coordinated a plan to help Lucian and the others return to the city without drawing attention."

Anja leaned forward. "You're going to help?"

"I'll be contacting a friend who can provide the vehicle and knows the less-traveled routes into Moscow," Nomad said. "However, given the increased security and random stops, I believe it would be better if you accompanied me, Anja."

Anja met his gaze, understanding immediately. "In case we encounter any difficulties at checkpoints."

"Exactly. Your abilities could help us avoid unnecessary complications."

Zoe's brow furrowed. "Should I go too?"

Nomad shook his head. "It's better if you stay here with Karolina."

Zoe tried to mask her disappointment, but couldn't help the slight pout that formed. "I understand," she said.

Anja reached out to touch Zoe's hand. "We'll be back before you know it, and with Lucian."

"Just be careful," Zoe urged.

Anja gave her a reassuring smile. "I will. We'll keep our link open. If anything comes up, you'll be the first to know."

Nomad glanced between them. "We'll need to leave within the hour. I have some arrangements to finalize first."

"Of course," Anja agreed. "I'll get ready."

As Nomad left the room, closing the door behind him, Zoe let out a small sigh. "I don't like the idea of you going without me."

"I know," Anja replied. "But this way, you'll be here to support Karolina, and I'll help ensure Lucian and the others make it back safely."

Zoe nodded slowly. "You're right. It's just—after everything that's happened, I prefer when we're together."

Anja moved closer, resting a hand on Zoe's cheek. "I feel the same. But sometimes we have to divide our efforts."

"Just promise me you'll stay in touch," Zoe said, her gaze earnest.

"Always," Anja affirmed. "Our connection won't waver."

Zoe managed a small smile. "All right. I suppose I should check on Karolina, then."

"She might appreciate the company," Anja agreed. "This place can be intimidating."

Zoe stood from the bed. "I'll see if she needs anything."

Anja watched her for a moment. "Zoe?"

"Yes?" Zoe paused at the door.

"Love you."

Lucian stirred awake, the remnants of sleep fading as a familiar sensation tugged at the edges of his consciousness. His psychic link with Anja was opening. He sat up; it was still pitch black.

"Lucian, we're approaching your location. Don't panic when you see us. Get everyone ready to load up."

He rubbed his eyes. *"Understood. We'll be ready."*

He glanced around the room. Mike was seated near the doorway, scanning the darkness outside through a gap in the boarded-up window. He looked alert but not overly tense.

"Mike," Lucian called softly. "Anja just contacted me. They're on their way. Said not to panic."

Mike raised an eyebrow. "Not to panic? Do they think we're that jumpy?"

Lucian chuckled. "Who knows?"

Graham emerged from the adjoining room, stretching his arms over his head. "What's going on?"

"Anja and Nomad are close," Lucian informed him. "She said to get ready to move."

Dora sat up. "Good timing. I was getting tired of this decor," she remarked, gesturing to the peeling wallpaper.

Emma padded over to Lucian in her feline form and leapt onto his shoulder. He gave her a reassuring scratch. "Time to go," he said.

Mike stood up, adjusting his gear. "I didn't see any vehicles approaching yet," he noted. "But I'll keep an eye out."

Graham moved to one of the grimy windows, wiping a spot with his sleeve. "Well, would you look at that? An ambulance is coming down the road."

"An ambulance?" Dora echoed, joining him at the window.

Lucian joined them, peering out. Sure enough, an ambulance was making its way along the dirt path leading to the farmhouse. Its sirens were off, but the vehicle's distinctive shape was unmistakable even in the darkness.

"That's one way to travel," Mike mused.

The ambulance pulled up outside, and the driver's door opened.

Nomad stepped out, his gaze sweeping over the area. Anja emerged from the passenger side, her eyes meeting Lucian's through the window.

Lucian felt a surge of relief and warmth. "Let's go," he said, heading toward the door with Emma on his shoulder.

They stepped outside into the crisp morning air. The sky was beginning to lighten, hints of dawn coloring the horizon. Anja approached, a smile spreading across her face.

"Anja," Lucian greeted.

Without hesitation, Anja closed the distance between them and pulled him into a deep kiss, causing Emma to leap clear. For a moment, the world around them faded away, and Lucian allowed himself to savor the reunion.

They parted slightly, and Anja whispered, "Missed you."

"Likewise," Lucian replied.

Nomad cleared his throat, a hint of amusement in his eyes. "We should get moving."

Lucian nodded, turning to the others. "Everyone, load up."

"Interesting choice of vehicle," Mike remarked as he approached Nomad.

Nomad shrugged. "In Moscow, it's not uncommon for the wealthy to own ambulances to bypass traffic. No one bats an eye."

Graham chuckled. "Huh."

Mike and Graham moved to the back of the ambulance, opening the doors to reveal a stretcher on one side and a bench on the other that could double as a bed. "Perfect," Mike said, climbing in and reclining onto the bench. "I could use a nap."

Graham took the stretcher, lying down with a satisfied sigh. "Wake me when we get there."

Dora climbed in and sat near the front of the cabin. "I suppose this beats that farmhouse," she remarked. "This seat is actually comfortable."

Lucian helped Anja secure the doors before he returned to the front seat. As he settled into the passenger side, he glanced at Nomad. "Thanks for coming to get us."

"Couldn't leave you out here, could we?" Nomad started the engine, and the ambulance eased forward.

As they pulled away from the farmhouse, Lucian felt a weight lifting from his shoulders. The past few days had been tense, but now they were moving forward together.

He could feel Anja reaching out to Zoe through their link to let her know they were on the way back.

Nomad said, "We should make good time. Traffic will be lighter at this hour."

As they drove on, the landscape gradually shifted from the countryside to the rural outskirts and then to the denser environment of the city. Nomad maneuvered the ambulance through the streets with ease. Lucian observed the city waking up—the storefronts opening, pedestrians beginning their day, the hum of activity increasing.

"Almost there," Nomad announced.

Behind them, Mike and Graham were dozing. Emma gazed out the window, her feline eyes reflecting the passing scenery.

Finally, they approached a discreet yet elegant building nestled among the bustling streets. Nomad parked the ambulance in a reserved spot around the back, away from prying eyes.

"Home, sweet home," Nomad quipped as they disembarked.

Graham stretched his arms above his head, yawning. "Best sleep I've had in days," he declared.

Mike laughed. "Speak for yourself. The padding on the bench wasn't exactly a feather bed."

Emma perched on her usual spot on Lucian's shoulder.

Dora asked, "This is Katya's place?"

"Yes," Nomad confirmed. "She keeps a low profile but has all the amenities we need. Good cover for Anja and Zoe, and a place where visitors come and go anonymously."

They gathered their belongings and headed inside. The interior was tastefully decorated, exuding an air of sophistication without drawing unnecessary attention. Katya herself greeted them in the foyer, her demeanor poised and welcoming, even at this early hour.

"Thank you for your hospitality," Lucian said.

She inclined her head. "Anything for friends of my friend. I owe him much."

They ascended the grand staircase. Lucian followed to the suite where Zoe and Karolina were waiting. As they entered, Zoe looked up from her seat, relief evident on her face.

"You're here," she said, standing to greet them.

Emma jumped down to the floor, apparently wary from Anja's greeting earlier, and looked around.

Lucian stepped forward. "Good to see y…"

Zoe wrapped her arms around him and shut him up with a deep kiss.

Anja moved to Zoe's side, joining in a group hug. "Careful, Lucian; I think I left her rather frustrated last night. We kept getting interrupted."

"Maybe we can fix that later."

Karolina stood a bit behind Zoe, offering a shy smile while watching the black cat that had approached her. Lucian nodded to her. "You must be Karolina. Do you like cats?"

She nodded. "Yes."

Dora stepped closer and extended a hand. "I'm Dora. We'll have to talk later. I know what you've been through. I was there myself once."

Karolina's eyes got bigger. "Oh…"

Mike and Graham settled into the room, finding seats and relaxing. Emma wandered over to Karolina and rubbed against her legs, letting out a soft purr.

Nomad addressed the group. "Now that we're all together, we can regroup and plan our next steps."

Lucian agreed. "First, though, I think we could all use some rest and perhaps a proper meal."

Zoe nodded. "Katya has arranged for food to be brought up. You should all eat." Her eyes met Lucian's. "I'm glad you're safe," she said.

He reached out to take her hand. "Thanks to all of you."

She smiled. "We do what we must."

Lucian looked around at his gathered friends and allies. "Indeed, we do."

"Meow?"

"Hmmm. Anja, Emma may want something to eat." He looked at Karolina and then back at Anja. "What are we going to do with Karolina? Do you think she can handle it?"

"There isn't much we can do other than keep her with us, so we might as well get the shock over with now."

"All right, Emma, let's get that collar off you."

The cat padded back over to Lucian, who reached down to pull the collar off. As soon as it was off, a glow enveloped the small feline. Karolina watched in disbelief as Emma's form began to shift and expand. The fur receded, and limbs elongated; paws transformed into hands and feet. Within moments, where the cat once stood, a woman appeared.

Emma stretched her arms above her head, her long, dark hair tumbling over her shoulders, strikingly similar to Karolina's own. Her emerald-green eyes met Karolina's wide-eyed gaze, a hint of amusement dancing within them. Realizing her lack of attire, Emma offered a sheepish smile.

Dora headed to the adjoining bathroom. She returned promptly with a plush robe and handed it to Emma. "Here you go," she said.

"Thanks," Emma replied, wrapping the robe around herself.

Karolina stood frozen, her mouth slightly open. She glanced around the room, noting that no one else seemed shocked by what had just transpired. "How...how she do that?" she finally managed to ask.

Anja exchanged a look with Lucian before responding. "It's a bit complicated," she said. "But Emma is...special."

"In my village in Ukraine...we had old story," Karolina began hesitantly. "About Koshka-Oboroten. Cat who can become woman. They say she walk forest, protect good people...help children who get lost."

Anja tilted her head, intrigued. "I've heard variations of that tale," she said.

Karolina stared at Emma, wide-eyed. "You...are...one of them?"

Emma smiled warmly. "You could say that stories often have roots in reality."

Karolina's brow furrowed. "Everyone here...like that?"

"We all have our roles to play," Lucian said. "But what's important is that you're safe with us."

She bit her lip. "I never see something like that before."

Dora offered a comforting smile. "Not many have. It can be a lot to take in, but we didn't want to keep this secret from you."

Anja moved closer to Karolina. "We understand this is

overwhelming. If you have questions, we'll do our best to answer them."

Karolina nodded slowly. "Thank you. It just…"

Emma adjusted the robe around her shoulders. "I hope you can accept us, even with our…quirks."

A shy smile appeared. "I think yes. In story people respect, not fear."

"That's reassuring," Lucian said. He then clapped his hands. "Now, Emma will be hungry."

Emma grinned. "Changing forms does work up an appetite."

"Food should be here soon," Zoe said.

As the group began to relax, the tension in the room eased. Karolina took a seat on one of the sofas, still glancing occasionally at Emma, who sat cross-legged opposite her.

"I can tell more if you want?" she offered.

Emma's eyes lit up. "I'd love to hear the story."

Karolina spoke slowly. "Story say was woman. She love forest. Always walk in trees. Birds, foxes, they not scared of her. People come to her for plants, for help, sometimes for secrets."

"Fascinating," Emma said. "I'll bet you it was true."

"But bad men came. They want hurt her. Take what she know. But she not let them. She change." Karolina's fingers stilled, and her voice grew softer. "She become big black cat. Very fast, very sharp. Bad men run away. Never come back." She hesitated, searching for the next words.

"People say she make…um…deal? With forest spirits. They let her change. Woman or cat, when she want. And she use this to help children who get lost. Bring them home. Scare wolves. And bad men." Karolina drew a shaky breath and glanced at Emma.

"Scare wolves. That's good." Emma chuckled.

"My babusia say people leave milk on door. Sometimes bread. Or coin. To say thank you. Or ask her watch them." Karolina's lips curved into the faintest smile, though her eyes still held a hint of doubt. "She was…little scary. But good. Not monster. Guardian. That what my babusia say." Karolina looked at Emma again, her voice dropping almost to a whisper. "Maybe still true. Yes?"

Emma's eyes glinted with a wide smile. "Yes, it must be true. You've seen. Not monster."

Anja sat beside Karolina. "Sometimes, old tales and reality aren't so far apart."

Karolina looked between them. "I never thought to see."

There was a knock on the door, and Nomad got up to answer. After a hushed conversation, Nomad wheeled in a cart with a selection of food.

They gathered around, helping themselves. The atmosphere grew more convivial, with conversations flowing more easily.

Karolina ventured, "I want say thank you for help me."

"You're part of our group now," Anja said warmly. "We'll look out for you."

Emma took a bite of her sandwich. "And maybe, in time, you'll find your place in all of this."

Karolina smiled shyly. "I like that."

As the evening wore on, the conversation shifted to lighter topics. Laughter filled the room as they shared stories and experiences, the earlier tensions fading.

Eventually, Karolina stifled a yawn.

"I'll get a blanket for you, and you can sleep on the sofa in the other room," Dora said.

"Thank you," Karolina replied, standing up.

As she left the room with Dora, Emma turned to Anja and Lucian. "She handled that better than I expected."

Anja nodded. "She's resilient and has been through a lot. Compared to being beaten and raped, I would imagine this is easy."

Lucian sighed. "We'll need to keep an eye on her, but I think she'll be okay."

Dora returned and said, "Thank you for helping her. She reminds me of myself at that age."

"We couldn't have done anything else," Zoe said.

"There are a couple of other rooms set aside. We should be safe for now," Nomad said.

Lucian agreed, "Yes, thank you. Let's meet again in the morning and start planning the next phase. We made it here. Now, we need to get started looking for the library."

Twenty-Eight

ANJA SAT ON a sofa in the sitting area. The scent of freshly brewed coffee mingled with the aroma of pastries that had arrived. Around her, the team was assembling.

"Is the call set up?" Lucian asked, taking a seat beside Dora.

"Just about," Dora replied, tapping a few keys on the laptop. "They should be connecting at any moment. This computer Nomad acquired isn't the greatest, but it isn't bad considering. He also obtained a few SIM cards. They should be anonymous, and we set up a hot spot with my phone."

The screen flickered, and soon, the faces of Ash, Ian, and Claire appeared in the call's window. Ash scanned the group while Ian smiled briefly.

"Morning, all," Ash began.

Lucian leaned forward. "We have much to cover, so let's get started."

Zoe nodded. "Anja and I have some updates regarding Marek's operation. We gathered substantial information on his trafficking network."

Anja added, "Names, locations, routes—we'll forward them to you. We think it's enough to significantly impact it if passed to the right authorities. Karolina helped to provide a few more names and places, including where she was taken." Anja didn't share that she had obtained some of his plans and contacts with Marek's feet dangling in the air.

Claire's eyes brightened. "My uncle Michael has connections with

ICAT at the UN and the International Rescue Committee in Poland. I'll pass this information to him."

"Spot on," Ash said with a smirk. "On another note, we've dug into those urban explorers you asked about—call themselves 'Diggerstvo.'"

"You've reviewed what Jonas gathered, right?" asked Zoe.

"That's right," Ash confirmed. "He's been tracking a few vloggers who've been poking about Moscow's underbelly. They've mapped a fair few tunnels and forgotten facilities. Could be useful as bolt-holes or ways out if it all goes pear-shaped. I've lined up a meet with one of them. Calls himself Deepcore. Best if only one or two of you speak to him at first, see how he plays it." Ash provided the name of a café and a time later in the day.

"Zoe, either you or Anja should go with Nomad. We need to make sure we can trust him," Lucian suggested.

"Watch yourselves," Ash warned. "They're adrenaline junkies, sure, but some of them run in circles you don't want to be caught dead in—or worse, they're stooges for the FSB."

"That's the issue," Nomad replied. "Some of them have cooperated with the FSB. Others will have avoided them. Many would want to avoid government entanglements, as they might lose access to the best places."

"Quite right. And another thing. Alerts have gone round to the authorities—photos and all—flagging 'Lev' and 'Kasia.' Word's out."

Dora frowned. "Oh, hell. Do they suspect who we really are?"

"No idea yet, but I'd rather keep it that way," Ash said. "The descriptions fit your cover identities to a tee. You'll want to keep your heads down."

Lucian exchanged a glance with Dora. "The real Lev is somewhere in Poland, likely unaware that his name is being used."

"That may work to our advantage," Zoe suggested. "If authorities focus their search elsewhere."

"Possibly," Ian conceded. "But don't count on it."

"Dora could dye her hair or keep it out of sight," Nomad said. "I'll see if we can figure something out for Mike and Graham. They fit in, but we shouldn't take chances."

Ash concluded the call. "Right. Stay sharp, all of you. I'll be in touch when we've more to go on."

“So, who goes with Nomad?” Lucian asked.

“Zoe might be less conspicuous,” Nomad said, “but she won’t be able to understand much of what is said. Is that a problem? Maybe Anja should go.”

Lucian considered. “I think Zoe and I should go along but not meet him. Provide some backup, just in case. Nomad?”

“I think we should minimize exposing more than two of us. You know where we’ll be. Anja should be able to contact you and Zoe if things go bad.” Nomad stood, checking his watch. “Anja, we should head out if we’re going to meet Deepcore on time. We’ll want to take an indirect route.”

“Right,” Anja agreed, gathering her jacket. She turned to the others. “We’ll keep in touch.”

Lucian gave a curt nod. “Be careful out there.”

“Always,” she replied with a smile.

As Anja headed out with Nomad, she felt exhilarated yet cautious. The streets of Moscow were busy, the morning rush filling the air with the sounds of car horns and distant conversations. They stepped out into the crisp air, blending with the flow of pedestrians.

“Deepcore agreed to meet at a café near the old metro station,” Nomad said, navigating through the crowd.

“I hope we can trust him.”

“Trust is a strong word,” Nomad replied. “But he was the one Ash suggested. If he doesn’t work out, there are others.”

“Let’s hope he’s as useful as we need him to be. Do you think the notices about Lev and Kasia will cause problems for us?”

“It’s possible,” Nomad admitted. “The sooner we can find the library, the better.”

Anja nodded. “Then let’s make this meeting count.”

They arrived at the café, a quaint establishment with a modest façade. The aroma of fresh coffee wafted through the air as they stepped inside. Seated at a corner table was a young man with a lean build, his dark hoodie pulled low over his eyes.

“Deepcore?” Nomad inquired as they approached.

The man looked up. “Depends on who’s asking.”

“Friends of Watcher,” Nomad said, using the handle Ash had been given to communicate with him. “He speaks highly of your skills.”

Deepcore gestured to the empty seats. "Then let's talk."

Dora sat at the large oak table in the center of the sitting room, a steaming cup of tea cradled between her hands. The hum of conversation filled the room as the team gathered around, waiting for Anja and Nomad to return from their meeting with Deepcore.

The ornate clock on the mantel chimed, marking the passing of another hour. Dora glanced around at her companions—Lucian was reviewing maps spread out before him, Mike was absentmindedly flipping a coin, Emma lounged on a velvet sofa in her feline form, and Zoe was typing away on their acquired laptop, occasionally exchanging words with Graham. Karolina sat nearby.

The door opened, drawing everyone's attention. Anja came in and Nomad followed carrying a large bag.

"How did it go?" Lucian asked, straightening up.

Anja offered a reassuring smile. "Productive. Deepcore is exactly who we hoped he would be."

Nomad nodded in agreement. "He's genuine. Broke away from one of the larger digger groups after they started cooperating with the Kremlin. He values his independence and the freedom to explore without oversight."

Dora leaned forward. "What about his online videos? Can we trust that he hasn't exposed sensitive locations?"

"His videos showcase only well-known sites among the diggers," Anja explained. "Tourist spots, so to speak. He keeps the more secret places to himself."

Lucian crossed his arms thoughtfully. "Did he agree to guide us?"

"Yes," Nomad confirmed. "But there's a catch. He wanted to take only three of us in."

Anja's eyes twinkled with a hint of mischief. "I managed to 'convince' him to allow five."

Mike raised an eyebrow. "How'd you pull that off?"

Anja shrugged. "I can be very persuasive."

A ripple of amusement passed through the group. Dora exchanged a knowing glance with Zoe.

"Five it is, then," Lucian said. "We need to decide who goes."

"You're one obvious choice," Nomad pointed out.

"And Nomad's experience with the training games under the Kremlin makes him another," Anja added. "I'll go as well. My... influence might be needed if we encounter any unexpected obstacles."

Mike pocketed his coin and leaned forward. "Count me in. My affinity with the earth could come in handy down there."

Dora felt a sudden pang of uncertainty. She wasn't sure if she would be included or left behind. Before she could speak, Anja turned to her. "Dora, you need to come with us."

Dora blinked. "Me? But I thought—"

Anja smiled. "Trust me."

"Anja's right. Trust her feelings," Zoe said.

Emma hopped down from the sofa, padding over on silent paws.

Anja chuckled. "Deepcore specified five people. He didn't say anything about pets." That earned her a glare from Emma.

Zoe's eyes gleamed with mischief. "She can move through tight spaces and scout ahead. Besides, there may be rats to chase."

Mike grinned. "Plus, who wouldn't want a lucky black cat on the team?"

A light-hearted laugh spread through the room. Karolina looked around, a puzzled expression on her face. "You...you make fun of her like this always?"

Emma hopped up to sit in Karolina's lap and rubbed her cheek against her chest.

Graham leaned back in his chair. "So that leaves Zoe, Karolina, and me here?"

"Yes," Lucian confirmed. "We need you three to coordinate from here. Zoe, you can keep in contact with Anja. Graham, you can coordinate with Ash and Ian."

Nomad glanced at his watch. "Deepcore will provide us with the necessary gear—lights, boots, and other equipment. We stopped and picked up some coveralls. We'll meet him at the entrance to the tunnels this evening. He gave me a location to meet at. He initially wanted to start in the Metro, but I nixed that."

"Why?" Dora asked.

"Too many cameras. The police may have our faces in their

system," Nomad explained.

"AI face ID?" Zoe asked.

"Yeah."

Dora asked, "Do we have any information on what we might encounter down there?"

"Not much," Anja admitted. "It's dirty, smelly, dark. Deepcore was cryptic, but he hinted at areas that even seasoned diggers avoid. That's why he was reluctant to take more than three. Remember what Howard described of Ivanov's search."

Lucian glanced at Anja. "Are you sure about this? If Deepcore was hesitant, there might be more danger than he's letting on."

Anja met her gaze. "I sensed he's holding back some concerns, but I believe we can handle it together."

Dora took a deep breath. "Sounds like we have a plan."

Dora tugged at her coveralls. The fabric was stiff and didn't fit very well, but it would serve its purpose. The early evening seemed colder than it should. Maybe that was just her projecting her unease. She stood with the others at the edge of a side street, the glow of streetlamps casting elongated shadows. Well, the lights that were working anyway.

Deepcore was a lean man with sharp features, his eyes constantly darting. He wore a dark hoodie pulled low over his forehead, and he gripped a long metal tool in gloved hands. Without a word, he approached a worn manhole cover embedded in the pavement. With practiced efficiency, he inserted the tool into a notch and lifted and pulled. The heavy cover slid aside with a scrape.

He motioned them forward. "Quickly," he whispered.

Nomad descended first. Anja followed, then Lucian, Mike, and Dora. Emma, in her cat form, leapt gracefully onto the edge before disappearing into the darkness below. Deepcore replaced the manhole cover before joining them. The clang of metal sealed them away from the world above.

Dora's eyes adjusted to the dim light cast by the lamps. The air was damp and carried the scent of mold and something metallic. The tunnel walls were lined with aged brick, slick with moisture. Deepcore pointed to a row of headlamps and waterproof boots laid out on a ledge.

"Put these on," he instructed. His gaze landed on the cat, who sat licking her paw. "I said five people."

Anja stepped forward. "That's what we have."

Deepcore frowned but didn't argue. Dora had the impression that he was wary of Anja, perhaps even intimidated. *Smart man.*

As they equipped themselves, Nomad addressed Deepcore. "We're particularly interested in areas beneath or near the Kremlin."

Deepcore raised an eyebrow. "Ambitious. All tunnels leading directly under have been sealed or are monitored. It's risky."

Anja met his gaze. "We understand the risks. Just get us as close as you can."

He hesitated, then shrugged. "Fine. Follow me, and stay close. Some passages we'll need to use aren't stable."

They set off, the beams of their headlamps cutting through the darkness. The tunnels twisted and turned, a maze of intersecting paths and forgotten passageways. The sounds of dripping water echoed around them, and occasionally, the distant rumble of the city's subway could be felt as a vibration underfoot.

Dora found herself walking beside Mike. "Do you feel anything unusual?" she asked.

Mike closed his eyes briefly, his footsteps never faltering. "There are more passages here," he murmured. "Old ones. The earth remembers."

Deepcore led them through a narrow corridor, the walls closing in. "Watch your step," he cautioned. "This area floods sometimes."

They came upon a fork where three tunnels diverged. Deepcore started toward the left, but Anja paused, scanning the other paths. "Wait," she said.

Deepcore glanced back impatiently. "What is it?"

Anja tilted her head as if listening to something distant. "The middle path. It feels…promising."

He shook his head. "That way is unstable. It hasn't been safe for years."

"Perhaps," she replied. "But it's the most direct route, isn't it?"

He hesitated. "In theory, yes. But it's dangerous."

Lucian stepped forward. "We're prepared to take the risk."

Deepcore sighed. "Your call. But don't say I didn't warn you."

They adjusted their course, entering the middle tunnel. The air grew colder, and the walls showed signs of greater age—stone blocks eroded by time, with inscriptions barely visible beneath layers of grime.

Emma darted ahead, her feline silhouette disappearing into the flickering shadows cast by their headlamps. The beams from their lights danced with each movement, causing shadows to leap and twist along the walls like restless spirits. The narrow tunnel walls pressed in on either side, damp with condensation that glistened. The air was thick, a mixture of musty earth and the lingering scent of stagnant water. Each step crunched, the sound swallowed by the seemingly endless passages.

Dora felt a chill despite the layers she wore. The oppressive darkness seemed to close in around them, their headlamps barely piercing the inky blackness. She kept close to Mike, who moved with a quiet confidence, his senses attuned to the subterranean environment.

"Stay close and watch your footing," Deepcore cautioned from the front of the line. "These tunnels are old."

As if on cue, a crack echoed from beneath. Nomad, walking just ahead of Lucian, paused. "Did anyone else hear that?" he asked, his voice low.

Before anyone could respond, the ground beneath Nomad gave way with a sudden lurch. "Look out!" Lucian shouted, reaching out to grab him, but it was too late. The floor crumbled, and Nomad disappeared into the darkness below.

"Nomad!" Anja cried out, rushing forward but stopping short at the edge of the newly formed hole.

They peered down to see Nomad lying on a ledge about ten feet below. He was moving but grimacing in pain. "I'm okay," he called up, his voice strained. "Twisted my ankle, though."

Emma, still in her cat form, was the first to reach Nomad. She leapt down into the hole, landing beside him. She circled him once, her emerald eyes reflecting concern. After a moment, she wandered off into the shadows of the space below.

"Hold on, we're coming down," Lucian said.

"Be careful," Deepcore warned. "I told you these tunnels are dangerous. I'm not going down there."

Anja glanced at Deepcore. "We need to help him. Stay here and keep watch."

Deepcore hesitated, crossing his arms. "I'll wait, but don't take too long."

Lucian secured a rope to a sturdy pipe on the tunnel wall. "I'll go first," he said. "Mike, you and Dora follow once I'm down."

Lucian descended, the rope taut under his weight. Once he reached the bottom, he moved to Nomad's side. "Let me see your ankle," he said.

Nomad winced as he shifted. "Feels like a bad sprain. I don't think it's broken."

Lucian placed his hand over Nomad's ankle, his eyes closing as he concentrated. A glow emanated from his hand, the light barely noticeable in the dimness. Dora watched from above.

Meanwhile, Emma reappeared from the shadows, padding over to Lucian. She nudged his leg insistently, looking up at him.

"What is it, Emma?" Lucian asked, glancing down at her.

She meowed, then turned and walked a few paces away, looking back to see if he was following.

Lucian looked at Nomad. "How's that feel?"

Nomad rotated his ankle cautiously. "Much better. Thanks."

"Good. Let's see what Emma's found."

By this time, Mike and Dora had climbed down to join them. "Everything all right?" Mike asked.

"Lucian healed my ankle," Nomad replied, getting to his feet.

Emma continued to beckon them, her tail flicking impatiently.

"I think she wants us to follow her," Dora observed.

Lucian called up to Anja. "I think we found something. We're going to check it out."

Anja peered down at them. "I'm coming down. Deepcore will wait here."

Deepcore shifted uneasily. "We shouldn't split up."

Anja gave him a reassuring smile. "We won't be long. Wait here," she repeated, adding a little power to the command.

He huffed but seemed resigned. "A friend of mine was hurt badly near here. She was in the hospital for weeks, healing. She's lucky to be alive."

Lucian watched uneasily as Anja scrambled down, then, once she was next to him, turned to follow Emma, who was already disappearing into a low tunnel branching off from the space they were in. The passage was narrow, forcing them to proceed single file.

"Watch your heads," Mike cautioned, ducking under a protruding beam.

The tunnel sloped downward, the air growing more still. Their headlamps illuminated specks of dust from the recent collapse. The limited visibility heightened the sense of unease, and every sound was amplified in the confined space.

"Where is she taking us?" Nomad wondered aloud.

"She must have sensed something," Dora replied. "Is it a good idea to go on without Deepcore?"

"He got us in unnoticed. We needed a starting point, and he gave us that," Anja said. "Besides, it's probably better he's not here if we find something we don't want him to see."

After several minutes, the tunnel opened up into a wider passage. The walls here were different, lined with aged bricks rather than cement or stone. Faded markings adorned the surfaces, symbols that Dora couldn't decipher. The atmosphere grew heavier, an unspoken tension settling over the group.

"These look old," she murmured, running her fingers over the marks.

Emma waited for them at the end of the passage, sitting beside an old wall. Some sort of plaster had flaked off, revealing bricks.

Lucian examined the wall. "It looks like someone sealed this off and tried to hide it."

Mike stepped forward, placing his palm flat against the brick. "There's something on the other side," he whispered.

"Now what?" Dora asked.

Mike held up a hand and closed his eyes in concentration. Dora was startled to see his hand darken. After a moment, Mike slammed his fist into the brick wall. It was like a battering ram. The bricks shifted and gave way, crumbling into a space beyond under his onslaught.

"Well, that works," Lucian said.

It didn't take Mike long to create an opening large enough for them to squeeze through. Mike relaxed, and his arm returned to normal.

Emma jumped over the rubble. They followed her lead, squeezing through the narrow opening one by one. On the other side, they found themselves in a large chamber, the ceiling arching high above them. The beams of their headlamps revealed massive stone columns, each carved with intricate designs eroded by time.

On the opposite side of the chamber stood a cell with iron bars, a chained skeleton lying within. Nearby, a fire pit held cold ashes as if abandoned only yesterday.

"This is incredible," Dora whispered, her eyes wide as she took in the scene. The eerie setting was both captivating and unsettling, the silence heavy around them.

"What is this place?" Nomad asked, his voice low.

Lucian stepped forward. "Some kind of prison maybe. Torture chamber? Hard to tell."

Mike closed his eyes, sensing the earth's energies. "There's something unusual about this place. The ground feels…different."

Dora felt a chill run down her spine. "How old do you think this is?"

"Centuries," Nomad replied, his voice hushed.

"This is like what Howard described—Ivanov's story." Dora felt an inexplicable pull toward the ashes. She knelt beside the fire pit, the others watching silently. *I need to see,* she thought but couldn't understand why.

"Be careful," Anja warned.

"It's okay," Dora reassured her. "I just want to see…" She reached out, hesitating for a moment before allowing her fingertips to brush the surface of the ashes.

Instantly, a surge of visions flooded her mind—flashes of torchlight, shadows dancing on stone walls, voices chanting in a language she didn't recognize. The air was thick with tension, fear, and something else—something ancient and powerful. The intensity of it all overwhelmed her senses, a cacophony of sights and sounds crashing over her like a tidal wave.

"Dora!" Anja exclaimed, rushing to her side as she collapsed onto the cold stone floor.

Everything went white.

Twenty-Nine

Igor Krakarov stood by the windows of his office, glaring down at the streets. A cold fury simmered beneath his composed exterior, his mind racing.

It had been a day since the fiasco. The team he had assembled, seasoned operatives known for their efficiency and discretion, had been wiped out. Not a single survivor. The mission had been straightforward: intercept Yakov's men and the supposed drug smugglers, eliminate any loose ends, and secure the shipment for themselves. Instead, all his men were dead, and the shipment was lost.

He turned away from the window. The folder on his desk remained open. Gruesome photographs of the aftermath stared back at him. Vehicles had been reduced to twisted charred metal, and bodies were strewn across the road. The initial analysis suggested explosions from unknown sources had demolished their SUVs. His men had been caught off guard—an embarrassment he could not tolerate.

Igor clenched his jaw as he reviewed the reports. The evidence pointed to a firefight breaking out between his team and Yakov's men. That in itself was perplexing; Yakov's men had been supposed to cooperate, unaware that they were being set up. The plan had accounted for their elimination, of course, but only after the transfer was complete. That they would end up dead prematurely was inconvenient but of little consequence. However, the loss of his own men and the cargo was another matter entirely.

One detail nagged at him. Among the dead was a man initially identified as Lev, but further investigation revealed he was one of Yakov's underlings. The real Lev was unaccounted for, which only added to the mounting list of concerns.

Igor picked up his phone and dialed. It rang twice before Yakov's gruff voice answered. "Yes?"

"We need to talk," Igor said, his tone icy.

"About what?"

"About why your men resisted my team's approach. They were supposed to cooperate, yet a firefight ensued. Care to explain?"

There was a brief pause on the other end. "I don't know what you're talking about. My men are reliable. They had orders to follow the plan."

"Reliable?" Igor scoffed. "They're all dead, along with my men. The shipment is missing. This debacle has your fingerprints all over it."

Yakov's voice sharpened. "Are you accusing me of something, Krakarov? Perhaps it was you who planned a double-cross, aiming to take everything for yourself. My men are dead? Why in hell is that my fault?"

Igor's grip tightened on the phone. "Watch your tongue. You forget who you're speaking to."

"No, you forget," Yakov snapped. "We had an arrangement. If things went wrong, perhaps you should look at your own incompetence."

A vein throbbed at Igor's temple. "Careful, Yakov. I don't take kindly to insults."

"Nor do I appreciate being set up," Yakov fired back. "Maybe you intended for my men to be collateral damage while you reaped the benefits."

Igor took a deep breath, reining in his temper. "This is getting us nowhere. What about Kasia? Do you have any information on her whereabouts?"

There was a bitter laugh from Yakov. "So, she's vanished again, has she? That woman is more trouble than she's worth."

"She was your responsibility. And now she's unaccounted for."

Yakov's tone turned mocking. "Seems like you're losing your touch, Krakarov. Lev and Kasia had the formula. The samples they left were perfect. The cunt always did have a knack for slipping away. Maybe you should handle your own mess."

Before Igor could respond, the line went dead. He stared at the phone, rage growing. Yakov's insolence was intolerable, but open conflict would be costly. For now, he needed information.

He pressed a button on his intercom. "Get me Yuri," he ordered.

"Right away, sir," his assistant replied.

Igor returned to his desk, closed the folder, and pushed it to one side. If Yakov was telling the truth, then someone else had interfered with the operation. Perhaps an unknown third party was making a move, or worse, someone within his organization was undermining him.

A knock at the door signaled Yuri's arrival. "You wanted to see me?"

"Yes," Igor said, motioning for him to enter. "I need you to dig deeper into the events of yesterday. Find out who else could have been involved. I want names, affiliations, and anything you can uncover. Put a trace on the missing IDs and phones. If they are used anywhere, I want to know. It's top priority. Also, increase the priority on face identification for the four missing. I want them found."

Yuri nodded. "Understood. I'll get on it immediately."

"And Yuri," Igor added, his gaze steely, "keep this discreet. I don't want word of our setbacks to reach the wrong ears. Figure out a cover story to explain the bodies."

"Of course."

As Yuri left, Igor leaned back in his chair, clenching his fists. The pieces weren't adding up, and he didn't like it. Whoever was responsible for this affront would pay dearly.

Igor stood and returned to the window. The city stretched out before him, a panorama of lights and shadows. He had risen to power through cunning and ruthlessness, and he would not let this setback derail his ambitions.

"Enjoy your games while you can, Yakov," he muttered to himself. "Soon enough, the board will be cleared."

Igor turned away from the nightscape. There was much to be done, and he would not rest until order was restored. Next on his list was following up on Helena. He doubted she was involved, but he couldn't be too careful.

Helena awoke with a start, the remnants of vivid dreams clinging to her consciousness like the morning mist. The first light of dawn filtered through the heavy drapes, casting a glow across the ornate bedroom. She turned her head to the side, her gaze settling on Jasmina, her maid, who lay asleep beside her. Jasmina's dark hair fanned out over the pillows, her features serene. Yet, even in repose, she couldn't compare to the ethereal beauty of Anja.

Anja. The very thought of her sent a heat coursing through Helena's veins. Memories of their encounter flooded back—the intensity of Anja's eyes, the electricity of her touch. Helena felt a familiar warmth stirring within her, but she quelled it swiftly. Such distractions were perilous.

She slipped from the silk sheets and pulled on a satin robe. She tied it securely around her waist and moved toward the window. Parting the heavy drapes, she looked out over the mist-shrouded lake below. The world beyond was waking, but inside, Helena's mind was already racing.

She knew she was treading a dangerous path. Her desire to ally with Anja and her group was fraught with risk. The Grandmaster was vigilant, and any hint of betrayal would seal her fate. She needed a new plan—one that would allow her to continue without arousing suspicion.

Leaving the bedroom, Helena made her way through the dimly lit corridors to her private study. The castle held secrets, much like the organization she served. Her footsteps echoed against the polished marble floors until she reached the heavy oak door.

She settled into the high-backed chair behind her intricately carved desk and activated the encrypted terminal. As the screen flickered to life, lines of data began to scroll.

Her fingers moved over the keyboard as she accessed the latest intelligence reports. First, she searched for any updates on Lucian. According to the surveillance, he'd been expected at NexGen's headquarters days ago. Yet the records showed that he had never arrived. There were no sightings, no communications—he had simply vanished.

Helena's brows knitted in concentration. She cross-referenced the data, searching for any anomalies that might explain his disappearance. Her search led her to another unsettling discovery: Isabelle, the CEO of NexGen, was also unaccounted for. Reports claimed she was working remotely, but there was no digital footprint to support this—not her typically active presence.

A sense of unease settled over Helena. Two influential figures disappearing was no coincidence.

She needed guidance—or at least, she needed to appear as though she sought it. With a measured breath, Helena initiated a secure communication channel with Grandmaster Eamon. The connection was established swiftly, and his stern visage materialized on the screen.

"Helena," he greeted, his voice as cold and precise as ever. "I trust you have news."

"Grandmaster." She inclined her head respectfully. "I have updates regarding Lucian and NexGen."

"Proceed," he commanded.

"Our surveillance indicates that Lucian did not arrive at NexGen as scheduled," she reported. "Also, there is no evidence of his presence at known facilities. Additionally, NexGen's CEO, Isabelle Sinclair, has withdrawn from all known engagements. She's reportedly working from a remote location, but we lack any verifiable data on her activities."

"That is…concerning. You need to find them."

"It appears they have another hole to hide in," Helena replied. It was a gamble. She did not want them to be found too soon. "Given their simultaneous absences, we must assume they're together. She appears to be associated with Anja and the others."

At the mention of Anja, the Grandmaster's expression hardened. "Anja continues to be a thorn in our side."

"Agreed," Helena said, suppressing any hint of personal interest. "I recommend increasing our surveillance efforts. Perhaps dispatching additional operatives to key locations could yield results."

Eamon regarded her thoughtfully. "Your initiative is noted. However, we must proceed with caution. Overextension could expose vulnerabilities."

"Of course, Grandmaster," she acquiesced.

He leaned forward slightly. "Helena, I trust you understand the gravity of this situation. Failure is not an option."

"Yes, Grandmaster. I'm fully committed to resolving these issues."

"See that you are," he replied curtly. "Keep me informed of any developments."

With that, the screen went dark, leaving Helena alone once more. She leaned back in her chair, exhaling slowly. Navigating the intricacies of politics was a delicate dance—one misstep could prove fatal.

She needed to act swiftly.

Her thoughts were interrupted by a knock at the door. "Enter," she called.

Jasmina stepped in. "I noticed you were gone when I woke," she said. "Is everything all right?"

Helena offered a reassuring smile. "Yes, Jasmina. Just attending to some early matters. There's much to be done."

"Can I bring you anything?" the maid asked. "Breakfast, perhaps? Or tea?"

"Tea would be lovely," Helena replied. "Thank you."

As Jasmina left to fulfill the request, Helena considered her next moves.

Returning to her desk, she began composing a series of encrypted messages. Codes within codes, designed to convey her intentions only to those who knew how to decipher them.

Minutes later, Jasmina returned with a silver tray bearing a delicate porcelain teapot and a single cup. She set it down on the desk. "Is there anything else you require?"

Helena looked up, momentarily appreciating the maid's loyalty. "That will be all for now," she said. "Thank you."

Jasmina hesitated for a moment. "If I may, mistress...you seem troubled."

Helena's gaze softened. "Just the weight of responsibility, my dear. Nothing more."

The maid nodded. "Very well. I'll be nearby if you need anything."

As Jasmina departed, Helena poured herself a cup of tea, the fragrant steam rising in delicate tendrils. She took a sip, allowing the warmth to steady her.

She had to outmaneuver the Grandmaster, forge an alliance with Anja, and ensure her own survival—all without revealing her hand too soon. She would have her revenge. It had already been too long coming.

She knew that leaving the safety of the castle was unwise. The Grandmaster's watchful eyes extended far, and any unexpected movements could arouse suspicion. Yet the need to uncover Lucian and Anja's whereabouts pressed heavily upon her. Yes, Eamon had assigned her the task of locating them, but she had to find them before he did. She did not doubt that he would use other avenues to search.

If she could not go to England herself, she would have to rely on trusted operatives to act on her behalf.

Turning to her desk, Helena activated the encrypted communication console again. Her fingers moved swiftly over the keyboard as she composed a secure message to the controller in London—a high-ranking member of the Sodality responsible for overseeing operations in the UK. Eamon would likely see this action, but that would just reinforce the narrative of her efforts.

Priority one directive, she typed. *Recent intelligence suggests activity at the Miller estate in Kent. Dispatch a discreet team to investigate and report any findings related to Lucian or associated parties. Maintain utmost secrecy. Awaiting confirmation.*

She encrypted the message using a cipher known only to the highest levels and sent it through a secure channel. Leaning back, she steepled her fingers and considered the implications. The controller was efficient and, more importantly, loyal—to Eamon.

Moments later, the console chimed. A response had arrived.

Directive received and acknowledged. Team will be mobilized. Will report findings directly to you. Controller out.

Satisfied, Helena allowed herself a brief respite. She rose from her chair and moved toward the fireplace, the warmth a stark contrast to the chill seeping into her bones. The flames danced hypnotically, and her thoughts drifted inevitably back to Anja.

Anja—enigmatic, powerful, and the source of an intrigue that

Helena found both exhilarating and dangerous. Their brief encounters had left a mark deeper than she cared to admit. Anja possessed qualities that could challenge even the Grandmaster, and perhaps, with the right alignment, they could confront him together.

But trust was a rare commodity. Could Helena truly trust Anja? And would Anja trust her, knowing her position within the Sodality?

She sat one more time and went back to scanning reports and files.

A knock at the door pulled her from her focus. "Enter," she called.

Jasmina stepped inside, her demeanor poised yet attentive. "You requested to be informed when dinner is served, mistress."

Startled by the passage of time, Helena looked at her maid and then the clock on her screen. "Thank you, Jasmina," Helena replied with a faint smile. "I will join you shortly."

The maid hesitated. "Is there anything else you require?"

Helena considered for a moment. "Actually, yes. Please ensure that I'm not disturbed for the remainder of the evening after dinner. I have matters that require my full attention."

"Of course." Jasmina nodded before exiting the room. Helena noted Jasmina's look of disappointment. Perhaps her dalliances were giving her maid ideas above her station. It did not matter and would not change the situation.

Waiting was always the most challenging part. She needed to keep herself occupied. Pulling out her leather-bound journal, she began to jot down her thoughts—encrypted musings that only she could decipher.

Anja's abilities could tip the balance, she wrote. *If we were to combine resources, perhaps the Grandmaster's hold could be broken. But the risks are immense. Mutual distrust must be overcome.*

She paused, tapping the pen against her lips. The Grandmaster was not invincible, she hoped, but he was deeply entrenched in power that spanned the globe. Any move against him would require meticulous planning and absolute secrecy.

Her mind wandered back to their last encounter—the intensity of Anja's gaze, the unspoken understanding that had passed between them. There was a connection. Perhaps Anja was bound by it, too, now. That thought gave her comfort.

Helena closed the journal and locked it away in a concealed

drawer. She needed to find a way to reach out to Anja without exposing herself. Waiting for Anja to return to her dreams was frustrating in more ways than she cared to admit to herself.

A vibration from the console indicated another incoming message. Her heartbeat quickened as she accessed it.

Preliminary report: team has arrived at Miller estate. It's occupied, but security is extensive. Will continue surveillance and listen for rumors among the locals. Further updates to follow.

She exhaled slowly. At least that operation was underway. With any luck, they would uncover something—an overlooked clue, a trace of their presence, anything that could guide her next steps.

The shadows in the room lengthened as evening settled in. Helena stood and made her way to the dining hall, where a solitary meal awaited her. The grandeur of the castle often felt hollow now, the vast spaces emphasizing her isolation and the absence of Anja.

As she dined, her thoughts remained on the unfolding situation. If Lucian and Anja were at the Miller estate or had left traces behind, it could provide the advantage she needed. Information was power, and with it, she could create a path toward an alliance, or at least an understanding, with Anja.

The Grandmaster's patience was finite, and his suspicions could be easily aroused.

Returning to her study after dinner, Helena settled into a high-backed chair by the fireplace, a glass of wine cradled in her hand. The warmth of the flames did little to ease the chill of uncertainty.

"Anja," she whispered into the quiet room. "What are you planning? Where are you? Will you come to me again?"

The crackling of the fire was her only reply.

If she reached out and Anja rejected her overture, it could spell disaster. Worse, if the Grandmaster learned of her intentions, there would be no escape from his wrath.

Yet doing nothing was equally perilous. The balance of power was shifting, and she needed to position herself.

As the night deepened, Helena resolved to take the chance. She would craft a message—carefully coded and routed through secure channels—that might reach Anja. It was a gamble, but one she was willing to take.

Rising, she moved to her desk and began drafting an email to the address in her file. Each word was chosen with precision, layers of meaning woven into the text. Only someone with Anja's insight would be able to interpret it.

Old paths converge once more, she wrote. *A shadow seeks the light, bound by common threads unseen. Trust is fragile, but necessity compels action. Should you wish to explore possibilities, a reply will find its way.*

She encrypted the message and set it to transmit through a series of relays that would mask its origin. Leaning back, she felt a mix of apprehension and anticipation.

Now, all she could do was wait.

The castle around her was silent, the weight of centuries pressing in. Helena gazed into the fire's dying embers, her thoughts a tangle of strategy and desire.

Perhaps, just perhaps, she and Anja could find a way to confront the Grandmaster together.

Thirty

DORA HAD FELT herself falling as visions had come crashing in. It had all gone white before resolving into another time long ago. She was not lying on the floor but floating above the fire in the same chamber beneath the Kremlin. The chamber was lit by flickering torches and the fire beneath her in the middle of the room. The air was thick with the scent of pine smoke, and the walls were adorned with tapestries depicting scenes of Russian grandeur. The grim chamber had been transformed.

A towering figure stood, draped in opulent robes of deep crimson and gold embroidery. His stature was imposing, his shoulders broad beneath layers of rich fabric. A long, silvery beard cascaded down his chest, framing a face etched with lines of authority and burden. His eyes, piercing and dark beneath heavy brows, held a fierce intensity. In his hand, he grasped a scepter adorned with intricate carvings and encrusted with precious gems that caught the firelight, casting prismatic reflections.

Kneeling before him was a man bound in heavy iron chains that clinked with his trembling. His once-fine garments were torn and soiled. His hair was disheveled, and a scrape darkened his cheekbone. Fear danced in his eyes as he glanced upward, only to avert his gaze under the weight of the towering man's stare.

Flanking the robed figure were two men. The younger stood calmly. He was of average height, and his build was sturdy. His dark hair was neatly kept, and a well-groomed beard framed his thoughtful face. Beside him, the other was slightly taller, his features sharper, with gray flecks in his beard. He looked wary.

The imposing man addressed the man in chains with cold authority. "You have betrayed me, Alexei. Whispers have reached my ears that you shared our most guarded secrets with those who would see me falter."

Dora recognized the harsh syllables of his words but somehow understood their meaning.

"You have betrayed my trust. For this, you shall be consigned to oblivion within these walls."

Alexei shook his head fervently. "Mercy, my tsar! I am loyal to you above all. Such accusations are falsehoods spread by my enemies."

"Silence!" the tsar commanded, his grip tightening on the scepter. "Do not take me for a fool. Documents bearing your seal have been seized—proof of your treachery. You consort with foreign spies, revealing knowledge that is forbidden. Betrayal against the tsar is a crime punishable by death."

The tsar turned to the men, and his gaze softened slightly, though the intensity remained. "Maksim, Nikita," he intoned, "the shadows creep upon us. Some covet my throne and the treasures embodying my legacy. Our realm's legacy. I will not bow to them or anyone. Maksim, Nikita, step forward."

They obeyed, bowing deeply. "Your Majesty," they said in unison.

"I have a matter of utmost importance," he began. "As you have witnessed, there are those who seek to undermine my work—work that is vital to the future of Russia. Certain…studies I have undertaken must be protected. Knowledge not meant for the unworthy must be kept far from prying eyes."

Nikita nodded. "We understand, sire. What would you have us do?"

"I entrust you with relocating my most precious volumes and artifacts—my Liberia," he said. "They must be moved from Moscow to a place where they will be safe from traitors and foreign agents until they are dealt with."

Dora suddenly realized she was witnessing Ivan the Terrible's greatest secret—the fate of the Golden Library.

Maksim glanced at Nikita before replying, "We are honored by your trust, Your Majesty. Our family's reach extends far; we can ensure the safe passage of your treasures."

"Good," Ivan responded. "Your family's ventures beyond the Urals are well known, and the House of Stroganov has earned my trust. The east holds vast lands where few dare to tread. Take my library there, and guard it with your lives."

"The east, sire?" Nikita inquired.

"Yes. To the forests and mountains, where the expanses are endless. There, my knowledge will remain hidden until the time is right."

"We are at your service, my tsar," Maksim replied.

Nikita inclined his head. "We are honored by your trust. We shall guard the library with our lives."

Maksim added, "No harm shall come to these artifacts, nor shall their existence be known."

The tsar nodded solemnly. "This oath must be sealed in blood." He unsheathed an ornate dagger.

The men each took the dagger without hesitation, drawing it across their palms. Crimson lines appeared on their skin. Ivan raised his scepter. "Place your hands upon it," he commanded.

They clasped the scepter, their bloodied hands curled around the shaft. A tremor seemed to ripple through the chamber—a fleeting sensation.

"By this oath," the tsar declared, his voice echoing, "you are bound to secrecy and unwavering loyalty. Let no force on earth or beyond break this vow."

They both repeated their oath, and Dora felt a pulse in the vision.

"We shall depart immediately to make preparations," Maksim assured him. "Your treasures will be secured."

Ivan's expression softened marginally. "See that it is done swiftly and without error. Erase all traces here and seal off these chambers."

"By your command, my tsar," both men replied, bowing again.

As they exited the hall, Dora trailed behind, her presence unnoticed as she moved like a ghost from one torch to the next. She listened to the two cousins speaking in hushed tones.

"This is a great responsibility," Nikita remarked. "The tsar places much faith in us."

"Indeed," Maksim agreed. "We must assemble a trusted entourage —men who will not question our mission."

"Do you think the rumors are true?" Nikita asked after a pause. "That the tsar dabbles in the arcane? Black magic?"

Maksim glanced around before answering. "It's not our place to judge. That's in God's hands. We serve as we are commanded."

"Still, moving such knowledge...it could bring unforeseen consequences."

"Perhaps," Maksim conceded. "But our family's legacy is built upon loyalty and duty. We will fulfill the tsar's wishes and ensure the library is hidden where no one can find it. Perhaps that is our divine calling."

They exited the palace into the crisp night air. The Kremlin stood silhouetted against a star-strewn sky. The cousins mounted and rode off to begin their preparations.

The scene shifted, and Dora found herself back inside the underground chamber. This time, Ivan stood alone before the fire—the same fire whose ashes Dora had touched. He held a small, ornate box, which he placed into the flames.

"Let all traces of betrayal be consumed," he intoned. "Only the loyal shall prevail."

A sense of finality settled over the room as the flames engulfed the box. Ivan turned and walked away, his footsteps fading into silence.

The vision began to fade, and Dora felt herself being pulled back to the present in another flash of white. The ancient chamber reformed around her, and the cold and darkness returned. She gasped, her senses reeling as she tried to process what she had witnessed.

Anja's voice broke through the haze. "...Dora! Are you all right?"

Dora blinked, focusing on Anja's face. "I...I saw them," she managed to say. "Ivan the Terrible, the Stroganov brothers. They were here."

Anja knelt beside her. "What did you see?"

Dora took a deep breath. "Ivan discovered a traitor—Alexei. After dealing with him, he entrusted his secret library to Maksim and Nikita of the Stroganov family. They were to take it eastward."

She recounted her vision. It was so vivid.

"The east..." Lucian mused.

Anja nodded thoughtfully. "It would explain why there's no record of it here—why it has never been found. They moved it."

Nomad folded his arms. "If that's true, then the library—or what's left of it—could still be out there. I guess this wasn't a fool's errand after all."

Dora looked around the room. "Perhaps not all could be moved. Or maybe this chamber served as a decoy to mislead those who might come searching."

Anja helped Dora to her feet. "What matters is that we have a new lead. The Stroganovs took the library east. We might uncover its resting place if we can trace its path."

Lucian agreed. "It's not here anymore."

As they exited the chamber, Dora looked back at the fire pit. The ashes were still cold and undisturbed, yet they had opened a window into a significant historical moment.

She whispered, "Anja?"

"Shhh, we can talk about this later," Anja whispered back.

Anja led the way through the dimly lit tunnel, her footsteps echoing against the damp stone walls. The air was thick with the scent of earth. Behind her, Lucian, Mike, Dora, Nomad, and Emma moved in a line, their faces illuminated by the glow of their headlamps.

Reaching the spot where the floor had collapsed under Nomad earlier, Anja paused. The rope they had used to descend dangled from the jagged edge above. She looked up, her keen eyes searching the opening. "We'll need to climb back up."

Nomad nodded. "I'll go first." He tested the rope's strength before hoisting himself upward, muscles straining as he moved along the uneven wall. One by one, the others followed until only Anja and Dora remained below.

"Go ahead," Anja urged.

Dora hesitated briefly before gripping the rope and ascending. Anja watched her until she disappeared over the edge, then followed.

At the top, they regrouped. The narrow passage was silent except for the distant drip of water. Anja looked around, her brow furrowing. "Where's Deepcore?"

Nomad knelt, examining the ground. "There are footprints leading away from here. Looks like he waited for a while, then left."

Anja sighed. "I told him to wait. I should have been more specific and told him to stay until we returned."

Mike shrugged. "Can't blame him entirely. This place would spook anyone."

"At least we know the way back," Lucian said. "Between the two of us, we won't get lost."

Anja nodded, pulling herself from her thoughts. "Let's keep moving. The sooner we're out of here, the better."

They followed the maze-like tunnels, retracing their steps. The oppressive darkness seemed to lighten as they neared the exit, the air growing less stagnant.

At the base of the final ladder, Mike gestured upward. "I'll go first and check."

He climbed, then paused beneath the manhole cover. With a push, he lifted it just enough to peer outside. After a moment, he glanced back down. "All clear," he whispered.

Mike turned off his headlamp and slipped out onto the street. He was followed closely by Nomad. Emma jumped up on Lucian's shoulders as he climbed out. Dora, and finally Anja, made it out onto the street. They moved away from the entrance, blending into the early morning shadows of Moscow's streets.

The trip back to Katya's establishment was silent and uneventful. Upon arrival, they entered through a discreet side entrance. Zoe had anticipated their return; fresh towels and clean clothes were laid out in the common area adjoining their suites.

"Let's get cleaned up," Nomad suggested, glancing down at his dirt-smudged attire. "We could all use it."

"What should we do with the lights and boots and stuff?" Graham asked.

"Stow them with the weapons," Lucian decided.

Emma and Zoe, more for relaxation than cleanliness, decided to share one of the larger bathrooms. Laughter and the sound of running water drifted through the hallway.

When Zoe emerged naked, she glanced around, then crouched next to the couch where Karolina sat with her legs folded under her. Karolina didn't seem to notice—or mind.

"I just wanted to check in with you," Zoe said. "You've been through…well, too much. If the way some of us—me, Emma, Anja—are about…you know, being naked sometimes? If that bothers you, you need to tell me. Okay?"

Karolina's brows furrowed for a second, then she shook her head, though her cheeks pinked a little. "No…no problem. Is fine."

"You're sure? It's not strange to you? I know you're young, and—"

Karolina cut in, shy but firm. "In Ukraine is not big thing. In house, at river, is okay. Just normal."

That drew a warm laugh out of Zoe, who grinned. "You're more grown-up about it than some adults I know."

Karolina gave a small, hesitant smile. "You worry much. But is okay. You all help me. I not judge."

"I think she'll fit in just fine. She'll be okay," Zoe sent to Anja.

"She will," Anja sent back as she went to find Dora. She was alone in the sitting room, a distant look in her eyes. Recognizing the weight of the visions Dora had experienced, Anja approached her gently. "Dora, could we talk for a moment?"

Dora looked up, her gaze clearing. "Of course."

"Let's go somewhere more private," Anja suggested.

They moved to one of the quieter rooms, away from the bustle of the others settling back in. Anja closed the door behind them and gestured for Dora to take a seat on a plush armchair. She settled across from her, the glow of a lamp casting warm light.

"How are you feeling?" Anja asked, her tone compassionate.

Dora sighed, clasping her hands in her lap. "I'm…not sure. What I saw down there—felt so real, like I was there in the past."

Anja nodded thoughtfully. "You experienced a powerful vision. Touching those ashes must have triggered something."

"I saw Ivan the Terrible," Dora continued. "He confronted a traitor and then entrusted his secret library to two of the Stroganov brothers to be taken east. I was watching history unfold firsthand."

Anja studied her closely. "This isn't the first time you've had visions, is it?"

Dora shook her head. "No, but they've never been this intense. Usually, it's just glimpses or feelings, not full scenes with dialogue and details."

Anja leaned forward slightly. "I think you have a unique gift, Dora. An ability to connect with the past, to witness events through remnants left behind."

"Like some form of psychometry?" Dora asked.

"Similar, but perhaps more specialized," Anja mused. "You seem to have an affinity for fire and ashes—a rebirth of history through the remnants of flames."

"It's strange. I've always felt a connection to fire, but I never understood why."

"Do you remember the fire that..." Anja paused. "The one from your childhood?"

Dora's eyes clouded. "When my father died. Yes, I survived, but I never knew how."

"Maybe it's not just a coincidence," Anja suggested. "Perhaps your connection to fire is deeper than you realize. It could be the source of your abilities—those you had before your awakening. Now, after the ritual, your abilities have grown."

Dora's cheeks flushed at the mention of the ritual. "What are you saying?"

Anja chose her words carefully. "I believe that you have a natural resilience to fire, an innate connection that protects you and allows you to access echoes of the past tied to it. Like a form of pyromancy—seeing visions through flames and ashes."

Dora absorbed this information, her mind racing. "But why me? How is that even possible?"

"There are many things in this world that defy explanation. Sometimes, our true natures are hidden, even from ourselves."

Dora looked down at her hands, turning them over as if seeing them for the first time. "It's overwhelming to think about."

"I understand," Anja assured her. "But you're not alone. We're all discovering parts of ourselves we didn't know existed."

Dora met her gaze. "Have you ever felt something similar?"

Anja smiled faintly. "In my way, yes. I sometimes glimpse versions of the future like yours of the past."

A comfortable silence settled between them. After a moment, Dora spoke again. "Do you think these visions are meant to guide us?"

"Yes," Anja said. "They're showing us the way forward, helping us piece together the mystery we're trying to solve."

Dora took a deep breath. "Then I want to understand this part of me better. Maybe it can help us find Ivan's library."

Anja reached out and placed a reassuring hand on Dora's arm. "It already has. It's out there somewhere. I'm more convinced of that than ever."

"Thank you," Dora replied sincerely. "That means a lot."

Just then, there was a knock on the door. Emma poked her head in, her damp hair cascading over her shoulders. "Sorry to interrupt," she said with an impish grin. "Zoe and I were wondering if anyone's hungry."

Anja glanced at Dora. "I think that's a great idea."

Dora stood up, her demeanor lighter. "Agreed. I'm starving."

They joined the others in the dining area, where the table was set with a variety of dishes. Someone, probably Mike, had lit the fireplace, creating a warm and lively atmosphere, the earlier tensions melting away. She noted that Zoe was still nude, and Emma seemed to be picking up the habit.

In this company, and after Zoe's conversation with Karolina, it didn't seem that strange. Nobody seemed to care. It was just a new normal.

As they ate, the conversation flowed easily. Mike recounted a humorous tale from their underground trek, exaggerating his heroics, and teased Emma about chasing after rats.

"Hey, being a cat has advantages, and I didn't chase the rats; they just ran in fear. Besides, Zoe is jealous that I don't have to wear anything as a cat. Kinda got used to it on the trip here. Too much bother dressing only to strip again."

"I guess I'm rubbing off on her," Zoe commented.

"You can rub…" Emma quipped before being cut off.

"We get the idea," Anja said, but couldn't help smiling.

Zoe rolled her eyes.

Later, as the evening wound down, Lucian approached Anja by the fireplace. "How's Dora holding up?" he asked.

"She's processing a lot," Anja replied. "But she's discovering new abilities."

Lucian nodded thoughtfully. "She's stronger than she realizes."

"Yes," Anja agreed. "And she'll need that strength for what's to come."

He looked at her, his eyes reflecting the flickering firelight. "We all will."

Anja reached out and took his hand. "We'll face it together."

He squeezed her hand gently. "Always."

As the rest of the team headed off to their rooms, exhausted from the day's events, Anja stayed behind for a moment. She stared into the fading embers of the fireplace, reflecting on Dora. Her mind wandered to the future—the quest for Ivan's lost library, its hidden secrets, and the inevitable challenges they would face.

Thirty-One

IGOR KRAKAROV SAT behind his desk, the dim glow of his computer screen casting sharp angles across his stern features. The opulence of his Moscow office did little to soften the hardened lines etched by years of his clandestine activities. He leaned back in his leather chair, eyes narrowed as he reviewed the latest reports from his operatives stationed near Zamec Echo—the imposing castle in Poland where Helena resided.

"Pretentious bitch," he muttered under his breath, a wry smirk tugging at the corner of his mouth. Despite the sparse reporting, it was clear she remained holed up there. She had not left, but Igor was nothing if not persistent.

He tapped a few keys, pulling up a log of her recent communications. One entry caught his attention: a secure message dispatched to the controller in England. Helena had ordered a pair of assets to investigate the Miller estate in Kent. "So, she's retracing old steps," he mused. "Perhaps Lucian and his little circle never made it to Geneva after all."

This development intrigued him. It warranted closer scrutiny if Helena suspected that Lucian was still at the Miller estate. Igor made a mental note to increase surveillance on the estate and intercept any findings from Helena's operatives. He couldn't afford to let valuable information slip by.

A knock on the door pulled him from his thoughts. Yuri, his trusted lieutenant, stepped inside, closing the door behind him.

"I have an update," Yuri announced.

"Go on," Igor prompted, steepling his fingers.

Yuri approached the desk and handed over a thin dossier. "Our teams conducted a routine sweep in the city center and picked up a known Diggerstvo—an urban explorer."

Igor arched an eyebrow. "And what of it? These diggers are a nuisance but hardly a priority."

"Normally, yes," Yuri conceded. "But during questioning, he admitted to guiding a group into the tunnels. They expressed interest in certain underground areas."

Igor's interest piqued. "Did he provide descriptions?"

Yuri nodded. "He described five individuals. I thought it prudent to show him photographs of the persons we're actively searching for."

"And?" Igor leaned forward, his gaze intense.

"He positively identified two of them," Yuri confirmed. "Kasia, and one of the two who were with her before. One of her muscle."

"Kasia again. She keeps turning up." Igor paused, considering the implications. "And the other three?"

"The digger described a man with dark hair of average build and a woman with deep red hair. He couldn't recall much more. The third man was Russian and seemed to be the one directing the group. I had the digger released and placed under surveillance, but so far, he's led us nowhere of significance."

Igor tapped his fingers on the desk. *So, Kasia is in Moscow, exploring underground tunnels with companions who match the descriptions of Lucian Miller and Anja Kinsey,* he thought. *Who was the other?* "This is quite the development. Good fortune."

"It seems so," Yuri agreed.

Igor's mind raced. "What of surveillance footage? Have we reviewed cameras in the area where the digger emerged?"

"Not yet," Yuri admitted. "I wanted to brief you first."

"Get on it immediately," Igor ordered. "I want eyes on every angle. If they didn't exit through the streets, they might still be underground or using alternative routes."

"Understood," Yuri replied. "I'll have the team start combing through the footage right away."

Igor pulled up the files on Anja Kinsey and Lucian Miller. "I'll forward you some photos that I suspect will match the redhead and one of the men the digger described. If they match, let me know immediately."

"Yes, sir."

"Good." Igor stood, moving to gaze out the window at the city lights sprawled beneath him. It changed things if Lucian and Anja were here. "Our priorities need to shift."

"Should we mobilize additional resources?"

"Yes, but discreetly. We don't want to alert them to our awareness. Pull in a DKRO agent to take charge of the search. Pick one of my better trainees whom they stole from me. Warn him to keep it quiet and report only to us."

"The FSB will not be happy loaning us one of theirs. They're focused on Ukraine and are overextended."

"They're better suited to operations like this inside of Russia."

Igor considered his options as Yuri left. The Grandmaster valued timely intelligence, and withholding information could have severe repercussions. However, delivering half-formed theories might reflect poorly on Igor.

Alone again, Igor returned to his desk. The convergence of Lucian, Anja, and Kasia in Moscow was an unexpected twist, but one that could play to his advantage. If he could apprehend them, or, better yet, uncover their plans, his standing with the Grandmaster would be significantly enhanced.

He pulled up profiles on Lucian Miller and Anja Kinsey again. Both were formidable in their own right—resourceful, intelligent, and notoriously difficult to track. Their involvement would suggest a deeper objective, perhaps something linked to the city's subterranean secrets.

"What are you after?" Igor murmured to himself. "And how does Kasia fit into all of this?"

His cellphone buzzed. "Report."

"Sir, we found surveillance video of a group approaching where the digger claimed to lead them underground. They match the images of Kasia, Lucian, Anja, and one of Kasia's guards. The fifth we still haven't identified."

There was no Sodality file on Kasia. She was more than she appeared, but who was she? He needed to find out. Their collective goal must be significant.

Igor's thoughts shifted to the Diggerstvo guide. If the group had been exploring the tunnels, perhaps they sought something hidden beneath the city. Moscow's underground was a labyrinth of history—catacombs, forgotten bunkers, and relics from eras past.

He picked up the phone and dialed a secure line. After a brief pause, a voice answered on the other end.

"Lieutenant General Krakarov," the voice acknowledged.

"Initiate a full sweep of all known access points to the underground tunnels," Igor commanded. "Deploy teams to monitor activity discreetly. Use unmarked units—no overt presence. Use some of my trainees. They like to play in the tunnels. I want real-time updates on any sightings or movements."

Ending the call, Igor leaned back. If he could outmaneuver Lucian and Anja, he could secure whatever prize they sought and eliminate them as threats in the process.

He glanced at the clock. It was late, but the Grandmaster would expect immediate notification of such developments. Igor steeled himself and began composing a detailed report, ensuring that all pertinent information was included without revealing any personal ambitions.

As he typed, a cold determination settled over him. The stakes had indeed skyrocketed, but Igor Krakarov was not one to shy away from high-risk, high-reward situations. This was his arena—a game of shadows and intrigue where only the cunning and ruthless prevailed.

"Let's see how you play your hand, Lucian," he said. "But know this—I've already begun to stack the deck."

With the report finalized, Igor prepared to send it through the encrypted channel reserved for communications with the Grandmaster. He hesitated for just a moment, contemplating the path ahead.

Then, with a decisive click, the message was sent.

Igor stood and gazed out once more at the sprawling cityscape of Moscow. Beneath its surface, secrets stirred, and he was determined to bring them to light.

Grandmaster Eamon Vale leaned back in his chair as he contemplated the report on the holographic screen.

Eagle's communiqué from Moscow flickered softly. It seemed a fortuitous coincidence that Eagle had been in place when Lucian and Anja had resurfaced. They were now trapped within Russia's borders. The thought brought a thin smile to Eamon's lips.

"Trapped like rats," he mused. But questions lingered. Were the rest of Lucian's circle with them? For them to risk venturing into such a place, their motive must be compelling.

"What could they be after?" he pondered aloud. "Are they trying to track Richard?" The possibility seemed remote. Helena had sent Richard's shoe, complete with its tracking device, to Moscow as a diversion. If Lucian and Anja were following that lead, they were chasing shadows.

Lucian's uncle Howard Miller had been captured in Rome during his ill-fated quest for lost knowledge. He had been rescued from Helena. That was one of her mounting failures. Eamon would need to determine her fate soon.

With a decisive motion, Eamon swiped his hand over the desk's surface, summoning his holographic AI assistant. The imp materialized—a translucent figure hovering above the desk.

"Access the digital archives," Eamon commanded. "Search for any significant underground locations near the Kremlin that might draw Lucian and his associates. Eagle reported their interest in the underground near the Kremlin."

The imp's eyes glowed as it processed the request. After a few seconds, it replied. "Search complete. The most probable point of interest is the lost library of Tsar Ivan IV, known as Ivan the Terrible. There are other possibilities, but the probabilities are lower."

Eamon arched an eyebrow. "What? Ivan's lost library?" He was well aware of the story—it was a vast collection of esoteric texts and forbidden knowledge. The Sodality had tried for centuries to locate it.

The imp continued, "Historical records indicate a Sodality operation during Ivan IV's reign, aimed at curbing his experimentation with the dark arts. The mission was partially successful but ultimately failed to secure the library."

Eamon leaned forward. "Elaborate."

"At that time, there was significant concern within the Sodality that Tsar Ivan's dabbling in the occult posed a substantial threat. Agents were dispatched to intervene. One agent, Nazar Lebedev, was captured and subsequently disappeared from all records."

"Nazar," Eamon murmured, recalling the name from old mission logs. "And the others?"

"A second person, Bogdan Belsky, was coerced into service to the Sodality through threats against his wife and blackmail. He was part of the tsar's inner circle and poisoned Ivan IV during a chess game. However, his mission to locate and secure the library failed. The library vanished, and its whereabouts have remained a mystery."

So Lucian and Anja might be seeking the library. It was a plausible objective, given their penchant for pursuing hidden knowledge. They were infants in this game.

"Imp, cross-reference any recent activities or patterns that suggest the library could be accessible or that new information has surfaced."

"Cross-referencing," the imp responded. "There are no significant developments in public records. However, there has been increased interest in underground explorations near the Kremlin."

Eamon's eyes narrowed thoughtfully. "So they may be searching beneath Moscow for the library. Bold, but reckless."

He considered the implications. The library, if found, could contain powerful artifacts or dangerous knowledge. Allowing it to fall into Lucian's hands was unthinkable. The only acceptable outcome was to take control of the library or destroy it. If they were killed before they found it, then he would renew efforts to locate it. This all supposed that the library was their goal. Either way, he needed to understand why they were taking such a risk.

"Imp, prepare a directive for Eagle," he ordered. "Instruct him to find and monitor Lucian and Anja closely. Do not engage unless an opportunity presents itself to capture them or secure their objective." He pondered whether it would be better to let them continue their search and capture it for himself, or eliminate them now when the opportunity presented itself and leave the dangerous library lost. The Sodality could always resume the search later.

On the other hand, Lucian's allies remained unaccounted for. There was the risk that they would find the library. It would be better to confirm their goal and take control of whatever they found.

"Do you wish information about the library included in the directive?"

He weighed the choice. He wasn't absolutely certain that was their goal, and the additional information could distract from finding the truth and eliminating the danger Lucian and his companions posed. "No. Only that they have an unknown objective, and if they somehow succeed, deal with them and inform me immediately."

"Directive prepared," the imp confirmed.

Eamon paused, his thoughts turning to Helena. She had sent the shoe with Richard's tracking device to Moscow. "Display Helena's recent communications," he commanded.

The imp brought up a series of encrypted messages. Eamon scanned them, noting her contact with the controller in England and the dispatch of assets to the Miller estate in Kent.

"Interesting," he mused. "Perhaps she suspects Lucian never left England, or maybe she's seeking something else entirely." He stroked his chin. "Could she be attempting to align with Lucian against me? Or is she merely covering her bases?"

The imp waited silently, its glowing eyes fixed on him. It seemed the imp could learn about rhetorical questions.

"Monitor Helena's activities closely," Eamon decided. "Intercept any communications between her and external parties. I want to know her every move."

"Understood," the imp replied.

He reflected on the history that the imp had recounted. The Sodality's past efforts to control the spread of dangerous knowledge were extensive. Agents like Alexei and Bogdan were instruments in a long game—a game Eamon now played with unmatched expertise.

"Centuries of searching," he whispered. "And now the trail resurfaces. What are the chances that Lucian and Anja will succeed where others have failed?"

"Probabilities are difficult to calculate without complete data," the imp replied. "However, given their resourcefulness and recent activities, the likelihood is higher than in previous attempts."

Eamon's expression hardened. The imp's learning was imperfect, after all.

Perhaps it was time to deploy additional assets—those skilled in more unconventional tactics. If Lucian and his circle could be captured, it would eliminate a persistent thorn in his side and might lead him to the library.

"Imp, initiate Protocol Seven," he commanded. "Authorize the deployment of sleeper operatives with full discretion to intercept Lucian's group. Put them under the direct control of Eagle."

"Protocol Seven initiated," the imp confirmed. "Operatives will be notified and await further instructions. Sending directive and contact details to Eagle."

Helena's maneuverings, Lucian's quest beneath the Kremlin—it all served to strengthen Eamon's position if handled correctly. "Is there anything else of note?" he asked.

"One additional item," the imp replied. "There have been searches for Ivan's library over the centuries, many guided by the Sodality. All have ended without success."

Eamon smiled thinly. "Perhaps it takes a fresh approach. Or perhaps letting others do the legwork will yield better results. Imp, send a notice to Helena. Order her to focus her efforts on locating the rest of Lucian's circle. Inform her that Lucian and Anja appear to be in Moscow, but none of their bodyguards have been spotted. She is to redouble her efforts to find them and to search for Zoe Ananda and Howard Miller as well."

"Done," the imp replied.

He dismissed the imp with a wave of his hand. The holographic assistant vanished, leaving him alone with his thoughts.

"Let them search," he murmured. "In the end, all paths lead back to me."

Late in the evening, Helena sat alone in her study within the ancient walls of Zamec Echo. The glow from the fireplace cast dancing shadows across the rich tapestries and polished wood panels. A stack of reports lay before her on the intricately carved desk, each bearing the insignias of the operatives she had dispatched to observe the Miller estate in Kent.

She sifted through the documents with a growing sense of frustration. The operatives had struggled to gather anything of substance. Edward Miller, Lucian's uncle, was reportedly in London at his apartment. As for the estate itself, they had been unable to approach it closely. Security measures were more intense than anticipated, and any attempt to get near had been challenged.

"Drones jammed and lost," she read aloud, a hint of irritation in her voice. The operatives had resorted to using drones to penetrate the estate's perimeter, but even those had been neutralized. It was as if someone very competent had anticipated every move.

Shifting her focus, Helena scanned the notes detailing interactions with the estate's servants. The operatives had tried to glean information when the staff ventured into town for supplies. Interestingly, the servants were purchasing unusually large quantities —enough to support a sizable group of guests. Yet no hints were dropped about who these guests might be. Every inquiry was met with polite but firm discretion.

"Too loyal for their own good," Helena muttered. She couldn't help but admire the Millers' ability to inspire such loyalty in their employees. But it complicated her efforts. A nagging concern crept into her thoughts: perhaps her operatives hadn't been as discreet as they should have been. Drawing attention to interest in the estate could jeopardize things.

As she closed the last folder, a chime alerted her to a new message. The emblem of the Grandmaster pulsed ominously on the screen. Helena's pulse quickened as she opened the encrypted communication. The message was brief but unsettling.

Lucian Miller and Anja Kinsey have been spotted in Moscow, it read. *Our sources have confirmed their presence. Double your efforts to find other members of his circle. Report any related findings immediately.*

Helena's eyes widened, her mind racing. "Moscow?" she whispered. This was unexpected—and dangerous. If Lucian and Anja were in Russia, they were walking into a trap. Eagle, known for his ruthless efficiency, held significant power and influence there. The Grandmaster's message confirmed her fears: they were in grave danger.

She reread the message, her thoughts a whirlwind. Her plans hinged on Lucian and Anja's success—or, at the very least, their survival. She had no idea why they had risked traveling to Russia. If Eagle captured or eliminated them, it would unravel everything she had been orchestrating.

Quickly, she composed a response to the Grandmaster. *Acknowledged. I will continue my efforts and remain vigilant for any further developments.* She sent the message, knowing that any display of undue interest might arouse suspicion.

Deciding she had done all she could for the night, Helena shut down her systems. The room plunged into deeper shadows as the screens darkened. She rose, the silk of her gown whispering against the polished floor as she made her way toward her chambers.

Entering the bedroom, she found Jasmina waiting for her in the dim light—a comforting presence amid the castle's loneliness. The maid looked up expectantly.

"Is everything all right, mistress?" Jasmina asked.

Helena offered a smile, though it didn't reach her eyes. "Yes, just a long day," she replied. "I won't be needing you tonight. You may retire."

Jasmina hesitated for a moment. "Very well. If you need anything..."

"I'll be fine," Helena said. "Thank you."

After the door closed behind the departing maid, Helena allowed the mask of composure to slip. She crossed the room slowly, her reflection in the antique mirror revealing the worry etched on her features. With deliberate movements, she shed her gown and slipped into the cool sheets of her bed.

Staring up at the canopy, Helena willed sleep to come. Her mind, however, refused to quiet. Images of Lucian and Anja navigating the treacherous streets of Moscow played out behind her closed eyes. This would explain the lack of response to the email she had crafted for Anja. If they were smart—and she believed they were—any communication devices, email, phones, anything would be left behind. She considered the possible consequences of their capture—not just for them but for herself.

Eagle won't show mercy, she thought grimly. *I need to warn Anja.*

Her attraction to Anja had become an obsession. She told herself it was helpful in her quest for vengeance. Images of Moscow faded to be replaced by Anja in all her glory. Helena's thighs clenched together, aching.

She remembered kisses and ecstasy as she let herself slip away toward sleep. Her last conscious thought was a plea. "Come for me tonight, Anja."

Thirty-Two

ANJA SLIPPED INTO the soft embrace of the bed, the weight of the day's revelations both exhausting and exhilarating. Lucian lay beside her, his breathing a comforting rhythm in the quiet room. On the other side, Zoe nestled close, her presence warm and reassuring. The success of their underground expedition had given them new hope in tracking Ivan's lost library, but it also meant they had much to plan for their travel eastward.

As the room settled into silence, Anja found herself unable to sleep. Restlessness stirred within her, an uneasy feeling that she couldn't quite place. She closed her eyes, attempting to calm her mind, but her inner demon—her succubus nature—began to stir.

"Someone is pining for your attention," a whisper echoed in her thoughts.

Anja sighed inwardly. She was low on energy, and the barriers she usually maintained were weaker tonight. Reluctantly, she allowed herself to drift deeper into the dreamscape that beckoned to her.

The scene around her shifted, and she found herself in a familiar chamber adorned with tapestries and lit by candlelight. The scent of jasmine lingered in the air. She recognized the room immediately. It was Helena's.

Helena lay next to her on the luxurious bed. "I need you tonight," Helena whispered, her voice tinged with vulnerability. "But there is more. I…I…You and Lucian have been noticed."

Anja's heart quickened. "Noticed by whom?" she asked, searching Helena's face for answers.

Helena's expression tightened before she turned away. "I can't say," she murmured. "I can't..."

"Eagle?" Anja asked.

"How..." Helena turned to her.

It was enough confirmation. The oaths Helena had sworn to the Grandmaster were powerful, constraining her even with Anja's ties threaded through them. "It's okay," Anja replied gently. "You've told me enough."

Helena reached out, her fingers brushing against Anja's cheek. "I wish things were different," she whispered.

"For now, this is enough," Anja said softly.

They remained together in the dream, sharing a brief moment of connection that transcended the complexities of their reality. The warmth of Helena's presence eased some of Anja's restlessness, but the underlying tension remained.

She stoked the desire in Helena as she lay with her. Helena's orgasm flushed across her skin as Anja fed. This was a quickie—a midnight snack.

Eventually, the dream began to fade, and Anja felt herself drifting back toward consciousness. Helena's image blurred, her final words echoing. "Come back," she whispered. "Please."

Anja opened her eyes. The weight of Helena's warning pressed heavily on her mind. She turned to see Lucian and Zoe still peacefully asleep beside her. She nudged them awake.

"What's wrong?" Lucian asked groggily.

"We need to talk," Anja said. "I had a dream—or, rather, a warning. We need to leave Moscow as soon as possible. Eagle—Krakarov—knows it's us now."

Zoe sat up, her expression alert. "Fuck. How?"

"I'm not sure," Anja admitted. "We can't afford to ignore this."

Lucian nodded, his jaw set. "All right. Let's get the others and make a plan."

They dressed and made their way to the common area, where the rest of their team was beginning to stir. Mike and Emma appeared from their rooms, curiosity aroused by the urgency in Anja's demeanor.

"What's going on?" Mike asked, rubbing sleep from his eyes.

Anja took a deep breath. "We may have been compromised. It's imperative that we leave Moscow immediately."

Nomad frowned. "Any specifics on the threat?"

"The Sodality knows we're here," Anja replied.

Lucian stepped forward. "Let's focus on securing transport out of the city. We'll need to plan our next moves on the way."

Dora looked thoughtful. "We were going to contact Ash, Howard, and Ian this morning. Should we still do that?"

"Yes," Anja affirmed. "They need to know what's happening. We'll just have to wake them up a bit early."

They gathered around the laptop, establishing an encrypted link to England. After a brief connection delay, Ash's face appeared on the screen. He looked a bit bleary.

"If you lot are ringing me at this hour, it can't be good," Ash muttered. "I've already pinged Claire to join us."

"Have her bring Ian and Howard, too. Listen, we have a situation. We need to leave Moscow immediately. We may already be compromised," Lucian stated.

Ash's expression tightened. He grabbed his mobile and tapped out another message without missing a beat. "Got it. Things aren't exactly quiet here, either. We've noticed more eyes on the estate lately. A few of your staff have even mentioned questions being asked about the estate in the village."

Claire came into view next to him. "We've decided it's best to relocate," she said. "We're heading to my aunt Fiona's house in the countryside. It's tucked away and easier to keep our heads down there."

"That's a good call," Lucian agreed. "We'll coordinate with you once we're clear of Moscow."

Dora leaned in. "We could use your help to pinpoint where to start our search. We believe Nikita and Maksim Stroganov moved the library eastward, possibly toward the Ural Mountains."

Howard looked especially rumpled with wild hair when he came into view. "That would track," he said, voice gravelly. "The Stroganovs had considerable holdings out there during the Siberian push. Ivan trusted them implicitly. I'll start combing through what records I can find on their settlements."

"I'll pull satellite data and recent geological surveys of the area," Ash added.

"Thanks," Dora replied. "That'll give us a solid head start."

Lucian checked his watch. "We've got to move. We'll be in touch once we're clear."

"Watch your backs out there," Ash said.

"You too," Lucian replied before ending the call.

Turning back to the group, Anja said, "All right, let's split up tasks. Nomad, can you arrange transport that won't draw attention?"

"Already on it," Nomad affirmed. "I've already contacted someone who owes me a favor. He can provide a couple of SUVs. I'll have him pick a location east of the city where we can swap the ambulance for them."

"Mike and Emma, pack up our stuff and make sure we leave nothing behind," Lucian continued.

They nodded and headed off.

"Dora, can you start analyzing any data Ash and Howard send over? We might need to make decisions on the fly."

"I'll keep at it until we need to leave," Dora said, already tapping away on the laptop.

Lucian approached Anja, placing a reassuring hand on her shoulder. "We'll get through this," he said.

She offered a small smile. "I know. This isn't as easy as I had hoped. Will we make it?"

He squeezed her shoulder. "We will."

Within the hour, they were ready to leave. Nomad had brought around the ambulance. It was as good a method as any to get out of the city quickly. It would not work in the country and would attract too much attention.

"Time to go," Lucian said, climbing into the vehicle.

Lucian sat in the passenger seat again. The back of the vehicle was a tight fit for the group and equipment. The scent of antiseptic mingled with the odor of fuel, creating a tense atmosphere. Nomad was behind the wheel as they drove through the dark streets of

Moscow. Behind Lucian, Anja leaned against the metal wall, her expression unreadable. Looking through the partition into the back cabin, Lucian saw that Mike, Dora, and Zoe sat on the bench across from Graham on the stretcher. Karolina sat in the EMT's chair with Emma curled in her lap.

The city seemed quiet, but Lucian attributed it to the early hour. They had decided that the ambulance would be the least suspicious means of transport—emergency vehicles often bypassed traffic and checkpoints without question. So far, their plan was unfolding smoothly.

"How much longer until we're clear of the city?" Lucian asked, keeping his voice low.

"Another twenty minutes if traffic stays this light," Nomad replied over his shoulder. "We'll be on the outskirts soon."

Lucian exhaled, trying to quell the unease gnawing at his gut. Just as he began to relax, a distant wail cut through the air. It started low but escalated into a piercing siren that sent a chill down his spine.

"What the hell is that?" Lucian exclaimed, sitting upright.

Nomad's eyes flicked to the rearview mirror and then met Lucian's gaze. "Air raid sirens," he said grimly. "Could be good for us—or very bad."

The wailing grew louder, joined by a chorus of other sirens from different parts of the city. The streetlights began to flicker before shutting off entirely, plunging the city into darkness. Buildings along the avenue went black.

Anja moved closer to a window, peering outside. "Everything is going dark," she said.

Nomad reached over and flipped on the ambulance's radio, tuning into the emergency frequency. Static crackled before a stern voice broke through in rapid Russian.

"Sounds like a drone attack," Nomad said.

Lucian's heart pounded. "A drone attack? This far from the Ukrainian border?"

Nomad nodded tightly. "There was a drone attack on the Kremlin earlier this month. Tensions are high. Looks like things are escalating."

"Does this help or hinder us?" Mike asked, his knuckles white as he gripped the edge of his seat.

"Depends," Nomad replied. "In the chaos, we might slip through unnoticed. But expect increased military presence and roadblocks."

The ambulance jolted as Nomad accelerated, weaving through the sparse traffic now reacting erratically to the sirens. Some cars pulled over, while others sped up in panic.

"Hang on," Nomad warned, flipping on the ambulance's lights and siren. The wail of their vehicle blended into the cacophony but granted them a semblance of authority.

They sped past intersections, the flashing lights casting eerie shadows on the buildings they passed. Above, the sky remained ominously calm, but the tension was palpable.

As they approached a main thoroughfare leading out of the city, the glow of headlights revealed a barricade ahead. Military vehicles blocked the road, soldiers waving flashlights and directing traffic to turn around.

"Checkpoint," Nomad announced tersely. "Looks like they're shutting traffic down."

Lucian's mind raced. "They'll question us if we try to pass."

Nomad met his gaze. "Options?"

Part Three

Thirty-Three

Moscow was awash with a tumult of sirens and distant explosions. Igor Krakarov stood by his office window, gazing out at the city shrouded in smoke and emergency lights flashing. The drone attack, allegedly launched by Ukraine, had thrown the city into disarray. His office seemed suffocating. He wanted to be out there in the action.

He scowled, turning away from the window. "Just what we needed," he muttered. The lockdown imposed by the authorities was siphoning resources he wanted to allocate to his search for Lucian and Anja and their elusive companions—including Kasia, who remained a mystery. The disruption threatened to let his quarry slip through his fingers.

Yuri entered the office, a tablet in hand and a furrow in his brow. "Sir, we've made some progress," he announced.

Igor turned from the window. "Report."

"We may have a lead on Kasia's associates. While we still haven't uncovered her true identity, our analysis pointed us toward an establishment—a brothel operated by a woman named Katya."

"Katya? Go on."

"Footage from street cameras in the vicinity shows a group matching the descriptions of Lucian, Anja, and others entering the premises several nights ago," Yuri continued. "More importantly, early this morning—just before the drone attack—a group was seen leaving the area in an ambulance."

"An ambulance?"

"Yes. They departed hastily just before the drone attack and the beginning of the city's lockdown procedures. I have the footage queued up in your feed."

Igor strode to his desk, tapped commands into his computer to bring up the relevant footage. Grainy images played across the screen, showing the ambulance pulling away from the curb.

"This has to be a coincidence," Igor mused. "They'll attempt to slip out amidst the chaos."

"Agreed," Yuri said. "I've already dispatched teams to track the ambulance's last known direction. Traffic cameras are sporadic, but we're piecing together their likely route."

"Good," Igor replied. "I want that vehicle found and stopped. They must not be allowed to escape. Go follow up on the progress."

Yuri left but returned quickly. "Our surveillance teams have been reviewing footage and checkpoint logs. We haven't located the ambulance, but we've identified a checkpoint on the outskirts where an ambulance matching the description exited the city."

Igor's eyes narrowed. "Why was it allowed past? How do the officers at the checkpoint explain that?"

"One of the men in the ambulance, a passenger, identified himself as Pavel Sokolov—one of our operatives."

Igor's jaw tightened. "Pavel Sokolov is dead. He was killed during the failed ambush."

"The officer insisted it was Sokolov. He presented SVR identification, and his appearance matched. They claimed to be on a critical mission. The driver said something about hazardous materials."

"Any idea where they were heading?"

"They left on the Entuaiastov Highway."

Igor leaned against his desk, processing the information. "So a dead man is in an ambulance leaving Moscow during a citywide lockdown. How is that possible?"

"Should we detain the officer for further questioning?" Yuri asked.

"No. We have too much else to focus on, and they're already gone. Check traffic cameras along the route to track that ambulance. They may be heading out along the M7."

"Yes, sir," Yuri said.

Igor straightened. "I've received authorization for the use of additional assets. They are now at our disposal. Has the DKRO agent reported in?"

Yuri's eyebrows rose slightly. "Yes, he has, but he's not happy."

"I don't care," Igor said. "These other operatives are highly skilled and operate outside conventional parameters. I want them deployed immediately to track the ambulance and any subsequent vehicles our targets may use. Put them under the DKRO agent to coordinate. My instructions are to track and follow them. Find out what they're after or if they're just seeking escape. They cannot be allowed to escape the country, but short of that, just track them."

"I'll coordinate with the DKRO agent at once," Yuri said.

"Also," Igor added, "cross-reference any known safe houses along their probable escape routes. They may attempt to disappear."

"Yes, sir."

Left alone, Igor returned to his desk, his mind racing through the implications. The fact that someone had impersonated one of his dead operatives added a new layer of complexity—and irritation. It was a bold move, bordering on reckless, but it had worked.

He pulled up Helena's profile on his computer, scrutinizing her recent activities once more. Despite his agents finding no evidence of her tipping off Lucian and Anja. Without concrete proof, he had to proceed cautiously. He would have captured them if they had not left when they had. He struggled to control his rage.

Igor's cell phone buzzed. He picked it up angrily to see a message confirming that the Protocol Seven operatives were en route. A thin smile formed on his lips. These assets were among the best. They were experts in tracking, infiltration, and elimination. If anyone could catch Lucian and his companions, it was them.

He tapped a finger on the desk, contemplating his next move. The ambulance had already left the city, but with the operatives deployed, the net was tightening.

Igor sat in his dimly lit office, the morning's chaos still echoing in the distance as sirens wailed and smoke lingered over the city skyline. The drone attack had not only disrupted Moscow but also complicated his pursuit of Lucian and Anja. Frustration gnawed at him. How were they operating so effectively on his turf? They were outsiders, unfamiliar with the intricacies of Russia's surveillance and security apparatus.

His thoughts turned to Kasia. Was she the key? Despite extensive efforts, her true identity remained elusive. But even with her possible connections, could she alone facilitate such seamless movements through Moscow's labyrinth of watchful eyes? Doubtful.

An unsettling possibility crept into his mind. One of Richard's operatives had gone missing some time ago, presumed captured or dead. Nomad was exceptionally skilled, trained in espionage, survival, and counterintelligence. Igor himself had recruited him into the Sodality, recognizing his unparalleled talents. He had kept a close watch on his progress.

"Could it be?" he whispered.

He accessed his database, pulling up Nomad's dossier. As he scanned the information, a sense of betrayal began to simmer. If Nomad was aiding Lucian and Anja, it would explain their uncanny ability to evade detection.

Igor retrieved the surveillance footage from outside Katya's bordello—the last known location of the group. The video was grainy and marred by interference, but it was all he had. He leaned forward, scrutinizing every frame. There—a figure entering the driver's seat of an ambulance. Igor froze the image and enhanced it as best he could. The resolution was poor, but the man's posture was unmistakable.

"Nomad," Igor muttered, his voice laced with cold fury.

The pieces fell into place. Nomad's expertise, combined with his intimate knowledge of the Sodality's methods, would make him a formidable ally and a significant threat to Igor's plans.

He clenched his jaw, anger seething. Nomad's defection was not just a professional setback; it was a personal affront.

Reaching for his phone, Igor dialed Yuri's number. The line connected almost immediately.

"Sir?" Yuri answered.

"Yuri, we have a new development," Igor said tersely. "Pull up the file on operative codename Nomad—missing and presumed captured some time ago."

There was a brief pause. "Yes, sir. I have it here."

"I believe Nomad is aiding Lucian Miller and his group. Review the surveillance footage from outside Katya's establishment. Focus on the individual entering the ambulance driver's seat."

"I'll examine it right away," Yuri replied.

"Good. I want an alert issued to all units. Nomad is to be considered a high-priority target. He's familiar with our operations and poses a significant risk."

"Understood, sir. I'll disseminate his picture immediately."

"This betrayal cannot go unanswered. Ensure that everyone understands the importance of capturing him. Alive is preferable. I would like to deal with him personally. Dead is likely, though. He will not surrender."

"Yes, sir. Understood."

Ending the call, Igor sat back, his mind racing. Nomad's involvement complicated matters significantly.

This is personal now, he thought grimly. *You chose the wrong side, Nomad.*

He stood and began pacing, strategizing his next moves. With a newfound clarity about his adversaries, he felt a trickle of control returning.

"Run all you like," he whispered into the empty room. "I'll find you. All of you."

Later that evening, Igor stepped out of the sleek black car, his polished shoes crunching against the cobblestone street. He was no closer to finding his quarry, and it grated. Katya's establishment loomed ahead—a discreet building nestled among others in a narrow lane near the Kremlin. Its unassuming exterior belied the secrets it harbored within. He hoped to find answers here.

He adjusted his coat and signaled to the two operatives flanking him. "Stay alert," he commanded in a low voice. They nodded, scanning the surroundings for any sign of trouble, but there would be none.

Pushing open the heavy wooden door, Igor entered the dimly lit foyer. The scent of expensive perfume mingled with that of aged wood and tobacco. A hostess approached, her smile was practiced but faded quickly.

"I am here to see Katya," Igor stated flatly.

"Of course, sir," she replied, bowing her head. "Right this way."

He followed her through a corridor adorned with ornate tapestries and subtle lighting. The muffled sounds of laughter and conversation seeped through closed doors.

They reached a lavish sitting room where Katya awaited, poised on a velvet chaise. Dressed in a stylish gown, she exuded an air of authority. Her eyes met Igor's without a hint of surprise.

"General Krakarov," she greeted. "To what do I owe the pleasure of this unexpected visit?"

He offered a thin smile. "Let's dispense with formalities, Katya. I have questions, and I require answers."

She gestured to a chair opposite her. "By all means. Please, sit."

"I prefer to stand," he replied, ignoring the invitation. He produced a folder from inside his coat and withdrew several photographs, laying them on the glass table between them. Images of Lucian, Anja, Zoe, and Nomad stared back, captured in various candid moments. He had been distracted by spotting Nomad. Discovering Zoe Ananda was another bonus. He made a mental note to task Yuri with backtracing Lucian, Anja, and Zoe to find out how they'd got here.

"These individuals were seen entering your establishment. I need to know everything about their visit."

Katya glanced down at the photos, her expression carefully neutral. "They were guests, like many others. They paid well and enjoyed our hospitality. Beyond that, I know little."

"You expect me to believe that? You run a tight operation. Surely, you keep track of who comes and goes."

"Discretion is the cornerstone of my business. My clients value their privacy, and I respect that."

He leaned forward. "These people are of particular interest to me. Cooperate, and it will be noted. Refuse, and there will be consequences."

Katya raised an eyebrow, a hint of defiance flickering in her eyes. "Threats are unnecessary, *General*. I've told you what I know. They were foreigners, they paid in cash, and they didn't cause any trouble."

Igor pulled out additional photographs—grainy images of Kasia and the two men accompanying her. "What about these individuals?"

She examined the photos briefly. "Yes, they were here as well. Acquaintances of the others, I believe. But names were not exchanged."

Igor's patience was wearing thin. "You're being deliberately evasive."

Katya sighed. "I'm sharing all the information I have. My establishment entertains many guests, some more notable than others. It's not my practice to inquire beyond what is necessary."

"There was also a young girl with them. What can you tell me about her?"

Katya's expression softened. "A quiet one. She seemed sweet and kept to herself. Again, no name was given."

Igor studied her face, searching for any sign of deception. "These people are dangerous. By withholding information, you may be aiding criminals."

"As I said, I run a business. I'm not involved in my clients' affairs beyond providing a service. Besides, disrupting my operations would not sit well with certain…influential individuals."

He understood the implication. Many of her patrons were powerful figures—members of the Duma and other high-ranking officials. Causing a scene here could have unintended repercussions.

"Are you threatening me, Katya?" he asked coldly.

"Not at all," she replied. "Simply reminding you that we all have alliances to consider."

Igor contemplated his next move. Pressing further would likely yield little, and he couldn't afford to ignite a conflict with her connections. Still, he wasn't willing to walk away empty-handed. "When did they arrive, and how long did they stay?"

"These three and the girl came in three nights ago." She pointed to the photos of Nomad, Anja, and Zoe. "The others arrived early one morning, I believe. I wasn't up yet."

"When did they leave?"

"Sometime early this morning, I'm told. Before all the excitement."

"All of them?"

"Yes."

As far as he could tell, she was telling the truth. The facts lined up with what she claimed, though he was certain she knew more than she let on. Kasia had arrived with Lucian and the two others the morning after his men were killed. Only Lucian had replaced Lev... He didn't remember his last name. Where was Lev now? Too many questions.

"Very well," he said after a moment. "If you recall anything else, anything at all, you will contact me immediately."

"Of course," she agreed, her tone amicable. "I'm always happy to assist the authorities."

He stared at her for a moment, then turned to leave. As he reached the door, Katya's voice stopped him.

"General Krakarov," she called.

He glanced back over his shoulder.

"A piece of advice. Sometimes, those who seek shadows become lost in them."

Without responding, he exited the room, his men falling in step behind him.

Outside, the city hummed with restless energy. Igor paused on the sidewalk, inhaling the cool air. The encounter had yielded minimal information, but it confirmed that Lucian and his group had been there, and that they had support in unexpected places.

Thirty-Four

CLAIRE STOOD NEAR the window of the estate's study, her thoughts drifting back to the video call. The early light of morning filtered through heavy curtains, illuminating dust motes that danced in the stillness. Ian and Howard lingered by a table cluttered with notes and maps while Ash stood in front of a bank of computer equipment he had set up near a distant wall. The atmosphere was tense—everyone felt the urgency borne of Lucian's warning from Moscow.

They needed to leave. Their presence at the estate was drawing too much attention. The increased surveillance, the suspicious inquiries in town, and now Lucian's call to relocate confirmed it: staying here was a risk they could no longer afford.

Claire drew a deep breath, steadying herself. "We all need to go," she said, breaking the heavy silence. "This place is compromised. We'll be safer at Aunt Fiona's. The farm's secluded—we can keep our heads down there."

Ash, arms folded, shot her a look. "Brilliant. I've just got all the kit set up here—secure lines, servers, everything humming along nicely—and now you want me to tear it all down and play travelling circus? Grand."

Claire turned to face him. "I know, Ash. But we can't stay. We'll need your skills more than ever—and we'll need them mobile. We'll figure out remote access for anything you can't carry. And your training...your experience...we'll need both of those." She softened, almost teasing. "Besides, you've come this far. You want to see how the story ends, don't you?"

Ash let out a long sigh. "Marvelous. I suppose the combat bonus makes up for the sleep deprivation. This job's turning out to be a hell of a lot less 'desk work' than advertised."

Claire allowed herself a small smile. "You wouldn't walk away now anyway."

"No," Ash admitted with a rueful shake of his head. "All right, I'll start packing the toys. Just make sure we actually have somewhere safe to set up again, yeah? I'm not running all this out of a bloody hayloft."

"We'll sort it," Ian assured him. "We're all adapting. We'll see what can be rigged at the farm."

Howard, who had been hunched over a stack of old papers, straightened and rubbed the back of his neck. His wild hair was as unruly as ever. "We know Fiona's place is tucked away. Less chance of watchful eyes there. Margaret will see the need. Best move, under the circumstances."

Claire nodded, feeling some of the tightness in her shoulders ease now that they had a direction. "I'll speak with Fiona and Mum," she said. "They'll know how best to manage the move quietly. No fanfare. No long convoys. Just what we can't do without for now. The staff's loyal—we'll need their discretion. Can't let whispers get out."

Ian fell in step beside her as she left the study. The corridor outside felt oddly still, each footstep echoing off the walls.

Fiona's sharp eyes went straight to Claire when she entered. "You look troubled, love," she said. Margaret, seated opposite her, wore much the same worried expression.

"We need to leave," Claire said. "We've had word from Lucian. The situation's escalated. We should relocate to Fiona's place in the country—quietly, and soon."

Margaret's eyes narrowed. "So the rumors are true, then?"

Fiona pressed her lips together, clearly turning it over in her mind. "I'll speak with Howard and see to it the servants keep their tongues still. But we've got to be clever about this. One word and people will catch wind. We can all fit at the farm, just...don't expect much in the way of luxury."

Margaret rose from her chair and crossed to Claire, resting a hand on her daughter's arm. "We'll manage. We always do. Best to move quickly and trust one another to see it through."

Claire exhaled, grateful for their quiet strength. "Ash is already breaking down his kit. Howard's gathering the most important documents and maps. Ian and I will see to the logistics. We'll split into smaller groups, leave at intervals, make it look like errands or short trips."

Margaret nodded, thoughtful. "If we keep the estate running as normal—staff carrying on as though nothing's changed—it should cover our tracks long enough. Timing will be everything."

A determination took root in Claire's chest as she caught Ian's eye. He gave her a nod, and she felt the familiar reassurance in it. They'd done all they could here. Time now to adapt and endure somewhere else.

As she and Ian stepped out into the corridor, she could already hear Fiona and Margaret discussing task assignments behind them, their voices quick and purposeful. Soon, the manor's grand halls would fall silent again, just another stately home, while they vanished into the folds of the countryside, out of sight, out of reach—for now. Whatever tomorrow held, they'd face it together.

Ian watched the discreet preparations that were underway for their departure. The staff loaded supplies into vehicles, each person avoiding any telltale signs that a mass relocation was imminent. Claire and Margaret had begun orchestrating the exodus, and Fiona supervised the loading of select boxes into a nondescript van. They had all agreed that stealth was the best option.

Ian stepped away, crossing to Ash's makeshift office, which was mostly packed for their move. Ash was waiting at a secure communication terminal. They had precious little time left here, and much to arrange before heading to Fiona's secluded country home.

Ian took a seat at the terminal and activated the encrypted link. After a few secure handshakes and key exchanges, the connection stabilized. Elín's familiar face appeared on-screen, the hum of Akar Labs' background noise audible even over the secure channel.

"Ian," Elín greeted, concern etched on her features. "I received your message. What's happening?"

Ian sighed, leaning forward. "We've run into complications. Our position at the Miller estate is no longer tenable. Surveillance has increased, and we believe we might be under close watch. We're relocating—today."

Elín's eyes widened. "That's not good. Do you need anything from us?"

Before Ian could answer, a chime sounded, and the screen split to include Isabelle and Sigri. Isabelle, her lab coat visible just at the edge of the frame, wasted no time. "Ian, I've been hearing rumors of infiltration attempts at NexGen in Geneva. Someone's been digging into our operations there. Files accessed, strange queries on our supply chains."

"That tracks what's been happening at many of Lucian's facilities," Ian replied. "We've had unexpected attention at the estate. It's all connected, I'm certain."

"What about Jonas Richter? He's head of security for Lucian's corporate interests. He might help identify where these leaks or intrusions are coming from."

"Good idea," Ian agreed. "We'll contact Jonas. He knows how to trace these threats. If anyone can help, it's him."

Elín cleared her throat. "The serum formulation for the wolves…did the awakenings proceed smoothly?"

A faint smile touched Ian's lips despite the tension. "They did. The serum's new formula worked as we hoped, stabilizing the transformations."

Isabelle nodded approvingly. "That's something at least. Progress amid all this chaos."

Ian's gaze shifted, his thoughts racing. "We'll be leaving for Fiona's countryside house soon. Once we're settled, we'll coordinate again. We'll need to collaborate closely—Lucian's team is heading east, searching for the library. We need to be ready to support them remotely."

Elín tapped at her console. "We'll help any way we can. Just keep us informed."

"Will do," Ian replied, adding, "Stay safe, all of you."

The call ended, and the screen went dark. Ian sat back, the sounds of distant preparations filtering through the closed door. He rose, going to where Ash hunched over his laptop and portable drives spread across a makeshift workstation. “Ash, we need to be ready to roll soon. We’ve got a lead—Howard’s pulling together some notes on the Stroganovs’ movements in Siberia. Dora’ll need it all mapped so she can cross-check possible sites.”

Ash’s brow knit as his fingers hovered mid-keystroke. “I’ll shove everything we’ve got onto the secure cloud drop. Dora can pull it down via the sat link.” He glanced up at Ian. “I’ve also got a contact in Kazan. Retired historian, runs an antiquarian bookshop. Might be worth tapping her for local context.”

Ian gave a short nod. “Good.”

Ash’s fingers danced back over the keyboard. “Right. That’s done. Upload complete. Dora should get the ping shortly—she can download what she needs on her end.”

Ian straightened. From somewhere beyond the study windows came the muted growl of an engine, another vehicle easing down the long drive, one more piece in their departure. “Right then. Let’s get the rest buttoned up. We won’t be far behind.”

Thirty-Five

To Dora's eye, Nomad seemed more wound up than she had ever seen him.

Nomad drummed his fingers on the steering wheel, eyes flicking to the rearview mirror. "We're coming up on Vladimir. We should leave the highway right after. I'm not in the mood to show up on traffic cameras any more than we already have. It's unlikely they know what to look for, but I don't want to take chances."

Lucian glanced over at him. "You think they're already looking for us?"

Nomad gave a curt nod. "Our departure from Moscow was too hasty. There's a good chance someone noticed. I'd rather not deal with any authorities, especially not Eagle."

Lucian coordinated with the other SUV, passing instructions from Nomad via Zoe to Graham so they could travel separately at times. It was a balance between distance and stealth. They could have traveled much farther, but covering their tracks was the better choice for now.

Dora leaned forward from the back seat. "Eagle...that's Igor Krakarov, right?"

Nomad pressed his lips together. "He's the biggest threat. If he catches wind we're here, he'll put everything he has into finding us, especially me. Better we slip away, find a place to rest and plan."

Mike looked up from his phone. "That bad?"

"Eagle is a powerful figure in both the Russian government and the Sodality. Call it being cautious," Nomad replied, checking the mirrors again. "We get off the highway, keep our heads down for a bit, and see if we can figure out how to stay off Eagle's radar. I hope it's not too late."

Dora cleared her throat, leaning forward from the back seat as Nomad guided the SUV onto a lonely stretch of road. "So," she began, trying to keep her voice steady, "this Eagle...Igor Krakarov. He's the one who recruited you to the Sodality?"

Nomad nodded, his posture tense behind the wheel. "Back when I was still under SVR command," he said. "He oversaw covert training —turning recruits into sleeper agents and illegals."

"So you had a whole life set up in America?" Mike asked.

A humorless smile twitched at the corner of Nomad's mouth. "House, job, everything. I was meant to blend in. That was the plan. Then I was approached by Eagle. A 'special assignment,' he claimed. I was sent to enhanced training. He said it was similar to swallow training."

"Swallow?" Dora prompted.

"Some of the most attractive and promising female agents were selected as swallows and sent to State School 4 earlier in training. Even some men were chosen for that—ravens. Sexpionage."

"Oh. Ummm, would you have done that?"

"Eagle had other plans for me," he replied gruffly.

That seemed a touchy subject, so she asked about his special training. "What was the training you received?"

Nomad's voice dipped lower. "Surveillance, infiltration, psychological warfare. I learned how to disappear, how to make my targets vanish with minimal fuss. They taught me to handle any weapon, plan assassinations, and endure interrogation without breaking. The Sodality added their own twist—techniques to induce obedience, punish defiance, and reward...efficiency."

Lucian turned slightly in his seat. "What was your name? Or should we still call you Nomad?"

Nomad's knuckles flexed against the wheel. He stared at the road ahead a moment too long before speaking. "My birth name doesn't matter. It vanished after enough missions. I've been 'Nomad' ever since."

Mike shifted uncomfortably. "You really don't remember it?"

Nomad shook his head once. "Remembering won't change what I

did. If anything, forgetting made it easier to follow orders. No ties, no emotions."

Dora watched the fields blur by, trying to absorb the weight of Nomad's words. The image of him as a faceless agent, shaped by indoctrination and training, unsettled her. "So Eagle is still out there, expecting you to fall in line if he calls?"

Nomad's eyes narrowed. "He thought he owned me, but I'm not his weapon anymore. I've defected. That has never happened before. Remember the controller, Richard? The Sodality must have figured out I set him up. Since I disappeared, they will assume I've turned. I'll be a priority target with a death warrant."

A heavy silence settled in the SUV as they continued along the rural road. Dora contemplated what might happen if the Sodality or the SVR discovered that Nomad's loyalties had changed. It was apparent that where there had once been respect, Nomad now hated both.

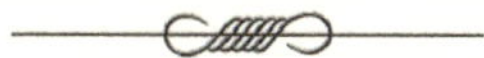

Dora stepped over the roots of a gnarled apple tree, her boots rustling through the wild raspberry brambles that crowded the path. Ahead, an abandoned cottage stood in the golden light of late afternoon, its sagging roof and peeling shingles testifying to decades of neglect. The warped front door was ajar. The breeze carried the scent of ripe berries and fields.

Dora paused at the threshold, taking in the cottage's leaning silhouette and the vines clinging to its walls. This was their waypoint —hidden, forlorn, but good enough for a short respite. The orchard around them was eerily quiet aside from the rustle of leaves and an occasional birdcall. A sense of weary relief washed over her; after hours on the road, they finally had a place to rest.

Behind her, Lucian approached, scanning the area for any sign of threat. Mike and Graham hovered nearby, weapons at hand but lowered. Anja and Zoe followed, ushering Karolina, who clutched Emma in cat form close to her chest. The cat's emerald eyes flickered as though attuned to every subtle movement.

"Looks clear," Mike remarked, nodding at the orchard. Graham moved ahead to push the door open fully. Dust motes swirled in the fading light, dancing in the still air.

Dora followed Graham inside, her gaze sweeping over the cramped interior. A wooden table, scarred by time and weather, stood crookedly in one corner. Empty shelves lined the walls, and the stale air hung in the gloom. It was far from comfortable, but it would do. Most of their travel would likely be off-grid from now on.

She set her pack down on the table, rummaging for the laptop. The sound of one of the SUVs departing seemed ominous somehow. With Nomad's history, he wouldn't get caught, but it still worried her. Turning to the others, she offered a small smile. "Let's settle in while Nomad is gone to find food, and we have some time to figure out our route."

They dispersed to find spots to sit—Lucian at a windowsill with a partial view of the orchard, Anja choosing a place near the door, and Zoe helping Karolina and Emma get comfortable in a dusty corner. Mike and Graham did a sweep of the cottage's two small rooms, returning to confirm it was deserted.

Satisfied they were alone, Dora sat at the table, clearing a space. She activated the laptop and waited as it linked to Ash's secure data drop. The SIM cards Nomad had procured were working and had a decent data connection. She hoped the laptop battery would hold up. A flurry of incoming files appeared on the screen—maps, historical records, and references compiled from Howard and Ash back in England.

"All right," Dora began. "Ash uploaded everything he and Howard could gather. It includes a few routes the Stroganovs might have taken when moving the library. Howard's notes also mention a Church of the Nativity of the Blessed Virgin Mary in Nizhny Novgorod, funded by the Stroganovs." She glanced around at her companions. "It might be worth investigating, but Ash's contact in Kazan could give us more direct leads. It's also closer to the main routes into Siberia, which they might have used."

Lucian inclined his head. "That lines up with what we'd expect."

Zoe leaned in, arms folded. "Nizhny Novgorod is closer, but Kazan's definitely on the direct path east. If we can talk to Ash's friend there, we could get local intel—maybe even old documents or legends."

Anja exchanged a look with Lucian. "Either approach could yield clues. The question is, which will give us better information about Ivan's library? Ash's description of his friend reminds me of Raymond. I think that would be a good place to start."

Mike huffed. "I hate guesswork. But Ash's contact is someone he recommends, so that's a strong point."

Graham tapped the butt of his rifle against his leg. "We might do both if time allows. But first, we should pick the one with the higher likelihood of success."

Karolina sat with Emma in her lap, stroking the cat's fur absentmindedly. Though still anxious, she seemed curious about the conversation.

"I think Kazan might be best. We still need to put more distance between us and Moscow," Dora said. Bringing up a digital map, she highlighted the route from Vladimir, where they currently found themselves near, around Novgorod toward Kazan. "We'll need to avoid major checkpoints," she noted. "But if we're lucky, we could reach Kazan in a day."

Lucian studied the screen over Dora's shoulder. "Nomad should be back soon with supplies. We'll figure out the final details when he returns."

A hush fell over them as they each considered the options. The setting sun cast a warm glow through the crooked windows, painting the dust motes golden in the stillness of the abandoned cottage.

Zoe broke the silence. "We'll find it."

Anja allowed a small, resolute smile. "Yes," she agreed. "One step at a time."

Her phone buzzed. Nomad, letting them know he was returning. Probably wise.

"Nomad is inbound," Dora announced.

They heard the distant rumble of an engine approaching, and Mike signaled for quiet. Moments later, Nomad's familiar figure appeared outside the orchard, maneuvering the SUV vehicle up to the cottage.

Dora powered down her laptop, stashing it away. "We'll finalize everything once we eat."

Dora beckoned Karolina to follow her out to meet Nomad. An evening breeze stirred her hair as Karolina wandered into the overgrown orchard. The fading sun cast dappled light across the wild raspberry brambles, their clusters of berries gleaming a soft red. Karolina began picking them tentatively, a small smile touching her lips, while Emma—still in cat form—padded after her, tail held high.

Dora watched with amusement as Karolina offered Emma a berry. The cat sniffed at it and then bit into one. She hadn't thought cats would care much for them, but apparently, she was wrong. However, she had to admit that a cat chewing on a raspberry was entertaining. As if sensing her thoughts, Emma turned her green eyes on her with a glare.

Nomad approached Dora with a pair of bags in hand, filled with newly acquired supplies. He nodded toward Karolina. "At least she's finding a moment of peace," he remarked.

Dora nodded. "We all needed a break. But we still have to finalize our route. I've been reviewing the data from Ash. He recommended Kazan because it's closer to the routes the Stroganovs might've taken into Siberia." She filled him in on the basics from their discussions.

Nomad shifted his stance, glancing at the orchard's shadows as if always on guard. "It makes sense. We can blend in there. We'll have an easier time re-supplying and gathering intel before continuing deeper east."

Dora exhaled, relief and anxiety mingling in her chest. "So we skip Nizhny Novgorod for now?"

"Howard's notes about that church could be useful, but time's against us. Kazan is more strategic and farther from Moscow. Hopefully, we'll find what we need there. Ash's contact sounds like a good bet to start."

She considered the half-dozen arguments swirling in her mind but ultimately conceded. "You're right. We can't do everything at once. And Kazan might be safer."

Nomad's gaze flicked toward the cottage. "One night's rest, then straight to Kazan."

Karolina returned, her hands stained pink from the berries, Emma padding at her heels. She offered a small handful of raspberries to Dora with a tentative smile. Dora accepted them gratefully, the sweet-tart flavor reminding her that, even amidst looming dangers, simple comforts could still be found.

Igor Krakarov waited impatiently at his desk, the click of the clock's pendulum marking each second. He had too many irons in the fire. A review of Helena's actions hadn't provided any more indications of treachery, though he knew they would eventually surface. He needed to focus on a single mission: find the targets who'd fled in that ambulance.

After a knock at the door, Yuri entered, followed by another operative. Agent Dmitri Kirilovich from the DKRO. Dmitri's footsteps were purposeful.

"Sir," Dmitri began, stopping a few paces away from the desk. "We've located the ambulance."

Igor's eyes sharpened. "Go on."

Dmitri set a small stack of photographs and printouts onto the desk, each bearing the insignia of traffic surveillance. "We traced the ambulance from the checkpoint just outside Moscow to a route leading through industrial zones. They left the main highway briefly, and we lost them. A search of the area revealed an old warehouse. The ambulance was parked inside, abandoned. Based on fresh tire tracks and witness statements, two SUVs departed shortly afterward."

Igor glanced over the images. Grainy captures of the ambulance, timestamps, some showing the checkpoint crossing, then the final exit from the highway. Another set of photos depicted the warehouse and the ambulance inside. "Did you confirm plates on these SUVs?"

Dmitri nodded. "Yes, sir. The numbers were captured by a local traffic camera east of the city—along the M7. The quality is poor, but we have enough fragments to run a trace. So far, the plates appear either falsified or belonging to defunct registrations."

Yuri leaned in to view the documents. "You said they headed east?"

"They did," Dmitri confirmed. "The last definite sighting was near Vladimir. We believe they went off the highway shortly after. Your men concluded they were likely going to ground, possibly lying low to avoid further detection. I've dispatched them to the area to search and inquire at likely places to pick up supplies. The group will need food and petrol."

"You provided the photos of the subjects to my men?"

"Yes, sir. They know who they're looking for."

"I doubt that," Igor grumbled.

"Sir?"

"Never mind. This one"—Igor pulled out a photo of Nomad from his file—"he is extremely dangerous. The others are likely to be as well. Four of them took out a skilled fire team—all dead. They didn't suffer any casualties in the encounter. That's why you'll track and not approach them until I give the word. Let your new detailees handle that when the time comes. Understand?"

"Yes, sir." Dmitri looked a bit paler.

Igor set down the photos with deliberate care. His jaw tightened, though his voice remained measured. "So, they slipped our net again."

"For the moment, yes," Dmitri acknowledged. "We've issued an alert to all relevant checkpoints, instructing them to report any sightings of these vehicles. They've been advised not to approach or engage—just to notify us immediately."

Igor allowed himself a brief nod. "Good. We can't afford more bungled operations. If they've moved beyond Vladimir, they may be out of our immediate reach. That is not acceptable."

Yuri studied Igor's face. "Shall I coordinate with local law enforcement or keep it internal?"

"Keep it internal," Igor replied. "We can't trust every patrol to handle this. We'll use our men and the men you've been assigned. They won't lose them again."

Dmitri gathered the documents neatly. "I'll relay the instructions, sir."

"No. I want you out there with them. Relay updates to Yuri."

"Sir?"

"You heard me."

"Yes, sir."

Igor waited until Dmitri departed. Then he turned to Yuri. "They're slipping away, but not for long. Increase the searches around the M7 corridor. They cannot vanish into thin air."

Yuri inclined his head. "Yes, sir. I'll see to it."

Igor's gaze fell again to the scattered images of the ambulance and the warehouse. They'd been so close, yet the circle had widened again. Still, this was progress—evidence, leads, directions. He pushed aside frustration, reminding himself that each clue inched him nearer to his goal.

“They’ve had their reprieve,” he muttered. “Now it’s our move.”

Thirty-Six

ANJA WATCHED AS Nomad drove away along the overgrown dirt road that had led to the cottage. Lucian was seated beside him with a map spread across his lap. Dora and Mike looked back at them as they departed. *"We'll be right behind you,"* Anja sent over the mental link she and Zoe shared with Lucian. This was how they intended to stay in touch—two vehicles traveling apart, stopping at different stations, avoiding too much notice.

Zoe stepped up, slipping her arm around Anja's waist. "They'll be fine," she murmured. "Nomad knows how to do this."

Anja nodded, keeping her voice calm. "And we'll know if anything happens," she said.

They climbed into the other vehicle behind Graham. Karolina and Emma took the front, and Emma hopped up onto the dash. The morning air had a nip, but the sky promised clear weather.

Anja leaned against the window, noticing patches of mist hovering above the tall grass. Wooden houses with brightly painted shutters dotted the countryside, and the occasional horse-drawn cart reminded her of how different life could be just a few hours from a major city.

Zoe shifted beside her in the back seat, brushing a hand against Anja's arm. "You see that church steeple? Looks centuries old," she said, her eyes flicking toward a distant village.

Anja nodded. "I wonder how many families have lived there," she replied, speaking softly so as not to disturb Graham, who was focused on the road.

Before long, they approached a quiet station—a small building with only a couple of pumps. Graham stretched his arms and walked around to check the tires while the tank was filling.

After refueling, they set off again, taking the southern route to Kazan. The others were to the north. The road led them onward.

In the back, Zoe slid closer to Anja, resting a hand on her thigh. It was a discreet gesture, meant to be unnoticed by those in the front seats. Emma had curled up in Karolina's lap, and they were both sleeping while Graham focused on the road. Besides, Graham would politely ignore them if he noticed anything untoward. Anja angled her body toward Zoe, enjoying the warmth as Zoe's arm slipped around her waist.

Anja gave a small smile. "At least we have a moment to catch our breath," she said, her voice low. "I feel like we've been running nonstop."

Zoe's fingertips moved in a reassuring pattern across Anja's hip. "We'll manage," Zoe said. "We keep getting interrupted, and I've been missing you."

Anja's breath hitched as Zoe unbuttoned her pants and slid her hand inside, stroking her heated folds. She shifted her hips, pressing into the touch as discreetly as possible. The thrill of engaging in such intimate acts in the backseat of the SUV while the others were so close only heightened the moment's intensity.

"Zoe," she breathed out, barely above a whisper, her heart pounding in her chest. *"We should be careful. Karolina..."*

"I know," Zoe purred in her ear, her voice caressing Anja's earlobe with its softness. "She's sound asleep, and I can't help myself." Her fingers found Anja's clit, circling it.

Anja bit her lip to muffle a moan that threatened to escape, arching her back slightly. It was all too much: the sensations coursing through her body, the risk of being caught, and the knowledge that they were embarking on an incredible adventure together. The ache between her thighs intensified as Zoe's touch became bolder, more insistent.

"Zoe," Anja gasped out, digging her nails into the seat beneath her coat. "I-I'm going to—"

Zoe sensed her impending climax, slowing down just enough to prolong the exquisite pleasure that was building inside of Anja. "Shh," she soothed, planting a series of feather-light kisses along Anja's jawline. *"Relax. We have time."*

They angled to lie across the back seat behind Graham. Zoe lay mostly atop her. Anja hesitated, but she could see Karolina still sleeping up front, so she slid her hand into Zoe's pants so she could return the favor. For some reason, she didn't know why she shouldn't continue. The road they were on was a two-lane country highway with little traffic. Her demon stirred, wanting more. *"Why the pretense? You should just go for it. The young one has surely seen more."*

Zoe responded. *"We don't want to distract the driver."*

"What are you two up to?" Lucian inquired.

"Oh!" Their link was still open, and Anja felt her cheeks burn as she realized that Lucian was well aware of their intimate activities. Despite the collective heat in the SUV, she felt a wave of warmth wash over her body. Zoe, however, seemed unfazed by the intrusion, her fingers still teasing Anja.

"Lucian, you're such a peeping tom," Zoe teased. *"Just keep your mind out of our pants, and you'll be fine."*

Anja couldn't help but chuckle. *"We were just…talking girl talk,"* she said innocently. *"Nothing to see here."*

"I wish I could watch, but I'll settle for eavesdropping."

"Ignore him," Zoe breathed against Anja's ear, her voice a low growl that sent shivers down Anja's spine. *"He's just jealous he can't join in."*

"All right, all right. Remember, soon, all bets are off," Lucian sent.

Anja couldn't help but giggle at Zoe's audacity. Instead of making her self-conscious, it only served to heighten her arousal further. She squeezed her thighs around Zoe's hand, silently urging her on.

Anja slipped a finger into Zoe while her palm ground into her pelvis and against her clit. Zoe continued to pleasure her. Their bodies were pressed close together as they tried not to be too obvious.

"Yes, that's what I need." Zoe's desire flooded through their link.

The combination of her building orgasm and the pleasure she was giving Zoe felt so good. Their tongues explored each other's mouths. Thankfully they didn't need to speak.

They were acutely aware of each other's touches, their heartbeats pounding in sync with the increasing rhythm of their passion. Anja's demon side craved more, urging her to cast aside all restraints and let loose with their desires.

Anja knew that they were both on the brink of orgasm, their breathing now ragged and uneven. She bit her lip harder, trying to muffle the moans that threatened to escape as Zoe expertly stroked her core. Anja's hips arched upward, seeking more contact, but Zoe held her steady.

"Z-Zoe," Anja panted, her voice a strained whisper. "I can't…I-I'm going to—"

"Shhh. Me too."

With one final, synchronized gasp, they both came undone, their orgasms crashing over them like a tidal wave. Anja's body shuddered beneath Zoe's as pulses of pleasure coursed through her body. The sounds of their muffled moans blended together as they rode out the powerful climaxes together.

As they finally came down from their respective highs, Anja collapsed back, her heart racing. Zoe's arm remained around her waist, their fingers intertwined as they tried to catch their breaths. Lucian's presence lingered at the back of their minds. They were very aware of how turned on Lucian was, and he would want to be with them soon.

When their breathing finally returned to normal, Anja could feel Zoe's heartbeat thudding against her chest.

"That was…wow."

Zoe chuckled, her body still pressed against Anja's. *"Told you we'd manage,"* she said smugly, letting Anja lick her fingers.

Anja playfully swatted her arm, unable to muster any real annoyance. *"You're insatiable,"* she teased.

"Guilty as charged," Zoe purred, kissing Anja's forehead. *"But you're one to talk."*

"You have no idea," Anja replied with a contented sigh. She brushed a stray strand of hair from Zoe's damp forehead, her touch leaving a trail of goosebumps in its wake.

As they continued down the deserted highway and readjusted their clothes, their bodies still humming from their shared release, Anja couldn't help but feel a sense of peace wash over her. She was exactly where she was supposed to be. And as long as she was with Zoe and Lucian, she knew they could face whatever darkness awaited them.

The day stretched, and the forest gave way to fields. By the time they neared Kazan, the sky had turned gold, streaked with deeper purples along the horizon. The city rose up with onion-domed towers and modern high-rises intermixed, the silhouettes cast against the fading light.

In the back seat, Anja's eyelids grew heavy. Zoe leaned over and touched her hand. "We're almost there," she murmured. "It'll be good to get out and walk around."

Anja appreciated the gentle pressure of her partner's thigh against hers. Their discreet interlude had taken the edge off, but there had been so few opportunities to simply exist. Even if this trip was all about caution, she would cling to these small moments.

Lucian relayed their destination. Anja passed the information to Graham and noted the glint in his eyes in the rearview mirror. Maybe he had noticed what they were up to after all. She remembered his awakening ceremony with Mike and Lucian. That had been a night to remember! She wondered if he was remembering it too. She allowed herself to glimpse his emotions, and…yep, he was.

Karolina stirred and looked around. Emma hopped back up onto the dash and settled there. She sniffed the air and turned to look at them in the back seat. Anja realized Emma's sense of smell would give them away. Oh, hell. Maybe they should have just gone for it. Only Karolina seemed unaware. Yes, they had rescued her from being trafficked, and she had already been with too many men for her tender age. Anja still didn't wish to think too hard about it. Her demon was not a good influence. They still needed to figure out what to do with the girl.

Graham wound through the evening traffic and found a route toward the quieter outskirts. The inn Nomad had chosen was modest, with a sloping roof and warm lights welcoming travelers. As the car rolled to a stop, Anja stretched, feeling Zoe squeeze her hand.

It was a small inn, a discreet spot that allowed both groups to reconvene without drawing attention. They stepped out into the cool evening air, each scanning for any sign of trouble. Yet, for once, the world offered a hint of calm. Kazan's skyline glowed in the distance, a reminder of the places and people beyond their small group—reminders of all that still lay ahead.

Anja spotted the other SUV parked around the side. Dora was already outside, stretching her legs. Lucian unloaded supplies with Mike while Nomad checked in. Emma, in her sleek cat form, hopped out and ambled toward Anja, tail swishing.

Nomad came back out and handed Lucian a key. "We have four rooms. It seems they're not very busy. I counted on that."

Lucian said, "One for the three of us." He indicated Anja and Zoe. "One for Graham and Mike, and one for Dora, Karolina, and Emma. Nomad, I guess you get your own room."

"Anja and I should try and find Ash's contact," Nomad said. "The rest of you get settled. We can figure out the rest after we get back."

"Nomad is right," Anja said. Both Lucian and Zoe looked disappointed but agreed.

"Ready?" Nomad asked, stepping toward the door. "Ash gave us that contact's address. Better to go now before it gets late. It's not too far from here."

Anja nodded. "Lead the way."

They walked several blocks from the inn, Emma trotting alongside them. Having Emma along might come in handy. The address led to a cramped row of shops. Each storefront bore signs of age, but one in particular caught Anja's attention—a small wooden sign reading 'Volkova's Archive.' Its display window revealed shelves stacked with leather-bound volumes and scattered trinkets reminiscent of Raymond's antique shop back in Brooklyn.

Inside, a smell of old paper and varnish greeted them. A tall woman with silver-streaked hair stood behind a sturdy counter, a catalog open. She wore round spectacles and an air of easy confidence.

"Dobro pozhalovat'...ah—velcome," she greeted in English, her accent unmistakable. "I am Inessa Volkova. You are friends Mr. Ash mention, da?"

Anja blinked at the greeting but quickly recovered, introducing herself and Nomad. Inessa gave a laugh, low and warm, and beckoned them closer.

"Da, da...come, come. No stand in doorvay," she said, rolling the "r" just slightly. The narrow aisles were crammed with centuries-old texts, scrolls, and a few relics that sparkled under dim lamps.

Inessa closed her catalog with a thump and leaned her elbow on the counter. "Ash, he did not tell me vot exactly you look for. Only say I might help. Description of you—ehhh, vas close enough. Long ago, I travel much, collect rare books. Historian by training. Now?" She gave a shrug, her smile wry. "Now I am just dealer of old things nobody care for."

Anja offered, "This is a lovely shop. It reminds me of a friend's place back in the States."

Inessa tilted her head, eyes bright. "Ah? And vot is name of this friend?"

"Raymond. Raymond Archambault."

Her expression warmed immediately. "Raymond! Da, ve have done business before. Very fine man. Always fair. Always polite."

Anja's brow rose. "You know Raymond?" she asked, tracing a row of faded spines nearby.

Inessa's smile widened, sly now. "He did not mention Inessa? Hah. This is fine. I prefer to stay, how you say, behind curtain. Not everybody need know my name." She straightened, brushing her fingers across the counter. "Now. Tell me—vot you hunt? Then I tell you if I help."

"Kazan," Igor said. "They have been located?"

"Not exactly, sir," Yuri replied. "One of the SUVs was spotted heading into the area. Surveillance and traffic cameras are not as prevalent that far from Moscow. The license plate was matched to one of the vehicles. We confirmed both were bogus."

"Was the other seen?"

"No, we believe they split up and we don't know…"

Igor cut him off. "They must be found."

"We're searching the area now and have put out an alert. Neither SUV has been seen leaving."

"I don't care if you have to search all night. When either or both are found—you better find them, or there will be hell to pay—your men are to plant GPS trackers and follow them. I still want to know what they're up to."

"I'll relay your instructions," Yuri said.

"We know Lucian and this Kasia and her two goons came in aided by Yakov supposedly to sell a new drug formula. Have you made any progress tracing the others?"

"Yes, sir. They showed up at Katya's place with a known sex trafficker named Marek. He was contacted but refused to say anything other than he was done with the business. He did mention a name. Blamed her for the whole mess."

"What name?"

"Kasia."

"Again? Who is she?"

"Nobody seems to know. There's an old Polish birth record by that name, which would be about the right age. Digging further, it appears her mother died of some illness, and her father perished in a house fire when she was young. Her body was never found. I could find no other references. If it is the same Kasia, what happened between then and now is a mystery."

"Assuming it's the same one, she was an orphan with nobody to turn to. I'm guessing Marek picked her up on the streets and put her to work. She was also somehow involved with the drug trade. If true, she would know players in both worlds. She set them up with a plan to get into Russia, undoubtedly with the help of Nomad."

"So they're all in this together."

"They will all die together," Igor said flatly. "Thank you, Yuri. Keep monitoring the situation in Kazan."

"Yes, sir," Yuri said as he left, closing the door behind him.

Igor sat at his desk, glaring at his computer screen. He needed to send an update to the Grandmaster.

Eamon sat in the center of his control room, the glow of monitors lending sharp angles to his features. Dark metal panels lined the walls, and the hum of hidden cooling systems underscored the beeps of incoming data feeds. A holographic interface hovered—the digitized extension of his will.

He flicked his fingers, and the image shifted. His imp flashed into existence. "Ready for your commands, sir," it announced.

"Begin summary of the NexGen report."

A panel displayed text and video fragments. The imp-like AI produced a brief overlay with highlighted points.

"Lucian has not been sighted at the facility," the AI droned. "Dr. Isabelle Celeste Sinclair has remained absent from NexGen labs, working remotely from an undisclosed location. Additionally, internal security shows no successful intrusion attempts."

Eamon's lips tightened. "No progress, then." He took a breath, waving a hand to minimize the NexGen report. "Have our asset there remain in place. I want Dr. Sinclair's location uncovered—quietly. No further moves until we know more."

"Understood," the AI replied. "Proceeding with directives."

Eamon turned to a second feed, the one marked with Eagle's seal. His mood darkened as he scanned through lines of coded references. "So Eagle finally has eyes on Lucian, along with Anja and Zoe," Eamon muttered under his breath. "That's something."

The AI flickered, presenting relevant bits of the report in bullet points.

- Lucian confirmed present
- Anja, Zoe confirmed
- Nomad also present, assisting Lucian

Eamon's jaw tightened at the mention of Nomad. "So the traitor resurfaces. He must've turned fully after the Richard incident." He paused, inhaling a measured breath. "That has to burn Eagle. Imp, record this note: I will personally handle Nomad's betrayal. I want him to suffer before the end."

"Note recorded," the AI responded.

Eamon paced across the cool metal floor, giving the holographic assistant space to slide the report aside and center the next. This update carried Helena's name. He flicked it open with a gesture, scanning the text.

"Unusual activity at the Miller estate in Kent has ceased entirely," he read.

He swept a hand, and a map of Kent overlaid itself onto the air in front of him, blinking with past data points. "It was probably just a diversion," he said, half to himself, half to the AI. "A smokescreen to hide Lucian's true whereabouts. Clever. But we're not so easily misled.

Have Helena continue her search for Lucian's uncle Howard and Lucian's bodyguards."

Eamon dismissed the hologram with a wave, the screens collapsing into a single projected feed again. He stood there in the sudden quiet, considering his next step. "Imp," he began, addressing the AI once more. "Strengthen our network's focus on identifying these unknown individuals." He pulled up Eagle's report again and indicated the images of Kasia and her two goons.

The AI nodded, a ripple traveling through its semi-transparent form. "Reallocating resources, sir."

Eamon glanced around the polished floors of his command center, the stark lines of screens, the subdued lighting. His empire extended beyond these walls, but it was here that he held the threads of all his schemes. "We're closing in," he said, more to himself than anyone else. "They might try to slip away, but they'll slide right into my hands."

He felt the urge to go to Russia himself to oversee the operation personally, but he had become too entrenched, too reliant on the infrastructure he had built here. Maybe it was time for a change.

Thirty-Seven

ANJA WAS STILL marvelling at how small the world of rare book traders felt, her eyes wandering over the rows of leather-bound tomes, when Emma leapt onto the counter and sat primly.

"Ah! This one must be yours," Inessa said, amused, watching the sleek black cat settle. "And vot is name of such curious creature?"

"Emma," Anja replied.

Inessa extended her hand, which Emma sniffed before butting her head against it. Inessa chuckled and gave her a scratch behind the ears, eliciting a deep purr.

"She seems to like you," Anja noted.

Inessa smiled, her fingers still trailing through Emma's fur. "Da, I like cats. They keep away little mice who try to make nests. Not good for books and papers, you understand."

Straightening, she leaned her elbows on the counter, her welcoming smile shifting toward Anja. "So, moya dorogaya, how may I help you and your very…interesting companions, hmmm? Tell me again."

Anja cleared her throat, aware of Nomad by the door, watching the street outside. "We're searching for information on two Stroganov brothers—Nikita and Maksim Anikeyevich. They travelled eastward, toward Siberia, shortly after Ivan the Fourth—Ivan the Terrible—died in 1584. There doesn't seem to be much recorded about them in the usual histories."

Inessa pressed a finger to her lips, thinking. "Ah…da, Stroganovs. Most people remember family for salt trade, for land, for supporting conquest of Siberia. But Nikita and Maksim specifically? Hmmm...not so prominent in official stories." Her brows lifted slightly. "If I remember correct, Nikita died only few years later. You are interested in those years?"

Anja nodded. "We are. We believe something about their travels might be relevant to our search. But so far, we've found little more than passing mentions."

Inessa drummed her nails on the counter, her gaze drifting to a half-open ledger at her elbow. "Da, they remain...how you say... footnotes, in most books. However..." She raised her head, her silver-streaked hair catching the light as her eyes sparkled. "There are archives kept at Nativity Church, in Nizhny Novgorod. Very old records, handwritten, some even from that time. Monastery and church kept very detailed logs. You may find something there."

Anja tilted her head. "You think they'd mention the brothers' expeditions? We've already checked a few sources, and no one seems to know much beyond vague statements."

Inessa shut the ledger with a snap. "Clerics there very thorough. They wrote who passed through, ven they left, who they hired, even vot they purchased for journeys east. If there is reference to Nikita and Maksim, it is likely hiding in those pages."

Anja glanced toward Nomad, then back to Inessa. "We were hoping you might know more. Anything else you can tell us about them? Any mention of...unusual circumstances?"

"Mmmm, nothing I can recall clearly, no. There are always little rumors, you understand—about Stroganovs making...how you say, arrangements, da—with local tribes. Some say they set up trading posts, even fortified them. But this is more gossip than record."

Anja pressed gently. "If you happen to have anything—documents, diaries—we're willing to pay for anything relevant."

Inessa shook her head, almost apologetically. "Eh...nyet, my dear. If I had such treasure, I would already have shown you. Best place still is church archive. But if you like, I can write note, say you are trusted. Archivists can be...how you say...prickly."

Anja felt some of the tension ease from her shoulders. "Thank you. That's kind of you. But honestly, I'd rather not go back through the church records if we can avoid it. I...don't think that's the best route just now. Are there any stories about other settlements the Stroganovs might have built? A monastery, perhaps? Somewhere remote—hidden?"

Inessa tapped her chin, lips pursed in thought. Then her eyes brightened. "Monastery, da. Now that you say, I remember hearing of one, somewhere near Cherdyn. Very remote. Stroganovs were religious family—at least, some of them." She turned and moved down a narrow aisle, fingers trailing along the spines of old books until she stopped at a worn leather-bound Bible. Carefully, she slid it out and carried it back to the counter. The book groaned as she opened it. "Let me see...it has been long time since I touched this one."

The pages were lined not only with printed scripture but also with handwritten notes in fading ink—family names, births, deaths. Inessa flipped through until her finger stopped on a margin inscription.

"This belonged to family whose son travelled with Stroganov brothers, east, in year 1585," she explained, adjusting her spectacles. "I bought it many years ago, kept it because of the notes. See here—he went with them, just after the death of Ivan Grozny. Ivan the Terrible. The family recorded every letter they received...until, suddenly, no more."

She skimmed a few more pages, then tapped one. "Here. They mention 'skete'—small, hidden monastic place. Said to be built in mountains beyond Cherdyn, along Vishera River." She set the Bible on the counter, letting Anja lean in to read the faded cursive. "Family never heard from boy again. Last note says he went to help build place of worship. They never learned if it vas finished...or abandoned."

Nomad stepped closer, peering down at the brittle page. "So this skete could still be out there," he murmured. "Buried by time."

Anja ran her fingertips over the delicate ink, heart quickening. "Thank you, Inessa. This is exactly the kind of lead we were hoping for."

Inessa gave a shrug and a smile, closing the book with care. "Official history has no room for such little people. But if you avoid church records, then perhaps you follow this path. Cherdyn is not so short trip—but if you find vot happened to skete, perhaps you also find vot became of Stroganovs. Mmmm…wait. Let me look…”

She turned to an old computer on the counter and began tapping at the keys, her round spectacles slipping a little as she leaned closer. After a few moments, she looked back at them, her expression glum. “It seems monastery vas shut down long ago. Records, I think, would have gone to church in Nizhny Novgorod.”

“Might any locals, or churches near Cherdyn, still know anything?” Anja asked, hope creeping into her voice.

Inessa gave a little shrug. “Eh, hard to say. You would need to ask there, maybe at one of older churches. Sometimes priest keeps old notes. Sometimes nothing at all.” She tapped at the keyboard a little more, squinting at the faded screen. “Mmmm, here. There is one church, I think they had…arrangement, da, with monastery centuries ago. Could be something there.” She tore a scrap of paper from a notepad, wrote in neat Cyrillic script followed by a Romanised version, then slid it across to Anja. “Here. Name of church, and address. Best I can do from here.”

Anja dipped her head in thanks, reaching down to scratch Emma behind the ears as the cat peered curiously at the closed Bible. She glanced at Nomad, who looked just as intrigued. “We appreciate this, Inessa. We’ll see if we can pick up the trail where the records leave off. Ash may follow up if more questions come to us.”

She was already starting to turn when her eyes fell again on the Bible. She hesitated, then gestured to it. “May we take this with us?” she asked.

Inessa arched an eyebrow, then gave a faint smile. “Ah…I have it for sale already, you understand. But it is not cheap, no.”

Anja glanced at Nomad. “Do you have cash on you?” she asked.

At his nod, she gestured toward the Bible, letting him take the lead. He raised a questioning brow but stepped closer to the counter, and he and Inessa began the familiar ritual of haggling, her tone sly.

Figuring it would take some time, Anja drifted among the shelves, trailing her fingers over the cracked spines of books, wishing she had the luxury of hours to lose herself in the shop.

Before long, they seemed to reach an agreement. Inessa wrapped the Bible in brown paper with a satisfied little smile, handing it to Nomad.

"Be careful, both of you," she said, voice softening as she glanced at the names she'd written. "Those mountains can be cruel, even now. And no one knows vot things might still sleep there."

Anja accepted the warning with a faint smile. "That's what we're hoping," she replied.

Emma padded behind Anja and Nomad through the inn's dim corridor, tail flicking with impatience. Seeing the world through feline eyes had its moments, but the novelty was wearing thin. She remembered waking from her nap in the SUV to the unmistakable aroma of sweat and desire lingering in the air. An itch had been simmering ever since. If she didn't scratch it soon, someone would feel her claws.

She listened to Nomad explain that the Bible was costly, but he figured he'd paid a fair price—only half a million. Sales had not been good recently. Anja seemed to choke on that, and Nomad laughed, reminding her it was rubles.

This conversation did nothing to ease the tension that continued to build.

After entering the inn, they paused at the door to their rooms, still discussing the newly discovered lead up north. Anja mentioned the colder conditions in the mountains, and Nomad agreed to acquire more provisions before they left. They had split off briefly to grab food for Emma, too—she had prowled after Lucian, Zoe, and Anja with a low, rumbling annoyance in her throat. No matter how discreet her cat form was, she wasn't into bestiality.

Once Lucian opened the door to their room, Emma raced in and wrestled free of the collar at her neck. The moment it clattered to the floor, the shift coursed through her. Fur receded, bones realigned, and within seconds, she stood upright, fully human, chest heaving—and fully naked. Lucian shut the door.

Anja raised an eyebrow. "I thought you'd stick with Karolina for now," Anja said, a slight question in her tone.

Emma shrugged and tossed her long black hair back. "Nope. I'm due more than a meal for traveling this way. Besides, there are certain things a cat can't enjoy quite as much."

She caught Anja's amused expression. The mention of heading north floated in from the hallway, but Emma's focus was on the promise of relief, both from hunger and from that itch that demanded satisfaction. *Which first? Food can wait…*

"I guess she figured out what we were up to in the back," Zoe said as she undressed. "God, it's good to get out of these clothes. I'm sure Lucian has similar thoughts in mind."

"It was all I could do to keep my composure while you two had all the fun," Lucian said.

"You knew?" Emma asked.

Anja answered for him, shrugging. "He did. And Graham figured it out, too."

Zoe looked at the bed. "Tight fit for all of us, but I think we can manage. Anja, strip. Emma is feeling needy."

When she heard her name, Emma went to Lucian and began helping him undress while Zoe started tugging at Anja's clothing.

Anja pushed Zoe to the bed and vanished her clothes before lying back next to Zoe to watch Lucian with Emma.

Emma's nimble fingers worked quickly, undoing the buttons on Lucian's shirt. She could feel his eyes on her, and their heated gazes met as she finished and discarded the garment. His chest rose and fell with each breath, an intoxicating sight that sent a shiver down her spine.

"So," she purred, her voice low and sultry as she pressed her body to him. "You've been watching, have you?" A mischievous grin played on her lips as she flicked her tongue out to trail over his collarbone.

Lucian's only response was a groan of surrender as he tangled his hands in her hair, tugging her even closer. Emma's heart raced in anticipation, every inch of her body aching. She knew Zoe and Anja were watching. She hoped this was a kind of payback for them sneaking in some fun time on the drive.

Emma trailed kisses down Lucian's chest, teasing him with her teeth and tongue as she went. Reaching his pants, she looked up at him. "Mmmm…what's the matter, Lucian? Cat got your tongue?" She laughed at her joke before unbuttoning his pants.

Lucian's erection sprang free. Emma circled it with one hand, squeezing gently before running her tongue along its length. His taste exploded across her senses—musky and salty—and she moaned appreciatively.

"Oh, yes," Zoe said from the bed behind them. "That's it, Emma."

Emboldened by Zoe's words, Emma took Lucian into her mouth completely, savoring the salty tang as she bobbed her head up and down his shaft. He filled her mouth, and she could feel him twitching against her tongue as pleasure coursed through him.

He groaned above her head. Emma sucked harder as she took him as deep as she could. Lucian's fingers tightened in her hair, but she welcomed the slight pain, using it to fuel her hunger. She could feel his cock twitching in her mouth, and she knew he was close.

"That's it," Zoe encouraged from the bed, her moans intermingling with Anja's.

Emma stood up and wiped her mouth with the back of her hand. She led him to the bed by his erection to join the others there. "More," she purred, guiding his still-hard cock to her entrance.

Lucian needed no further prompting. He slid into her with a low growl, gripping her hips as he began to thrust in and out. Emma arched her back to meet each powerful thrust. His cock filled her. She was happy she was very bisexual. With her eyes closed, Zoe or Anja, she didn't know or care which, started fondling her breasts.

"Oh, fuck," she moaned, rocking against him. "Yes!"

Lucian picked up the pace as their bodies slapped together with a wet rhythm. Sweat glistened as they lost themselves in the throes of passion. Next to them, Zoe and Anja urged them on, their moans and gasps adding fuel to the fire that burned between all of them.

Suddenly, Emma felt herself teetering on the edge of orgasm. "Lucian!" she cried out as pleasure exploded through her body in bright white flashes of light. She clenched around him as she shuddered through her climax. Lucian growled in response, his hips jerking as he drove himself deep inside her one last time before he, too, came.

As their breathing slowed, Lucian collapsed against her, his forehead resting against her chest as they both caught their breath. The room was filled with the sounds of their ragged breathing and the quiet moans from Zoe and Anja, who were still at it next to them.

Emma couldn't help but smile to herself. It seemed like they all needed this release.

After a few minutes, Lucian rolled off her to be next to Zoe and Anja. He moved over and presented his resurgent erection between their passionate kisses.

Lucian groaned in anticipation as Anja took him into her mouth, mirroring Emma's actions from earlier. He tangled his fingers in her hair as she bobbed her head up and down his shaft, as Emma had done moments ago.

"My turn," she breathed before he entered her with a moan of pleasure. Lucian's eyes rolled back, her wetness enveloping him. Her breasts bounced enticingly with each thrust, and he reached up to cup them in his hands, squeezing them roughly as they fucked.

Zoe and Emma found themselves entwined in each other's arms, making out passionately as they watched Lucian pump into Anja. Zoe's hand slipped down between Emma's thighs, finding her clit and rubbing it.

"Oh, fuck," Emma moaned into Zoe's mouth as her skilled fingers brought her back to the edge of orgasm. "Don't stop."

Zoe's tongue danced with Emma's as her fingers picked up the pace. Emma bucked her hips against Zoe's hand, desperate for more friction. Gods, she was close again already.

Lucian and Anja grunted and moaned just inches away, their bodies slapping together in wanton rhythm. Lucian gripped Anja's hips tightly as he pounded up into her.

Anja panted, her eyes half-lidded with pleasure. "I'm going to... aaah!" Her body stiffened, and she came with a loud cry as she shuddered through her climax. Lucian groaned and followed suit moments later, burying himself deep inside her.

As their breathing returned to normal, they collapsed onto the bed in a tangled heap of limbs, spent and sated. Zoe and Emma exchanged a heated look before their lips met in a fiery kiss once more. Their tongues tangled together in a sensual dance that left them both panting for air.

"You two are insatiable," Anja said with a laugh, propping herself up on one elbow to watch them.

"Jealous?" Zoe teased between kisses. She slipped two fingers inside of Emma, curling them expertly against the textured spot she knew would drive Emma wild.

Emma cried out as Zoe hit just the right spot, sending her over the edge again in another shattering orgasm that left her trembling and gasping for air. Zoe withdrew her fingers and sucked them clean before smirking at Anja and Lucian. "Ready for another?" she asked before straddling Lucian's lap.

Anja touched his member, and it sprang to life again. He groaned as Anja guided him into Zoe. Emma watched, transfixed, as Zoe began to ride him slowly, her eyes closed in pleasure. Soon, Lucian was moving with her, his hands on her hips guiding her pace.

As if sensing her thoughts, Zoe opened one eye and caught Emma staring at them. "You started it," she said, winking before returning her attention to Lucian.

Emma moved back and spread her legs, encouraging Anja to go down on her while she watched Lucian and Zoe.

"Gods, you're beautiful," Lucian breathed, unable to take his eyes off Zoe's bouncing breasts as she rode him.

Lucian growled, flipping them over so he was on top. He entered her with one swift stroke, and they began to move together in that familiar rhythm.

Emma closed her eyes and lost herself in the sensation of Anja's mouth devouring her. She felt a hand on her thigh and opened her eyes to find Zoe reaching for her hand and bringing it to her breast.

Anja came up for air and pulled her hips down, making room to move up and straddle Emma's face. Anja went back to licking her, and she returned the favor. She was on the edge, and it would be only moments before...

With a cry, she came apart, her entire body shaking with the force of her climax. Anja's scream was muffled as the sound vibrated against her. Lucian buried himself one last time inside Zoe. They all collapsed, their bodies slick with sweat and spent from their exertions.

Zoe propped herself up on one elbow, trying to make sense of the tangled limbs and the lingering heat. Her eyes flicked to Anja, who was breathing heavily, hair clinging damp against her cheeks. Lucian leaned back against the headboard, his expression indecipherable. Emma's hand rested on Anja's calf as if uncertain whether to stay close or retreat.

There were no words for several minutes as they all caught their breaths. "What the fuck just happened?" Zoe directed the question at Anja. "Is everyone all right?"

Anja's demonic side answered. *"See, you should have just gone for it earlier. It would've saved a lot of tension. That was only a light snack, and she doesn't let me feed deeply on you two."*

"I think I've been losing control. It's been too long since I last fed. I was afraid this might happen. At least it was just us… It could've been worse if the others were here."

Emma brushed a strand of damp hair from Anja's face. "Do you mean you could have pulled them in too?"

Zoe cleared her throat. "Her demonic side is real. Lucian and I accepted that a while ago, but it has, well…side effects. So, yes, she could have…might have."

Emma's eyes flicked to Anja. "Succubus. Yeah. I see what you mean."

Zoe nodded slowly, recalling the times she had helped contain that part of Anja. "Normally, we make sure she feeds before it gets this bad. But everything's been hectic. We should plan better."

Lucian massaged the back of his neck. "We're not exactly in a safe zone for this. If it'd happened in front of Graham or Mike, Dora, or especially Karolina…"

Emma exhaled and looked at Anja and then Zoe. "I'm okay with this, if that's what you're worried about. I just wasn't expecting it. Well, I might have been hoping for it. I can roll with it. I like sex—a lot. It would probably help to know when you need to feed. I thought it was just me."

Anja sat up a little. "This is my fault, I know. I shouldn't have waited so long. Next time, I'll warn everyone."

Zoe traced a pattern across Anja's shoulder. "We'll handle it. Just remember, we can't let your demonic side run wild."

Anja gave a nod, her demeanor shifting back toward her human half. "Lucian, Zoe, I'm sorry."

Lucian shrugged, offering a wry smile. "We've done this before," he said, indicating the four of them. "Together and apart. We adapt."

Emma snorted softly. "Adapt, sure. I just need a heads-up. Or maybe a safeword."

Zoe glanced around the rumpled bed. "Not sure a safeword would help. At least we're all in one piece. Think we can move past the awkwardness?"

Anja's demonic half chimed in again, her lips curling slightly. **"Awkward is such a mortal concept."**

Emma stretched her arms over her head. "I don't think it's awkward. I'm available. I know you three have a special arrangement, but if there's anything I can do to keep it from spiraling, tell me."

"See?"

Anja reached for Emma's hand. "Thank you. We just have to be careful. I don't want to feed on innocent bystanders."

Thirty-Eight

DORA WOKE TO a shaft of sunlight sneaking through the gap in the curtains. She stretched, blinking the sleep from her eyes, and tried to shake off the anxiety lingering from the previous day's events. The muffled sounds of movement drifted through the thin walls of the inn, signaling that she wasn't the first awake.

The sounds from the next room last night had also been muffled, but it had been obvious what those sounds signaled. Emma had stayed there with them and enjoyed it loudly as well.

Dora's sex life had been non-existent until Anja and Zoe. She wondered if there might be an opportunity for another session with them. Her past had switched that part of her off, but it had been reawakened along with whatever else she was. Anja was still being tight-lipped about it.

When she stepped into the hallway, Lucian was already waiting by a small table near the stairwell. A few half-empty cups of tea hinted that others had been up earlier. Dora joined him, catching a glimpse of Anja and Zoe further down the corridor, discussing something.

Karolina followed her out, and Emma jumped into her arms and onto her shoulder. She smiled happily as the cat rubbed her cheek.

"Morning," Lucian greeted, rubbing a hand over his stubbled jaw. He looked tired but determined. "We're rearranging who rides where. After…ummm, yesterday, we want to make sure Karolina won't be put in a tense situation if things get unpredictable again."

"What did I miss?"

"Have them explain after we get on the road again," Lucian replied.

"I'd like you to swap places with Karolina."

Before Dora could question further, Nomad emerged from around the corner, motioning for Anja to follow him. They walked toward the front desk of the inn, where the innkeeper was busy with a ledger. Dora watched as Nomad slipped the man a neat roll of rubles, nodding in approval when Anja leaned in to speak in low tones.

Lucian angled himself so he could keep an eye on them from a distance. "Nomad wants the innkeeper to call him if anyone starts asking about us," he explained. "We aren't hiding that we were here, but we do want a heads-up if someone picks up our trail."

Dora brushed a loose strand of hair behind her ear. "So he's asking for a courtesy phone call."

"Yes," Lucian said, casting a quick glance at Anja. Dora could sense that ripple of her gift—it always made the air feel a bit charged, as though gravity had shifted by a fraction.

Moments later, Nomad clapped the innkeeper on the shoulder, and the man nodded, stowing the rubles away. The pair returned to where Dora and Lucian stood.

Anja's eyes flicked to Lucian. "We're all set here," she said. "He'll answer honestly, then call the number we gave him. We'll be long gone by then."

Dora exhaled, relieved at how smoothly that exchange had gone, given everything else that had happened recently. "I'll get my things," she said. "Let Karolina know I'm taking her place. We'll head out soon, right?"

Nomad nodded. "The sooner we're on the road, the better. We'll need the extra time if we're going up toward Perm and then Cherdyn." He paused, looking between them. "We'll still travel in separate vehicles, keep a gap between us. Stay connected by... whatever methods we have."

Lucian offered a tight smile, and Dora knew he was thinking of his link with Anja and Zoe. "Let's get moving," he said.

They regrouped in the parking lot, reorganizing their seating arrangements. Dora hopped in next to Graham, with Anja and Zoe in the back seat. In the other SUV, Karolina took Dora's old seat in the back with Mike. They rolled out, leaving the modest inn behind.

The roads stretched out before them, the route shifting into long expanses of empty countryside. Dora glanced in the side mirror, spotting the second vehicle trailing far enough behind to avoid suspicion. She settled back into her seat, letting the rhythmic hum of the engine fill the silence.

"So, what did I miss?" Dora asked after a while.

Graham chuckled. "Those two had some fun in the backseat while the girl napped. They were trying to be discreet, so I was a gentleman and didn't say anything. It was kinda hard to miss, though."

"Ummm, sorry, but I guess we got carried away," Zoe said.

"I didn't mind. It brought back some good memories."

"Memories?" Dora asked.

"His awakening. Lucian and I helped him and Mike through the ritual," Anja said.

"All of them? At the same time? Like with me?"

"Yeah. A good time was had by all," Anja confirmed.

"Oh."

"And last night? The walls were kind of thin..." Dora trailed off, looking back and seeing Zoe and Anja exchange a quick glance. Dora guessed they were 'talking' to each other mentally. That bond of theirs would certainly come in handy.

"We should tell you both, seeing as it could happen again," Zoe said.

"What?" and "Tell us?" came from Dora and Graham in near unison.

Anja cleared her throat. "Ummm, go ahead, Zoe."

Zoe twisted in her seat, meeting Dora's eyes. "You're both aware that Anja is...well, part demon. Her succubus side can manifest if she goes too long without feeding. It's usually fine, but if she's stressed or hasn't taken care of her needs, things can...escalate."

Dora took a moment to process it, recalling the noise she'd heard through the thin wall at the inn. "So that's what happened last night? She lost control, and it just—spilled over?"

Anja shifted uncomfortably. "I'm sorry. But when I'm too hungry, that side of me tries to take over. I think I was too far gone to even think about control. We didn't want Karolina stuck in a car with me if that happened on the road. We trust you two to handle it. If it flares again..."

Graham tapped the steering wheel lightly. "I think I get it. So you're saying we might need to be…food? As in, have sex? I'm good with that, by the way. Beats crashing the SUV if Anja's demon side surfaces at a hundred klicks."

Dora nodded in agreement, cheeks warming a little. "Same here. I mean, it's not the first time we've…I mean my awakening." She paused, swallowing. "I've actually been thinking about that…that time. I never really figured out how to bring it up. Or how to ask if we could…you know, do something like that again."

Zoe smiled. "We'd be open to that."

Anja exhaled, her expression gentler than a moment before. "Yes, if you're both volunteering, it'll help me keep things balanced. I'd rather not explode with lust while we're racing down the highway."

Dora managed a hesitant laugh. "Okay."

Zoe reached out and gave Dora's shoulder a squeeze. "We appreciate it."

"What about Lucian?" Graham asked.

"Lucian understands the need. Even with him and Zoe, it's not enough. I can only sip from them. I'm too afraid of weakening or draining them completely."

Graham glanced over his shoulder, one eyebrow raised. "So to recap: before things get too out of hand, we just pull over and, ummm…"

"That's the gist, yeah," Zoe said. "Maybe we need to set up a rotation schedule for other times. Lucian claimed there would be no shortage of volunteers."

"That's true," Graham confirmed.

Dora looked out at the rolling countryside. It wasn't the typical conversation, but their group wasn't exactly normal. She settled back and let the engine's hum fill the silence, her mind spinning. She clenched her legs together, wondering if it was just anticipation or spillover.

Dora's gaze wandered across the passing landscape as she tried to calm the scattered thoughts rattling in her head. Her mind kept drifting to her awkward confession about wanting another round—and how Zoe and Anja had welcomed the idea. She let out a slow breath, wondering if Anja could feed on a self-induced orgasm from the back seat. That might be a pleasant distraction for the long drive, and it didn't seem like anyone would mind. She just didn't know how to ask—or if it would bring on the situation they were trying to avoid.

Anja's voice broke Dora's reverie. "Nomad said to stop for fuel whenever we can, but with everything going on in Ukraine, there might be supply problems out here."

Graham nodded at the news. "Makes sense. We've already seen a couple of stations that looked deserted."

Up ahead, a weather-beaten sign advertised petrol. As they drew closer, the station appeared old but still functional, with a single attendant visible in a worn gray uniform. Dora could see two pumps that looked like they had stood through decades of harsh winters.

"That's probably our best chance for the next hundred kilometers," Dora said. "Let's pull in."

Graham steered the vehicle off the main road and alongside one of the pumps. The attendant, a wiry man with a heavy mustache, waved them forward, indicating they should stay in the car while he handled the fueling. Zoe slumped down in the back seat to avoid drawing any extra attention, and Anja rolled down her window to speak with the attendant in Russian.

Dora watched as the man nodded, reaching for the pump. Then Anja glanced over her shoulder. "I'll go inside and grab whatever snacks they've got, if any. My Russian's decent."

Dora watched as Anja stepped out, exchanging a few quick words with the attendant. Her Russian seemed to flow with practiced ease, and the man nodded curtly before returning to the pump.

Zoe shifted, glancing at Dora. "Let's hope they have something better than stale crackers."

Graham snorted in agreement. "I'm guessing our choices are going to be pretty limited."

A few minutes passed in companionable silence while the attendant filled the tank, glancing occasionally at their vehicle. Dora kept an eye out for anything suspicious, but the place seemed deserted apart from a flickering light inside the station's mini-mart.

Eventually, Anja emerged with a small bag in hand. She cut across to the SUV, her boots crunching over bits of gravel. The attendant finished up, accepted a payment of rubles, and then returned to the shack.

Sliding back into the passenger seat, Anja exhaled a weary sigh. "It's pretty picked over," she said, lifting the bag for them to see. "I found some chocolate bars—they look like Alyonka, hopefully edible—plus a few packs of crackers, some dried fish, and these dusty pryaniki. No fresh stuff, so I grabbed bottled water, too."

She passed the bag around. Zoe perked up when she spotted the chocolate bars. "This'll keep us going a bit longer," she said, unwrapping one with a crinkle.

Dora took a bottle of water from the bag, twisting off the cap for a quick sip. "Thank you," she murmured, giving Anja a small smile. "Better than nothing. Maybe."

Graham checked the fuel gauge, then eased the car back onto the road.

"Nomad and the others will stop there as well. I let Lucian know it was open," Anja remarked, stowing her purchases near her feet. "We'll reconnect eventually. Until then, we just keep moving."

Dora nodded and let her gaze wander to the passing scenery. Maybe that would distract her from thoughts of Anja and Zoe.

Igor rubbed his stinging eyes as he pushed himself up from the worn leather sofa in his office. He hadn't intended to doze off, but exhaustion had won out sometime after midnight. Now, it was mid-morning, and he must look disheveled—an unusual state for someone who prided himself on meticulous presentation. He shot a glance at his wristwatch and cursed under his breath.

He barked a hoarse "Enter!" as a knock sounded at his door. Yuri stepped in, shutting the door behind him. Igor raked a hand through his hair, feeling the stiffness in his neck. "There better be good news," he growled, his voice rasping.

"I think you'll be pleased, sir. We've had some developments."

Igor leveled a stare at him. "Go on."

"Our men finally located an inn where the targets stayed last night," Yuri began. "They left early this morning, but we confirmed photos with the innkeeper—he recognized the group. They're still together, using the same two SUVs."

Igor nodded slowly, crossing his arms over his rumpled shirt. "Any idea where they're headed now?"

"That's the best part," Yuri said, lowering his voice with a hint of satisfaction. "We placed some of your special men on standby along the main routes out of Kazan. One replaced the normal attendant at a small petrol station on the northeastern road, hoping to see them if they stopped to refuel. Fuel can be scarce on those country roads. He managed to plant trackers on both vehicles without being noticed. They traveled about half an hour apart, so one SUV is ahead of the other."

Igor's exhaustion gave way to a surge of dark satisfaction. "Finally, some competent work." He dropped into his office chair, gesturing for Yuri to continue.

"The attendant—our man—called it in as soon as they were out of sight," Yuri said. "He's following at a distance, keeping to your standing orders not to engage. All assigned teams are converging. The next city on that route is Perm."

Igor frowned at the mention of Perm. A mental map of the region flickered through his mind, and he recalled its industrial sprawl and the routes deeper into the Ural Mountains. There were missile production facilities there. Did they intend sabotage for the Ukrainians? They had escaped Moscow during a drone attack. He dismissed that as a coincidence. "Perm," he echoed, letting the word hang. "What are they after out there?"

Yuri shifted his weight. "We're not certain, sir. Possibly something old—there are historical sites, mining interests… Could be a step toward Siberia."

Igor drummed his fingertips on the desk. "They have a reason. If Lucian, that traitorous Nomad, and the others are all headed north, there's something they want. Something they think they can find in or beyond Perm." His gaze sharpened. "I want every piece of intelligence we have on that region—old accounts, secret facilities, everything. Understand?"

"Yes, sir." Yuri paused. "Do you want us to tighten the net, maybe force a confrontation in Perm?"

Igor inhaled slowly, trying to regain a measure of composure. "Not yet. Let them think they're in the clear. I want to know exactly what they're after before we strike. If we lunge too soon, they'll scatter like rats. Keep tracking them. Do not tip them off, especially not Nomad. I want that traitor alive long enough to face me."

He remembered the Grandmaster's request to have Nomad sent to him. He might grudgingly allow that, but send Nomad alive? He wasn't so sure of that.

"Understood."

Igor glanced at the couch where he had slept. He'd need more than a power nap to stay ahead of this. "Send in some coffee, will you? And arrange for a hot meal. I'll need to make some calls."

Yuri bowed his head in acknowledgment. "Right away, sir."

With that, Igor's subordinate exited, leaving him alone once more. He gripped the arms of his chair, mind racing through the possibilities of what lay in Perm. Staring at the swirl of data on the screen in front of him, he allowed himself a rare, cold smile. Sooner or later, they would run out of road—and he would be waiting. He composed a quick update to the Grandmaster and sent it off.

After coffee and a few bites of food, he could think again. Igor tapped his fingertips on the edge of his desk. His eyes flicked to his watch. Waiting around here felt like a waste of time. If there was any chance he could intercept Lucian and the others in Perm before they disappeared into the mountainous wilderness, he intended to seize it.

His decision made, Igor rose to his feet, crossing to the door in a few long strides. He threw it open, barking Yuri's name. The subordinate appeared almost instantly, standing at attention.

"I'm leaving," Igor announced. "Arrange a flight to Perm—right now. I'll head directly to the airfield, and you can handle the rest from here."

Yuri blinked, then gave a sharp nod. "Understood, sir. Shall I alert the men there to meet you on the ground?"

Igor paused, considering. "Yes, but keep them on standby until I arrive. I want to see the situation firsthand before we commit to anything."

"I'll have a car brought around immediately. The helicopter will be ready within the hour."

"Get it done quicker," Igor growled. Without waiting for a response, he snatched an automatic pistol from his desk, threw on his coat, and stormed out of the office.

He settled into the back seat of a waiting car minutes later, drumming his fingers impatiently against the armrest as they wove through city traffic. The driver sped them along, and the sprawling airfield came into view. Igor's phone buzzed with an update—his transport was fueled and cleared for takeoff.

Stepping onto the tarmac, he was greeted by the pale gray silhouette of a Russian Mi-8 Hip helicopter, an older but durable workhorse capable of ferrying troops or cargo under challenging conditions. The rhythmic thump of the main rotor carried across the airfield. A flight officer stood at the open side door, offering Igor a salute, which he returned with a curt nod before climbing inside.

The interior of the Hip was spare and functional: bench seating along either side, harnesses for passengers, and little else. Igor moved toward a seat near the cockpit and secured his straps. The air filled with the pungent smell of aviation fuel and hot metal, evoking memories of training operations. It had been years since he had seen any real action.

As the helicopter lifted off, the cabin shook. Igor allowed himself a brief, tight-lipped smile. No more pacing around his office, reliant on patchy secondhand intel. If Lucian, Nomad, and the rest were heading north for some unknown reason, he would discover it himself—and be waiting for them in Perm. They wouldn't even know he was coming.

Banking eastward, the rotor blades drummed overhead. The final confrontation was not far off now. He had waited long enough.

It was time to show them exactly why Eagle's reputation preceded him—and why no one escaped his talons.

Thirty-Nine

THE SMELL OF fresh-baked bread greeted Anja as she stepped out of the SUV, stretching her legs after hours on the road. Perm's crisp air carried a hint of earthiness that reminded her how far they'd come from Moscow's chaos. She glanced around for anything out of place. It felt too peaceful, too still.

Nomad emerged from the bakery a few moments later, balancing a paper bag brimming with meat-stuffed pirozhki. The steam rising from the pastries mingled with the cool air, but his grim expression didn't match the comforting warmth of the food.

"We've got news," he said, distributing the pastries to the group. "Good and bad."

Anja raised an eyebrow, taking a pirozhok and passing another to Zoe, who leaned against the car, her pistol discreetly holstered under her jacket.

"Start with the bad," Lucian said.

Nomad sighed, leaning against the hood of the SUV. "The innkeeper called me. A man came by asking questions. Showed pictures—mine, yours, Dora's, even Karolina's. All of us. Said he was with the authorities. He didn't buy the story we left behind. Eagle knows I'm helping you. It's only a matter of time before he tracks our movements."

A cold weight settled in Anja's chest. "Did the innkeeper tell him anything?"

"No. Just confirmed we were there. But it doesn't matter. They likely have our plate numbers. We're marked now. The good news is, they're behind us. For now."

Lucian nodded thoughtfully. "That means we need to keep moving."

"Agreed," Nomad said. "We'll skip any long stops. We head straight to the church in Cherdyn."

"What's the plan?" Dora asked as she joined the group.

"Keep driving," Nomad replied, scanning the street for any sign of trouble. "The sooner we're out of here, the better."

Anja bit into her pirozhok, the savory filling doing little to ease her rising anxiety. She caught Zoe's eye and sent a silent thought through their link. "*We can't outrun them forever.*"

"*We can try.*"

With their breakfast finished, they piled back into their vehicles. Nomad took the lead again, the SUV's engine growling to life as they pulled out of the street. The city of Perm faded behind them as they headed deeper into the countryside.

The church in Cherdyn came into view as they rounded a bend in the winding road. Its weathered stone walls and bell tower stood out against the backdrop of dense forests, the morning sunlight casting long shadows across the rural landscape. Something about it exuded a quiet power that drew Anja's attention.

Nomad parked the SUV near the entrance, and the group stepped out, stretching their limbs and surveying the surroundings.

"This is it," Nomad said, nodding toward the church. "Let's hope we find what we're looking for."

Anja glanced at Lucian. "Let's move quickly. The longer we stay in one place, the more vulnerable we are."

Lucian nodded, his dark eyes scanning the area as they approached the church doors. They had made it this far, but the weight of the pursuit behind them was palpable, a shadow stretching ever closer.

The church's cool, dim interior carried the weight of centuries. Worn wooden pews stood in rows, their varnish faded from time and use. The scent of beeswax and incense lingered. Anja led the way, Zoe and Dora trailing behind her.

At the front of the sanctuary, an elderly priest stood near the altar, his robe a faded black and his beard as white as the snow that blanketed the Ural winters. He turned as they approached, his piercing blue eyes studying them with a mixture of curiosity and wariness.

"Father," Anja greeted in Russian. "Thank you for your time. We're travelers, seeking guidance."

"Guidance of what kind?"

Anja reached into her bag and produced the worn Bible Inessa had given them. She opened it to reveal the handwritten notes scrawled along the margins. "This belonged to a relative of ours. We've been tracing his steps to learn what happened to him. Inessa from Kazan suggested we come here."

The priest's gaze softened at the mention of Inessa, and he stepped closer to examine the Bible. His gnarled fingers brushed the pages with a reverence that spoke of decades of devotion. "Ah, Inessa...a kind woman, though troubled by many things. And this...this is old."

"Yes," Anja said, leaning in slightly. "And we believe it might lead us to something important. Something tied to our family's past. We were hoping you might help us."

The priest glanced at her, his gaze lingering on her face as though trying to discern the truth. "Family, you say? What is it you seek to find?"

"Closure," Anja said. "There are men hunting us—evil men. We need to understand where our family came from to fight them."

Dora stepped forward, pulling out her phone. She opened a map of the surrounding area and held it out to the priest. "We're looking for places connected to this Bible's owner. Any old settlements, churches, or monasteries nearby?"

The priest hesitated, his eyes flickering between Anja, Dora, and the phone. After a long moment, he pointed to a spot on the map.

"There was a monastery here, many years ago," he said. "It was abandoned long before my time, and now it's no more than ruins. I've heard tales of it, but I know nothing more."

"Thank you, Father," Anja said, her gratitude genuine. "Your help means a great deal to us."

"If you are being hunted, this is dangerous knowledge. Be cautious where you go."

Anja placed a hand on his arm, her succubus nature lending a subtle nudge to her words. "We are only pilgrims, stopping to pray.

We mean no harm, and we will not bring harm to your church."

The priest nodded reluctantly. "Then I will pray for your safety. May God guide you."

Anja, Zoe, and Dora bowed their heads in thanks before retreating from the sanctuary. The air outside felt brighter.

As they returned to the vehicles, Nomad's expression was grim, his eyes scanning the parking area.

"What's wrong?" Lucian asked.

Nomad knelt by the front tire of one SUV, holding up a small, sleek device. Its blinking light was unmistakable. "Found this in the wheel well. GPS tracker. Freshly planted."

Anja's lips tightened, and Zoe moved to check the other SUV. "Here's another one," Zoe called, pulling a similar device from beneath the rear bumper of the second vehicle.

Nomad stood and brushed his hands on his jeans. "It's likely whoever filled us up at that station planted them. They probably guessed we'd stop there. You have to get close to place them."

Lucian's expression darkened. "That means they're not just following us; they're starting to anticipate our moves."

Anja folded her arms, her mind working through the implications. "If they had the opportunity to plant these, why not just apprehend us? What are they waiting for?"

"Maybe they were only guessing we'd be there, and one lone attendant would not have tried to detain all of us. They must have somehow tied these vehicles to the ambulance and monitored traffic and surveillance cameras," Nomad answered grimly. "They found the inn we stayed at last night. They're tracking us. They want to know what we're after."

"These guys are smart," Graham said.

"Eagle," Nomad muttered. "He's throwing everything he has at us."

Lucian's jaw tightened. "So, what do we do? Ditch the trackers and run?"

Nomad shook his head. "No. If we ditch them, they'll know we're onto them, and they'll switch tactics. If we leave them in place, we can turn the tables—lure them into a situation we control." Nomad got in and started the engine. "Let's not waste time."

They climbed back into the SUVs, and as they pulled onto the road,

Anja glanced at Lucian. "We have a lead—a monastery in ruins. It's the best we've got."

"We could face them in the mountains," Dora suggested. "The monastery is isolated, and the terrain could give us an advantage."

Graham nodded. "Yes. They'll think they've cornered us, but we'll be ready for them."

The group fell silent, absorbing the weight of the decision. After a moment, Dora spoke. "If we're going to face them, we need to rest first. We won't be any good if we're exhausted."

"I agree," Graham said. "One night. However, we set watches and stay on alert in case they change their minds. Maybe staying the night will make us appear unaware and complacent, whereas the reverse will be true."

Dora pulled out her phone, scanning for nearby accommodations. "There's an inn not far from here. Two rooms. It'll have to do."

Anja passed the information to Lucian.

The inn was small, nestled at the edge of the town, its weathered wooden sign creaking in the wind. Inside, the air was warm with the smell of stew and fresh bread. The group secured two adjoining rooms.

As night fell, they settled in. Lucian, Anja, and Zoe shared a room with Dora and Karolina, while Nomad, Graham, and Mike took the other. Emma stuck with Karolina.

Emma could feel the tension in the air, the unspoken acknowledgment that they were being watched. She slipped out through a slightly ajar window, her feline form blending seamlessly with the night. Moving across rooftops and down shadowed alleys, she confirmed their suspicions.

Two figures were stationed in a parked SUV down the street. Another lingered by a lamppost, his eyes flicking to the inn's entrance every few minutes.

Emma returned, slipped back through the window and nudged Anja awake. Since she had refused the collar, she just changed shape and related what she had seen.

"They're here," Emma murmured, her voice barely above a whisper.

Igor sat in the passenger seat of the black SUV, his fingers drumming an irregular pattern on the armrest. Dmitri, the DKRO agent, glanced at him briefly. Igor had landed in Perm too late. The group they were pursuing had already moved on, and while the trackers had continued to provide updates, their elusive prey seemed to always be one step ahead.

The vehicle pulled up to the small church that Dmitri had mentioned in earlier reports from the advance team. That team had tracked them to an inn where they appeared to be staying the night, completely unaware they were being tracked. He wanted to know why they'd stopped at this church, which had no known significance.

Its stone exterior showed the years of wear and weather, its modest bell tower rising above. Igor stepped out, adjusting his coat against the crisp air. Dmitri followed close behind as they approached the building.

The old priest, clearly roused from his sleep, stood at the front of the modest altar, his robes hastily thrown over his shoulders. His wrinkled hands clasped in front of him, he offered a shallow bow as they entered.

"Father," Igor began, his voice cold and commanding, "I understand you had visitors earlier. A group traveling east."

The priest nodded. "Yes, they came seeking sanctuary."

"And what did they want?" Igor pressed. "What did they tell you?"

The priest's weathered face betrayed no fear as he replied, "They said they were hunted by evil and sought to pray for protection. They spoke of no other business."

Igor's jaw tightened. He had heard this kind of evasion before, and it grated on his patience. They were not hunted by evil—it was they who embodied evil to be crushed. "They stopped here for a reason. They were looking for something—or someone. What did they want?"

The priest shook his head. "They sought divine guidance. They prayed and left, nothing more."

Dmitri stepped forward, his tone more aggressive. "Did they show you anything? Maps? Documents?"

The priest's gaze did not waver. "They were weary travelers seeking God's grace. I have told you all I know."

Igor exhaled sharply, his temper barely restrained. He turned to Dmitri. "We're wasting time."

The priest bowed his head.

Outside, Dmitri asked, "Should we take them tonight at the inn? It would be simple."

Igor shook his head, his mind racing. "No. They've gone to great lengths to avoid us. If we take them now, we'll lose the chance to find out where they're headed. We can track them now—we'll know where they go." His orders were clear. Find their goal, then handle them. Making Nomad suffer would be a bonus.

Dmitri frowned but nodded. "Understood."

Back in the SUV, Igor reviewed the latest tracker updates on his tablet. They hadn't left the inn yet, but dawn was not far off. A check with the surveillance team confirmed they hadn't moved.

Igor leaned his seat back. "Wake me when they start moving. Tell the team to back off and ensure they aren't observed. Place a camera if you need to. If someone is spotted, they will answer to me."

The crackle of a radio woke him. Dawn was casting the town in pale shadows. He glared at Dmitri, who provided an update.

"The group loaded up in their vehicles. They appeared unconcerned and unhurried. There was no indication that they suspect they're under observation. The display here shows their current location and route."

The small blinking dots marked the progress of the two vehicles, both heading steadily east. Their route roughly paralleled the Vishera River.

"They're moving deeper into the wilderness," Dmitri observed. "There's little out there but mountains and old settlements."

Igor nodded. "Which means whatever they're after is either well-hidden or long-forgotten."

His mind worked quickly, piecing together the fragments of intelligence they had gathered. A stop at a church, a route paralleling the river—these were not the actions of mere fugitives. They were searching for something specific, something valuable. The

Grandmaster's instructions were to let them find whatever it was before capturing or killing them. It must be valuable indeed.

"They've become complacent," Igor said, almost to himself. "They must think they've evaded detection. The vehicles are staying together now, but they haven't abandoned their goal. Whatever they're after, they're risking their lives for it. Dmitri, have the advance team continue following the vehicles at a safe distance and report any stops. We'll let them lead us to their prize, and then we'll take it from them."

As the SUV sped along the winding road, Igor's mind drifted back to the grainy footage of Nomad behind the wheel of the ambulance. The betrayal stung more sharply with each passing moment.

Soon, Nomad, we will meet again.

Forty

Claire stood on the back terrace of her aunt Fiona's countryside house, the early morning light revealing the gentle slopes and rolling pastures that stretched beyond. She inhaled deeply, savoring the fresh scent of dew-coated grass.

Though far from the Miller estate's grandeur, Fiona's home exuded a warm, lived-in comfort. Fiona had inherited it from her mother Judith in a matriarchal line that traced back generations all the way to Isobel and beyond.

Claire hoped they were safe, since they had escaped the Sodality's notice for so long. Unfortunately, that would end if their secret were to be discovered. *We have to be ready,* she thought.

They had arrived only a few days prior, and already the compound felt crowded with the wolves milling about—some newly awakened, others still unsure of themselves, and more still to come. There was still so much to be done.

Shaking her head with a smile, Claire stepped off the terrace and walked through the courtyard, then into the main house. It would be a tight squeeze to accommodate everyone, but she found solace in the calm of the rural setting. The corners of her mouth quirked up at the sight of various sleeping bags and bedrolls laid out in Fiona's sitting room.

She, Ian, and a handful of others had been rearranging furniture and converting spare nooks into more bedrooms. They had started with five bedrooms on the second floor and one on the main level—that one was Fiona's. There were three small bedrooms in one of the outbuildings that had been for stable hands and farm workers.

Claire drifted toward the kitchen, drawn by the smell of tea, fresh scones, and sausage. She found Fiona and her mum, Margaret, seated at a small wooden table. Simon and Bee were moving around in the background, setting up a buffet with fruit, bread, and various spreads, including Ian's contribution of Scotch eggs, to keep the wolves fueled for the day.

"Morning, love," Margaret said as Claire came in. "Grab yourself a plate. Tea's piping."

Claire poured herself a proper cup and glanced at Fiona, noting the shadows under her aunt's eyes. "You all right, Auntie?" she asked.

Fiona managed a tired smile. "Oh, I've been better, pet, but I'll muddle through," she replied. "Had a word with the university—I'm taking next term off. Told them it was a family emergency. Could hardly say we've an influx of werewolves needing a roof over their heads, could I?"

Margaret reached over and gave Fiona's hand a squeeze. "Thank you, for everything you're doing," she murmured.

Fiona patted her hand in return, letting out a dry little chuckle. "We do what needs must," she said, then cast a glance at the bustling hallway where Simon and Bee were steering everyone towards the buffet tables. "For all the bedlam, it's good to have the clan back under one roof. This place had gone ever so quiet."

Claire nodded, blowing on her tea before taking a sip. "It does feel right," she said simply.

Fiona's expression softened. "Yes, dear. And thank you for bringing us all together again."

Claire spotted a cluster of wolves working through their morning drills and set off towards them, her boots crunching over the gravel drive. Ian was already there, guiding three newly awakened wolves through the basics of combat stances. His voice was low but clipped as he demonstrated how to turn and brace properly while in human form. A small knot of more seasoned wolves darted through agility drills in their shifted forms, weaving between the trees at the edge of the woods further uphill.

On the back terrace, Howard and Diana Forester sat under the morning sun, a contrast to the more boisterous drills below. Diana's light auburn hair gleamed as she moved through a series of precise hand gestures and spoken words, her expression focused. Howard watched with the faintest glint of pride, occasionally leaning in to adjust her motions or correct her phrasing.

Since her awakening, Diana had surprised them all—not only had the ritual unlocked her ability to shift to wolf form, but the reawakening of dormant strands of flux had also stirred something deeper within her. Though untrained, she had proven unusually sensitive to the subtle currents of energy Howard worked with. Given her background in psychology and medicine, and her long-standing fascination with holistic practices, it had been agreed—by her own choice as much as the council's—that her focus would remain on learning the shamanic arts rather than combat. Watching her now, tracing sigils of light into the air, Claire couldn't help but feel pride in her cousin's growing confidence.

"Claire!" Dillon called when he shifted back to human. "Am I doing it right? I'm trying not to overthink it—just…feel it, like you said." It seemed his modesty had fallen away along with his fur as he stood starkers.

She smiled warmly. "You're smashing it," she called back. "That's the trick, love—trust your instincts. The more you try to overthink it, the more you'll trip yourself up."

He'd come on leaps and bounds since those early, hesitant days when the idea of being 'otherkin' had seemed more curse than gift. Now, shifting between boy and wolf was second nature, the spark in his expression showing how badly he wanted to prove himself, to take his place among them.

He grinned, wiping the sweat off his brow, and behind him, another wolf shifted back with some difficulty, wobbling slightly as they found their footing again. Not everyone took to it as fast as Dillon—he was a natural, really.

Claire picked up a wooden practice staff from the rack and gave it an experimental swing, her muscle memory of Royal Protective days kicking in at once. "Your stance is everything," she said, catching the eye of a woman in trackies who was watching her, clearly unsure. "If you're wobbly on two legs, you'll be about as easy to knock over on four."

The woman set her jaw and squared up again. Claire stepped in and adjusted her position, nudging her into a firmer, more balanced stance. "That's better," she murmured, pleased to see the woman straighten with a bit more confidence.

She looked up just in time to see Fiona coming out from the house, arms full of neatly folded towels and a basket—hopefully full of sandwiches. Her aunt set them on a bench with a knowing smile.

"Don't forget to feed them," Fiona called cheerfully as she caught Claire's eye. "Else you'll have a pack of fainting wolves on your hands by noon."

When the session broke for a breather, Claire circled over to Ian. He handed a baton to one of the others and then turned to her. "They're coming along nicely. Dillon's doing great. He's got youth on his side, and he hasn't had time to pick up bad habits yet. Blank slate, that one."

Claire nodded, watching Dillon laugh with one of the others. "He'll be a force before long. We just need to make sure he keeps his feet on the ground."

Ian gave her a sidelong look. "Well, that's what you've got me for. Keeping hot-headed wolves out of trouble's practically a full-time job. And you lot don't even come with hazard pay."

She huffed a laugh and shook her head. "And yet here you are."

"Mmmm. You're welcome," he replied, though his eyes glinted with humor.

She brushed a stray lock of hair from her cheek, letting her gaze sweep across the yard. The wolves moved with a growing confidence now, weapons training blending with raw instinct. They'd come a long way from the precarious days back at the estate, finding their rhythm here amongst Fiona's fields.

Yes, the house was modest. The situation wasn't what any of them would have chosen. And time was short. But the beat of purpose in her chest was steady and sure. She drew in a long breath, letting hope settle.

They had each other. They had wolves eager to learn. And if luck was on their side, they might just have a chance.

Ash sat at the dining table, resolutely pretending not to be overwhelmed by the cacophony around him. The kitchen was cramped, noisy, and bloody full of wolves. He'd worked briefings in warzones that felt less chaotic. Dishes clinked and clattered as they were passed from hand to hand, and bursts of laughter ricocheted off the low ceiling. Through the open window came the scent of earth, livestock, and something faintly feral. Charming, really.

He'd ended up next to Dillon, who was animatedly describing some half-crumbled castle he'd spotted during one of his runs—as a wolf, naturally. Ash hid a smirk. He was still wrapping his head round the fact that the kid had paws at all, never mind a fondness for a good ruin.

Fiona leaned in, resting her elbows on the table, clearly enjoying herself. "Oh, that old thing? It's not even a proper ruin, just a folly. Some ancestor of ours built it to show off—waste of stone if you ask me."

Dillon's grin faltered, but only for a moment. "We could still use it for training though, right?" he asked, glancing around for backup.

Claire and Ian exchanged one of their loaded looks. Ash knew that look well—MI6 teams used it whenever someone suggested a plan that sounded clever until you actually had to execute it.

Ian shrugged. "Might be fine. But we'll need to check it over first."

"Check for rotten beams, holes, maybe the odd badger sett," Fiona chimed in. "Even fake castles have a habit of falling on your head if you're not careful. But a more varied training ground wouldn't hurt."

Dillon turned to Ash with bright eyes. "What do you think?"

Ash met the boy's gaze and took his time, swallowing a spoonful of stew before answering. "Well, lad, I'm all for using every tool in the box. If it helps you lot train without maiming yourselves in the process, then crack on. Just don't go playing at king of the castle before we've swept it properly."

Truth be told, Ash still found the whole bloody werewolf business surreal. But fieldwork taught you early on to adjust your expectations

—or die. And if nothing else, these people needed every advantage they could get.

He set his spoon down. "Considering one of Claire and Ian's jaunts involved laying siege to a castle full of zombies, you could do worse than get a bit of practice in."

That drew a sudden hush around the table. Ah. Touched a nerve, had he? In the flickering lamplight, their expressions looked half-amused, half-haunted.

"I still don't believe that one," Dillon muttered after a beat.

Ash raised a brow. "And this coming from a werewolf?"

That earned him another round of chuckles and broke the tension nicely.

The conversation moved on—training schedules, supply runs, who was due for what drills next week. Ash just listened, leaning back in his chair, taking stock. The energy of the room was different now. Not quite a unit yet, but not far off either. Given half a chance, this lot might actually pull it together.

One by one, the family began to drift away. Plates scraped clean, dishes stacked, leftovers boxed. Bee swept in and spirited the last of the crockery away, the kitchen quieting as the pack thinned.

Ash stayed where he was for a moment longer, watching the door swing shut behind the last pair of departing wolves. His fingers drummed against the table absentmindedly.

A makeshift family. A pack. Bloody strange business. But—he admitted to himself—it was starting to feel like something worth fighting for.

Now the hubbub had finally ebbed, Ash caught Ian's eye. Claire, too, gave him a subtle nod. Right. Time for the pow-wow.

He pushed himself up from the table and followed them out of the kitchen into the snug—a modest sitting room he'd more or less commandeered as his operations center. Cozy enough, but the smell of dog, or maybe wolf, still clung to everything. He didn't dwell on that.

Ash dropped into the chair nearest his kit, flipping a laptop open. "Right then," he began briskly. "Latest from Dora. They've got a decent lead in the Urals—some monastery, supposedly abandoned donkey's years ago, tied to the Stroganovs. Not much in the way of hard intel, mind. I scraped together satellite imagery, a handful of mineral surveys, and a smattering of historical mentions. Nothing you'd call comprehensive, but it's something."

Ian, as ever, was economical with his reaction. Just a short nod. "So they're pushing deeper into the wilderness. If they're still being tailed, it's only a matter of time before they lose coverage—or someone makes a move." He glanced at Claire. "We should be ready if they call for rescue."

Ash gave a dry little laugh, no mirth in it. "On that note...they're being tailed. Nomad found a tracker in the wheel well of their vehicle, and the other wasn't any luckier. Emma clocked surveillance at the inn they stopped at last night. Current plan, if you can call it that, is to play dumb, lull whoever's watching into thinking they haven't twigged, and pick their moment for a counter."

Ian swore softly. "Bloody hell."

"My sentiment exactly," Ash muttered.

Claire's brow furrowed, arms folded. "They'll have quite the element of surprise. I can see the logic...but I hope it's worth the risk."

Ian shot her a glance. "Any chance of calling this whole thing off?"

Ash shook his head. "Not a chance. They're dug in now. Too far along to turn back. Can't believe I signed on for this madness. Knew it'd turn pear-shaped sooner or later." He let out a sharp breath through his nose. "I'll keep the lights on here and do what I can to help them. But if Krakarov himself comes bearing down on them..."

Claire dragged her fingers through her hair, tension written in the line of her shoulders. "We can't do any more from here. All we can do is plan for the worst and hope it doesn't come to that."

Ash gave a bitter little chuckle. "Too bloody right. Here's hoping they find whatever it is they're chasing up there, and that we can all get through a single day without them having to pull another miracle out of their backsides at the last possible second."

He tapped the laptop lid shut, leaning back with a weary sigh. Quiet fell between them, and for once, he didn't bother filling it. No point dressing up the fact that the odds weren't getting better.

Ian offered one of his faint little smiles. Supportive, understated, annoyingly calm. "We could ring up Elín. See if she'd be able to provide air cover."

"Air cover?" Ash asked, staring at Ian like he'd grown a second head.

Claire gave Ian a sidelong glance, the corners of her mouth quirking. "Oh, right. Guess we forgot to mention that bit. You know about the wolves here and the grumpy bear." Ian didn't bother denying it. "Well…Elín is a dragon. So. Air cover."

Ash blinked. Then he blinked again, shut his mouth with a clack, and shook his head slowly.

After a beat, he chuckled. "I swear to God, I keep having to pinch myself just to make sure I'm not in some bloody fever dream. Or a nightmare. Still not sure which, mind. Honestly, you lot could tell me just about anything at this point, and I'd have to believe you. You planning to tell me next week that someone's actually a unicorn in disguise?"

Ian didn't even crack a smile. "I'll call her. See what she says—or if she's got a better idea."

Oh, marvelous—a bloody unicorn, Ash thought. *Why not? Let's just tick that one off the list while we're at it.*

He blew out a breath, the faintest of smirks tugging at his mouth. The tension in the snug eased just a fraction, the air lighter now.

After a few more details were hashed out, Claire stood and stretched, graceful but weary. "Let's call it a night," she said.

Fine by him.

Ash followed them out, the warmth of Fiona's house settling around him as the others found their rooms or commandeered floor space. Upstairs, he could hear low murmurs, the occasional laugh. This wasn't the polished, bloody intimidating grandeur of the Miller estate—but it was alive, and it was…something. Something he'd almost missed having, though he'd never say it out loud.

Climbing the stairs to his borrowed bedroom, he muttered under his breath about dragons and wolves and whatever the hell else he'd signed on for, then fell quiet. In the stillness of the hall, he found himself thinking—hoping—that Nomad, Lucian, and the rest were keeping their skins intact out there in Russia.

Because for now, all he could bloody well do was wait. Like the rest of them.

Helena paced within the confines of her study. An ornate window overlooked the grounds, but its view offered little comfort. She had spent the past week watching the Miller estate from afar through the streams of data her operatives provided.

However, the latest report was infuriating. The estate, once teeming with activity, now lay silent. The presence of so many guests and staff had dissipated—and apparently without leaving so much as a whisper of their new destination. Helena's jaw tightened. Those people had managed to vanish yet again.

She set her encrypted tablet on the desk, tapping through the last set of images: shots of vehicles leaving in different directions at different times, staff refusing to disclose even the simplest details. They weren't frightened; they were loyal—and that loyalty baffled her. She had hoped the staff might become more pliable once the guests had departed, but they were as unyielding as ever.

A chime signaled a new message from the Grandmaster. She keyed in her authorization, eyes narrowing at the file that opened. It detailed an update from Eagle, confirming known associates involved: Lucian, Nomad, and Anja, among other individuals. There were photos attached. Zoe Ananda was there. A woman named Kasia and two other men were described as her muscle. There was even a young waif. Cute little girl, but Helena had no idea how or why she was with them. It seemed Eagle was just as in the dark.

The fact that Nomad was assisting Lucian drew Helena's brows together. This confirmed he was compromised. If Anja's seductive power could snare her, it made sense Nomad might be similarly bound.

Helena let out a slow breath, the tension in her chest easing. After all the cat-and-mouse games, the group had eluded the Eagle's forces—her plan's best outcome. So much of what Helena intended hinged upon Anja's continued survival and the strengthening of her allies. *Let them vanish,* she mused. *Let them grow stronger and survive.*

Absently, she tapped at her tablet again, confirming no new leads on Lucian's four personal guards. They had simply disappeared from all surveillance. She sighed, refusing to let her frustration linger too long. If Lucian's team remained free, so did the possibility of her greater plan.

Turning away from the desk, Helena drew a cloak tighter around her shoulders. She moved across the echoing corridors of Zamec Echo to a small window seat. Shadows slanted in the moonlight. Her silent contemplation gave way to a renewed determination. If Eagle's intel was correct, then the Grandmaster's net would only tighten. Helena's part lay in weaving gaps into that net, ensuring its flaws multiplied.

Her eyes lingered on the silent lake beyond.

Forty-One

Dora sat in the passenger seat of the lead SUV. She glanced up occasionally to check their surroundings, then back down to cross-reference Ash's digital maps and satellite imagery with the location of the abandoned monastery. It was supposed to be deep in the forest near a river, far from the conveniences of modern life.

At a self-serve filling station, they stopped briefly. Graham exited the SUV and began fueling. The other vehicle pulled up on the other side of the pump, and Nomad started filling that one.

"How are we doing this morning?" Dora asked, glancing over her shoulder. "You've both been quiet."

Zoe, reclining against the door, gave a mischievous grin. "I'm just saving my energy for witty commentary later."

Anja, seated next to her, met Dora's gaze with a serene smile. "I'm fine. A bit tired, but...my hunger's under control, if that's what you're asking." Her voice dropped slightly. "The night with Zoe, Emma, and Lucian...helped."

"Hmmm," Dora murmured. "On the drive yesterday, I couldn't stop thinking about that. My awakening also seems to have reminded me I do have a sex drive. I had suppressed it for a long time. I kept thinking about you two passing the time on the long drive and considered amusing myself. I figured nobody would mind after our conversation, but I wasn't sure if it would trigger something more."

"I wouldn't have objected." Zoe grinned.

"You wouldn't," Anja responded. "I don't know, Dora. This is all new to me, and...it might have complicated things now that we know we're being followed."

"Oh, don't worry about her, Dora." Zoe winked. "I'm still trying to get her to loosen up more. Then again, look where that's got us so far," she added in a stage whisper.

Anja rolled her eyes with a mock sigh. "You're impossible."

"I prefer irresistible," Zoe countered with a playful shrug. "Keeping morale up while we're driving into the great unknown."

Dora stifled a laugh.

The pump clicked off, and Graham tapped the hood. Dora turned back to the front as he climbed back in and started the engine. As soon as Nomad was done, they pulled out onto the road, heading east.

"Anything worth noting?" Graham asked.

"Just that we're heading into the middle of nowhere," Dora replied with a half smile. "But Anja's sure it's right. We'll need to follow these logging roads past the village and onto even less inviting trails. It's going to be rough."

"We're looking at maybe six hours to the spot, assuming we don't get turned around. Once we get close, we may have to hike."

Graham grunted his acknowledgment, scanning the gravel road ahead. They maintained a steady pace, the occasional bump in the road jarring the vehicle.

Dora's mind drifted as they drove. She tried to imagine what this trip might have been like five hundred years ago. Back then, ox-drawn carts and trudging on foot would have been the only way to traverse the region. The harsh and unforgiving terrain must have stretched the travel into weeks, perhaps longer. Given bandits, wild animals, and the biting cold of Russian winters, it was no wonder the monastery had been forgotten over time. Even now, with GPS and maps, it felt like they were chasing shadows.

The road narrowed, flanked by dense pines. It was well-maintained for such a remote area, which puzzled Dora until they crossed a bridge into a village. She caught sight of a sign she couldn't read and nudged Graham to slow down.

The village was active despite its small size. Men milled about, their flannel shirts and heavy boots giving them a rugged appearance. A massive mill was surrounded by stacks of logs piled high like giant matchsticks. A truck loaded with timber rumbled past.

"This must be the hub for logging operations around here," Dora said, gesturing toward the sprawling yard. "The road's so well-kept because they need to move timber."

"Good news for us," Graham replied, maneuvering through the dusty streets. Workers paused to watch them pass.

As they left the village behind, the road narrowed further. Dora checked the map again, tracing their route toward the monastery. "These are all logging roads from here on out," she said. "At least for now, the path is clear. But once we're off these main trails..."

"It's going to get tricky," Graham finished for her.

The SUVs rumbled along a dirt track that had veered off the main road some miles back. Beyond the windows, vast swaths of forest stretched out, broken up by rectangular patches where trees had been harvested. In a few of these sections, rows of saplings showed signs of replanting—green hope rising from the scarred earth.

Further on, they passed a region stripped of vegetation altogether, the ground pitted and raw from mining operations. The mountains loomed closer now, mostly rocky and bare. The air felt different here—sharper, tinged with the scent of resin and moist soil.

Dora felt the SUV slow as Graham followed a winding path riddled with ruts. They rounded a bend to find themselves at a shallow stream, the water glinting in the midday sun. On the opposite bank lay the remnants of an ancient bridge—its arch collapsed into the waters, leaving only jagged outcroppings on either side.

"Well," Dora said, scanning the scene with a resigned sigh, "I guess this is where we stop. The monastery should be uphill through the trees about a mile or two that way." She pointed toward a path that disappeared into the undergrowth.

Anja slid out of the SUV, her boots crunching on the ground.

Lucian climbed out and surveyed the area. "All right. Let's park off to the side."

Nomad hopped down, adjusting his jacket. "I'll help camouflage them. Mike, give me a hand?"

Karolina lingered nearby, hands folded nervously. She glanced at the track behind them, then back to Dora.

"You're coming with us," Dora reassured her. "We're staying

together."

Karolina mustered a small nod. Meanwhile, Emma stretched, stepping a few paces away from the group. Within moments, she transformed from her feline form back to human and rummaged in the back of the SUV for clothing and running shoes. She looked somewhat reluctant as she dressed.

Zoe checked her sidearm, slid up beside Emma, and handed her one of the handguns and some spare magazines. "So we're doing this?" she asked.

"Yeah," Emma responded. "Let's just get there and set up a welcome party before our shadows show up."

Lucian joined them, double-checking his gear. "We'll move quietly—one group, single file. If anything happens, we regroup and find cover in the monastery ruins."

Emma looked over the pack slung across her shoulders, then touched Karolina's arm. "Stay close to me. If you need to rest or anything, let me know."

Karolina nodded, offering a small smile. "Thank you. I be okay."

With the vehicles now concealed amid branches and brush, the team gathered near the path. Nomad and Graham each carried rifles at the ready while Emma cradled her newly checked weapon. Dora and Anja positioned themselves to lead, and Zoe fell in behind them.

"All set," Nomad said, scanning each face in turn.

Dora looked at the ruined bridge. "Well, here we go."

Anja walked along what seemed to be a narrow game trail, the press of old pines and towering birches hemming them in on both sides. Her senses were keenly attuned to the forest's hush—the rustle of a small creature darting through the undergrowth, the fragrance of damp earth. The air felt charged, as though centuries of secrets lay buried beneath the ground.

Ahead, the path curved upward, and they followed it until the rise leveled off. A stone marker stood near a gnarled tree, its surface worn by time. Anja brushed aside a curtain of moss and lichen, revealing a crude cross etched into the rock.

She paused, calling to the others. "Look at this. It might've been a marker for the monastery's path once."

Lucian ran a hand over the lines of the cross. "Judging from the underbrush, no one's used this path in a long time."

Zoe craned her neck to peer down the slope behind them, scanning for any movement that might indicate pursuit. "Wish Carlos was here."

Lucian's gaze drifted across the dense woods. Carlos was a special forces sniper. He'd spot anyone tailing them long before they got close. "Yeah, me too."

Emma shifted her rifle on her shoulder. "Hate to admit it, but Claire and Ian would be welcome too," she muttered. "We could use their firepower and...well, they're good in a fight."

Anja offered a faint smile. "We'll manage. Carlos, Claire, and Ian would help, but we've come this far."

They lingered for a moment, drinking water from their canteens and catching their breath at the crest of the rise. The vista was dominated by forest stretching in every direction, with no sign of anyone following. Still, an unsettling sense of being watched hovered at the edges of Anja's mind.

"All right," Lucian murmured at last. "We move on."

The group pressed forward along the meandering trail. Soon, the forest opened into a clearing, and before them lay the remnants of a once-modest monastery. Portions of stone walls jutted from the ground, their edges worn smooth by weather and time. Timbers that had once formed the structure's roof were scattered in heaps, charred in some places, rotten in others. A collapsed archway hinted at an entrance hall, now carpeted in moss.

Anja's heart sank at the sight. Even from a distance, it was clear that the ruin held little more than ghosts of history. Still, they approached with caution. Karolina hesitated at the edge of the rubble.

Stepping into what remained of the main hall, Anja ran her fingertips over the cold stone. Vines wound through cracked mortar, nature reclaiming what had once been a place of worship and refuge. She glanced at Lucian. His expression was resigned.

"No hidden passages," Zoe remarked, shining a flashlight into a dark corner. "No chest of scrolls. Nothing that looks like a library."

Dora, kneeling by a collapsed beam, glanced up at them. "All these years…it's just ruined. There's no sign of any records or archives here."

Nomad exhaled slowly. "So much for our monastery lead."

Anja closed her eyes, listening to the rustle of the wind through the broken walls. She felt disappointment tug at her, though she wasn't entirely surprised. "We'll have to look elsewhere," she said at last.

Then she noticed Dora kneeling by what was once a hearth. And time seemed to slow.

Dora knelt before the massive fireplace, its maw easily large enough to hold the logs that had once heated the monastery. She couldn't tear her eyes away from the blackened stones charred by countless winters long past. Something within her stirred—a pull she couldn't resist. As if from a distance, she registered Anja's voice: "We'll have to look elsewhere."

Then Dora's fingertips brushed the sooty interior, and the world went white.

In an instant, she was no longer in the ruined monastery. Instead, she stood in a scene bathed in the muted glow of burning logs. Two men, cloaked in traveling furs, conferred in a corner alcove. She recognized them from her earlier vision: Nikita and Maksim. A hush surrounded them, punctuated only by the crackle of the fire in the hearth.

They spoke of venturing east, their resolve undimmed by the trek that had brought them to this remote place. Small bands would traverse old trade paths across forgotten fords lying in the upper reaches of half-silted rivers.

Time rippled around them like a curtain shifting in the breeze. Dora saw them discover a depleted mine hidden in the folds of a mountain. It lay near a river crossing that was once used by merchants bound for farther east. Here, the Stroganov brothers envisioned a second outpost: discreet, concealed from prying eyes, destined to hold the great treasures entrusted to them.

In fleeting images, devout and skilled brethren gathered timbers, iron nails, and sacks of grain. Dora felt the cold sting of water across her ankles, as if she too waded through the ravines. Within a rocky hollow, the monks erected a modest skete—a small chapel, unadorned except for icons hung at precise angles. Beeswax candles glowed in the gloom, while somewhere below, passages were cut through stone, leading to a secret vault. Scrolls and sealed chests rested in silent vigil there, guarded by the stale air of the mine intermingling with fragrant incense.

Days gave way to months and then years. Nikita and Maksim visited seldom, each trip more grueling than the last. Dora felt a pang of empathy as she witnessed Nikita's strength fade; a shadow seemed to cling to him, telling of hard experiences and something else. On their final trip, they arrived with a bound codex and an ornate wrought-iron seal. Voices whispered of Nikita's failing health, and Dora saw Maksim stand alone at the threshold of the skete, head bowed in sorrow before turning away.

When the last of the brothers passed on, the mountain retreat stood complete. The vault below remained sealed, containing the library safe in hushed and candlelit watchfulness. Monks continued their routines—tending small gardens in harsh soil, oiling hinges to keep them from rusting, and lighting torches against the ever-deepening dusk. As the years passed, fewer and fewer of the monks remained until the embers in the hearth flickered out for the last time.

A whisper, almost a gust of wind, brushed Dora's ear: *They protected it, always. And the secret died with them.*

And then, just as suddenly, the whiteness flashed again and receded. Dora found herself back at the abandoned monastery's hearth. The blackened stone was cool under her hands. The corners of her vision refocused on the present, where Anja stood a few paces away.

"Dora?" Anja asked, voice taut with worry. "Are you all right?"

Heart pounding, Dora nodded slowly. The echoes of distant footsteps and the glow of a candlelit vault left her mind. "Yes…yes, I think I've found something more. They built another place—hidden. The library is there."

Igor Krakarov stood at the edge of a shallow stream, the sound of running water filling the crisp mountain air. Ahead lay the remains of a collapsed bridge—massive stones and timbers long fallen into disrepair. He crouched by the bank, eyes narrowed as he examined the muddy tire tracks leading to a makeshift parking spot. Two vehicles sat among the tall grass, covered by hastily cut pine boughs. Their engines were cold.

Igor rose to his feet, scanning the deserted scene. "The trackers on these cars won't help us anymore," he said.

Seven men—heavily armed and trained for such pursuits—fanned out. The hush of the wilderness settled over them, broken only by the gush of the stream.

Igor's gaze settled on the ruin of the bridge. Now, at last, they were within reach. Their prey had no easy way to retreat.

One of the operatives, a sniper named Oleg, returned from a quick scout of the vicinity. "Sir, looks like they followed that trail," he said, gesturing to a winding path that cut upslope through the pine forest.

Igor's lip curled. "They have seven, plus a child," he murmured. "We're seven men here, all highly trained, well-armed. They're nothing but a ragtag group running on luck."

Alexei shuffled, recalling the earlier failed ambush. "Respectfully, sir, Nomad is with them. He knows our tactics."

Igor ground his teeth at the mention of Nomad. "No matter. Now that I know it's him, I'll deal with Nomad myself. I didn't teach him all my tricks," he said coldly.

He glanced at the vantage point where the path climbed a small rise. A crude cross carved in a mossy stone stood like a sentinel next to a gnarled tree. "The priest lied," he muttered under his breath, recalling how the old man in Cherdyn had insisted they'd only come to pray. "He sent them here. I'll deal with him later."

Turning his attention to his men, Igor let his voice harden. "We push on. Once we find them, they cannot be allowed to slip away again. Keep your intervals. Watch for any signs of a trap."

A wave of acknowledgment swept through the group. Weapons clicked as magazines were checked, safeties flicked off. Each man readied for a decisive encounter.

They followed the path down the incline. The pine branches overhead filtered the sunlight into shifting patterns on the ground, casting dancing shadows around the team. Silence reigned except for cautious footsteps and the occasional rustle of gear.

The path opened into an overgrown clearing with the crumbling ruins of what must have been an ancient monastery. Stone walls were half-collapsed under the weight of years, blackened timbers rotting away. It stood empty—fresh footprints in the dust and a set leading out the far side. Igor felt a surge of frustration as he realized his quarry had come and gone.

No matter. They were close. He could feel it.

Igor signaled for his men to spread out, searching for any clue that might reveal the group's direction. Broken weeds, displaced stones—they discovered the continuation of the tracks through the trees beyond the ruins. That had to be the path.

He straightened, face set with cold determination. "They've taken another trail. We go after them immediately."

They murmured assent, adrenaline already simmering in the lengthening shadows. It would be night soon, and he wanted this finished before dark.

His jaw clenched. The chase would end today in the hush of these forests and the shadow of these mountains. They were following the path the fugitives thought was safe.

"Move out," Igor said grimly, and the men advanced, forging deeper into the wilderness, prepared to finish what they had started.

Forty-Two

Zoe crouched near a fallen timber, heart pounding in her chest as the dusky sky bled into night. They were deep in these woods, menaced by killers who wanted them dead—and she refused to go quietly. The enemy had followed rather than attacked earlier. That meant the enemy wanted to find out what they were after. That detail might just give them a chance.

A strange calm settled over her, tinged by an unexpected surge of arousal. Perhaps it was the thrill of danger or the realization that she'd do anything to keep her friends alive, even if it meant dying for them.

They'd found the skete near a steep rock wall, rubble and half-burned timbers marking where a small wooden chapel had once stood. Mike stood before a large stone that he said was out of place. A black void was revealed when Mike and Graham levered the hefty stone slab to the side. A hush fell over the group.

"That must be it," Dora murmured, pointing her flashlight into the void. "An old mine shaft, or maybe the vault. I can't see how far it goes."

Lucian nodded, his jaw set. "We're cornered here. Graham, Mike—take positions uphill with rifles. Keep eyes on the approach." The two men gathered their gear and vanished into the trees, soft footfalls barely stirring the pine needles.

Zoe swallowed hard. Her hands tightened around the pistol's grip. *"I hate this, but we can't let them catch us. It's us or them."* She flashed back to all the Sodality had done—torture, killings, people left in ruin. She forced down her revulsion. *"I won't let them hurt you two, or any of us."*

Nomad stepped away from the mine entrance, nodding at Lucian. "I'll wait here. Eagle wants me, so I'll give him a target."

"Emma," Lucian said, "stick with Zoe. We need pairs."

Emma checked her weapon again and turned to her with a quick grin. "Ready?"

Zoe grinned back. "Yeah. Let's make it count. This will be better than shooting zombies."

"How could I forget?" Emma replied wryly.

"Dora," Lucian said, "take Karolina inside. Keep her safe, and see if there's a spot in there you can hide or barricade."

Dora guided Karolina inside, ushering the trembling girl into the shadows. Karolina shot a last worried glance at Emma and Zoe before disappearing into the darkness.

"I'm heading uphill, but on a different route than Mike and Graham. They're in for a few surprises," Anja declared.

Lucian squeezed Anja's shoulder. "We'll distract them here. Be careful."

Zoe heard a dark chuckle through their link. *"Feeding time?"*

"Uh-huh."

"Do I want to know what you're planning?" Zoe asked silently.

"I can guess," Lucian sent.

As the sky dimmed, the group split, heading up into the trees on the hillsides. Zoe found a hidden vantage behind a fallen log, and Emma crouched beside her.

Lucian gathered some dried branches into a pile near the entrance, then waved toward Mike and Graham. In a few moments, the pile burst into flame.

"That's handy," Nomad said.

"They have no idea what they're walking into," was all Zoe heard before they lowered their voices to continue whispering.

With Graham, Mike, and Anja scattered above, they waited in a tense silence for the night to descend—and for their pursuers to walk into the teeth of their defense.

Igor Krakarov crouched at the edge of a sparse copse of trees, the dusk blurring outlines into hazy shapes. In the distance, a glow flickered through the undergrowth—firelight dancing under the twilight sky. He signaled for his men to halt. The hush of the forest swallowed every sound, save for the wind through the pine needles.

By now, darkness had almost completely fallen, the last streaks of daylight fading from the horizon. One of Igor's men, Oleg, slipped off to scout, moving with practiced stealth among the pines. Igor waited, heart pounding with anticipation, until Oleg returned, breath shallow, eyes narrowed with excitement.

"Two men," Oleg whispered. "They're warming their hands over a fire near an old mine entrance. It's definitely Lucian and Nomad. No sign of the others."

Igor's lips curled into a cold smile. The Grandmaster would be pleased indeed if he delivered both Lucian and Nomad in one strike. He waved his other operatives closer, then gave short, precise orders. "The rest are likely inside the mine exploring, unsuspecting of their doom. Surround the clearing, keep quiet, and stand ready for complications. No mistakes this time."

A sense of triumph filled him as he rose from his crouch and stepped past the final line of trees. The forest seemed to hold its breath at his approach. Ahead, the two figures huddled near a small fire. Their faces were revealed by the fire, and their shadows danced against the rock wall. They appeared unaware of their predicament.

Igor walked forward, each footstep deliberate on the forest floor. He stopped at the edge of the flickering light, his men forming a silent semicircle behind him in the darkness.

He drew his sidearm and raised his voice to carry above the crackle of flames, "Nomad. Lucian. You are surrounded. Would you care to surrender?"

Nomad stood slowly. The flames reflected in his eyes in some unnerving way, almost like he was burning inside.

"Eagle," Nomad called out. "It's been a long time. I'm surprised to see you here. I thought you would send your minions to do your dirty work for you, like you sent me."

"I wanted to see your treason for myself. You've betrayed me, and that's something I'll have trouble forgiving."

Nomad laughed. "Forgive me? Do you really believe I would ever trust you again?"

"I see. I think I'm going to enjoy this." Igor began to raise his arm to signal his men to close in.

A piercing shriek erupted, and the night shattered. A flash—a swift extinguishing of light—then absolute blackness enveloped the clearing. Not the normal darkness of a forest night, but something deeper, suffocating, as though the moon, stars, and even the fire had been snuffed out—as if the world itself had gone blind. Igor's unseeing eyes widened, his breath catching in his chest. Screams rang from behind him, followed by erratic bursts of gunfire, too rapid and chaotic to be controlled.

He sensed, rather than saw, movement all around. The crack of a branch, the rustle of clothing, a sharp intake of breath—then silence. The quiet was deafening, an impenetrable wall of nothingness.

Igor fired blindly toward where Lucian and Nomad had stood moments before. He felt the recoil jerk his arm, then pivoted to bolt for the cover of the forest. His vision swam, darkness giving way to stars bursting and shifting behind his eyelids, colors blooming violently as he stumbled forward. Confusion gripped him, nausea building, as he realized he had been too confident. Too sure of himself.

He had been wrong. The others were not inside exploring. A trap had been set, and he had led his team into its jaws.

It wasn't over yet. His vision was slowly returning. Ahead, he could make out blurry silhouettes of his men fleeing. His mind struggled to comprehend the scene, the panic infectious, spreading like wildfire. These were trained men. They should be better than this.

Footsteps pounded behind him, and Igor turned abruptly, firing again. Nomad ducked low, rolling despite the bullet grazing his wrist, blood splattering dark against his sleeve. Lucian faltered, clutching his thigh as he hissed in pain.

Nomad surged forward, closing the distance with frightening speed despite his injury. Igor snarled and aimed his pistol at Nomad's head, but the shot missed as Nomad ducked, driving upward into Igor's ribs with brutal precision. Air exploded from Igor's lungs, pain radiating outward as he staggered backward.

Recovering quickly, Igor lunged, grabbing Nomad's injured wrist. Nomad growled through clenched teeth, eyes blazing, and Igor twisted viciously. Nomad's blood-soaked arm slipped from his grip as Nomad grabbed his weapon hand. Igor's legs were swept out from under him. They both sprawled onto the ground in a tangle of limbs.

Igor grappled desperately, clawing at Nomad's throat, while Nomad drove elbows and fists into Igor's sides, each strike precise, efficient, trained. Their breathing mingled harshly, the scent of blood and sweat heavy between them. Igor's strength waned under the relentless assault, frustration and panic clouding his senses.

From the corner of his blurred vision, Igor saw Lucian limping closer, determination etched across his face as he raised his weapon. The sight sent a surge of desperation through Igor, and he bucked upward, catching Nomad briefly off guard.

Nomad's gaze locked with Igor's for a split second, a dark satisfaction glittering in his eyes. "This ends now," Nomad growled, delivering a powerful strike to Igor's temple.

Stars exploded anew in Igor's vision. His world spun violently as consciousness ebbed. His body no longer obeyed, and his senses spiraled toward darkness. The last thing he heard was another bloodcurdling shriek like a demon from hell.

The forest night swallowed him whole.

Anja stood in a dense stand of pines, heart pounding as she focused on the scene below. The glow of the fire danced against the rocky wall while the day faded into night.

"We rule the night," her demon mused.

She sensed men ghosting into position around the clearing, waiting for their moment to strike. Only seven men. A fury stirred in her chest.

She closed her eyes, shutting out the world, and banished her clothes. She let her inner demon rise. Not the subtle, sensuous succubus, but the other demon—stronger, darker, wicked, and filled with lust. Bloodlust. Her skin darkened like night brought to life, and her eyes burned red. Vicious horns curled above her head like a fanged crown, and massive wings unfurled from her back, their tips ending in cruel spikes. Her hands stretched, and wicked claws sprouted. Her tail grew, ready to strike with its spade-shaped tip.

Anja inhaled, calling forth the armor from the nexus—the cupless red leather cuirass, bracers, and the greaves that glinted with arcane runes. She summoned her razor-tipped whip, the metal humming with dark energy. The transformation tugged at her soul, and a hunger swelled in her chest as her demon self took the fore.

She caught Zoe's mental query—*"Anja?"*

"Call me vengeance." She closed the link. Her bloodlust would be too much for Zoe. She would spare her that much. And Lucian, too. Anja would be alone in this. Well, except her other self.

Adrenaline and other chemicals flooded through her. Her senses sharpened, and the fading light seemed to brighten. She could hear the crackle of the fire, and the scent of smoke kindled some inner flame.

Below, she spied a man stepping from the trees. She watched as he pulled his pistol and called out to Lucian and Nomad, asking for them to surrender.

Nomad stood and called out, "Eagle," and then said other words she didn't pay much attention to. Her focus was on Eagle, who was here in person. An unexpected bonus. One that would make this night even more eventful. Her grin showed sharpened fangs.

A flicker of triumph crossed Eagle's features as he raised his hand to signal the ambush.

Anja's face twisted, and a shriek tore from her throat, echoing through the dusk—a monstrous battle cry directed at Eagle that reverberated across the tree-covered slope. She leapt skyward with a single powerful thrust of her wings, cutting through the air like a blade of living night. The rush of wind stung her face, and her red eyes gleamed as she spotted Eagle's men in the shadows—rifles and sidearms at the ready. She let the demon's wrath flow as she streaked downward.

One man yelped as his assault rifle began to glow, burning his hands and spontaneously firing off stuttering rounds. He cursed, tossing the gun aside in panic, and turned to flee. She angled toward another pair. That one had been too easy.

Anja descended among the trees, claws extended, whip crackling with malevolent force. She hit the ground in a swirl of dark wings and lashing tail, her momentum carrying her straight into the nearest man. A savage blow tore out his throat, and blood slashed her face and body. She spun, whip flicking out to wrap around the other's arm, the razors cutting to the bone.

Shots rang out—a muzzle flash in the gloom—but she slid to the side, wings buffeting the shooter, spikes tearing flesh. She ignored the pain that lanced through her wing. Her tail whipped forward, the sharp tip plunging into his chest and finding his heart. Another man stumbled, fear etched in his eyes as he scrambled back.

Bloodlust roared in her veins. She felt a thrumming at her core, feeding on the terror, blood, and deaths of men who had come to kill them. Every strike, every shriek of pain, poured more vitality into her limbs, fueling her savage strength.

Amid the fray, she glimpsed Eagle. He was running to the trees as Nomad and Lucian chased him. *Later,* she thought, fangs bared in a predatory grin. *He's last.*

For now, she reveled in the chaos. The sounds of gunfire shattered the night's earlier quiet. The hiss of her whip and screams of the wounded formed a melody she relished. She was vengeance incarnate, claiming the battlefield for her own.

The shriek Emma heard was chilling, but it stirred something in her blood. The shape that launched into the air and streaked towards the woods was terrifying. "Remind me not to get on Anja's bad side," Emma said.

Zoe began firing at movement in the trees. The woods only held the enemy, even if they couldn't get a clear line of sight—for the moment.

More shots came from Graham and Mike's direction.

"They're running!" Emma yelled. "Can't let them get away!"

The shooting stopped, but screams erupted in the trees where Anja had landed. Emma heard another pistol shot, then a man's gurgling scream.

She dropped her pistol and tore at her clothes, trying to strip. "Damn it. I shouldn't have bothered putting these on." She kicked off her shoes.

"What are you doing?"

"I'll run them down. Hunt them in the dark." She had the urge to taste blood. *Is that from Anja, or is that me?* she wondered.

"I won't be able to keep up."

"Go help Lucian and Nomad. They're chasing Eagle," she said as the shift started.

Zoe exclaimed, "Fuck."

Emma pushed her change faster than ever before. It hurt. A lot! The sound that escaped her throat wasn't human anymore, part yowl and part growl. She lay there for a moment, painting. Zoe was watching her warily. She had seen the large pather before, but now the lethality of her other form hit hard.

Emma rose and looked down the slope. She shook herself, then bounded over the log and away.

As she hit the tree line on the far side of the clearing, she heard a dark laugh and gurgling near where Anja was fighting—more like slaughter now.

Emma's senses sharpened. The scent of her prey and fear was strong. Colors were muted, but it almost seemed like daylight. It would be easy to track her quarry. She sped on almost silent paws, leaping over fallen logs and dodging trees and low branches. Her prey's scent grew stronger, and she could hear someone crashing through the underbrush, running in panic.

There.

He slowed, then stopped, doubled over. She leapt and landed on his back, driving him to the ground. She sank her claws into him as her powerful jaws clamped on the back of his neck and bit down, jerking back and forth. The taste of blood filled her mouth as his neck snapped with a crack. He lay still, but other odors soon followed.

She trotted off to the side and stopped. She could hear the distant sounds of fighting near the ruined skete and clearing.

Raising her head, she opened her mouth slightly, lips curling up, and inhaled. It probably looked like a smile or, more likely, a grimace. Flehmen, she recalled, and chuffed.

The scent of blood was strong, but she filtered it out. The other forest smells faded into the background as well. What was left was two distinct men who were somewhere upwind. One had used cologne; the other had not and had a mild smell. Not fear, but... maybe determination. She needed more experience to understand what these scents meant.

She tilted her head to gauge the breeze on her whiskers—that way, upwind.

She crept slowly on silent paws, careful to avoid dry branches. Her tail flicked behind her. She could still taste blood, but she wanted more. It was just ahead, and from the sounds of footfalls, it was coming her way. She crouched down, waiting—stealth hunter in the darkness.

There. A man stepped behind a tree, looking back toward the battle. He did not seem anxious to rejoin the fight. He looked around and listened. After a moment, he continued to slowly, cautiously move toward her.

Emma launched into the air. He screamed, then—

An explosion of sound and pain. She realized her mistake too late. The other man, who had smelled determined, had been hiding in the trees as the other man moved. With a cry that tried to rival Anja's, she crashed to the forest floor and lay still, her blood seeping into the pine needles. Just before it all went black, she heard a rush of air and another bloodcurdling shriek. *Anja...I'm sorry,* she thought.

Anja looked down at the torn, bloody form and smiled.

"So good," her demon purred. It was like an orgasm of power. She felt alive like never before. Energy thrummed through her veins.

She tasted the blood on her claws, salty and metallic. Warm blood trickled down her chest and dripped off her breasts. *So much like the other fluids of life,* she thought, unsure which of her selves that thought came from.

She looked around. She had killed three, and the sounds of another death after Emma had joined the fun made four. That left only two and Eagle. They were trying to flee. Maybe to get help or maybe just to run. It didn't matter.

Her demon gazed into the forest's darkness, away from the old skete and the library that awaited them. Two men and another sleek figure—Emma.

Anja looked up, looking for a way through the boughs, then leapt into the air on her mighty wings to glide above the treetops, seeking those motes in the forest below.

As her dark shape flew above, the black feline shape pounced on one while the other hid. The shot flashed out with an explosion of sound that echoed off the hills. The scream Emma let out was soon accompanied by Anja's own. She took the head off the man who had shot Emma with her whip as she rushed past. The other man was wounded, but his suffering ended abruptly as she grabbed his spine with her talons and twisted.

Emma lay unmoving as blood pumped from the wound in her side. Her breathing was shallow. Still alive, but for how long?

"Can we fly with her?" she asked her demon.

"No, not fly far enough to get back. You are strong enough to carry her."

"She needs Lucian."

"Then grab her and run."

Anja didn't take much care, and it was a mercy of sorts that Emma was unconscious while she lifted the massive cat and ran.

She reopened her link to reach out to Zoe and Lucian as she ran. *"Emma is hurt badly. I'm bringing her back."*

"Fuck. Lucian was shot in the thigh, and Nomad was shot in the wrist trying to protect him. Lucian healed Nomad and himself enough to stop the bleeding."

"Anja, I'm out of power. I don't know if I can heal her."

"I have plenty. It has to be enough to save her."

In only a minute or two, which felt much longer, she entered the clearing and set Emma down next to where Lucian sat. Eagle was bound, gagged, and unconscious. The others were gathering.

Karolina gasped and started to cry. Anja wasn't sure if it was her appearance or that Emma was so badly hurt. Probably both. Dora hugged her when she buried her face and sobbed.

Lucian rested his hand on Emma's wound and closed his eyes. Anja rested her bloody hand on his shoulder and willed power into him as she had before. If they had saved Richard from dying, then they would save Emma. Anja would not let her die.

The look on Lucian's face told her as much as his thoughts. *"It's really bad...I don't know..."*

"You can do it, Lucian," Zoe said.

"You must do it," Anja added.

His hand glowed over Emma's side where the blood had slowed to a seep. Her flesh was healing, but it wasn't going to be enough.

"The shift! But she doesn't have enough power for that either," Lucian said. "I don't even know if she can change while unconscious."

"I can take what you need from Eagle and feed it to you both. Make her body remember."

"Anja, what are you saying?" Zoe asked.

"Take Karolina inside. She doesn't need to see this," Anja told Dora.

Dora took Karolina's hand and led her into the mine.

"Anja?"

"Would you rather Emma die?" she asked, looking into Zoe's eyes.

"But cold-blooded murder..."

Anja approached Eagle and raised his chin. **"Hear me... See me,"** she commanded, pulling him to consciousness.

His eyes slowly focused, and he stared at her. She must be a sight. Covered in blood was the least of it. Nomad had once looked at her that way what felt like such a long time ago.

She used a claw to cut off Eagle's gag. "Nomad. You are a witness to his crimes. Crimes that should carry the penalty of death. Is he guilty?"

"Many times over," Nomad said quietly.

"Igor Krakarov. How do you plead?" she asked.

"Demon whore! You should all die!"

"I hear that as guilty. There. See, Zoe? Justice that the world's laws are not ready to mete out." She looked back at Zoe.

Zoe looked on the verge of tears, shaking her head. Then she dropped her gaze and nodded.

"Anyone who doesn't want to bear witness should go inside." Anja looked around. Nobody moved.

Anja knelt next to Igor. "Eagle of the Sodality of the Thorns. Igor

Krakarov, your life is forfeit. But take heart in the fact that your life will save another, one that is infinitely more worthy."

She plunged her talons into his chest under his sternum and reached inside to grasp his beating heart. Her fingers twisted, talons cutting tissue, and extracted his heart. More blood spurted over her as it pulsed, and she held it up to glisten in the firelight as power flooded into her again.

"Now!" She willed power into both Lucian and Emma.

She followed Lucian into the essence of Emma's being, deep into the twisting helices of her DNA. Wonder swept over the link, spilling into both her and Zoe. It was a small blessing that Zoe could witness this miracle to replace the horror that had preceded it.

Emma's form changed slowly before the process sped up. In minutes, Emma lay on the ground. Unconscious, still, but alive.

Mike wasn't so lucky. He was near the trees, emptying his stomach. Graham looked grim but steady.

"It's done," Lucian said. "She'll live. Probably be out cold for a while."

Anja took a last look at the heart and tossed it into the fire.

Nomad said, "We'll need to gather the bodies. What do we do with them?"

"I'll bet there are crypts or at least some abandoned tunnels inside. Mike, do you think you can get one of the SUVs over here or at least hike some of our supplies in? You probably have the most off-roading experience."

"I can try it."

"Good. Grab all of our things and anything useful from theirs. Remember to destroy the tracking devices."

"On it," he said before heading into the woods.

"Graham, Nomad. Can you drag the bodies here?" Lucian asked.

"I'll help," Zoe volunteered.

"You okay?" Anja asked Zoe.

"No, but I will be."

Forty-Three

ANJA STOOD NEAR the charred remains of the old wooden skete, the night's chill pressing against her face. She had debated staying in her dark form, but at Zoe's urging, and with the blood starting to dry and itch, it was time to change. The hole in her wing had also started to ache. Shifting to her human form felt like a relief, but came with other feelings she had suppressed. Maybe her demon had taken too much control. She had ripped a still-beating heart from a man's chest and felt the power rush. It was like a powerful drug that she hoped would not be addictive. Counseling might be in order. *Well, Zoe will be there to talk to, anyway,* she thought.

She shivered as she surveyed the grim work they had done. Bodies—those men who had come to kill them—were stacked among the broken timbers. Even in the faint moonlight, she could see the smear of blood on the scorched beams, their damp surfaces reflecting the recent struggle. Eagle's wide-eyed stare of horror and the gaping hole in his chest were a macabre sight as Graham added him to their makeshift pyre. It was a harrowing sight, but she had no illusions about the path they walked.

The crunch of boots drew her attention. Mike approached, stepping around the scattered debris, carrying two large duffels he had trekked back. The flicker of headlamps and tactical flashlights illuminated the night, casting stark, dancing shadows on the ruined walls.

Nomad stood to one side, wrestling a half-splintered log into place. Lucian and Zoe worked in silence, passing stray beams to bolster the pile, their expressions grim.

"This should be sufficient," Lucian said. He locked eyes with Anja. She sensed his exhaustion but also his resolve.

"We'll need to get this done," Anja said. "I hope the fire doesn't draw even more attention."

"Agreed," Mike said. He pointed at a battered set of flashlights, some presumably taken from the fallen men, and others from their underground expedition. "At least they left us these. We'll have plenty of illumination in the mine."

Emma, who was standing watch by the edge of the clearing, tossed back a final piece of broken wood. "They won't be missed," she muttered under her breath, referencing the dead men.

Anja gave a nod. "Let's do it. Mike, do the honors." His fire salamander side had its uses.

Mike concentrated on the stone of the foundation beneath the pyre. They began to glow, and the logs smoldered before flames whooshed up, bright and hungry, devouring the timbers and corpses. The glare forced them back a few steps, as did the blast of heat. For a moment, no one spoke. The roar of fire swept over the silence.

As they watched, Dora said, "I updated Ash via the satellite link. He's still wondering what our plans are for getting out of here. Especially if we have to move…whatever we find. He said he might have a few options, but all of them are risky."

"As if getting here wasn't," Lucian muttered.

"He even mentioned the 'dragon lady,'" Dora continued. "I guess he's been getting up to speed on our group. He said they'd settled into their new location successfully and had been making progress."

Anja said, "We'll figure it out, but first, we need to find that library."

They turned from the blazing pyre and headed toward the mine entrance. The cliff face seemed to dance in the light of the fire. The crackling roar echoed all around. Just inside the mine entrance, a corridor led into darkness, the stale air carrying a tang of old minerals and damp earth, replacing the reek of smoke outside.

Anja ducked under a warped timber, her boots crunching over gravel and ancient dust. Their flashlights cut through the darkness in arcs, revealing damp stone walls lined with rotted supports and half-collapsed beams.

The passage widened into a chamber, clearly excavated by hand centuries before. Chisel marks gouged deep into the dark stone walls, primitive but purposeful. Rusted iron spikes protruded from the rock, holding remnants of ropes long rotted away. To one side, stacks of splintered wooden crates and barrels sagged, bound in iron bands gone brittle with age, their contents long since decayed.

Nearby, broken mining picks and hammers lay scattered in heaps, their handles reduced to splinters, heads rusted almost beyond recognition. A faded emblem etched into the wall—perhaps a Stroganov crest—overlooked the ruin. The very air seemed reluctant to yield its secrets.

They searched for what felt like hours. Room after room, corridor after corridor, each one empty but for scraps of wood, piles of rock, and dark, stagnant pools. Zoe's muttered swears carried through the echoing space as she swept her light over yet another dead end. Dora knelt now and then to examine markings on walls or the uneven floor, but nothing she found offered hope. Even Lucian's usual confidence had dulled, his gaze darting down the corridors as though the walls themselves mocked them.

Anja felt frustration simmering, and she could sense the same creeping into the others. It had taken everything just to get here, and for what? Her demon coiled in her mind like a restless serpent, whispering darkly about failure and futility.

Dora joined her, wiping dust from her hands. "I checked some side chambers. Mostly empty—at least at first glance. But if there's a hidden route, that's where we'll find anything left of Ivan's library, if it truly exists."

"You think this is where Nikita and Maksim hid the library?" Anja asked.

"I do," Dora said. "They sealed most of the library deeper underground, where the small monastic community once guarded it. This is it. It has to be."

"I think I've got something," Mike called from farther down one of the side passages.

Anja's head shot up, the small flare of hope burning through her weariness. They hurried toward his voice.

They found Mike crouched near a collapsed support beam, tracing along a seemingly solid wall. "Here," he said, his eyes glinting in the harsh light. "Feel this. There's a seam here. The air's cooler, too—there's a hollow behind it."

Anja pressed her palm to the wall where he indicated, feeling along the thin, uneven line in the stone. There—just the faintest shift of air, the barest hint of a crack.

For a moment, she only breathed, her heart thudding. Then she glanced back at the others, who had all gathered now, their expressions brightening despite the exhaustion in their eyes and their lights beginning to dim.

"You think it leads deeper?" she asked.

Mike nodded, certainty in his voice. "It has to. Look at the stone floor. It's worn more from here to the entrance, but not so much further in. This has been closed off. Hidden."

Dora crouched beside him, brushing her fingers over the seam as well. "This would fit," she murmured. "It wouldn't have been left in plain sight. I didn't see this in the vision."

Nomad checked his sidearm out of habit as he eyed the narrow space. "Then let's see where it goes. We didn't come all this way to quit now."

Anja straightened, feeling the familiar chill of anticipation washing over her, mingled with the burn of her own dark hunger. She gave a nod, the faintest of smiles curling her lips as she raised her flashlight.

"All right," she said. "Let's see what's been waiting for us all these centuries."

One by one, they pried the hidden stones loose, revealing the way forward.

Sure enough, a gap led into a cramped tunnel. Broken timbers braced the walls. The floor looked damp, with rivulets of water trickling down from cracks above. Anja crouched low, shining her light into the gloom. The beam revealed slick walls and a ceiling blackened with soot from ancient torches. From somewhere ahead came the rhythmic drip of water, echoing as if counting the years.

Mike moved up next to her. "Stay alert. The next part of the mine might be flooded," he warned. "See the water?"

Anja let out a breath. "We can handle some water if it's passable. Let's be mindful of any traps—though I doubt the monks would have set anything."

"All right, let's move," Lucian said. "Mike, lead the way."

Anja felt a surge of mingled excitement and apprehension. The trail of legends, scrawled notes, and midnight escapes had led them here. Their footfalls echoed. The light from their lamps illuminated more of the passage with each step—a lost world beneath the Urals, whispering secrets across the centuries.

They followed the corridor as it sloped downward, turning at unexpected angles. The rock walls narrowed until they felt like they were threading through the belly of the earth. The air was heavy here, thick with the scent of old earth and forgotten time.

Occasionally, they passed carvings on the stone—crosses, Cyrillic letters worn to near invisibility, icons depicting saints or stylized eagles—remnants of a time when pious guardians had once trodden these passages, carrying the tsar's fabled library to its hiding place.

It was a dreamlike trek, the tension from the battle above overshadowed by the awe of what they might find. Anja breathed in the cold, damp air, reminding herself that Eagle's forces lay smoldering out there in the darkness. Now, the real treasure might be within their grasp.

Anja steadied herself against the cavern wall, the sound of dripping water amplified by the natural hollow. Their lights swept across rock formations that glistened with mineral deposits, stalactites hanging like daggers overhead. At their feet sprawled a wide, dark pool of unknown depth, the surface reflecting flashes of light from the group's headlamps. She felt a chill skitter up her spine. Moisture was bad. She hoped that the library wouldn't be a moldering pile.

Mike took the lead, testing each step with care. "This is a natural cavern," he announced, shining his flashlight along the far edge. "And there"—he paused, training the beam on a section of rock behind a cluster of stalagmites—"there's another passage."

"Great," Zoe murmured from just behind Anja, trying for humor. "Let's just hope there's not some giant tentacle monster waiting to drag us under, like in *The Fellowship of the Ring*. You know—the creepy thing in the water outside the Mines of Moria? I told you movie nights were educational."

"Well, thanks for that image, Zoe. Just what we needed," Dora said dryly.

Anja glanced back at Zoe with a smirk despite the tension. "If anything grabs you, Lucian will make sure it regrets it."

They made their way around the pool, boots slipping on the wet stone. After Zoe's comment, everyone seemed to take extra care and eyed the water suspiciously.

Once they passed the limestone outcrops, Anja spotted the tunnel carved into the wall, almost obscured by a fallen stalactite. It sloped upward, its sides and ceiling drier than the path behind them. Relief washed through her: they were finally escaping the water.

They pressed on, single file. The air changed from the damp of the cavern to dryness, laced with centuries-old dust. At the passage's end stood a timber door, remarkably intact despite the passage of time—its surface hardened as though the wood had petrified under the mountain's embrace. Mike ran his hand along the planks, feeling for a latch or handle.

Zoe and Nomad moved to either side, guns at the ready, just in case. Lucian joined Anja, and together they watched Mike pry back a simple, hand-forged iron bolt. With a low groan, the door swung inward.

A stillness greeted them—no air currents, no wildlife stirring. Only their footsteps broke the silence as they stepped into a chamber shaped more by human hands than natural forces. Their flashlights revealed rows of carved stone shelves laden with stacked chests and sealed containers. On one side sat a collection of cylindrical canisters stamped with strange sigils. Anja's pulse quickened—scroll cases.

"This is it," Dora whispered, stepping around Mike to shine her beam farther along. Several thick volumes lay in a neat stack, their covers edged in gold. Words in Cyrillic embossed the spines. Some books displayed stylized double-headed eagles or intricately wrought crosses, designs still discernible under years of dust.

"It is," Lucian breathed, moving closer to the largest chest. Its lock had rusted shut, but the wood seemed sturdy, embossed with regal motifs.

Emma joined them, touching the edges of a volume. "Unbelievable," she murmured. This was the trove of religious texts and historical records once prized by Ivan.

Nomad remained at the door, while Zoe knelt near a battered trunk of scrolls. She picked one up, swallowing her awe. "We found it…"

Anja couldn't deny the surge of reverence she felt, gazing at these artifacts. Legends whispered about the tsar's fabled knowledge—holy texts, forbidden lore, chronicles of a brutal but culturally significant reign. To think it all lay here, sealed away by devout keepers.

She brushed dust off a set of gilt-edged tomes and felt their weight—an echo of countless centuries. A wave of relief, excitement, and unease settled over her. For even as they uncovered this sacred legacy, enemies waited.

"Use your phones to photograph everything," Anja said. "Document it, then we need to get ready to move it. Once we get it out of here, we can decide how to protect it, just as those who came before us did. And use it," she added.

Graham groaned, then asked, "And how do we get it out? Cart it up to the SUVs? I don't think it will all fit. Once we do that, drive out and wave as we pass Moscow, maybe? Those men and Eagle are bound to be missed soon. This is not ideal."

Anja noted his sarcasm and knew the others would be just as uneasy. "I have an idea. The pool out there…"

"Open a portal to your nexus? You think that will work?" Lucian asked silently.

"We've been there, but what about the others?" Zoe asked.

"I don't know. What else do we have?"

"Let's try it," Lucian said out loud. "If that doesn't work, maybe call for an airlift like Ash mentioned. Although I don't know if Elín could fly that far or carry this much."

Zoe chuckled. "Dragons do tend to appreciate a good treasure hoard."

"What? Fly?" Dora asked. "What was the other option?"

"A portal at the pool to my nexus. I'm not sure it will work, but I'll try."

Dora watched from the water's edge, her pulse quickening with each breath. Anja stood near the dark pool, eyes closed as if listening to something beneath the surface. Dora sincerely hoped no tentacles appeared.

Graham, Nomad, Emma, and Karolina hovered nearby, exchanging uncertain looks as if none were entirely sure what Anja intended to do. Not surprising, since Dora didn't either.

Zoe had explained earlier that only she and Lucian had experienced Anja's nexus firsthand, and Mike had seen them vanish and reappear in Iceland. Dora still had trouble believing it.

She and Mike had spent much of the last hour at the mine entrance relaying directions to Ash, who passed them on to Elín, hoping the same principle that let Anja travel between planes from Iceland would hold here. If it failed, well...there was no Plan B. Flying by dragon didn't seem practical as far as Dora could tell.

Anja let out a slow exhale and shook her head, causing Dora's heart to sink. Had it not worked? But then Anja lifted her gaze, and Dora's breath caught at the sight. Anja's clothes vanished, revealing her body as it shifted into a form both sensual and inhumanly captivating. She radiated an allure that made Dora's heart race and her cheeks flush with a rush of desire.

Part of Dora wanted to offer herself—she knew that Anja's succubus hunger could need fueling. A thrill coiled in her belly at the notion of being more than just an observer.

Anja closed her eyes once more, concentrating. The air grew colder, and a haze of mist swirled over the pool's surface. A shiver of energy rippled outward, a subtle pulse that Dora felt in her bones.

A shimmering portal flickered into existence—mist parted like a curtain, revealing an opening beyond. Anja nodded to Lucian and Zoe, taking their hands. Together, they stepped forward and vanished into the swirling haze.

Moments later, Anja reappeared, wearing that same beguiling form but smiling reassuringly. "It worked." Her voice held a tremor of triumph. She extended her hand to Dora. "Come on."

Dora's stomach lurched. Butterflies of anticipation and nerves warred inside her. Yet the warmth in Anja's eyes settled her doubts. Accepting the offered hand, she let herself be guided into the swirling vortex of mist.

Icy air prickled against her skin. One step became two, and then the dull grayness faded into something else—a shimmering lake nestled in a forest at the foot of a cliff. Dora blinked, trying to steady her racing heart, until she saw Zoe and Lucian waiting a few steps from the water's edge. Whatever this place was, it existed between reality and fantasy.

Zoe greeted her with a grin of relief. "Welcome," she said, motioning Dora forward. Lucian offered a nod, though he watched for Anja, who had emerged with Dora in a swirl of red wings and that mesmerizing shape.

Anja turned and disappeared into the icy mist. Dora exhaled, letting the tension ease. Her arousal, however, did nothing of the sort. She suspected she was feeling the effects they had described that led to the 'spillover' that night at the inn.

When Anja reappeared, Nomad held one of her hands and Karolina the other. Nomad looked uncomfortable, but Karolina looked around in wonder.

"Magic," she said happily. Dora thought Karolina's acceptance came from her youth and innocence...well, her youth, at least. She had lost most of her innocence through her experiences with Marek and others, just as Dora had.

"Yes, magic," Dora said. That was what it was.

Soon, Anja went back, then appeared again to start passing chests and boxes through. Her demon form was stronger than it looked.

Lucian guided them to a cave entrance in the cliff wall and had them start carting their treasure inside.

The stone steps led to a spacious room filled with shelves. Karolina chipped in, moving the smaller items out of the way and onto the shelves.

Zoe commented, "Anja's nexus seems different every time. Maybe to suit her wants or needs. Kinda like a fae burrow."

Dora had to ask. "Fae?"

"The...oh, never mind, later. Let's get things across before Anja runs out of energy. This has to be draining."

Soon, the last artifacts were through and stored. Anja brought Mike, Emma, and finally Graham through. As she stepped onto the pebbles of the shore, the misty vortex dissipated.

"Mike, do you think Elín will have someone waiting yet?" Anja asked.

"Should. The idea was to put someone on watch with transport."

"Good, Nomad, Karolina, let's get at least you two through. I don't think I can go much longer."

Anja held her hands out for them. Karolina took a hand readily, and Nomad reluctantly.

A new portal opened with that bone-jarring pulse, and Dora swore the air was colder than before. They disappeared through the mist, and it was several minutes before Anja returned.

Anja looked weary. "Sigri and Carlos were waiting. I think my appearance startled them, though Sigri looked intrigued," she said, indicating her succubus form. "I requested they upgrade Nomad's quarters and provide a pass to access the common areas. He's proven his new loyalties and will brief Elín and the others. Sigri agreed to have someone wait there for when we return." She sighed and said, "I can't do any more. You may have to be my guests for a while until I can regain my strength. I'm hungry."

"Is this where you say, 'Come into my parlor?'" Zoe asked, grinning.

"Yes, Miss Fly," Anja replied and winked. "'Will you walk into my parlor?' said a spider to a fly; 'Tis the prettiest little parlor that ever you did spy. The way into my parlor is up a winding stair, And I have many pretty things to shew when you are there.'"

Anja guided them through the varied chambers of her nexus, soon stopping in a room with a huge bed surrounded by mirrors. "This is one of those many curious things," she said, gesturing around.

"Now that's what I call a bed." Zoe grinned while removing her clothes. Emma quickly joined her in her lack of attire.

"This is going to be fun," came her inner voice. *"Hungry."*

"Zoe, time to let loose. We all deserve this," Anja sent.

She could feel Zoe's subtle influence swirling with her more overt sexual energy. This time, she was in control and on the same page as her inner demon.

"Ummm, is that what's called orgy size?" Dora inquired, pointing to the bed.

"Is it? I suppose that fits and should handle us." Anja glanced at Mike. He was the only one here who had not explicitly agreed to provide sustenance, but she could sense his dawning understanding and willingness. No, that was eagerness. Maybe it was her and Zoe's cocktail of vibes, but that thought faded as clothes were being discarded.

"Everyone okay with this?" Lucian asked.

"You don't have to ask us," Zoe said as she started to make out with Emma at the edge of the bed.

Mike looked at Graham. "Same as last time?"

"Looks like it might be wilder. We're good," Graham supplied.

"I hope so," Zoe said, taking her mouth from Emma's breast. "Anja told me all about her adventure with you three. I've been hoping for a chance to be the center of all that attention."

"What about me?" Emma asked, pouting.

"Go play with Dora," Zoe said. "And Anja." She was already beckoning the men to join her on the bed.

In an instant, the room transformed into a whirlwind of sensations and bodies entwined. Anja watched as Zoe, a vision of unbridled lust, lay back on the large bed, her legs spread invitingly wide. Mike and Graham flanked her, their hardened members poised to either side. Lucian knelt before her, teasing her clit with his tongue.

Emma crawled towards Dora and Anja, a mischievous glint in her eyes. "Zoe insisted that I join you two," she purred, running a finger along Dora's bare thigh. Dora's cheeks flushed crimson, but she nodded in agreement.

Anja's heart raced as Emma's lips and tongue trailed hot patterns down her stomach. When she looked over at Zoe again, Zoe writhed in ecstasy as Graham thrust into her from below and Mike from behind. Zoe was taking Lucian deep in her throat as he knelt. She could sense what Zoe felt, both from having experienced it firsthand and through their psychic link. Zoe was as full as she had been then, and she was relishing this new experience.

Lucian glanced over, his eyes meeting Anja's in the mirrored reflection on the wall. He grinned and closed his eyes. Anja strengthened their connection with Zoe and felt him slip into Zoe's perspective. He sensed himself in her mouth, then seemed to swap bodies with Zoe.

"Holy fuck!" Zoe exclaimed in Lucian's voice.

Lucian's barriers were obliterated.

"I wonder if I should remind Lucian that he could probably change to female?" The thought slipped out through the link.

"I don't know if I'm ready for that..." Lucian sent.

"Too late." Zoe's thoughts echoed in their minds.

"Well, the cat's out of the bag now. We'll add that to our growing list," Anja responded. It was hard for her to control her thoughts and what was being sent, especially while Dora and Emma focused on her.

The room filled with moans and groans, wet flesh slapping against eager skin, and the creaking of the bedframe under the weight of so much desire. Anja could feel Zoe's arousal feeding hers, intertwining like the tangled limbs of those caught up in the throes of passion around them.

They all moved together in a primal rhythm—a symphony of lust played out on their bodies as they brought each other to new heights of pleasure. No barriers were left, only shared needs and a seemingly insatiable hunger.

Giving in to the sensations flooding her body, Anja arched her back as Emma's fingers found her clit, rubbing her in time with her tail's movements, plunging into Dora and twisting. The room spun around her as Zoe's and Lucian's orgasms crashed into hers. They rode out the climaxes together, their shared pleasure multiplied by their connection. It was a veritable feast as her demon fed.

As they all came down from their respective highs, bodies slick with sweat and spent from their exertions, Anja couldn't help but smile lazily at the debauchery they had just partaken in. Sated and content, she curled up against Dora, who had fallen asleep against her chest. She looked around the room. Zoe was fast asleep between Mike and Graham. Lucian and Emma were tangled together on the other side of the bed.

They had done it. They had discovered the Golden Library and dealt a blow to the Sodality. And tonight they could bask in the afterglow of their shared experiences, both physical and emotional. Tomorrow would bring new challenges, but for now...for now, they would rest.

Forty-Four

Lucian stood at the edge of the lake. A cool Icelandic wind contrasted with the warmth of Anja's nexus. The sky stretched above him in broad, pale arcs, and the surrounding mountains loomed, witnesses to their return. Only minutes ago he and the others had emerged from the shimmering portal onto the shores of this hidden body of water, Sigri waiting in anxious silence.

His mind still reeled from what they had just experienced. In that pocket reality—Anja's realm, an echo of desire and power—they had all ended up on a bed larger than anything he'd seen, surrounded by mirrors that threw reflections of reflections until the scene spiraled into an infinite array of bodies. It was a feeding, yes, but far more than that: Anja's succubus weaving them together in a swirl of sensual communion. At some point, he'd realized he could switch to a feminine form—an ability that should have startled him but, in retrospect, seemed obvious. Through the haze of shared pleasure and mental links, he'd felt what Zoe felt. More than that, he had experienced her body as his own. It was a whole new perspective.

He drew a deep breath of the crisp air, letting the swirl of dreamlike recollections settle. It was one thing to know his shapeshifting talent existed and quite another to consider the other implications. Anja's succubus nature and their link had blurred the boundaries of identity and body. He would have plenty of time to process that—and to think about the possibilities it presented. Later.

But here and now, reality pressed in. Sigri stepped forward, greeting them with a relieved nod. "We were worried." She glanced at

Anja, who wore her human body, no longer the embodiment of sexuality. It seemed Sigri was looking at her in a new light. Sigri did not remark on their disheveled appearances.

Lucian ran a hand through his hair. “We’re fine,” he murmured. “We had to…recover…but it was necessary.”

Sigri nodded, offering a small smile that suggested she understood more than she let on. “Ready to head back home?”

“Home. Yes.”

Behind them, the last wisps of Anja’s portal faded, leaving only the tranquil surface of the lake. The water shimmered as though carrying echoes of the realm they had just left. When the last spark vanished, Anja came to Lucian’s side, her eyes meeting his. He could still feel a faint yet comforting hum of connection through their link. A part of him wanted to slip right back into that place, but the real world called.

“All right,” he said, turning back to Sigri. “Let’s head in.”

They loaded into the van and Sigri drove them to the lab. A subdued hush fell over them, and each was lost in private thoughts about what had transpired. Lucian kept replaying scattered fragments in his mind: the bed, the infinite mirrors, the perspective shift, and the pleasure. His cheeks heated, and he cleared his throat as Sigri pulled through the gates and to the back entrance to their living complex.

“Elín said to let you settle in and rest. She also asked if she could stop in later this evening. Would that be okay?”

“Of course. You should come with her and bring Nomad and Karolina. Lynn too. We have a lot to share,” he replied.

Once they had retreated to their living area, he sank into a chair, allowing the events of the last few hours to settle. Through the relief in Dora’s posture and Anja’s contented smile, he knew they were all processing a whirlwind of emotions.

Despite the lingering tension—and the danger that still lurked—they had made it here. They had each other, they had some measure of safety, and Lucian could still feel the memory of that dreamlike union sparking through his every nerve. He closed his eyes, taking a moment to cherish the closeness he felt for all of them.

There would be time to plan the next steps. For now, though, the hush of Iceland's lab offered a reprieve from the hazards they had left behind. And for Lucian, the echoes of what they'd shared in Anja's nexus—the boundless warmth of bodies and the freedom to explore parts of himself he'd never dared imagine—still thrummed in his chest, reminding him that for all their perils, they had discovered a deeper unity that no enemy could ever shatter.

Zoe, clad in her usual attire, as in none, leaned against the plush arm of the sofa next to Anja and Lucian. They all laughed as Sigri and Emma bounded from one side of the spacious living area to the other. Sigri's fox form darted across the floor, bushy tail sweeping the air, while Emma, as her usual sleek black cat, pounced and spun in an endless game of tag. The two shifters vaulted over the coffee table, nearly colliding in midair, before Emma darted behind an armchair and Sigri chased after her.

She couldn't tell if Emma was holding back—cats were famously agile, after all—but Sigri's fox more than compensated with enthusiasm. Every so often, Sigri yipped, ears perked in delight, and Emma replied with a hiss or a chirp-like call. Just watching them chase each other was enough to lift any lingering worry from Zoe's mind.

A half smile tugged at Nomad's lips, though he quickly masked it. Karolina, perched beside Dora on another wide sofa, let out a gasp of delight each time the two creatures zoomed past, nearly toppling a lamp. Karolina was adapting well, Zoe noted. Far better than the timid figure she'd been weeks ago. Dora was doing wonders acting as a big sister, guiding her through both the mundane and the realities of this new life.

From the corner of her eye, Zoe spotted Mike rising to answer the chime at the entrance. She heard murmured voices as the door opened. Elín and Lynn stepped in. Both wore curious, amused expressions that turned to open laughter when they spotted Sigri-the-fox making a flying leap over the back of a chair, hotly pursued by Emma-the-cat.

Lynn burst into giggles, and Elín clapped her hands for attention.

"All right, children, settle down." Her tone was part exasperated, part amused.

Sigri and Emma skidded to a halt. With a shimmer of energy, they resumed human forms, each breathing heavily from the romp. Neither appeared inclined to put on clothes, which hardly surprised Zoe; the lack of modesty felt almost normal now. Sigri's cheeks glowed with exhilaration, her eyes bright. Emma's grin was downright impish.

"Well," Zoe said, clearing her throat with a conspiratorial smile, "it looks like we might need to invest in some more durable furniture if this becomes a habit."

Sigri tried to tame her long raven hair and shrugged with no sign of embarrassment. "Sorry. Fox instincts," she offered.

Emma draped herself on the edge of the sofa. "Cat instincts aren't any more polite," she retorted. "That was fun."

Elín and Lynn exchanged a look of bemused acceptance, like they'd interrupted a children's birthday party run wild. *Not far off,* Zoe thought.

Elín addressed the group: "We've sorted the emergency. Sorry we're late. Graham should be here in a few minutes. He was right behind us."

"No worries, Elín. Everything's under control here…well, sort of," Zoe teased, gesturing at the scattered pillows.

Karolina tucked a lock of hair behind her ear. "I wish I can learn to change." She looked at Emma, her eyes hopeful. "You can teach me secret? How you do?"

"I'm…" Emma started.

Dora came to Emma's rescue. "We can talk about that later. Not all of us can change. Will you be able to? Maybe. I don't know. Let's let you get settled here in your new home first, okay?"

"Home? Okay." Karolina smiled.

The question pulled at Zoe's heart. They had dragged her into their world. They'd really had no choice. They could save her, so they had. What was next was still a question.

Graham walked in, setting his bag down by a chair. He greeted everyone with a nod, weariness etched on his face. "Spoke with Isabelle," he said, meeting Lucian's eyes. "She won't make it tonight. She's got some developments at NexGen—it's still under control, but it's tying her up. She can't risk exposing her location."

Lucian nodded, an undercurrent of concern in his voice. "All right. We'll have to catch her tomorrow. Did she say anything about the problem there?"

"Just that Jonas, your corporate security chief, is on top of it," Graham replied. "Isabelle has to maintain her cover, so she's imitating another time zone and schedule."

They all made themselves comfortable in the living room. Sigri, still flushed from her earlier romp, offered to fetch refreshments. She bounced out and returned with a tray of bottled drinks and an assortment of snacks. The group welcomed them with thanks. Graham raised an eyebrow at this new aspect of Sigri, but he shrugged and tipped his beer toward Zoe and Emma. Zoe caught Emma's eye, sharing a private grin.

"I guess it's time to discuss practicalities," Lucian began, sipping his drink. "Ash wants to set up something more permanent here. It's secure, and we can coordinate with Elín to keep everything under wraps."

Elín nodded, her gaze flicking around the space. "Howard informed me that he's trained one of the new wolves in the ritual and some minor magics. He wants to return here and work with Anja on cataloging the library. He said it was getting a bit too crowded. Ian and Claire will stay behind in England with so many new wolves to guide. He also mentioned he'd like to bring in Raymond."

"There may be problems with that. I think leaving the books in my nexus is safest." Anja tilted her head thoughtfully. "But there are concerns. If someone's in my nexus alone and something happens... well, it's complicated. I'd need to be present to ensure no one's stranded."

Nomad spoke up next, his tone subdued. "We should also consider Eagle's death. The Grandmaster won't take it lightly. If anything, we'll be facing more pressure. We have to prepare for the day they find us."

Lucian exhaled slowly. "Agreed. Mike, I'd like you to figure out additions we can build onto this place. Enough to accommodate everyone comfortably. And talk with Ash and Nomad—come up with some decoys in case they trace us to Iceland."

"Consider it done," Mike said.

They continued to talk for a while about new rooms, expansions, and security strategies. Eventually, fatigue settled over all of them. The buzz of conversation began to fade. Lucian glanced at Zoe and Anja before standing up. "I think we've earned a good night's rest."

A round of murmured assent followed as the group dispersed to their respective rooms. Zoe stretched, a wave of drowsiness washing over her. Gathering her thoughts, she and Anja followed Lucian down the hall.

In the quiet of the bedroom, Zoe let out a sigh. It was just her, Anja, and Lucian again—like before. The bed felt familiar, a balm after so much upheaval. She glanced between them, a small smile curving her lips. She sensed Anja's softness and Lucian's steady presence. It all felt strangely normal, if this life of shapeshifters, nexus realms, and ancient libraries could be called normal.

As she drifted off, Zoe mused that maybe, for them, this was exactly what normal had become—and it wasn't so bad after all.

Epilog

GRANDMASTER EAMON Vale stood in his private study in the Vault, deep beneath centuries of secrets and shadows. Silence reigned. His gaze settled on a glowing display embedded in the black marble desk before him. Rows of data scrolled past, each line an unanswered message to Eagle.

Something was wrong. Igor should have reported back long before now. Lucian's group had outmaneuvered skilled agents in the past, yes, but Eagle's cunning and efficiency were legendary. Even if he had failed to capture them, Eamon would have expected some word. Instead, there was only silence.

He recalled Richard's fate, how he had disappeared trying to capture Lucian. Impatience gnawed at Eamon. "I have no time for repeated failures," he muttered under his breath.

Stirring from behind his cold mask, an ember of frustration ignited. The oath that bound Eagle to him was a failsafe that allowed him to sense his agent's presence, yet he felt nothing. Eamon reached outward through that arcane link, searching for the resonance of Eagle's devotion. There was no response; the binding itself was gone.

A roar of fury ripped from his throat, reverberating off the walls. His facade slipped, revealing for an instant a visage no living witness had observed—something edged with an ancient, wrathful power. Then he steadied himself, forcing composure to return. Fury gave way to planning.

Messages flew through his secure network. Helena's name came to mind—someone else tethered by oath, though she had tested his limits before. Eamon initiated an encrypted video channel, eyes narrowing when Helena's familiar face blinked into view. Her expression flickered with concern at his uncharacteristically severe tone.

"Eagle is dead," Eamon announced without preamble. "You will return to the Vault immediately."

She drew a ragged breath, shock flitting across her features. "Dead? I—"

The news had caught her by surprise. That was only somewhat reassuring.

"You will come at once," Eamon said. "You have no choice. Do not force me to summon you through more drastic means."

Whatever she might have felt or planned was swallowed by her acquiescence. The call ended with her promise to comply. Eamon breathed once, calm beginning to return.

He called up the files from Eagle's last reports. A name popped up repeatedly—Yuri, his assistant. Eamon recalled Eagle's notes that Yuri was fully indoctrinated. Perfect. With Eagle gone, this Yuri might be the key to gleaning what had taken place and how Lucian's group had wriggled free again.

Eamon reviewed the messages: Yuri's account of a pursuit that led to Perm, followed by intermittent signals from tracking devices. Then silence. The devices relied on local cell networks. When they entered remote territory, the coverage stopped, and so did their trail.

He tapped the desk, lines of data flickering. The Vault seemed colder than usual, yet a pulse of excitement thrummed beneath his rage. Lucian Miller… Eamon recalled how he'd first read a slender dossier about that young heir, so restless, always seeking new challenges. *I, too, once found relief from ennui in the world's petty intrigues,* Eamon mused. But Lucian was beginning to awaken something in him—memories of the past.

He closed his eyes for a moment, letting the hush of the Vault envelop him. He was Grandmaster: unyielding, unstoppable. He opened his eyes, exhaling slowly.

"They have not escaped. Not truly. I will see to that," he declared. Sitting alone in this cold room was becoming intolerable. Perhaps it was past time to take a more active role.

Soon, Helena would stand before him to account for her actions, and Yuri would provide fresh leads. He needed to understand what had happened and if they had accomplished their goal. The pursuit hadn't ended with Eagle's demise—it had only begun in earnest.

Helena stood by the tall window of her bedchamber, dawn light casting shadows across the chamber's marble floor. The summons from the Grandmaster weighed upon her like an iron yoke. Eamon demanded her presence at the Vault—no delays, no excuses. The tension in his message echoed that harsh fury she had glimpsed when he spoke of Eagle's death. She knew what it meant: if she failed him, a single misstep could end her life.

She turned away from the window, letting her gaze linger on the great oak desk. A spread of parchment and a slim, leather-bound journal awaited her there, pages filled with cryptic marks. She approached, the rustle of her gown emphasizing the hush in the room.

Sinking into the chair, Helena traced a finger along the entry she had penned the night before—her coded confessions, part diary, part contingency plan. The script conveyed truths through hidden ciphers—rune substitutions and archaic languages she had dabbled in for centuries. If this proved to be her final testament, she wanted to give someone, perhaps Anja, a fighting chance to unravel her secrets.

She started writing:

...Should I fall, let this journal serve as a map. The language is layered—first in archaic Norse, then a runic shift. I've left references to the key on folios seven, nineteen, and twenty-three. Anja, if you ever find this, follow the margins. The scribbled references are not random. If you can interpret them, you'll uncover what I've concealed...

Helena paused, nibbling the feather end of her quill, mind drifting to Anja. A flicker of longing stirred. Before Anja, she had never imagined tethering her fate to anyone else, nor feeling so vulnerable. The memory of Anja's dream visits set her heart pounding. If the worst happened at the Vault, she hoped Anja might reach her one last time—save her, or at least read her final confession.

She added a final line in the journal:

...The girl I was, the woman I became—these pages hold both. If Anja dreams again, I pray she finds the key to decode this.

Closing the book, she let out a slow breath. Her gaze settled on a simple iron-bound chest by her wardrobe. In it lay several volumes—some truly precious, others false leads for the Grandmaster's agents if they pried. Atop the chest sat a sealed note for Jasmina.

Helena's ever-loyal maid, who had borne witness to Helena's darkest moods and cruelties, yet never deserted her. If Helena did not return, those instructions would guide Jasmina to pass the chest to Anja or to anyone from Anja's circle. If the worst were to occur, let them have these volumes. Even a fraction of her knowledge might aid in the Sodality's destruction. That was the goal she pursued.

She drew a smaller parchment from her desk. She wrote instructions and descriptions of possible scenarios for Jasmina to follow. The final line read:

If she returns, go with her. Serve her as you served me. Let no one betray your vow. I release you from my command, Jasmina, on the condition that you aid my once-captive. She is no enemy. She is someone I never intended to care for—but do.

Folding it, she pressed her signet ring's impression onto red wax to seal the note. Another old affectation to the old ways. *I have no illusions,* she told herself. *Eamon will sense any hint of betrayal. But Jasmina deserves something more than captivity or death.*

Soft footsteps behind her made Helena glance up. Jasmina stood in the doorway, cheeks flushed. The woman's eyes flickered from Helena to the chest, then back again. She must have grasped the situation well enough.

"Madam," Jasmina said in a tremulous voice, "is it...? You are truly leaving tonight?"

Helena rose, brushing a hand across Jasmina's cheek. The affection in that gesture startled her. Only in the last months, under Anja's lingering influence, had Helena even recognized the shape of this maid's adoration. Was it a weakness? Perhaps. But it was also a deeper stirring of Helena's long-buried heart.

"I must," Helena replied. "If I don't return, follow what is written. And if fortune smiles on us, we shall see each other again."

A quiver ran through Jasmina's lips, tears threatening to form. "I...I don't want you to go, not like this."

Helena forced a wry smile, burying her own fear. "Nor do I, but we have no choice. I must obey." She hesitated, then added in a quieter tone, "I once thought caring for people was a flaw, a door to exploitation. Maybe it is—but it's also the only reason I stand a chance now."

Wrapping her arms around the maid, Helena shut her eyes. For a fleeting heartbeat, she imagined a different fate—one not overshadowed by Eamon's wrath. But reality crashed over her, and she released Jasmina. She handed her note to Jasmina and indicated the chest.

Jasmina clutched the note to her chest and stepped forward. "I will wait as long as it takes," she whispered, leaning her forehead against Helena's shoulder.

"Lock everything once I'm gone," Helena said, stepping out into the corridor. "This note will guide you."

With that, she slipped through the castle's winding halls, heading for the vehicle that would take her to the airport—and from there, to Eamon's Vault. Tension coiled in her gut, the knowledge that the Grandmaster's rage might consume her flickering like a dark flame.

Yet a fragile hope lingered in her chest. *As long as Anja and Lucian live, there's a chance at least for them.* She thought of the coded diary, and each footstep echoed the silent vow she'd made. If she died, her truth would remain. If she survived, she still might see that demon's eyes and feel her touch again.

Thus, with her final illusions burned away, Helena set forth, carrying both fear and a strange feeling blossoming in her heart.

About the authors

THE DUO behind Morgan Emerson Fox is a husband-and-wife team that has ventured into the realms of urban fantasy. They weave tales that are not only entertaining but resonate on a deeper level with the readers.

Their journey into writing began as a shared passion, a way to create worlds and explore the complexities of characters and narratives together. During the dark days of the pandemic, they were running out of novels to read, audiobooks, and podcasts to listen to, and tried writing as a creative and emotional outlet.

Writing under a pseudonym has allowed them to blend their voices, thoughts, and ideas into a singular stream of storytelling that reflects both our imaginations. It's a partnership that challenges and inspires them, pushing them to explore the intricacies of plot and character development.

For more information, please visit morganemersonfox.com

www.ingramcontent.com/pod-product-compliance
Lightning Source LLC
Chambersburg PA
CBHW020603310726
48979CB00008B/1327/J

* 9 7 8 1 9 6 5 2 8 0 0 7 2 *